Capture the Empress

Fantasy Erotica

By S.W. Lupine

Copyright ©2024 by S.W. Lupine

All rights reserved. No part of this book may be reproduced or transmitted in any form or by any means, electronic or mechanical, including photocopy, recording, or any information storage and retrieval systems, without prior permission from the publisher (except for reviewers who may quote brief passages).

First Edition

Printed in the United States of America

Paperback ISBN: 978-1-965770-03-0

Ebook ISBNs: 978-1-965770-01-6 & 9798230935452

Cover design by: Carder Wicker Writing

Published by Carder Wicker Writing

www.carderwickerwriting.com

To my readers, followers, and those who have supported me. Thank you. May this present an escape from the real world.

To my family, those of blood and those chosen, without you I could not live my dream.

Chapter 1

Two living mirrors met her in her lava lit chambers. Her Bloodsworn sisters smiled as she did, keeping up the eerie effect. To greet her, as Klava, for she was, and they were for their people, too.

"Klava, Klava, my sisters." She said, warmth spreading in her chest, watching their most trusted servants stare in awe at the three. Despite the passage of time, seeing herself twice remained unsettling.

After the assassination of the first Klava, her daughter devised and implemented a brilliant plan. The same daughter, the second Klava, chose a pair of families to breed daughters to look exactly like Kavkan royalty to safeguard the bloodline. Mating techniques and synchronized sessions ensured each woman birthed close to the same time. Every Klava thereafter had two Bloodsworn who resembled her perfectly. Decoys. Those households gave birth to the duo with the true Klava. They took them from their mothers when they were still suckling and molded them into exact replicas of Klava.

Now grown, these Klavas awaited the disarmament. Her servant, Gyrna, stepped forward, in sync with the other maids, and began unlatching the black and flame armor from their mistresses. The metal, seemingly insubstantial but nearly impenetrable, created the illusion of walking amidst eternal flames. They took each piece to be polished, replace any needed straps, and rework them into brighter and stronger metals.

Stripped down to the thin, breathable charcoal underthings, Klava's body grew weightless. It was only in front of them she took off the armor. Such was her curse as the Ruler of Kavkan, the greatest kingdom of killers the world had ever known.

Silence filled the room after the servants bowed and departed.

Their black hair gleamed in the molten light cascading in from the wall to ceiling windows. The lava's force couldn't melt them, nor would they let it in. Kavkan was a volcanic dominion of fire magics, and the most northern kingdom on the continent. A home of the best mercenaries, assassins, and army. Birthed amid lava lakes surrounded by blue ice glaciers, and hot springs made native born ready for any element the world could toss at them.

As it were, social classes barely existed in their country. The superior Kavkans became the Bloodsworn. The trio being the deadliest; as flames of infinite fire. Like the infinity star flower that never died, and the three had tattooed on their wrist. That's what the masses believed for generations.

As soon as the large doors carved from snowflake obsidian closed behind the servants, the Klavas relaxed.

"Hava, Nava." She spoke their names with a smile even as she whispered. A full year had passed since they were in this room together. Stepping into the curve of their arms, she pressed her forehead to theirs. Comfort. Home. Three women, sisters, bound by blood, and unique in the world.

"Mylva." They replied, her name so rarely spoken she hardly remembered the last time she heard it. They knew her mind, and she theirs.

"Ready?"

Two windows of spilling lava bracketed them as they strode toward their duty. She placed her hand upon the curve of the gray basalt wall, she spoke a singular word 'asdui' meaning open in their ancient language. A language nearly forgotten, except for those in the royal household, generals, and messengers.

It slid seamlessly, revealing a glass hallway thrusting through the molten fall. The trio stepped into the hall, following the short path to another basalt wall, which opened with the same word. A chamber of obsidian glistening with the orange light from the central pool of clear water steaming over yet more serous fire. Magic of the Goddess Kasvuki saved the holdings from turning to ash. Low red, gold, and purple pillows lined the cool floors amid thin blankets of violet and blue.

Klava let her Bloodsworn to an alcove on the right, boasting of weapons from all over the world. Sharp and deadly, they glistened in the fiery glow of the room. Central to the space was a table laden with gauze, ointments, needle and threads.

"Neither of you better have any new paper cuts. Those are the worst." Hava glared at each of her sisters as her cloth belt fell to the floor, followed by her tunic and pants.

Nava grinned following suit, but she gathered her clothes and folded them, and placed them neatly on the edge of the first aid table. "I thought you hated whip lashes the most."

"Yes, but they're rare for us," Hava replied.

Mylva eyed the Sarvaren leather embedded with gemstone shards and grimaced, "Only once. That was enough." She joined her sisters in their nakedness. "I have no new wounds." She thanked the gods, for she detested wounding them.

"Nor I," Hava added.

Both swung their eyes to Nava, who sighed heavily. They watched her turn to reveal a scarred gash, like a wide claw had dragged over her flesh from hip joint to spine.

"It liked belly rubs." She said in explanation as the others groaned.

Mylva grabbed a circle of blades from the wall. She sized each blade against the scar, measuring which one would fit it. Settling on the third to largest, she handed it to Hava and turned. Placing her hands on the lip of the table, she gave a nod.

The sign received, Hava dragged the edge from hip bone to spine, deepening the cut on the meatiest parts, just as the healed wound on Nava looked. Orange blood spurted from the fresh slash, spilling down Mylva's scarred thigh. Nava added a thick swatch of ointment across the lesion from a blue vial. The bleeding stopped. Her skin hardened into scar tissue.

Mylva watched the medicine, "I adore this new gel."

"It makes our lives so much easier. Where was this ten years ago?" Nava asked, rolling her eyes.

"If someone wouldn't try to pet every little clawed thing, we might not have to use it as often!" Hava bit out.

"They're cute!"

Mylva shook her head, "Hava, you're just as lousy with cooking."

"You mean murdering fruit and vegetables in such a way they are unrecognizable and tasteless in a meal?" Nava interjected.

Hava glanced at her hands, "I didn't cut any off this time! See?" she asked as she held them up, the circle of knives jangling dangerously close to her forearm.

"Fire and smoke, woman, give me those!" Nava snatched the circlet from Hava's hooked fingers.

"Nothing terrible was going to happen!"

"Says the one who thinks a bit of extra blood in the meal is spice." Nava and Hava eyed each other, then grinned.

"Your turn." Mylva plucked blades from Nava's palm and waited for Hava to situate herself.

The key was to stay calm, breathe, and understand the pain was temporary. She thanked the gods for the ointment. Newly rendered by magician healers in her employ, the three Klavas were grateful for their ingenuity.

So much so, she made sure they wouldn't dream of selling to anyone else, nor live anywhere but in Kavkan. She gave them free housing in her wealthy district, plus a salary and royalties from medicinal purchases. Her people were experts at keeping secrets.

Cutting the matching swath into Hava, Mylva kept her thoughts to herself as Hava growled curses under her breath. Her lifesblood was the normal reddish orange of her Bloodsworn, not bronze like hers. Only through proximity or witnessing her blood on a white cloth could someone discern the dissimilarity.

Hava was the clumsy one out of them. Among the three, she lacked grace the most. Nava was the kin who would likely act without thinking first, especially if it was a cute animal distracting her. Mylva held her anger on her sleeve and had a disdain for all things too feminine.

Because of this, their long hair resulted from a challenge not of her daring. She hated it the most of all the attributes she'd given Nava and Hava leave to wear or do. The day she would shave her head was nearing, for she could feel the annoyance reaching the boiling point with the straight inky tresses.

Nava covered the wound with the ointment as soon as Mylva cleared the blade from Hava's flesh. "It's not so bad, right?"

Mylva rolled her eyes as Hava poked Nava in the forehead and asked, "Anything else?"

"Ah, these new exercises I learned!" Hava grinned, "They tighten the canal for ultimate pleasure."

The two groaned, but listened intently as Hava explained the drill.

"We will get a visual next door." Mylva held up her hand, stopping Hava from grabbing one of the metal balls from the table. "That'll be enough."

She took them to the furthest alcove in the grand room. The absence of wars made this part of the yearly ritual the hardest. For during battles, the trio were inseparable. In times of peace, they had affairs of state to attend.

Klava's triplets from three generations back contributed to much of Kavkan. Making it supreme. The gods had blessed Klava Walva with three girls, and the Bloodsworn families had struggled to find six babes to mold into their likenesses. With nine acting Klavas, a spread of new lands like no other, and none since, fell into Kavkan hands. Even though the kingdoms under their rule called themselves allies, it was an empire. The triplets had built the fortress in the volcano of their god, which to this day was called their capital, Xlanvka.

Their capital, their fortress, and the ways of the ancient Klavas were still practiced. Mostly. A low table of onyx held a large diamond vessel suspended above it. They sat around it, upon wide pillows of soft, cool cloth. Each woman stretched forward, pricking a finger on the sharp corners of the clear gem. Into the bowl, they each squeezed three droplets of blood.

Then, settling back, she reached for their hands. The basin swirled their blood together; the diamond throwing sparks of light and color upon the walls as it spun. They closed their eyes, and the Klavas spoke the three words that would unite their minds into one yet again, "Galavs tso tsulv."

As if she lived it herself, Hava and Nava's lives entered her memories. Every detail, from their morning breath to the nightly armor pinch, mattered. The past year of her life infiltrated theirs, too. This way, if one were to encounter someone the other had met, they knew the names and previous interactions.

Once finished, after hours of soaking in each other, she opened her eyes and grinned at her Bloodsworn, "Hava. Nava."

"Mylva." They said in unison.

She turned to Nava and questioned the story of the king with twenty sons. Broaching a subject while the brain was cataloging information was quicker at times. And she was impatient.

"I am not sure. There were whispers of this kingdom's hostile maneuvers. Conquering, somehow."

"Any of ours?" Hava asked.

"No, not yet. I believe the one spoken of was an island kingdom far to the south and west. A place I've never heard of," Nava explained, "There is fear. More people talk of this threat there."

Nava had spent her year in the south, tightening the bonds that held their empire together. Alliance. That's what the kingdoms under her rule wanted to call themselves, the Alliance. Allied. Allies. She'd agreed. After all, the words Empire and such created unrest among those that didn't hold the highest rank of Empress or Emperor. And the kingdoms needed that emotional boost after losing. Klavas weren't one for titles, just power.

"We should prepare, then. If fear sows discord in the south, then we should assume this threat is real." Mylva stated, looking at Hava and Nava. "What of the west, any rumors there?"

"Not a word." Hava responded, "This is new for me as well. What of the north?"

"Nothing." Mylva shook her head, leaning forward to prop her chin up on her fist. It felt odd being bare. The situation was simultaneously glorious and worrying. Every minute of every day spent in the metal meant her armor became like a second skin. But getting to live in her flesh, to remember where each of her scars came from, whether they were hers or her sisters', was sublime.

"What is the significance of twenty sons?" Hava asked, leaning back on her pillow, stretching long legs riddled with identical scarred slashes and jagged stab wounds.

"Twenty kingdoms," Mylva mused aloud, for that's what she controlled.

"Ridiculous. Not all have birthright inheritance like we do." Nava shook her head, then stared at the diamond, empty of their blood. Its magic completed. "If that is the case, then they intend to conquer us."

"May the gods be on their side, because there is no chance in smoke we will yield." Hava grinned at the ceiling, "Twenty sons become none."

Mylva chuckled, "May that be true, and that king has to start all over again with whatever plan he had."

They lounged on pillows some more, allowing the ointment to finish, and their memories to settle. Quiet was comfortable among them. Silence was as warm as a blanket upon the glacier encampment with the sisters. A year of solitude, without familiar companions, was truly hellish. Sometimes, it needed to be done.

United, they would quell rumors or conquer the king with many sons.

Afterward, back in their bedchamber, "You think we can grow this here?" Hava turned the ceramic pot on her bedside table. Planted in the dark soil of the vessel was a single stem curving up in an arch. Along the tapered end were delicate petals that looked like white raindrops.

"We'll see if it survives." Nava said from her place, lounging on her bed.

Kavka's plants were hardy, as were the people. They had to withstand extremes, flourish in either the coldest of temperatures, or upon the steaming, burning soils of the volcanic mountain. Hardly any plant or person from the outside could stand such a country.

A knock made the Klavas prepare. Mylva tensed, Hava reached for a mace in her nightstand, and Nava stood. Only Mylva answered, "Enter."

The three maidservants entered one at a time, bearing trays laden with vivid clothes.

This was the part of the Memory Merge she hated the most: a thin dress, with no armor. The decorative plates did little to make her feel less naked. Gyrna bowed before her, holding the tray out from her stocky body. One look at the bright oranges and reds made her cringe.

Gyrna clucked her tongue and set it down on her dressing stool, anyway. "You wear that expression once a year, no matter what your advisors pick for you to put on."

"I shall replace them all for their terrible tastes," Mylva said through her clenched teeth.

Hava sighed, "It's pretty. And so soft!" She was already hugging the dress to her.

"Uchloye," Nava warned with the single word for 'same likeness' in the ancient tongue.

Hava sobered, schooling her face into a neutral expression that still held a slight smile on her lips. Gone were the moments where the trio could be entirely themselves. Even their maid servants barely knew the differences between them. Relying on their Klava being by their furnishings.

"Go ahead, Gyrna." Mylva stated, holding her arms out so the shorter woman could dress her.

"Goddess of Fire, no."

Hava and Mylva turned their heads to Nava. Her attire was on, if one could call it such. Sheer orange fabric haltered her breasts up and together, leaving ribs, hips, stomach, and legs bare from the flowing gauzy stuff. The gloves held more substance than the dress, Mylva observed.

"It is the year, my Klavas." Gyrna bowed.

Five years had passed since the last atilos, the night when important Kavkan families saw their ruler and her Bloodsworn in such a state. Only Warmonger, the title for her supreme warrior, being half naked, made these nights better. Warmonger, or Praedae, hated it more than all three Klavas put together. Four generations ago, the Klava and her court started the practice of hosting numerous extra-marital and mating gatherings.

Gyrna pressed the matching attire upon her body, and she slid on the flame colored gloves. Most of the more delicate families who held their titles through other means than battle honors didn't care for the roughness of weapon wielding palms and fingers. Though they still enjoyed gawking at the myriad scars, asking for the story of each honored wound. She noted the dress did little to hide the many flaws. Marks like theirs repulsed the weak. It was the reason she hadn't felt disappointed at all for the scars her Bloodsworn gathered during their year apart. The more, the better.

After sitting down at the mirror, she watched as they pulled, teased, and fashioned their long tresses into an intricate monstrosity just so their hair could hold feathers and magical flames. She failed to abolish this sole celebration, not for lack of effort. But she had amended it.

A lottery system for the less fortunate to taste, touch, whatever their higher counterparts. Each family had to put their 'of age' offspring into a diamond bowl, much like their Memory Merge. From there, an advisor drew twelve names. Those heirs of the advisors were to be present at parties in lower ranked soldier's homes, or merchant dances, or various similar gatherings.

With the addendum, she'd hoped there would be enough hate for the lottery system to allow her to abolish the five-year skin party. Alas, most didn't care as long as they got to ogle the Klava. "Expression?"

Her two sisters sighed before Hava answered, "If they're pretty, be flirty. If they're gross, kick them."

According to Hava's memories, anything with a fair smile and large hands was considered pretty.

"My standards of beauty." Nava added, smirking as Hava pouted.

That narrowed it down. Nava's choices in mates were those of strategic minds with attractive smiles and strength enough to lift her. With their height and level of muscles, few could handle them.

"Perfect." Klava agreed, only to frown at the weak-looking thing she'd become in the mirror. Were she her adversary, this evening would be the opportune moment for an assault.

The armor for the night was simple chain mail that only covered her ass and cunt in small triangles, and a plate for the middle of her back to hold two of her dainty maces. The ones she usually used for throwing at rodents. Or those that acted like them.

Once adorned, they rose in unison, their maids as attuned to each other as the Klavas were. A few quick finger motions in battle sign language, they decided on a game to determine the first to enter the fray. They reached up, picking a single strand of hair in the ridiculous hairdo. From the count of three, they yanked it free.

Hava's was the shortest, Mylva's the middle length, and Nava's was the longest.

Following Hava through the halls and spiraling staircase up to the top of the mountain to the dance hall, she listened to the two incessantly talking. Nava whined she would rather be in the stables, or in their gardens, or asleep. A continuous admiration spilled from Hava about how their breasts had less bounce and more hold this time.

If no one had interfered, Hava's chest would have been flat, but she would have had the thickest buttocks and legs among the three of them. The fat in her thighs added to her chest to make her even with the other two. While Mylva had to have fat taken out of her breasts to reduce them to the proper size appropriate for the true Klava. She had to wield any weapon and nurse her child, after all.

In another life, Nava would have been an expert keeper of animals. A stable hand or breeder of sorts, perhaps. Or a gardener. Were it not for the curse of being Bloodsworn.

Before Mylva's thoughts could flounder in the dark recesses of her hatred for the practices of her people and her title, Hava cleared her throat. They were at the molten glass entrance of the dance hall. Mylva gave Hava a curt nod. Hava pushed open the door, and it swung in on silent hinges. Golden light and the glacial floral perfumes spilled out into the hall. Chandeliers of glistening crystals hung from diamond chains at equal distances along the ceiling. The crystal walls arched upward, meeting in the dome at puzzled intervals to create a cacophony of black irises set against the starlit sky. Onyx pillars held sconce rings with golden flames and created seating space away from the marble dance floor at their bases.

"I present to you our Klavas!" the crier at the door announced in his thunderous voice once a wave of his hand silenced the music.

Hava entered first, then Mylva and Nava behind her. Each step was in perfect sync, as was each smile, nod, and handshake. And the attendees were already either half naked in attire like theirs, or bare. After the throng of one hundred and twelve revelers finished their greetings, the music began again.

Complete with a denial from a blustering Warmonger that carried over the first strains of string instruments, "For the love of flames, no!"

The Klavas shared a grin before separating to mingle.

The echoes of his voice guided her to discover him in the far corner. Surrounded. He brandished a wine bottle as if it were a sword.

They had denied Praedae weapons for the past two parties like this.

"Leave him be," her command whipped out, before she added with a knowing smile, "For now, at least."

Warmonger's rippled muscles in his arms and thighs flexed until his orange eyes rested upon her. His gaze softened for a moment before he bowed, "Klava, I beseech you. Release me from this torture."

She waited until the throng of people surrounding him dispersed. They were alone in the corner, given a wide berth by those resting nearby. "Stay until you discover a way for me to avoid attending, too."

Those orange eyes blazed as he straightened. "I'll kill them all, then."

She held up a hand to keep him from making good on his words. He was the same height as her, same black hair, though a little thinner. He had the burnt tan of her people on full display, as whoever had dared to clothe him had given him something akin to a loincloth to wear. She wondered if her staff would have to find yet another servant for him this year, as they had the past soiree. His flesh bore countless scars, perhaps even more than hers. Many sought after him, his scars trophies to be admired by her people.

"Calm down, my flame. Breathe," Mylva wasn't a soother, but she had to try before there was a bloodbath. "They may be the most annoying in our country, but they are needed." Somehow.

"Why do I have to be here?"

"Because wetting your dick in one of them might help satisfy some of that rage in you?"

He snorted, tossing the wine bottle. It shattered against the far wall. Such was his strength, even when he didn't mean it. "They are beneath me."

"I'm sure most of them wouldn't mind that position with you." Mylva retorted, watching a few servants scurry to clean up his mess.

"What are you wearing?" His gaze trailed down her body, the flickers of rage coloring his flesh again.

She sighed, observing his anger build. His veins glowed. Then she reached out a hand and brushed his loose hair behind one ear.

A charm only Klavas knew.

The flames and rage cooled. His orange eyes widened, the pupils dilating, and he leaned into her palm. She moved to stand directly before him, so no one else could see her trick.

"You cheat against me." He murmured, his lips moving against her wrist.

She grinned, "I am protecting my people from your rage, my flame."

"These deserve it. Not one has entered the battles with us." His eyes searched hers, "Not one has a scar from an enemy. They are not needed."

"Lies. Our generals are here, too. Can you calculate how much grain we need to purchase from Parvis to feed us during the winter?"

He pulled away from her, frowning as he scanned the dancers in the middle of the room. "They are," he said, spotting one of his fellow warriors. "Still." He dropped his gaze, answering her, "No."

"How about running the diamond mines and what to sell them for?" Mylva tossed the questions at him that she had to use for herself when dealing with the snivelling advisors.

"I can figure that one out."

"Figuring that out wouldn't happen on the battlefield."

"I can do two things at once," he huffed, his gaze swinging back to her.

She laughed, returning her fingertips to the magical spot behind his ear, "I know, my flame. I know."

"Keep doing that and I'll show you how well I function outside the battlefield, my Klava."

"You are the only one here stronger than me."

"Barely." He smiled, then ripped her glove off before replacing her hand against his cheek. He glared at the fabric dangling from his fingers in shreds, "I had to train for twelve hours a day to best you. I don't think I can do it again."

He glanced around and stepped into her before she could answer, "Klava, there are whispers."

She frowned, and leaned in, "What whispers?"

He groaned, "I uh…"

"Two things at once, hm?" She felt his jaw clench under her palm. Then he gripped her thighs, lifted her, and slammed her against the glass wall behind him. She hadn't time to even gasp.

"My Klava, I shall tell you if I may sate my rage by wetting my dick in you. Isn't that how you put it?" His grin was feral, his eyes ablaze with a new flame.

"It is. I'll agree, if you spar with me in the morning."

"Agreed." He growled before cupping where her neck and shoulder met in his mouth, biting and sucking. Marking her. He released when she hissed, pressing a kiss to the mark as if to seal it.

"I suppose I'll have to notch the other two the same, hm, my Klava?"

"Finish what you start with me first, Warmonger."

"As you wish." His body leaned back, he slipped his hand between them, moving the thin chain mail and fabric to the side. His calloused and scarred fingers parted her folds until they found her clit. "There is a threat to us."

"From where?" She asked as she wrapped her arms around his neck, tangling her hands into his dark hair. Warmth spread from his fingers into her and she grew wet under his touch. Perhaps the party wouldn't be so bad this time, with him between her legs.

"A kingdom there is little knowledge about, I'm afraid." He nipped her ear. Since he was free to move his other hand, he cupped her left breast as she held her balance on him against the wall herself. "I've heard that they conquer through infiltration tactics. However, this word is from a foreign island nation, so my resources suggest that studying this rumor may not be ideal."

She arched into his hands, then rocked her hips, urging him to continue growing her pleasure with his fingertips. "Is this more of the twenty sons?"

His smile was dazzling under the burning flames of desire showing in his eyes, "Yes, my Klava. I should know information always finds you before it finds me."

The callouses on his large hands caught and tugged on the sheer fabric of her garb, "Continue. You may yet have something I don't." Her breathing was ragged. As if she'd sparred with him for hours. She forgot the wondrous pleasure of an adept and potent lover.

"One thing I have is begging to enter you." He chuckled, pinching her nipple. "Twenty sons to a king. I suspect they are a kingdom of information and assassins. Large numbers for collateral losses." He slid his fingers inside her, the area between his index finger and thumb still rubbing her clit, until his thumb slid into place over the nubbin.

She moaned.

He cursed. "Another sound like that and I will spill my seed readily."

She smirked, tangling his hair into a fist and pulling back to capture his lips with hers. She pulled away, talking against his mouth, "Enter me and finish."

"Not until you finish first. I shall give you two, as is far less than you deserve, but all I may manage, my Klava." His words were deep and breathy against her chin, his hot breath feathering down her neck.

"Faster, then."

Praedae obeyed her order. His fingers worked her into a frenzy. Her body warmed. At the moment she crested, she kept her cry at bay with another kiss; she rode the orgasm. "Now."

She wasn't sure when he had moved his loincloth, but she felt his hand leave and then clasp the fleshy part between thigh and buttocks. Then the head of his shaft parted her, touching her heated core, before it slid inside her. It filled her better than fingers and was glorious.

His thrusts steadied into a deep rhythm. His forehead was against hers, looking down at her body. She watched the flames in his eyes grow darker in hue, his obsession overpowering all his senses and control. The wildness of her Warmonger had always attracted her. She loved driving it from him in any manner she could. This was one of her favorites.

Feeling his power. Lust. Rebellion. It was one reason of three she kept him around.

Another cliff's lip, and she urged him to go faster with the movement of her hips. He obliged. He thrust harder into her, his hands crushing into her flesh. Controlling her when she never lost control.

Then he was done. The desperate, instinctual thrusts of him into her drew her over to the edge again.

She rested herself against the glass, held up by his body, grinding until she gained another orgasm.

He chuckled, rolling his forehead gently against hers, "My Klava, I shall follow you like a child begging for a mother's love for the rest of the night, if I may gain a promise."

"And what promise would that be?" she inquired, raising a brow.

"Stop the tiny rodents from nibbling on me."

Klava laughed, "You will have to do more than follow me." She paused, thinking of something. "Perhaps on your hands and knees, then I shall ride you as a steed."

He grinned, "If I hold you like this, no one would dare nibble at you either. Except I. If you're on my back, I cannot make any promises of not watching as you gain pleasure from others."

"Will you keep your cock in me, then?"

"Hm, interesting challenge." His eyes flashed the lustful flame again, "If that is your wish, I shall do my best to bear it true."

Chapter 2

This strange flesh show was uncharacteristic of Kavkan, or so he thought. When invited, Ryven had readily agreed, before the other generals filled him in on the every fifth year party. It wasn't often he was welcomed beyond the barracks and training grounds. To be inside the core of the fortress, and then on top of it. Well, he couldn't resist that.

For this country believed scars were beautiful. He had few. Kavkan also believed that wearing one's armor until the stench mandated a bath and cleaning was normal. He didn't have to worry about using his magic to 'fit in' with scars when in armor every moment.

But when his attire arrived for the party, he second guessed his decision. Triple. Ryven spent too long contemplating it, whether or not he could pull this off.

The little white swath of cloth covered his balls and penis. It tightened them down, so he'd erect when released, but not before. Breathing was impossible. Controlling how everyone in the room saw him and his imaginary scars was nigh so.

Where was he supposed to hide his tools?

He tugged on the cloth, loosening it from his privates for a moment's relief as he considered the transportation spherules on his cot. He needed at least three of them. The six he had left would be ideal, but shoving all of them somewhere on his person was not happening.

It took him four years to gain access to the fortress and the higher ranks. He cursed himself for not beating the brawny Praedae, who held the highest rank of Warmonger, and taking the title for himself. But he knew that would be too much for him to control. Too many people talked to Praedae. As second rank general, he already had too many people interacting with him. Too many minds to control. Too many backstories of how they met to insert into their brains.

The Generals here were treacherous. Not simply physically dangerous, but smart. Each time he had to insert some memory to cover a gap they thought of, he gained massive headaches for the hoops he had to jump through to get through their analytic minds.

For the life of him, he still hadn't memorized all the signals, Kavkan's secret language, because of how complicated it was to infiltrate their minds to learn them. A slight finger twitch or twist of the wrist and he could've commanded something entirely unnecessary. Like dumping out all the pudding in the mess hall for the soldiers to lick up.

He still felt terrible about that.

Kavkan passed these signals down by word-of-mouth. They learned them as infants. It was the toughest language in the world to understand. He knew twenty other languages. Comprehended them easily. Not this one.

One day, he'd learn it. And implement it into his armies. After he took care of what he needed.

He popped two of the transportation balls into his mouth, pressing them into the pockets of his jaw, and hoped he wouldn't swallow them. The other he placed in between the cloth, the base of his cock, and his sack. It had to do. Even if his breathing turned shallower.

A harsh rap sounded on the paneled door. "Enter," he barked, depositing the remaining spheres in his dresser bolted to the floor beside the bed.

"Ready, General Ryv?"

No, he thought to himself. "Ready." He turned and gave a smile to General Drak, thankful he'd already seen his own outfit. Scars covered the older general's body, and the cloth didn't secure him as well as Ryven's did.

The ache in his temples began as he painted himself in what would be suitable scarring for a person of his rank in Kavkan in Drak's mind. The old man rivaled him in strategy games, and was one of the worst to read. Which meant there would be trouble with him soon.

He followed the general, listening to the old man grumble about how they were to see too many dicks tonight and there wouldn't be enough perky tits to make the night better. Saggy bits were his bane, and the elite had plenty of those.

An additional difficulty arose in the form of General Drak's muscled rear in his face as he ascended the stairs behind the wisened, but fit, man. An eyebrow twitch accompanied the twinge of pain in his temples. The glass doors Drak pushed open didn't make a sound, but glittered in the constant glow from the lava all around them. Orange and red spikes danced across their flesh and the obsidian stones before getting lost in the crowd.

"Presenting Generals Drak and Ryv!" the crier blasted as Ryven passed him.

At least it was cooler here, even if he was deaf in one ear at the moment.

When he arrived, he thought he'd melt if he breathed too deep. He remained thankful for his research ahead of time; he made sure he and his soldiers that entered the country knew the measures and spells to save themselves from baking alive in Kavkan. Or freezing to death in its glaciers.

"Good luck. Stay away from anything that wears green." Drak slapped a large hand on his shoulder before sauntering through the crowd.

Green. Outside merchants were to wear something green, symbolizing their weakness. And for Kavkan's to not trust them with any secrets. Ryv was surprised some would be here.

Mating noises washed out the sound of the music coming somewhere from the left. Merchants rich enough to buy their way into Kavkan could easily purchase an invitation. A mountain of gold for the pounding of flesh.

Ryven wove his way through the sex crazed crowd. Initially, removing himself from any instance of touching another. Then it became a game, as it was nigh impossible to take a step without the brushing of exposed skin against his own. A quiet section of the wall appeared, and he sighed. Pressing his back against the icy walls, he took a drink from a naked maid and swallowed half of it down as he deposited one sphere into the glass. He sloshed the rest of the drink against the wall, watching the transport ball tap and roll its way onto the floor, before melting into the stone at his feet. One down. If he may plant the rest, several of his soldiers could enter the fortress from the top and work their way down as the rest worked their way up.

"I present to you, our Klavas!" The crier's announcement tore his attention away from his duty. His gaze rested on the doors and then on the women that entered.

Analytics. Five years of analytics disappearing at the sight of a single woman. She'd done this to him before. Several times. Too many instances where his superior mind hit rock bottom and relied completely on survival instinct.

Tonight was the worst.

They substituted the armor of black and flames with sheer cloth. He only thought them gorgeous in the armor. Now that he saw their muscled figures, he knew he'd made the right decision to take the initiative here. Kavkan would have eaten any of his siblings alive without pause.

For he wanted the bloodline that could control an army of the deadliest in the world and subjugate twenty countries with it. He feared for his army, still, if he slipped and didn't proceed with the plan correctly. He never feared for the lives of his men, for they were the best he knew. Until he entered Kavkan.

Just like he never felt intimidated; until he looked into the eyes of Klava Mylva. Her mind was the most difficult to touch. Their first encounter set him in bed for the rest of the night, moaning and holding his throbbing head like a child with their first headache. But he could only tell the three apart by touching their minds.

Hava. Nava. And then Mylva. Mylva was the one that waxed and waned in his dreams, and entered his plans like a tree busting hammer. The rumors didn't do her justice. She was as formidable as the goddess Kavkans worshiped. Fire, sulfur, and molten to the core.

What he wouldn't give to worship her with every breath she allowed him.

The sisters were nearly as terror inducing, but their minds were easier to crack. And it was in their minds he uncovered the horrors of being Klava. From that moment, his plans changed.

The awe he felt for them endured even doubled in some ways. Ryven knew they needed to be released from their cages. There wasn't much hope in physical healing, but he dreamed they could heal from the mental and emotional torture.

For Mylva, he'd bestow everything on her. A larger place than she knew. And after he gave her that, he'd fight to give her more. If there were other worlds, he'd give her those, too.

Even now, Hava and Nava were having fun, while Mylva was tethering her wild Praedae down before he killed the crowd. Always a strategy based upon what she observed. Fluid mind, ever changing plans to make the most of every situation. A mind that kept him guessing, and working to build his own stratagem around.

He rolled the next orb onto the tip of his tongue. The muscles in his jaw twitched, as Praedae took a position he'd kill to have. There were two things he did better than her precious warrior. He smirked, knowing that he'd get to prove those two to her one day. If she'd have him. If he could get near her again.

He mingled. Ryven shuddered at the sight of Drak's predicament with an elder and a younger genderfluid advisor. The honored general reduced to a toy. At least when his homeland had orgies, all there were willing, and all were happy and content.

"Ryv."

He turned, scanning the crowd for whoever called his name. Fingertips trailed down his biceps. He switched the orb back into his cheek and smiled, "Klava." He bowed his head. This one was Hava. The one that appreciated pretty things. Probably the only one he wouldn't have to paint his scars on for, but he did anyway.

Her mind dwelled on a ritual. Her love of her sisters, her Bloodsworn, was there, but the pain of getting slashed was processed, repeatedly. Along with the memories of the others. Her mind was a cluster of hives intertwined as her subconscious worked through whatever that tradition did to them.

The horror of going through with such a ritual every year tore his heart asunder.

Without thinking, he cupped her cheek in his palm, rested his forehead against hers. The only thing that stopped him from erasing her pain was her saying his name again. He straightened, *right. Not his place,* he thought. "Hm?"

"Think you deserve your Klava?"

He grinned, letting the Kavkan ego loose, "I'm not sure you can handle me, Klava. You do well in battle, but this sword is mightier than what I wield in armor." Her laughter washed over him, and he wondered if Mylva had the same laugh, or if it was a note or two different.

Someone bowed beside them and asked for Klava's attention. He slipped away from Hava and her new suitor, moving the orb back to the tip of his tongue before he spit it. Standing still long enough to watch it sink into the floor, he learned, was a terrible idea. Hands slid up his thighs and curled to the inside. He caught them before they touched the cloth. He turned his head enough to watch the woman's eyes widen over his shoulder.

"Advisor Nular," he stated as his brows rose. She was the Sevinland representative, marrying a Kavkan native to gain her title. Gossip around the halls claimed the couple had complete devotion to one another. Rumors were not true in this case.

"General." Her teeth grit between black painted lips, those a stark contrast to her milky white skin. Paleness was an oddity in Kavkan, and she was indeed pale all over. "You are hurting me."

Kavkan's never admitted pain freely. He stepped from the circle of her arms and released her wrists. Drak's comment about sagging bits crossed his mind before he settled his gaze on hers.

"You haven't enjoyed yourself yet."

She at least had the ego of a Kavkan down. "I have." He licked his lips with the lie.

Nular took it as an invitation. Her thin frame pressed into him and those black lips tilted toward his. The full bodily shudder from her flesh on his had him stepping away quicker than was tactful. Then again, this party was anything but polite.

"General, you should partake. Everyone else is."

"If you know my name, you can have a taste." He smirked as her eyes widened.

"It's General…"

He didn't give her time to fail as he maneuvered through the crowd, "That's a title. Nine others have the same." He waved at her over his shoulder as he turned and began processing the rest of the room.

Ryven bent his mind to making himself invisible or uninteresting to the room at large. The pain between his temples spiked as he hit six walls with his powers. "I can fend off six, I think." He said to himself with a sigh. Tugging at the cloth, he hissed as blood began circulating again, and the spherule dropped to imbed in the floor with the other two.

"To be naked, or not to be." He eyed his crotch as he used two fingers to keep the cloth binding loose.

"Nakedness is preferred by most here."

His ears pricked, and he felt his blood rush throughout. He met her gaze, then immediately bowed.

"Nevermind the formalities. Undo the cloth. I won't have one of my best castrated because of the night." She handed him bits of sheer cloth, "Not sure if this will be much better." She lifted a shoulder.

He nodded, tying it around him as best as he could. It was like a loincloth that hid nothing. So he tugged the string until it broke between his cheeks, and let the white cloth hang too. "I appreciate it." He kept his eyes high on her. "Without armor, I am naked."

Her mouth twisted, her eyes scanning the chamber as she crossed her thick arms under her bare breasts. "As are most Kavkans worth their breath."

"Why do you allow this?" He motioned to the room with one hand.

"It's the one thing I haven't been able to abolish that I desperately want to. These advisors… they fear we will be too powerful if we don't have things like this knocking us down to the mud with them from time to time." Mylva finished her scan and turned to face him. "General Ryv, have you heard anyone speaking of the king with twenty sons?"

I am the first of the twenty, Mylva, he desired to say. Pieces were in place. A perfectly timed game. "I have only heard of that. Twenty sons to one king. But it seems rather impossible. One screeching child would be enough to dry up seed, let alone twenty, don't you think?" After having over twenty siblings, he surprised himself with still wanting an heir of his own.

"Mm." She stared at him, before adding, "One is enough for you, then?"

"Yes, Klava." *What was it about that look that set his blood rushing to his newly freed sword?*

"Male or female?"

What he wouldn't give to have her brain a touch easier to read. "How should I take that question, Klava?"

She grinned, "By the way your body reacts, I know you prefer females." Her eyes trailed down, then flicked back up to his eyes, "I am asking if you prefer male or female offspring."

"Ah. Yes." He cleared his throat. Thinking of the worst things imaginable to get his blood to quiet or slow its rush downward, "As long as the child is born to the best of our abilities, all I can hope for is for it to be healthy."

"Our?"

Smoke and fire, he cursed himself. "You brought it up, Klava."

That seemed to satisfy her as her eyes gleamed with mischief. "Perhaps, General Ryv. You are the type that would suit."

Kavkans liked to keep things simple. Klava and their kin were black-haired, tanned skin, obsidian or green-eyed, and had a frame to carry mountains. Somehow, the gods had blessed him with such looks, and he hoped that his luck continued. He desired her and to be hers.

Thinking about it would do him nothing. He reached for her mind, tapping into her memories to make sure General Ryv was solidified in there. Then he prodded a little deeper. His head pained him, as if a hammer beat his skull like it was a drum. Each path in her mind was thick walled, fortressed to protect her god-like intellect.

It was like trying to break into his mother's mind.

Worse.

Day after the morrow, he gathered after ramming through the walls in her mind. Frozen dicks. She was moving pieces into place tomorrow.

Quickly, he rethought his plan. Shifting things up and ordering them into place. His thoughts splintered, the pummeling in his mind developing into sharp pin pricks that deepened as he sent orders. Once finished, his vision tunneled, his hearing was a roar, and cold sweat goose pimpled his feverish flesh.

"General Ryv?"

He swallowed down the nausea, focusing on her mouth, "Yes, Klava. Do you have need of me?"

"Perhaps another time. I believe the nakedness is getting to you, or perhaps you're already castrated and I was late to salvage. Go. You are released from this pit of mockery." Klava waved a maid over, "Make sure General Ryv is unmolested on his way to the barracks."

It was when they arrived at the barracks that the order was off the table, it seemed. The half naked maid's hand squeezed his ass cheek, pulling him to lean on her more. Each step sent shoots of pain up his spinal column as he shoved her out of his room and used the weight of his body to slam his door shut. If Klava had been of a mind, he wouldn't have the strength to deter her. Compared to the empress, the maid was petite.

Empress Klava Mylva. He thought of her name to shut out the spear of pain the sound of his locks clicking in place caused. Two steps, and he fell on his cot and didn't move. Twenty countries were hers. The whole of this island and a few smaller bodies in the near oceans. This empire explored, but not the other.

She was too great a woman to have only twenty. Mylva. She deserved the world. And he owned most of it.

Throughout the night, he lay in bed. The pricks of pain ebbing and flowing as he relayed messages and orders to his men throughout Klava's Empire. His siblings were warriors in their way, and half already had their prey in hand. The others would follow soon enough. He rolled from his kip as the sound of the birds and beasts of dawn trickled through the barrack's slotted windows.

Taking a slip of paper and pen out, he wrote in the code his father created and took out the largest of the transport orbs from under his pillow. He tapped the slip against it and watched as a red hued light enveloped the slip before it disappeared.

Ryven poured tepid water into the washtub and bathed quickly. His eyes stayed on the orb. Frowning as he dried off, he tapped the orb to make sure it was still working. Red flashed twice before it turned into its usual gray. "Quit dicking Mother and answer me."

Halfway through dressing into his armor, the orb activated and spit out a slip of paper. Ryven snatched it before it hit the ground. "I'll see you when you get home, son. We've missed you."

He knew his smile looked strange, even without checking a mirror.

His father, Licthan, was an orphan. A war between two countries wiped out Licthan's parents and nearly the entire village. At six, his father vowed to sow love into the world. Although his plan was a bit… much, it helped Ryven with his.

Licthan charmed his way into having a harem, including Ryven's mother, who was another survivor of the village massacre. He moved his harem to an island country, took its queen as wife, and became king. This day, Ryven's family numbered in the hundreds. While his father didn't want to touch an army, he had a strategic mind. He knew numbers intimidated, and rumors of numerous deadly warriors caused submission.

The women of his harem were a strategic move itself. Queens, princesses, women of deadly assassin clans, and those like Ryven's mother, Moonapsa, with a mind worthy of a goddess. Not to mention, Licthan loved her, had since he was seven and she eight.

While Ryven didn't have the luxury of a childhood sweetheart, he had his dream woman in Klava Mylva. Smart. Deadly. Ambitious. And while her country lived for war, she could have wiped out the continent. But she didn't.

He hoped it was compassion hiding under the armor that kept people alive around her.

It was while reading a report about an empress that called herself Klava that he knew he had to have her. He formulated the plan. Every step to finish his father's dream, and then to gift Empress Klava the entirety of the world. His plan was falling into place quicker than he anticipated.

He'd expected to be in Kavkan for another year. A long game to gain a beautiful mind. It didn't hurt that she was pretty. Ryven was certain she could snap him in half if she wanted to.

His induction in the Kavkan army was priceless. His father had already implemented some of their practices for elite instruction, per his request. He couldn't wait to torture his siblings with his new strength in the training rounds.

He made his way to the mess hall after hiding his communication tools. A few dabs of a strong herb over his temples and sniffing it twice eased some of the pain. The light of the sun nearly blinded him, but he had to make do. He was a general. He needed to make an appearance.

Ryv arrived in time to see Klava leaving with Praedae. He debated for a moment on following them, but caught some stares from a few soldiers and decided against it. He gathered a heaping plate of meat and fried potatoes with an egg on top of them before sitting at the table reserved for the generals.

"Best eat well, boy. We're about to be sent to Klava knows where."

He smiled at the wisened woman, her bright blue eyes a stark contrast to the rest of them. Instead of swearing to gods, or cursing by them, Kavkan people swore by their leader. For it was she that kept them safe or destroyed them. "Rebellion, again?"

She shook her head, but another answered, "No. A threat to the south."

Ryven raised his brows, even as his inner self grinned, "Threat?" He snorted before adding, "Who's foolish enough to do that?"

"Apparently someone with plenty of seed or has a way to impregnate multiple at once," Drak muttered as he sat down beside Ryv.

"I'm betting on two cocks and he doesn't shit. Just pisses everything." The blue-eyed general, Mabis, raised her fist with a grin.

Drak grinned in return, raising his fist, "I'll take that and claim four ball sacks and a dragon cock because he has to charm them somehow."

"Not everyone has dead balls like you, Drak. I'll wager they're not all his. He claims them." General Tinir raised her fist, incomplete with two missing fingers, and a nasty scar running the length of the back of her hand until her gauntlet edge.

After General Yerv placed her bet of finger cocks, all eyes turned to Ryven. He cleared his throat, taking his time swallowing a bit of water before raising his fist, "I bet he doesn't even exist. It's just a big group run by twenty souls."

Drak chuckled as knuckles rapped into each other, sealing the bet. In Kavkan, bets were always teeth, a weapon, and the helm. The winner also got to land a punch wherever they liked on the losers. None of them would land any punches, or gain any teeth on this bet. Ryven felt his throat tighten and hoped they had as much sense as he knew they had.

For they'd either die by his order on the morrow, or surrender and bend their heads in shame. He didn't care for either outcome, but most didn't appreciate their control being challenged or taken. If the rest of his plans fell into place, they wouldn't be resentful for long.

Mylva and Praedae returned, sweat on their faces, panting. He stood with the rest of the generals and the soldiers in the mess hall. He envied a training match with either. Both were formidable, even if he had beaten Praedae once. Technically, he had to let Praedae win. It would be too much to gain that much notoriety and keep his cover entrenched in all their minds.

Klava grabbed a plate, downed one cup of water, and brought another to the table. She nodded for them to sit as she did. "Ready in the morn at the tower."

"Of course, Klava." The generals acknowledged in unison.

Ryv watched Praedae bark orders at the soldiers to finish up and get to the training grounds over his own black stone cup.

"When did you gain generalship, Ryv?"

He turned, catching her sharp gaze, and holding it as he dove into her mind, slamming through wall after wall, rebuilt as pain in his head. His hold on her was slipping, and continued to slip because he wasn't paying attention to it. He was too close. He had to move too many pieces between now and the morning for him to mess it up.

"A year ago, wasn't it, boy?" Yerv spoke in a tone that resembled everyone else's tone as they ordered their underlings around. She never let up. He learned quickly that she was close to deaf, but still fearsome enough to keep her general title.

"Yes, just." Ryv answered both. He kept digging through her barriers, chasing her mental timeline of him. He discovered more of what he found last night. A ritual. Memories shared. The maze overwhelmed him. He planted the thought, and left, hoping the merge of minds from last night was enough to let it tie in where it needed to.

"Your first battle as general will be soon." Mylva grinned, flames of war raging in her eyes.

Five years in Kavkan and he found their minds to be the best he'd encountered, and the worst. Rage. War bent. With trauma shut up tightly behind locked doors in the back. Enough suffering to fuel bloodshed.

Praedae thought with rage and hormones, if one could even call it thought. Ego and pain fettered Drak's intelligence. Arthritis had consumed the man; at his age, Ryv only hoped he could still move that well. Yerv's hearing hindered her from reading the room, but she was still sharp on threats and attacks. The others were a grade or two down from Drak and Yerv, and never touched Mylva's cunning.

The greatest test of his life would be at dawn.

Chapter 3

As soon as Mylva stepped foot in the dining hall of her officers, silverware clattered to the dishes and they stood. In unison, they bowed and cried, "Good morning, Klava." By the rich fatty scent, she could tell pork was on all their plates.

"Good morning. Finish your meal." At her order, they sat down and completed their meal. All except one. He loomed over those at the head of the middle table, the plate before him scraped clean. Before giving her a nod, he quickly finished his drink.

She slowed her pace down the open corridor, but not for long, so he could catch up. The training grounds and the corridors surrounding were empty. Sconces were still lit. The sun hadn't risen yet.

"Did you sleep well, Klava?"

She grunted a yes before asking him the same question.

"After bedding the other two Klavas to give them matching marks, I did."

She looked at him out of the corner of her eye when his voice had a bite to it. His eyes were the orange they took on before rage erupted. "Praedae, you mean to tell me you are displeased with having your Klava ride you?"

His boot scraped, the only sign of his faltering thoughts, "No, not at all, Klava." He answered as they walked through an intersection of corridors and entered the training grounds she had built for her personal use. And that of her Bloodsworn, of course.

While open like the other grounds, a shield of magic covered it, preventing anyone from seeing inside or hearing anything from within. Nor could they enter, unless she gave them permission. The gift from her Praedae was a secret room for her exclusive use.

"Enter." She said as she strode through the shield.

He followed her.

She turned on him, "Did they disappoint you?"

He stood still, staring into her eyes, "No, Klava."

"How do you know it is me, and not them you speak to?"

Here his lips twisted into a snarl, "I can tell the difference between the three of you. I may be the only one, other than maybe Gyrna, but I know you. I know you are the Klava I..." His jaw cracked with the click of his mouth shutting. He looked away.

"The Klava you, what?" She grabbed his jaw, forcing him to look into her eyes. His were boiling with red and orange alike. A war of emotions she never saw in him.

A silence between them was long before he answered, his voice filled with conviction, "The Klava I swore my life to. The Klava I have trained with so she may protect herself and her people without fear. The Klava I have battled with, always at her side, because her ideals and strategies are what I breathe for. You. You are my Klava."

She yanked her hand back from his jaw as if stung.

"I am already Bloodsworn. I shall never speak your secrets." He went down on one knee. If he had his helm, he would have set it at her feet. Ready for death or her blessing.

"Are you in love with me?"

His head jerked up at the question. He gaped at her. The colors that betrayed his emotion warring in them again, before he squeezed them shut. "No."

She had to believe him. Otherwise, things would become complicated. Klavas didn't take husbands. They mated with a suitable partner. Love for a mate was a weakness. "You are Bloodsworn. That must be enough for you."

"Yes, my Klava."

"You say that to the other two as well, in public. You cannot just call me 'my Klava', understand?"

"Yes, my Klava."

She let him stay on his knees for a few moments longer. "Let's spar." The sun's first rays made the rubies glisten along his back, as if they were new droplets of blood.

"As you wish, my Klava." He stood.

His black armor gleamed like hers. Instead of gold intricacies added to the edges and designs, his were glistening red. The mark of his status as Warmonger. The tear shaped rubies signified the number of lives he'd conquered. Something he had started in the first war they fought together.

The years of peace ensured that the last three slots remained unfilled, keeping him from hanging it up with the other two in his chambers to start another afresh.

No wonder his emotions warred within him. It had been too long since he spilled blood. Perhaps the new threat would set his mind straight. War was when they were at their best.

"A Sparrow arrived today."

She picked up a spear. They started with long distance first. "And?"

He did likewise, walking to the ring's center. "A few more details on the twenty sons."

She faced him, two body lengths away. "Go on." She smirked, motioning him to take the first shot. Mylva took in a deep breath of the fresh air, readying herself.

His spear slid through his hand until he held the end. He stepped forward, swinging the weapon in an arc, and again. "They are here, on the mainland. They confirm one is in Parvis as we speak."

Parvis. Like the last thrust, it was too close. She knocked his spear from the smooth arc of his swing with the butt of hers, relishing the clang of metal against metal. She stepped on the end, leaping to throw herself to his side and jab at him with her first attack.

"Any action taken?" Her neighbors in Parvis were rich. Their mines held as many jewels as hers, but were far less dangerous to dig in as they had dormant volcanoes. The farmland there was mighty prosperous and fed several countries in her empire. Parvis paid a handsome sum for the use of the Kavkan armies before allied.

They still paid handsomely for the Kavkan guards.

"No, not as we know." He grinned, knocking her thrust away with his gauntlet, and grabbing at her shaft in the next breath. "I have trusted men scouring our lands."

She jerked the spear toward him again, avoiding his grasp, while trying for another attack on his open side. "We have had no one enter, other than myself lately."

"This is true. But I would rather be safe than sorry." He clasped the sharp head between his arm and chest plate, swinging his to knock her weapon out of her hand.

In retaliation, she grabbed the shaft just under the blade, using his upward momentum and strength to swing her legs forward and planted her boots in his diaphragm. He grunted and fell back with her; the spears falling to the ground in a clatter. She expected his next move as she spoke, "Before me, were there any arrivals that would be beneath my advisors reporting to me?"

As she predicted, he swung his legs up behind her, going to use his falling momentum to roll her to the ground and he on top of her. Thwarting him, she pushed off his breastplate, slamming her shoulders into his shins, and rolling back over his feet to gain hers.

He thrust his hips up, planting himself to stand and face her. "Draw."

"Draw." She agreed and strode over to the weapons rack and chose a two-handed sword. The scent of weapons was one of her favorite metals and woods with pristine oiled edges.

"Only one caravan from Parvis of fruit and vegetables, a small delegation from the upper Kavkan glacier who attended the party last night, and a shipment of cloth from… wherever it is we get cloth." Praedae lifted a shoulder with the mention of cloth, hefting and then swinging the longsword with one hand.

"Gagaint." She did the same, not to be outdone, showing off that she was just as strong as he was. Gagaint was distant, possibly allowing someone from an island country to hide in, as it did little to watch their borders since the kingdoms fell under her. It was landlocked by a coastal country on one side, Slifth, and Dreindank on the other.

He made a face, mentioning the fields.

She smirked, he'd hated those battles. Their armies were out in the open. Only a few trees dotted the flat landscape of Gagaint, and those were never tall enough to provide shade. The storms there whipped up out of nowhere and lightning strikes always hit the dry grasses, causing fires. The fires were constant until the winter torrential rains that caused deep mud fields that lasted for days, or lakes if another few storms popped up in the same area before the land could dry out.

Praedae prized his boots and hated feeling like a drowned rat.

He motioned for her to take the initiative. This time he talked to her through the sign language of her armies, and spies. It came naturally to both of them. His favorite thing to do was to tell her the opposite of his next move.

"I assume you checked the carts properly?" She lunged, then danced away, only to swing at his head. He motioned he was going to take it and die.

"Yes, of course." He blocked the swing with his gauntlet and shoulder, grunting as the strength of her move knocked him off balance.

She kicked the sword from his hand. He frowned as it landed near the forgotten spears. She grinned and pulled her sword from his shoulder armor and gauntlet. "Nothing to worry about at the moment." She tossed her blade down, picking a pair from the racks for the next round.

"Yet." He mimicked, rolling his shoulders as he chose a long blade and then a dagger.

As the swords clanged, and daggers slid along armor, she came up with a plan. "Call the armies to the tower in the morning. We're going to help our allies weed out these infiltrators."

"As you wish, my Klava." He said with a smirk as he crossed his blades in front of her neck.

ᘒ ᘒ ᘒ

Mistake. Ryven cursed under his breath as he wiped sweat from his brow. He eyed the soldier at his side, one of his half-siblings. *Young. Foolish.*

"This was not to be." He wiped the froth from Klava's mouth with a kitchen apron.

"What then?"

The gurgled question made his stomach flip, the stench of her breath enveloped his nose in acidic burns. Panic gripped him, and his powers evaded his use. He couldn't tell, even this close, if she was the real ruler of a decoy. His powers continued to elude him. "You were to live. To have a choice."

Eyes with newly popped vessels in them stared up at him, a deep green amid the sea of white and red rivers. "Free?"

"Free."

"Klava… she will be free, then?" Her fist gripped his collar, fingernails digging into his neck. Her other hand still blindly reached for something, anything, on the floor to their side.

"Yes. She will be." This wasn't Mylva then? A decoy. He leaned into her hand, her thoughts spilling into him. Relief spilled in with her thoughts, as she was not Mylva. He watched her, knowing Hava was finding peace, and there was no pain.

"She needs it." Hava swallowed hard, liquid spilling from the corners of her mouth faster than he could wipe it away. "If you lie…" Hava showed her teeth, her glassy eyes flashing for the last time as her grip slid free of his collar and her body fell limp in his arms.

Ryven gritted his teeth to keep from cursing.

"It was supposed to be just in case! Not…" His young half-sibling's voice faded away as his attention jerked toward the door. "Someone…"

"Hide." Ryven hissed, lying Hava down as gently as he could in her armor on the stone of the kitchen floor. He lunged toward a pantry door, barely fitting in it.

He took the blame for Hava's death like a knife in his chest.

The other one. A sharp gasp before she landed on her knees beside Hava. Working her fingers into her sister's mouth, dragging out what she could. Her slick fingers fumbled at the leather and buckles, desperately pulling the chest plate. With a scream, she lifted her sister by the armor and shook it, willing it to free her.

Ryven couldn't take any more. "Klava." He stepped out, holding his sword so its point was at her neck. "I didn't mean for this to happen."

Those eyes. They were the same. How? Same height. Same build. This close to them and their resemblance sent chills down his spine. It was a once a year thing for them to be together like this. He'd never gotten this close to more than one at a time. It was the eyes that made him feel like he was about to burn alive. "She was to live. Like you. And the other. Live and choose."

A bark of a laugh as she stood with tears spilling down her cheeks. "Choose? Choose what? Poison or beheading?" Klava's fingers flexed at her sides.

"No. You were all supposed to live. I don't like needless killing." The snort made the hairs on the back of his neck stand up, and he dove into her mind as his resolve finally settled the panic of a broken plan. Kavkans killed their enemies without thought. "I have an idea to take the world and give it to the true Klava. She… I feel she deserves it. Don't you?" His head ached with the clang of her thoughts, raging forward like the ring of metal upon metal.

The dark brows of the female warrior drew close, a crease forming between them. Her eyes seemed to search for something behind him. To read or remember something. "As long as one of us lives, there will be no choice for Klava. We will fight, always fight, always… keep our scars together. No rest."

After another pause, she began again, "You killed her. The nicest one of us." The sneer was sharp. Her voice biting, "You should have gotten me first." She hit her knees, hand cupping Hava's cheek, then she took her sister's hand in hers, her body slumping in the stiff armor with a heavy sigh of release. "She looks at peace. Doesn't she?"

He nodded, her desire for an end washed out the clanging rage like an avalanche.

"I hope what you say is true. We are… I am tired. I cannot take this without Hava. I can't… without both of us, Klava will fight you or lose her will to live." Her eyes trailed up to him, "If you give her freedom, our deaths will be worth it. I ask you, give me my peace with that sword. If you point it, use it."

Ryvan shook his head, "I cannot."

"You will."

He swallowed, watching her face and knowing her resolve. He'd seen something like that before. A desire for death. He knew little, and could imagine even less of their suffering. For her to want this, to desire her end like this? Her torture must have been great indeed. "Very well."

She smiled up at him, "Be free, my sister," she whispered as she closed her eyes and dropped her head.

Liquid ice flowed through Mylva's chest to her toes and fingertips. A golden light burned through her eyelids. The sticky stubbornness of slumber held her lashes together. A golden orange beam of sunlight poured through the window she faced.

Afraid the ice in her fingertips would make the burning in her face worse, she blinked a few times to clear the sleep. The motion caused a matching flutter of throbs in her skull. Thoughts raced across her hazy mind. Where was she? Why was she waking? Hadn't she been in the tower moments before?

The image of her army in their black and silver armor stretching before the fortress walls washed through her memory. The speech she had written to inspire them and herself still upon her lips. Then an ache at her temples. The bliss of nothing followed. Blackness.

She lifted her hand. The black of her gloves blocking the sunlight. Tentatively, she touched her cheek. The burning in neither her cheek nor her fingers doubled with the action. Whatever it was, the burning was inside her. Not outside. She cleared her eyelashes with a few rough swipes of her gloves.

A black iris on a red field stained the clear glass of the arched window. The other windows, she'd never counted them, met in the middle, creating a cacophony of her kingdom's symbol upon the roof. She was home, still. In the dancing hall above the mountain and her beloved lava pits.

She pushed up, the familiar weight of her armor absent. The marble floor cooled her palms. Her right cheek and ear cooled from their contact with the marble while she slept, Mylva realized. An odd taste was in her dry mouth.

Why didn't they carry her to her bedchambers? Had she passed out in the tower? Had she gotten too excited about the prospect of war? Looking down at herself, she found the plain black clothes she wore under her armor intact. Had she gotten too hot? The thought made her snort. She was born of fire and lava. Fire magic ran through her veins. Too hot and too excited was not an option.

A door hinge creaked. She turned, seeking a mace that was absent and a blade that was missing. Weaponless. Gyrna entered. The maidservant she trusted with her very life. She was pale, like the old tales of spirits of the dead, and she moved with a dragging motion in her right leg. As Gyrna looked at her, those dark eyes sparked with something.

Hope.

"You're awake, my Master."

It was odd for Gyrna to call her that. Despite being master and servant, they had addressed each other by name since teens. "What's going on, Gyrna?"

"I believe I can answer that."

She turned as Gyrna came to her side and pulled her to her feet. She leaned on her maidservant's stocky frame as the ice in her blood threatened to topple her. Poison? Once she held steady, she stood on her own. Facing the voice, she gazed at a helm of white with a cream crest of horsehair shining like starlight. Shadows covered their face and eyes. He was twice her size, a feat even giants from the south found difficult. The armor gleamed polished silver. Carved on the breastplate was a symbol she had never seen upon armor or on the war banners on a field.

She should have picked up on his presence before Gyrna entered. "Who are you?"

"One question at a time. I have infiltrated your country, Klava." As he spoke, a trio of soldiers rose from the ground before her, bowed to the stranger, and marched toward the door. "I have you. Kavkan is full of my army, ready to tame it and make it my father's. Unless you willingly release it to me." The voice resonated in the glass room.

She snorted, glancing at Gyrna. Covering her surprise at the soldiers appearing out of thin air, she kept her gaze steady on her friend. With the gentle and minute flicks of her fingers, her maidservant verified the words. Gyrna also signed that no one told him she was the true volcano born Klava.

Gyrna was one of four that knew the secret of the sisters. Bloodsworn herself, Gyrna was incapable of telling anyone she was the true Klava, or else the oath would burn her from the inside out. As were the other maids belonging to Hava and Nava, and the Praedae - the most powerful general of their army and most loyal protector.

Where were they, her sisters?

"I am but a mere warrior. Not the Klava you seek."

His head tilted, and white teeth showed between shadows. Not a grin, not a snarl, something else. Thick fingers, ungloved, snapped. The door opened again, and another wearing matching armor entered. This one carried a covered platter from her own kitchens. "Show her." The helmed enemy demanded.

The soldier bowed when he stopped a body's length away. He took the oval covering off.

She swallowed the bile that rose before her rage swept it away. Hair, black and silky, poured over the edge of the platter, matching her own. Their clouded eyes stared up at her. Dried reddish-orange blood spilled from Nava's mouth while Hava's flesh was an eerie green. Blood pooled beneath their heads, lapping at the black edges of the oval platter, lending a coppery and sulfur scent to the air.

Countless ways to eliminate the men in the room crossed her mind.

"I believe they own the name Nava and Hava, a secret known by few. Second and third Klava. Don't worry, they didn't speak of your truth. Honorable to the end."

Gyrna's shoulders shook with silent sobs at her side. She swallowed down the screams in her throat and closed her eyes against the threat of tears rarely spilled. She was nothing. No one without them.

"I know you are the true Klava. Ruler of this land. Love of your people. Strategist. Inspirer. But no one has called your name. What is it?"

"Klava." The millionth way for them to die raced through her mind, and her fingertips craved to soak in their blood. She had to find out what they wanted. How they had manipulated their way into her holdings… or had enough magic to grow from her floors? She had too many questions to spill their life blood over the lava pits.

His smile didn't gleam again under the helm, one point for intelligence in his favor. "Klava, what?"

"My Master's name is too precious to be defiled by your lips!"

"No matter. We can take all the time we need to know each other." He waved away the soldier holding the platter. "Keep them well for funeral rites. Do you burn your bodies like Sevinland or bury like Parvis?"

At the mention of her neighboring countries, Mylva watched him. "Tell me what you know about Sevinland and Parvis." Something about him pricked familiarity.

Was this the kingdom of twenty sons? Had they already taken Sevinland and Parvis? Why didn't anyone inform her? How did she not know the simple symbols of her enemy until one of them stood in her dance hall?

Had she slipped?

"They find themselves in the same situation as you. My siblings are there, with their armies, talking to a ruler."

"You are a son of the King with twenty sons?" She murmured as it settled into reality. For once, rumors were true. *Why did his voice call to her like a friend?*

"One for each of you."

Her empire. Her countries, including her own beloved Kavkan. Twenty of them were being held like this. "Each of us? Why?"

Another mirthless smile before he answered, "A son to marry into each of the ruling families of each country in this land."

"You are mad to think I would believe that." She sneered, noting where each of his blades was. "No army is enormous enough to hold twenty countries hostage." Not even her army could be spread so thin.

He had to have weapons hidden, too.

"Yes, our father's army is large enough."

When he didn't expound, she held out her hand, "Dagger."

His chuckle was low and echoed off the glass walls, "No."

"You are preparing Nava and Hava for death rites. My hair goes with them. Give me your dagger or send for some scissors." She pulled her thick braid from under her shirt. The end slapped against her hip. Years of growth. All because Hava wished to see how long it took for Mylva to break and cut it. The weakest willed would remain unknown.

A rare burning began behind her eyes as she ran her hand down the length of inky hair. The women who were as much a part of her as her hands were gone. She studied the man in armor before her. Had they died by his hand? Or just by his words? Either way, she would have a pound of his flesh for each of them.

Nava. Hava. Names given to them by her mother, not by theirs, as was the custom for Bloodsworn of Klavas. She missed their whispered advice and the silent motions of their hands. Only Gyrna remained, maybe her Warmonger, if he was smarter than her.

She watched the armor flicker in the sunlight, then fade to shadows before glinting again as he walked from one stream of sunlight to the other. Not once moving closer to her, but not escaping her line of sight, either. His pace was deliberate. Not slow enough for a warring debate in his mind, but one of consideration. Measuring.

Pondering if she was worthy of his blade or not, perhaps.

"Why your hair?"

She felt her lips twist, but before she could answer, Gyrna scoffed. "As if my master needs to explain herself to you."

"If she wants it done, yes, she does." Another smile made his shadowed countenance look feral. "Name or an explanation. Your choice."

Her name held more devotion among her people than the gods' names. Its sacredness far surpassed the ritual of grieving. To her, Nava and Hava were far more important than her name. Still, a name was power, especially with her orange blood running through her veins. Her name could bind her for life.

"This hair was a bet we had. I've lost it."

"I see."

He pulled the silver handle from his left hip, sliding free a shining silver blade. Her enemy moved toward her, clasping the hilt in his hand. He raised the blade, reaching for her braid with his other hand.

She stepped away, shaking her head as Gyrna jumped between them.

"To cut my Master's hair is to turn her into your slave."

He tilted his head, the horsehair on his helm swinging from the center of his back to the broad shoulder. "Do your people never have your hair cut, then?"

"Yes, but not by an enemy." Gyrna answered, her voice holding another scoff as if the answer had been staring at him.

"I cannot give you the blade."

Klava smirked, "Why?"

"Your reputation, of course."

"A blade is only marginally superior to my bare hands. You trust me with them. Why not a tiny blade like that?"

"Excellent question, for I have another. Why have you been so submissive? You are not at all how the rumors painted you."

"Rumors are often less clever lies masquerading as hidden truths." She answered readily enough. It was one of Nava's favorite quotes. "What do you want?"

"Place your army on standby. Come back to Rothland with me." His voice softened at the last of his words.

"Only to gain Rothland's surrender."

"Then I will hold your country hostage until you agree to my terms." Another clanking shrug.

Seeing her opening, Mylva grasped the dagger, jerking it free from his hand. Gyrna flung herself against the armored man, causing him to grunt and fall back a few steps. The Klava raked the blade through her tresses at the back of her neck. Her braid in one hand, she flicked the weapon round and round with her fingers twice before Gyrna swung free of his grasp.

Mylva crouched, then launched herself at the man. They fell. His armor clattering against the marble. She ripped his helm free. With her braid, she wrapped one of his wrists in it, pulling his arm down to pin it under her knee. Once held there, she moved both of her hands to the dagger, using her full weight to push the point closer to his right eye. His arm shook with the effort of holding her at bay.

"Klava!"

She glanced toward the scream from Gyrna. Three armored soldiers surrounded her Bloodsworn with a spiked mace raised to strike while short silver blades held the maidservant still. She turned her gaze back to the man underneath her and raised her brows.

"I die. She dies. Then they subject you to thirty-two years of torture."

"Why thirty-two?" She asked, taking in his features. He'd be a suitable sire for the Bloodsworn, or to make her daughter. If she ever had one. Black hair, dark eyes, flesh the same tanned tone as hers. Familiar.

He grunted, "That's how long I've lived, dear Klava. That is one of our sacred traditions."

She sat back, still holding the dagger, but no longer pointing it at his flesh. "What do you want with me?" She watched as the soldiers around Gyrna slightly relaxed. Not enough slack for her to take a chance.

His now free hand, thick and warm, rested on her thigh, "You are to become my wife, or one of my sister-in-laws."

She snorted, taking her eyes off Gyrna to stare down at him. "Marrying into royal families won't work here. I am my family. We breed. We don't marry." A general. He was General Ryv. One of her very own underneath her... how had he become one of hers?

"That's about to change. I have infiltrated your country with thousands of warriors. They live and breed among you."

"Is it?" As she mulled over his words, she saw a flash just inside her peripheral vision. Golden and swift. She flicked her fingers wide on her free hand. The flashes started relaying a quick code.

The report confirmed what she suspected and what he'd revealed. Her blood kin were dead. Only Gyrna remained of her Bloodsworn. Captors held her generals Mavis, Ada, and Tayna captive while another three were dead. Drak and Praedae were missing. Her ten personal assassins lifeless. So were her twelve guardians, who protected Hava, Nava, and herself in shifts.

"It is." Her enemy stated, still underneath her.

"Your magic... is shifting into another person? One familiar to me? And the magic of your army, those who infiltrated, is the same?" That was the only explanation her brain could fathom while keeping him distracted from the window, and her Sparrow.

"In a way." His words fell from his mouth as if that was answer enough.

Just two of her Sparrows survived or made contact. The one reporting to her, and the one stationed in Parvis. She released her faithful Sparrow from their duties with a few motions of her fingers and told them to save themselves and those they loved, if possible.

She didn't spot another flash.

Her best was gone. Kavkan hostage. She stared into the eyes of her enemy. Her general. Her rage boiled. She tamped it down. Patience.

"Gyrna, it seems I am about to take a long journey."

Chapter 4

The thick white mourning cloth fit better now that she was grown. Gyrna wrapped it over the black irises of her shoulder plates, then let the ends trail down to the ground. Mylva had burned the ends the last time she wore the wrap, leaving them ragged and ashen. When her mother died, nearly twenty years ago. On that day, she'd inherited the cloth of the death rites.

Back then, they had to wrap it twice over her abdomen, and then swaths over her arms, and still the garment had trailed too far behind her ten-year-old self in the cavern of their dead.

This day, the day she grieved her Bloodsworn, the ashen ends of the white linen barely touched the ground.

Within her hands was the diamond bowl where just the other day she had shared in the Memory Merge with the two lying in the iron caskets on either side of her. The trio were in the volcano's depths; where only her ancestors and those of her two Bloodsworn sisters returned to the flames that birthed them. The families of her generals held the same ritual for them, three chambers above her.

In these hallowed depths, she and Gyrna stood to see her sisters off. The man who killed them was not of honor, but curiosity, she was sure. He stood in his pale armor a step behind Gyrna. She looked at her maidservant and nodded.

Gyrna pushed the caskets forward, the magic lending the rest as Klava kept pace with them. Ahead were crystalline doors, keeping most of the heat at bay. The doors parted, allowing her to enter with her sisters, and they snicked shut behind her, locking Gyrna and her enemy out of the room of her gods.

Her power swelled, feeding off the earth's blood surrounding the long basalt embarcadere into its depths.

She walked with the caskets down toward the end. The magma sizzled and spat around her, held apart from the pier by the magic of her god like a wall of impenetrable glass.

She reached down into the casket to her right, Hava, poking the sharp edge of her gauntlet into a finger. Blood tainted the linen that wrapped the body before it dribbled three drops, which deposited into the diamond bowl in her free hand. She repeated the action with the other, Nava.

At the pier's end, she stopped. The caskets floated on without her, into the wall of magma. She began her prayer as the mountain's blood swallowed up the last of the iron caskets. A prayer in the ancient tongue she hoped would never leave her lips again. It roughly translated as: *I give to you my heart. For these are my sisters, Bloodsworn to you and I, oh fire goddess Kasvuki. Take them into your heart whence they came as my own shatters in despair. Give me strength to carry on without them. For I will see them again. Soon.*

Mylva knelt, pretending this was part of the service as well. Into the bowl, she dropped three droplets of her own blood. Swirling them together, she uttered the phrase she wasn't supposed to for another year. Her hands clutched the bowl to her chest as their last memories flooded in a riot of sounds, smells, tastes, noises, words, and emotions.

She felt their amusement at watching her being fucked by Praedae during the party. Their climax mirrored her own as he gave them the same marks. She felt despair as Hava threw out the dead flower before she and Nava succumbed to sleep.

Peace. A soft melody as Hava hummed, readying her tea in an empty kitchen, pale moonlight slipping into the predawn glow out the window. She alone suffered from an acidic stomach, often set off by the greasy foods served at the party. A shadow in the doorway. A wide-eyed boy, clutching the small basin of water she used for her tea. Hava's fingers twitched toward the kitchen knives hanging on the wall. Hurried words in a cracking voice, a promise of peace, of freedom. Of healing. She didn't need to drink that tea, for it was poison, all she had to do was join them. As the cup emptied through her lips, she grew sleepy. Numbness entered her hands and feet. She stared at them, the boy, the shadow turned man. The boy's sobs were quiet as his thin body shook, as her nail beds turned green. Sadness flowered as she spoke her last words: *I shall miss you, my sisters. My heart is full because of each of you, I have lived a grand life.*

Rage erupted, swallowing Mylva whole as she relived the memory of their enemy attacking Nava when she found Hava slumped over the table in the kitchen. She stopped, listening to his words, the promise of marrying the true Klava, explaining the choice Hava had. A bloom of hope swarmed the rage, and Nava smiled as she dropped her maces and knelt. She moved her hair to the side, waiting for the sword to fall on her neck, a smile still on her face as she mouthed the words: *You should be free Mylva, this is your chance. Change our world.*

Salty tears evaporated before they could fall into the diamond bowl. Those who knew her best had departed. She shared her world with no one.

A thud sounded behind her. She turned her face to stare at the strange open palm stretched over the glass partition. Freedom? She could step into the magma. End her line.

Free for her.

Her gaze flicked to Gyrna. She took in the line of her mouth, the darkness of her brow from too much time spent in the sun on battlefields right beside her, and the rage in her eyes. Rage that would burn away her future. Gyrna wouldn't live life as she should. Not without revenge.

Her passing might destroy the privileged life her people led. How had he tricked her sisters so quickly? Mylva prodded at their memories, trying to pick things apart to see the conviction or the trickery. His words, peace, marriage, what was behind them?

She soaked up the last of the mountain she could into her veins, tamping it down so it didn't show in her face, but burned wildly in storage within her heart. Mylva stood. The bowl in her hands grew heavy. She took it in. The beautiful facets, the sheen of magic over it. She tossed it into the liquid that replicated the blood of her goddess.

No other would face this sorrow, whether they were of her loins, or another.

Mylva's spine cracked as she saluted her remaining generals. She hoped it wouldn't be the final encounter. The women were the best fighters and minds left alive in her country. In their hands, her Kavkan would rest until her return. If she returned.

"Treat our invaders as guests, but don't let them ruin us." She stated after motioning them to relax. "I shall see you again."

"I shall see you again." Her generals repeated back to her as one. Then they bowed.

The Klava stared at them. The sunlight of the early morning made the cast gold upon their ebony armor gleam. All of them bore the dark black hair and tan flesh of their people. They were broad, powerful, and proud. Bowing was a gesture reserved for rank promotion and paying respects to the fallen.

Now they bowed to her. As if they were honoring her. Fallen. And she was. Dishonored. Her power taken in a day.

She gave them a nod. Her newly shorn hair fluttering around her face was still an odd phenomenon. She swallowed back the tears, holding her head high as her enemy's men flanked her.

The Floral Courtyard smelled of passion flower, orchids, and golden swords. Scents she was sure to miss again. She allowed herself to look. To memorize the tall red pillars whose only job was to allow the long tendrils of fruiting vines to flourish. The Klava watched the sunlight sparkle through the dew upon the flowers.

Swiftly, they passed through the welcoming courtyard and reached the shadowy onyx wall with its iron gate. She saw him, once a friend, now the enemy, leaning against a tall gray stallion. The itch to kill him roared to life. Reason rose in a wave to douse it. What was the use of killing him if there were nineteen more to take his place?

Enormous horses for the area stomped and snorted under his men. The hair over their hooves alone could make a bald man happy. Not to mention kindling for fire. As she approached, the deceiver straightened his armor. He seemed too uncomfortable, ensconced in the heavy plates. He didn't wear his horsehair helm; it rested on his saddle horn.

The black of his hair, his build, unsettled her. All but for the squareness of him, especially his brow line, kept her from thinking he was kin. They did not at all match her green eyes or her rounded face shape. He would have definitely made a better sire to her child's Bloodsworn.

"This isn't all, is it?" He motioned to the lone trunk of hers on a wagon hitched to titanic horses that could rival the ones his guards rode.

"Yes."

He frowned at it, "It's light."

"As it should be for travel."

He shook his head, "Your dresses, attire for state, extra armor, underthings… where are those?"

"My one dress is in there. I wear armor for meetings which is on my person. Extra undergarments are in there. Shall I show you?" She strode toward the wagon.

"No." He met her gaze, "A cloak?"

"On my horse."

"That should be a blanket to sleep in."

She sneered, "What is a cloak if not a blanket with buckles?"

"I…" He pressed his lips together when one of his men cleared his throat. "Very well."

He moved to her horse, capturing her stirrup in his hand before bending down to one knee.

She stared down at him, "What are you doing?"

"Aiding your mount." He glared up at her, "What does it look like I'm doing?"

Mylva laughed, plucking his hand from her stirrup before placing her boot in it. She rested her hand on her mare's mane, grounding them both in their partnership. She gathered her reins and, with slight pressure on the stirrup and her mare's withers, swung up with ease. "Even the smallest child learns to mount their horse on their own before learning to walk in my country."

He stood. "Your armor…" His voice trailed off as he fingered the plates along her calf. "This is light enough to move freely."

When his fingers explored up her thigh, she leaned down, "To take it is to kill me. To have it off, my body is to begin a bargain for offspring. Which is it you wish, Prince?"

His dark gaze bored into her soul, his lips twisting into a smirk. "We shall see soon enough."

As he walked back toward his horse, the Klava ground her teeth. His filth had touched her. She could've killed him. Easily. A boot to the head. Pulling her mare down upon him. Mylva bit back each urge, and took a deep, calming breath of sulfuric air.

Her attention turned to a huffing and kicking Gyrna being dragged toward the wagons.

"She is to stay here." Mylva growled the order, glaring at his men who handled her Bloodsworn like a sack between them.

"You need a maid. I also need leverage for when you get out of sorts." The trickster stated after being pushed up onto his horse by two other guards.

She couldn't fault him for that logic. She observed the loading of a few other trunks onto the wagon with Gyrna. "Finally pillaging?"

"Just enough supplies to get us to Parvis, Klava." He smirked at her, "I wouldn't want to steal from my family so soon in our relationship." He turned, kicking his horse into a canter, "Ride beside me," the once General Ryv called over his shoulder.

"Commands do little for me." She muttered as she adjusted her gloves and then gauntlets. Her mare agreed, cantering amidst the surrounding stallions. Fiery nostrils flared as she bent her neck with a snort. Kavkan's never named their horses. To do such was to sully and weaken the bond during battle.

She felt barren. A stranger to herself, as many parts of her were gone. Shattered. And they were departing from the sole place she healed best.

The Empress turned in her saddle, her mare slowing to follow her movements, until they both faced their volcanic home. Six towers speared up into the sky, natural wonders. Her ancestors added the winding stairs in their sides and the flattened gardens up top. Each garden held a statue of the six founding warriors of her country, of her ancestors. Below the towers that pierced the gray skies stretched her home. Built in and over natural lava flows, or in the sheer cliffs where windows magicked into place, reflected the flickering fires here and there. It was rough around the edges. Dangerous. The great plains of glaciers lay beyond, stretching to the northern ice filled seas. A single path stretched along the border of fire and ice, hand hewn, and a favorite pastime for many, including herself. She would miss the clarity the path lent her thoughts until her return.

Mylva watched as a snowflake survived its fall from the soft gray clouds above, through the heated air down to her. She let it settle on her gloved knuckle, but peace nor clarity stilled her mind with its demise. Nowhere in the world compared to her home. No people like hers either. Hearty, kind, and built with fire in their veins.

"Klava."

She held up her hand. Knowing she only needed a few more seconds. It was almost time.

A low rumble vibrated the stone path underneath her mare's hooves. She smiled up at the old mountain. The Klava turned back, nudging her mare along and rose beside an open wagon.

"Happy birthday, Klava." Gyrna reached out, brushing her fingertips along the black iris crest upon her shoulder.

Heat stung her eyes from behind, "Happy birthday, Nava. Hava."

She allowed her mare to catch up to the head of the column, and stopped her beside the prancing steed of the bearer of her fury. "When we return here, my mountain will soak up your blood as it drips from my hands."

Ryven let the threat hang in the air between them. Her face was a pale reflection of what it'd been at the party. Now, dark red rings lined her green hued obsidian eyes. He did not dream of these filled with hatred and exhaustion, but the ones from the party of amusement and a touch of ire. He knew, looking into them, she would not be the easiest to convince.

He turned, nudging his stallion into a steady, smooth canter that ate up the steaming ground. When he was sure she wouldn't overhear, he slipped into prayer, asking the gods to help her heal from the deaths suffered by his hands. Then, he returned to his work. Riding in silence, he peered into her maid's mind.

Gyrna. Bloodsworn. She knew her Klava like the back of her own hands. How she moved in battle. The care she took of her armor and weapons. How Mylva desperately planned and organized ways to tear down traditions that harmed those she loved. There.

He followed that thread. The next memory nearly had his stomach contents breach his mouth. *Surgeries on babes. Matching them to one another perfectly. Breaking and molding of bones. Metal pieces inserted where bones wouldn't shape properly.* His temples throbbed as he dug deeper.

Blood spattered across her face, spraying her eye and she closed it while making a tight swing to crack open her enemy's helm. Another mace followed, sinking into the skull like it was a rotten melon. Then there was a whip of fire down her thigh as a sword slashed through her leathers. Gyrna screamed, and Ryven gritted his teeth with her pain, hitting his mind as if he'd taken the hit. *Black and gold armor flamed like a bonfire as an unearthly roar poured from Klava's mouth.*

Gyrna hit the ground, watching the fire pour out, swallowing every body not bearing a black iris. The roar gave in to the crackling thunder of a wall of fire sweeping through the muddy battlefield. Shields gathered, blocking the wall, some of the black irised warriors were too slow, and screamed along with their enemy until an ally soaked the fire off them.

No.

He replayed the memory from when Gyrna fell to the fire raging. *She pulled it back.* To let her magic rage wild, then be able to control the minute details like that… he'd never witnessed an equivalent. *Mylva strode right behind the wall, her head high. Once fire touched a soldier that couldn't take the fire, her eyes swung to them and the flames swirled away from them.*

Ryven paused in searching Gyrna's mind. He'd known many who could control fire. Some of his half-siblings were experts in fire manipulation. But even they were wary of their powers. Fire was a fickle thing, having a mind of its own. Not Mylva's. Hers was an extension of her.

He was pretty sure that he would die.

That battle was unrecorded. Had to be. In his study of Kavkan, he'd never read about a battle Mylva ended with a firewall. Was it a dream Gyrna had?

Real. He realized after reviewing the memory. Minds had a way of melting things together, but something as awe-inspiring as that did not hold hints of dream fog.

Kavkans and their secrets. She didn't leave survivors, making it an easy secret to keep. And to keep her deadly army in check under her thumb.

Ryven pulled himself further along the thread. Funerals. The sisters coming together each year. Birthday. Battle. Battle. Meetings. How she'd not killed the whining advisors was a salvation from the gods in Gyrna's mind.

Birthday?

Ryven frowned, pinpointing the date. This day. This very day where he spit on her world as she knew it and made her all alone. Smoke and Fire he was the lowest being on earth. Did Kavkan not hold a celebration for their beloved Klavas? Surely the skin party wasn't it.

"Is there anything special about today?" He asked after pulling the reins to still his horse.

He watched Mylva lift a shoulder, listened to the clank of her armor as she settled in her saddle like it was her favorite sitting chair. "Other than having to listen to a battalion of strange dialects. No. Nothing special." Her lips twisted as she speared him with her eyes, "A day like before, where you presented me with my Bloodsworn's heads, is not a day like this. A better day, perhaps." Her lips turned, teeth flashed in a gritted smile, "Might not be for you."

The heat of the fireball aiming at his head warmed his scalp, even through his helm, as he lay on his horse so the danger would pass him. His second in command doused the Klava in a wave of water before he could sit back up. His armor screeched a little in his ears as he breathed too heavily. Too close.

The laughter pouring from her lips sent his spine tingling and his mouth clamping shut. Steam wafted off her like she was a lava flow in the rain. In two breaths, he couldn't see his hand in front of his face, much less the dangerous woman at his side. His mind flexed thoughts of calmness and sleep toward hers. He hit her defenses, blundering through them as pain erupted behind his eyes like the volcano behind them.

An orange glow from his left was his only warning before another ball of fire arced toward him. He urged his horse forward, out of harm's way. The beast heeded and, as a well-trained war horse should, turned to face the flame throwing danger. At least, he thought, that's what his steed did. He felt her in front of him. Her thoughts steady, calculating her next attack.

A scream rent the air, followed by another. "Vish!" he cursed. His horse took initiative and rammed into something. He spotted a shadow in the steam, large, laughing. He launched himself at her.

He wrapped his arms around Mylva's abdomen, armor clanging together. He felt like he hung there for longer than he should have. His weight suspended because she didn't give. Until she did, and they both toppled off the side of her horse. Ryven twisted, taking the brunt of the hewn stone road in his shoulder and hip.

He snaked his hand up, trying for the skin of her throat under her helm. Something wet closed around his first knuckle and into his palm before teeth sank in. "Smoke and fire! Off." The idea of not wearing gloves was a terrible one, but he needed to touch her skin.

Her thoughts flowed to him as freely as his own as he felt his flesh break under her teeth. *I've got them. I do. I have him. It's the traitor, the son, isn't it? Feels big enough to be him. I'll taste his blood and then feed it to my mountain.*

A slight amusement broke through the pain as he realized she growled in her mind more than she did out her mouth. *Focus, Ryv.*

He bucked, metal plates grating across each other as she slid, scrambling for purchase with her gloved hands on his steam slick armor. Ryven rolled, using the finger in her mouth as leverage just as much as his hips shoving hers over. Her helm cracked against the stone as he pinned her down. Her jaw gave, and he jerked his hand free before wrapping it around her throat. "Sleep."

Instead of slumping and complying with his order like he was used to, she relaxed. For a breath. Then the heel of her hand found his chin. He noted the snow cloud sky. The steam was dissolving.

Take that you sack of filth! Why is he so heavy? It's like I'm trying to move a horse, her screams filled his mind.

Had he gained weight? Ryven shook his head, clearing his mind so he could focus another order on her before she punched and writhed her way out from his grip. It took all he had to stay atop her, and his hand on her flesh. "Sleep! Now!"

Ryven thought it didn't work and was about to push it again when she stopped struggling, her body limp under his. He waited a beat, then another. He loosened his hold and rested his palm on her chest plate. Steady breaths, deep. He groaned, sitting back on his butt in the road, and leaning his head back against his horse.

"Prince Ryven, are you harmed?" His younger half sibling asked.

"No. Anyone else?" Ryven noted the boy kept a distance. Fear for Mylva, or fear she knew he'd killed Hava by mistake, it was a smart move on his part.

"Commander Gar is dead."

Ryven closed his eyes, his heart dropping to his stomach. Gar was a fine man, a better friend than he'd deserved. His thoughts trailed to Mylva's mind, she dreamed of her sisters. Of their deaths, over and over again. How had she received those memories?

He shook his head, letting the hot tears fall, "The Kavkan way."

"Sir?" The kid's voice broke on the single word.

"Nothing." It was his fault. He'd harmed hers. Killed them. It was only fair for her to kill his. As was her right, in Kavkan.

Ryven wondered if his plan was going to work. It had to work. They had little time left, down to mere months, until their enemy took action. He needed Kavkan. He wanted and needed Klava.

Chapter 5

He put her to sleep, knocked her out. Something, somehow. Mylva remembered being pinned. The trickster telling her to sleep. Why had she obeyed? Rage was a fickle thing. The dangerous mood traveled from Klava to Klava, down the bloodline, along with the fire burning within their veins. An instance of overwhelming rage could destroy the strategies she built in an instant.

This time, it would get her killed. At least then she would be with her sisters.

"You have my word." Ryven's voice held notes of sincerity.

That meant nothing. The Klava watched him, his eyes. His soul burned brightly through them. Nearly as bright as the low wispy lava falls behind him in the southern portion of her Kavkan. She wished the heat bothered him more, like a true stranger to her lands.

The blade resting against her neck tickled. Death after killing her enemy was a fine way to return to the gods. The dagger held to Gyrna's throat bothered her more than it should have. With only one Bloodsworn left, it was not a welcome threat to her sanity, or lack thereof.

"Release me here, she dies, and then you shall be tortured with her death for thirty-two years."

She pulled him toward her, off the stone railing of the bridge, and allowed him to steady himself on his own two feet. Mylva remembered him telling her of the custom upon murder.

He forced her hand from his neck, straightening his armor and underclothing with the movement and another shrug. "I've told you, a handful of times now… no more harm shall come to your kingdom, nor the people within it."

"Unless you continue to do stupid things." The guard, still holding his sword against her throat, said in a low, growling lilt.

"Any warrior would do the same. Would you not try to free yourself of capture if given the chance?" She asked, biting her cheek to keep the anger down. She almost had him. If not for his quick reflexes, she would have allowed her mountain to swallow him. And her too.

"Prince, I would advise you to not ride next to her." A slender man spoke with a broken voice from behind the angry guard.

The black eyes of said prince burned into her soul, "It would not have mattered if I were before her, behind her, or in the sky. She could have, and may yet, find a way."

"How perceptive of you." The Klava swept her gaze to the fall of lava, observing it pool and swirl before forming a river flowing swiftly down the mountain. This stream fed a lake. There, the fiery blood of the goddess delved back into the depths of the earth. Melting a path to the core. She wouldn't see the earth's center, maybe her great-great-grandchildren would.

The bridge they were on had witnessed blood fed to fire and mountains. It was the Bridge of Konu, or sacrifice. The same overpass she was planning on killing the prince at, if they ever returned. Though she had plenty of plans of murdering him all throughout her kingdom.

She wriggled her toes in her boots. Distraction. Focus. Which strategy would work best to make sure she didn't cause Gyrna's death?

"It's too hot," One guard whined for the thousandth time since their voyage began.

"It can be hotter. Allow me to show you?" Smiling sweetly, Mylva turned towards him, as a good hostess would to a guest.

He had to be ten years her junior. His eyes widened, the knot in his throat bobbing with a hard swallow. When he looked away from her, she strode to her mare and mounted. He was the same mouthy runt from before that hid behind others.

"She just flew from her horse to the Prince. Maybe we should tie her to her saddle?" A larger guard suggested.

"She's a guest." The Prince barked, silencing his companions. "Ride." He ordered after being pushed up on his steed.

By the time they entered Parvis, Mylva's enemies were more relaxed. Each soldier had a weakness she could exploit. In the four days it took them to cross through her fiery mountains to the plains of Parvis, she had three additional plans should the first fail. Each one would fall by her hand. But not until she could release her last Sparrow. She couldn't risk being locked down until she could free them.

She had to assess Parvis's subjugation to one of these twenty.

"Klava, don't you like this country better?" The Prince waved a hand, encompassing the thick trees that scrapped the blue sky with their bare branches. A light powder of snow covered the wide road of frozen mud and leaf litter.

Before her kin took strides to unite the kingdoms, the ruling powers of Parvis had risen and fallen like the seasons passed. They never survived long enough to establish a reputation. Not until the royal family of Hephaene. The family that bought Kavkan's armies to crush the others vying for Parvis' throne.

Pazai Haphaene, the current Queen of Parvis, was the latest. One of many brains, but average beauty, Mylva liked Pazai well enough. The brother, less so.

"It's a pleasant vacation spot," Mylva said, drawing her gaze to the prince with nineteen siblings. She watched as he shook his head at her, the white horsehair of his helm swinging. What was it like to grow up with that many siblings?

"When you are used to fire and volcanic stench, I guess anywhere could be a 'nice vacation spot'." One soldier spoke in a snide tone.

He had a penchant for drink and little taste. He hadn't noticed the hemlock oil she kept squeezing into his canteen. The plant was easy to find on the lower mountain passes. Just like other men, none of them paid much attention when females needed to answer nature's call. The snide drinker would be dead in five days once the hemlock's poison built in his system enough.

The small party rode through the trees into the rich rolling hills of farmland. As winter approached, farmers planted only the hardiest crops. Soon, they would be barren, then the snows would bury them in a white blanket. Then the isolated farmers and their families would move to their cold season homes within the small villages close to the cities for Parvis' restful holidays.

In another few hours, before the sun touched the horizon, the company rode into the second largest city of the country, Edgewhere. The city, aptly named for its proximity to Kavkan, sat on a plateau with one entrance and one exit.

The party took the road to the right, up to Edgewhere instead of the route to the capital city of Drana. Their horses worked up a sweat on the steepness, weaving back and forth on the plateau's side. A silver-clad guard stood on the platform over the gate, "Prince Ryven, welcome! Your brother awaits."

Mylva's fingers flowed around her reins, feeling the soft leather between her gloved digits. Ryven. How quaint. She expected a king with over twenty children to give them simple, single syllable names for memory's sake, Ryv, for instance, as she knew him as when he was her general.

Her general. Was he Bloodsworn? Half of her generals were, the other half had not been. The new ones too untested, not enough battles to satisfy the traditions of becoming sworn. Pouring over the memories of her siblings and her own, she couldn't pinpoint if he'd taken the oath, and her blood. Surely, he had not. He wasn't Kavkan. He wouldn't survive such an ordeal.

Then again, she realized she'd been wrong more often in the last week than her entire life.

The thick gate rattled open, sliding into pockets on either side. The wide walls, made from the plateau's blue-gray stone, had iron plates fortifying them on both sides. Her own grandfather had taught the metal workers of Edgewhere, and little three-year-old Mylva, the unbreakable welding technique himself. It was the perfect fortress for a flatland without geographical protection.

Ten walls circled the city in intervals within each other, devising the city in tenths, before the eleventh wall surrounded the cathedral and mansion. All broken by a single gate, built with solid metal as thick as she was and secured with seven locks each. Rooms made of equally dense iron encased the systems to open each gate. Nothing in them but the operators were flammable. They changed the numeric codes for the locks daily.

The gates of the inner walls remained open until a threat arose. She had held hope that Edgewhere was untouched. The gates were open.

Silver clad soldiers ran amok in the city as they did hers.

"Klava."

She looked down into the wagon she rode beside, and then followed Gyrna's gaze.

Pazai.

The queen was regal in her midnight blue dress. She always wore the color of her country. Her arm was around her brother's. The Prince of Parvis bore the black of mourning under the midnight blue cape. Their hair, blonde and shining, had an orange hue as the sun threatened to set behind them. His hair shorn so short that he might as well have shaved his cranium bald. While Pazai's thick golden tresses wrapped around her head in various twists with blue ribbons.

Mylva counted ten of the enemy's silver soldiers, and the ones that had kept her under control joined them.

Pazai smiled, looking up as her new guests stopped before her. She was short, only reaching her own brother's shoulder, and he barely reached the height of Klava's chin. A trait of the Haphaenes. Her smile faltered for a blink as she recognized her ruler, then it returned to a bright radiance, "Klava, welcome."

She caught Pazai's hand clutching her brother's arm, and it didn't relax. The queen was decent at keeping her thoughts off her face, but her hands always gave her emotions away. Klava was not her savior this day. Parvis' coin didn't purchase their enemies off.

"Queen Pazai. Prince Carlan." She greeted after swinging down from her mare and giving them a nod each. The royal males of Parvis always received names that echoed those of Klava lineage. They even shared a bit of blood. Parvis' bastard Prince Glaff was born of her father's seed. At some point, she was to provide Parvis a child of hers and Prince Carlan's making unless she chose a mate. Then she could pawn him off on Pazai to bear a Klava blooded Parvian.

"I see you have met our new neighbors." Pazai's elegant smile belied the clutch of her hands on her brother's sleeve.

"As have you. Same demands, I assume? Marry one of them?" She asked, stretching her limbs and letting her gaze roam, calculating how many more of the enemy were around them.

"Yes. Yes, of course. It is nice to see you again, Klava. It has been too long. They spotted your train from a few lengths away and had us meet you, as if we wouldn't greet an old friend on our own." Prince Carlan's grin was far more feral than his sister's. He'd always reminded her of a canine. Overly loyal, easily influenced, and prone to biting when threatened or being pleasured.

With a wave of her dainty hand to encompass the new arrivals, Pazai said with a tight smile, "Come, let's go back to our stronghold. You can meet our other guests and introduce your new friend." Not deigning to give Prince Ryven another glance, the queen turned away with a swish of her skirts.

Mylva watched the two Parvis royals walk to their glossy carriage parked just up the hard packed road. She remounted her mare, smirking to herself with the silent dismissal of Ryven. Pazai and her brother were proud people. It had insulted them that Ryven hadn't deigned to dismount or introduce himself to them.

For one meant to conquer through marriage, Ryven had few charms.

Winding through the city streets, Klava noted little fear in the residents of Edgewhere. Many went about their day as if nothing unusual had occurred. As if there wasn't a strange soldier stationed at every intersection. A flash of silver hinted at one enemy on the rooftop ahead. Only for a moment would a civilian pause, as if feeling the weight of being infiltrated, of the threat against their rulers, or spotting someone strange among them.

Exactly the same as her people.

Her enemy was like no other she'd ever encountered before.

How had they infiltrated? How had they entered Edgewhere, which was nearly as well guarded and sentried as her capital? She knew, as half the guards here were hired from Kavkan.

Once within the eleventh wall, she dismounted again and helped Pazai out of the carriage. Gyrna was at their side in an instant, pressing two fingers against the leather under her armor at her hip. Signaling her Sparrow was watching and had news. They were mid-wall of the mansion, hence the pressure on her hip and not her shoulder.

"Distract them." She whispered in Prince Carlan's ear as he stepped out after his sister.

"Well, then, since you're new here, let me introduce you to..." He flicked his gaze back to her.

She nodded toward the horses.

"Stables! We have the best horses on the plateau housed here. Possibly in all of Parvis." He urged the party to follow him to the stables beside the mansion.

For once, she was glad Hava taught Carlan some of their nonverbal cues. Just this once, though. She motioned she would join them in a moment.

Except Ryven didn't follow the prince.

His eyes were only on her.

Carlan laughed, and asked, "My dear sir, are you worried she will escape with so many of you here?"

"No. Something more heinous, perhaps. I shall catch you up once she is finished."

"Go ahead, I won't do anything." Mylva smiled, trying for sweet, but grimacing instead.

"That is not at all reassuring." Ryven said with a twitch of his brow.

With a flick of her wrists, she motioned for her Sparrow to find another spot. Mylva's gaze staying halfway up the mansion walls would make him too curious. He might follow her line of sight, and see the flashes her Sparrows communicated with.

Spending five days with these individuals was enough. How was she to keep her anger in check for longer? Her eyes flowed to Gyrna, then to the Hephaenes. That was how. She had to remember that her last Bloodsworn, and her people, held greater worth than her current vengeance. She had to make her revenge count and not cost more.

After Carlan's long-winded explanation of the bloodlines of his stallions and mares' bloodlines, the mansion's staff allowed her flock of enemies and herself to have rooms. Much to Mylva's chagrin, they assigned Gyrna her own chambers.

Ryven followed her into hers. The white-haired steward exclaimed, "Sir, the adjacent room is yours."

"No need for it. I shall monitor her." He dismissed the steward's concern. "Bring another tub and a screen."

"But, sir, with all due respect…"

"Do it." Ryven's dark eyes narrowed upon the man once he took his helm off and ran a gloved hand through his black hair to get the strands to loosen their sweaty hold on his brow and scalp.

"It's fine." Mylva waved it off when the sweating, loyal elder looked at her for guidance. To him, she was the epitome of power. Not the invaders.

"As you wish, Empress." The butler stated after a bow. He motioned two chamber servants into the room before closing the door behind them.

The mansion was decorated in Parvis's signature hues: blue, silver, and white. Walls were one light, and one dark shade of blue in wide vertical stripes while the trims along them and the furniture were silver or white. One large bed covered in midnight sheets and a thick comforter took up the dais in the middle back of the enormous room. The seating area spanned the plush rectangle rug from the bed to the screen separating the bathing area from the rest. A pastoral scene picture covered one wall with an intricately carved silver frame.

"You intend to bed me so soon after dragging me from my country?" She hated the obstacle of imagining them together, keeping her from formulating a plan to kill him if he should try.

Ryven held his arms out as one of the chamber servants unclipped his armor from his person. "Sleep in the same bed, yes. Have sex with you, no." He smirked, "Unless you are already in love with me?"

"Love is an emotion I'm hardly capable of. Not in the sense you would want." Mylva watched his protection leave him piece by piece, "Are you confident enough to remove your armor in my presence?"

"I commend you on not falling for me." Ryven's smirk fell to his resting countenance, "And as far as my life being in constant danger in your presence, seeing as how you have yet to kill me, I believe you are in search of more answers than vengeance now. Are you not?"

Intelligent or an idiot, she wasn't sure which he was at the moment. She saw him as more than what met the eye, like other formidable adversaries. "Do I have a choice in your father's offspring, or am I to settle for you?"

He chuckled, "You will find my siblings to be less than me, so you would not be settling if you chose me for a husband."

"I have a choice." She didn't mean to say it out loud. No advisors to suggest. No man thrown into her chambers by power hungry parents. Perhaps she would have a true choice. As much of one as twenty of them would give her.

"Yes." He rolled his shoulders, then neck, and stretched his hands up to the ceiling while rolling up onto the toes of his boots before continuing their conversation as a quartet of servants entered their chamber bearing another tub. "One of them is here, choosing between the Queen and her brother as to who would be suitable for marriage and ruling this part of my father's domain. We strive to minimize disruption to the way of life in each country." He said, his eyes on her, "Bathe. No harm shall come to you. Think of this as a vacation from always being poised for the next threat or battle."

"No need. I have ways of keeping a stench away, and my physiology allows me cleanliness without taking my armor off." There was no way to relax with him. The fact that he held himself in such high regard made her blood boil.

A woman approached, "Empress, if I may say, I guarantee that no harm may come to you here," her maidservant spoke softly with a deep bow. A Kavkan harshness to her 'k's tickled Mylva's ears, "I shall make sure of that upon my life."

All her people, whether rented out or not, were lethal. Starting from the time they crawled, Kavkans were taught to cause harm. A flash of mirror-sheen metal from the top of the maidservant's slender hand made Klava smile.

Her Sparrow had found another spot.

"Very well. It's not like I need protection, but if you insist." She nodded, and her country-woman made quick work of removing her light armor. Her last Sparrow, who could melt into shadows with ease, was out in plain sight.

As Klava went to the farthest tub, servants spread the screen promptly. They swiftly departed, bowing and trotting away from the room. She stripped herself of her underclothes, as this woman was too high to be treated like a servant, motioning for the Sparrow to report.

Sinking into the lukewarm water, Mylva frowned. Her flesh was hotter after a bath in snow than the water in the tub. She let her fire slip into the tub, the water temperature quickly rising and it steamed. The Sparrow handed her a sponge.

She watched the hands of her countrywoman.

"They are in every one of our countries. Each one selected or is selecting a suitable royal to join the fleet at Frystwaithe. From there, I believe they are to take you to their country. It is called Rothland. They talk of your captor, Ryven, as if he orchestrated all of this alone and received their father's approval. He's revered among them. Please be wary of him, my Klava."

She held up a hand, stopping her Sparrow from communicating more as she processed the information. Washing all the while. Frystwaithe was three days away, with just one night's sleep. With as slow as Ryven and his men moved, it would take five days. If they made no more stops in other cities, like they had here. He said he had another sibling here, too. That meant a larger entourage if the sibling had guards like Ryven did.

If Ryven was revered by his siblings, that many people... perhaps his pride was validated. If he possessed such strategic skills as to enter and keep Frysthwaithe, she would face difficulties. An adversary three steps ahead of her. What caused her to hesitate, and her heart to race in a touch of fear, was her inability to discern his thoughts or intentions.

And the fact she fell victim to his commands from time to time.

Had he been ready for her to kill him at the bridge? Was that why he was so calm?

"Anything else?" She signed to her Sparrow.

"The infiltration, his plan, began five years ago."

She motioned for her Sparrow to tell her that again. Surely she had been mistaken in her interpretation. A five-year plan to take over her empire? Just days ago, she learned about this kingdom and its sons. Five years?

She had read her Sparrow correctly. Her blood turned to ice. For five years, she had not seen a threat. Other than the rebellions.

Did he play a part in orchestrating those as well? As distractions? Five years ago, the Vixtan Rebellion began along the eastern border. The opposite side of her empire from Frystwaithe. It lasted a year, that rebellion. It would have been easy to get several ships ported at Frystwaithe carrying princes and a small battalion. Only one rebellion had come close to Frystwaithe, and the battles were still a day's ride from the port.

She couldn't have planned it better herself if Ryven and his father set those pieces in place.

Refugees from the rebellions flooded her countries. Mylva remembered her plans to take in most at the foothills of Kavkan, where the air wasn't as poisonous to outsiders. Then she remembered Rovinlan, and how a swell of refugees entered it. Rovinlan was her weakest kingdom, and the least populated. They barely held guards at their ports and borders. Those refugees were all Ryven's people. They had to be. Why would refugees deign to run to a country with the least protection?

Mylva looked into the eyes of her last Sparrow. Loyalty. Hope. The fires of Kavkan burned in the souls of her people.

"You are released from your duties." She signed, *"Live life as you wish. Return to Kavkan or travel to wherever. You will be in my heart, always adding to the flames of my blood."*

"I will still live in service to you, Klava. In some form." Her former Sparrow signed before giving her a deep bow. She said, "Are you ready to get dressed, Klava?"

Before she could reply, Ryven interjected, "There are new clothes. I had them prepared for you before our arrival."

She shared a look of disgust with her Sparrow before standing to step out of the thin metal tub onto the clean layers of towels on the tile floor. Her Sparrow dried her off, then wrapped a dry blue towel around her. Klava walked past her screen, stopping to stare down at Ryven, still stretched out in his tub.

His brawny arms curled around the tub's back lip and sides. The layer of soap bubbles and scented oils on top of the water hindered her ability to see well beneath the surface. Scars were a mark of honor among Kavkans. Ryven held a handful of them along his arms, only three that she could see on his chest. As honorable as a soldier who had only fought in four battles, perhaps.

Not at all of the numerous scars he'd sported during gambling spars.

"Where are we going after this?"

Ryven didn't flinch as she studied his body. "We'll stay overnight, leave for Sugawa in the morning, and then to Frystwaithe."

She nodded and then followed her Sparrow into the next section of their chambers. The monstrosity on the bed made her pause. Nightclothes, made in the style of Kavkan. The designers created the fabric to allow free movement, fit snugly, cool the body, and could be worn under armor if necessary.

A look at her armor resting on the nearby chair, and she nearly motioned for it.

"Wear the gown, Klava."

She turned, meeting Ryven's gaze. He had a full view of the bedroom. She supposed it was only fair. Dropping her towel, she stepped into the gown and pulled it up over her arms and shoulders. It was nice, despite feeling like her buttocks were about to fall and her thighs would eventually chafe.

"He didn't watch." Her former Sparrow signed, her brows drawn low over her dark eyes.

Honor among warriors.

Servants entered, carrying trays. They set them on the intricately carved round table between two equally delicate chairs near the narrow windows with iron muntin. They pulled off the silver tops and a heavenly scent of honeyed meat, sweet fruits, and baked vegetables filled the room. Afterward, they disappeared, swift and effective.

"Another doing of yours?"

He smirked as he stood, the water sheeting off his muscles. His entire body had the same tan color, except for slightly darker hands, neck, and face. "I thought I should aid you in your decision between me or my siblings."

She wouldn't give him the same respect as he did her. His servant dried him off, taking particular care of the crevices and bends, and wrapped a robe around him. Ryven wasn't the worst male specimen she'd ever laid eyes on, but he had fewer scars than she liked in her bedmates. He didn't seem to mind her gaze at all. "Am I to understand that you would choose me?"

"Yes," came the simple answer as he walked to the table and sat down.

"Why?" She followed suit, sitting across from him.

"There are many reasons." As he smoothed his hair and wiped his wet hand on his robe, "The more you get to know me, the more I shall show you why."

"Do you know all about me?"

"I know five years of you." He stated as if it was nothing. He piled his plate high with honeyed red meat, and only a few vegetables.

She glanced at her Sparrow as the woman poured her a drink. The sweet scent of mead filled her nose as she picked up the glass and took a sip of the golden liquid. Could she have accomplished what he did in the span of five years in her Kavkan? Yes. She frowned, or perhaps not.

"Closer to six, actually, but I had to work my way up the ranks in order to get access to you," Ryven said without prompting before he took a hefty bite of meat.

She felt her heart drop. Ranking up to become closer to her within a year indicated he had surpassed her elite. Even Praedae struggled for seven years to gain the rank of general, then another two to gain Warmonger. In a year, not four like she'd first thought. A general in a year? Impossible.

"The one called Praedae, I almost had him."

He'd fought Praedae. It was like she was on the glacier to the north of her city. Frozen blind. They had been in close contact with their formidable enemy. "How did you…"

"Fool everyone?" He smiled, "Your accent is not that difficult to mimic." He made sure to sound Kavkan with the hard 'k' sounds. "I have a few other tricks up my sleeve."

She tried to remember if she'd seen him fight Praedae. It meant he was eligible to take Praedae's status. He hadn't, though. Something else just as grand that wouldn't bring suspicions to him, then. General. She liked her generals, for the most part, as they were prone to stoicism. The least emotion the person showcased, the better. "I should have seen you."

"You did. Many times." When she stared at him, gripping her fork like a dagger, he smiled, "Another trick I have up my sleeve is that I blend in well. Forgettable."

Mylva found it hard to believe. She'd battled beside her enemy. Probably talked with him. Trusted him with some task during one of the many rebellions he fought with her in. And probably began. She was no longer fit to be Klava. Her mind and heart were more of a traitor than the man before her. Disillusioned in her pride, and her pride was her comfort giving way to her downfall.

In the event that she ever found Praedae again, she would grant him the privilege of ending her life.

The food turned to ash in her mouth, but she forced herself to choke some of it down. She needed her strength. The mead went down her throat a lot easier. "Since you were there so long, you learned some of the survival magics, didn't you?"

"I did. I passed them on to my men."

How long had he been alone in her country? How long did she have to squash the infiltration before he had friends among her countrymen? Before his army was in place amid Kavkan? She'd lost to someone right under her nose for the past five years. "Impressive," she stated flatly.

"Thank you, Klava." He paused, leaning forward to prop his chin on his hand. He smirked, deciding to test how much she knew of him or had figured out, "Imagine me saying that with your actual name."

Her name wasn't sacred. Not as long as she had failed her country so greatly. Not only hers, her empire. They were in Parvis. Parvis, who was under her protection. Her words and deeds were invalid. Nothing had survived them. Had it?

Klava Mylva had to make this up. This situation required something new. A new strategy. A new plan. She would regain her empire.

And more.

Her blood heated again as a strategy formed in her mind. A single king with twenty children and armies, too. With all that at her disposal, what could she accomplish? If her Sparrow was correct about Ryven's revered status…

"Mylva."

His eyes widened, then narrowed from his smile, "Mylva," he repeated after her. "That is not a common Kavkan name, is it?"

Ryven was to be hers, and his empire too. "I am not common."

Chapter 6

Mylva had shared beds with many men, sometimes all at once. Women too, and those in between. Not all were as big as the one she halved with Ryven last night. She bit back another yawn. Sleep had eluded her.

He didn't snore. That seemed impossible to her. A man of his size, not snoring. Had he slept?

Like her, he hadn't moved once. That was odd too, wasn't it? Someone not moving at all in their sleep. She assumed he hadn't slept.

Mylva slid her gaze to him as they walked down the dark, tapestried hall. Both were back in their armor. He hadn't yawned once, nor did he look tired.

A normal servant of the house had replaced her Sparrow that morning. Something akin to hope bloomed knowing that one of her own had made it out, and was living as free as possible. She wondered how long that would last. No conqueror could preserve all traditions at once. Kavkans' alone was enough to drive her mad.

All her thoughts halted as they stopped before the ornate iron and dark wood doors in the middle of the west wing's wide hallway.

"Ah, so you have decided to show her off at last." A tall redheaded man grinned as soon as they entered the grand dining hall.

The men clasped arms. Ryven's face finally displayed a genuine smile, a first for her. They had the same skin complexion, the same fluctuations in their voice. The other was taller, which made him appear lanky against Ryven's bulk.

"Klava, I've heard so much about you. I'm Sihfe. Ryven is my eldest brother from another mother." Sihfe gave her a charming wink and curl of his lips as he held his arm out to her.

She took it, clasping the silver metal over his forearm as she saw them do, but he pulled her into his chest. His shirt gaped open, revealing almost all of his chest.

Grunting, she tried to pull away. His long arms had a lot of strength to them. The one wrapped around her locked her into place for a moment.

Sihfe's breath warmed the shell of her ear, "I hope you haven't fallen in love with him, because you are going to be the one everyone wants. You'll have your pick of the litter. Or should I say… litters." He chuckled and released her.

"Klava, come eat." Queen Pazai's warm voice was a welcome respite from the redhead's excitement, even if her lips pinched at the show of affection among strangers. Parvis was a country of little touching, and fewer obscenities.

Klava found her way to the table, large enough to hold 200 people. As usual in Parvis, she took the seat at the head. Someone had pre prepared her plate, featuring a few mouth watering cutlets, fluffy eggs to the side, and candied fruit. As Ryven paused, she looked up, and he sat rigidly in the chair to her left. Pazai was already to her right, with her brother Carlan beside her.

Sihfe chose the seat beside Ryven.

"Who have you chosen?" Ryven asked as he drizzled a cream over his pork.

"Queen Pazai," Sihfe said with no pause, his dark eyes on Klava, his attention quickly turning to Pazai, "Is it tradition to welcome a ruler of another country to the head of your table?"

Carlan scoffed, "Another ruler? She is the ruler."

Ryven settled into his meal, "A true Empress."

Sihfe whistled under his breath, "She's really going to be fought over now, brother. Maybe you should just stay here with her and make her yours."

"She deserves a choice. A chance."

Sihfe had a turn to scoff, "Alright poetic warrior brother of mine, don't come crying to me when she chooses someone she can push around."

Klava shared a look with Pazai. Smiling at the guests, "Perhaps I should invite you to my womb tournament, hmm?"

Carlan muttered as he stabbed at his breakfast, "I had dibs. Until these idiot conquerors."

"It will be more than your womb we want, Klava. Believe you me," Sihfe said with a grin, even as he eyed Carlan like he was a bug.

The trotting to Sagawa was four long days. Much longer than it would her and her army. All because Pazai didn't know how to ride a horse and the royal carriage wasn't suitable for gravel paths and rutted mud. Even though these roads were far better than those in the mountains of Kavkan. In the night, the Princes took turns sleeping in the same tents as the Empress and the Queen.

Pazai's countenance remained pale, livid at the invidious actions of her captors.

Not that they had physically touched the queen. Other than to pass her up into the top heavy carriage with too thin wheels. Klava made sure she handed Pazai into the stifling compartment on the third day; preventing the queen's permanent disdain and throwing away her own amusement.

"You must have a plan." Pazai hissed as she settled on the plush cushions within her all too thick and long midnight dress.

"Perhaps." Mylva moved to allow Gyrna in the carriage. At least her last Bloodsworn didn't have to ride in a wagon like a crate of apples.

"Tell me what I can do to help."

Klava smiled sweetly, "Just remain your charming self, my dear queen," she answered quickly as Sihfe and Ryven neared.

"I don't like that look. What does that mean? Is she about to kill someone?" Sihfe spoke quickly, only taking a breath after he asked his questions.

Ryven lifted a shoulder, "Perhaps."

Sihfe sighed, "Now is not the time to tease!"

As Ryven stated, he did not tease, one of his soldiers mimicked his voice while saying: "He does not tease."

These siblings were nearly as close to one another as she had been with her Bloodsworn sisters. Her heart ached as she pulled herself up in her saddle. Only fitting that they died on their birthday. After everyone settled in their wagons and on their horses, they began the last leg to Sagawa, the city on the horizon.

Sagawa remained one of the most beautiful cities in her empire, according to those she deemed worthy of listening to. The people of Sagawa, settled in the rolling hills of Juliant, were famous for creating stained glass that enhanced the city's beauty. Vibrant shades made the city appear like a glistening rainbow from afar, with the skies above and waters below glimmering with the same hues, though muted in comparison. Bridges, buildings, towers, and even down to little chimes were stained glass.

Sagawa's glass makers had a knack for making their craft durable without being too thick.

Klava had hired a few of their craftspeople to create long-lasting panes for her fortresses, able to withstand fire and ice interchangeably. Her people loved it, often sitting in the bay windows to read under the hues of light that were not fiery red or blue of the normal panes.

The clunk-tink of the horses' hooves on glass spooked most of them. The beasts tossed their heads, dancing back and to each side before their soldiers regained control over them. Klava twisted her lips in a smirk, waiting in the middle of the rainbow bridge that spanned the River Frawn, one of three entrances into the city of glass. Her mare snorted, watching her fellows act like fools.

Klava reached down, running her hand down the soft neck. "That's my beauty," she crooned. Keeping her war horse from getting annoyed at the slow pace had been a job in itself in the past week and then some. More than once, the fires in her steed's heart threatened to erupt and send her mare on the path of destruction.

"Not yet." She soothed as the horse stomped a hoof against the glass bridge. Ryven finally urged his beast forward, the rest of the soldiers and even his siblings had to dismount and continued to cajole and pull at theirs.

He met her, his stallion snorting and bumping noses with her mare, who returned the favor with a clack of her teeth, a warning nip. "I see you've been here before."

"Many years ago."

He eyed her mare as his stallion arched his neck, mouth frothing. "Being born in a country of lava keeps your horses from being spooked by much, yeah?"

"Yes." She turned her horse, going across the bridge as the carriage driver finally grew annoyed and pushed through the fearful ones. "A well-trained horse trusts their rider." She shot a glance over her shoulder at his soldiers, "Yours are disgraceful."

A few of his soldiers trotted up, forming their pattern of protection again.

"Perhaps you can lend your expertise to making my army better once we're married."

She felt like that was a challenge. Mylva scoffed and shook her head, "Why would I train an army not worth my efforts?" She smiled as the soldiers near them glared at her, or stiffened in their saddles. She had used similar words to test her military, to see if she could rile them into doing something out of haste.

"They are worth your time and knowledge, Klava. Most are on par with any of yours." Ryven's voice had a soothing tone, even as he turned in his saddle to study the progress of the rest of his soldiers.

Her mare pranced sideways into his horse, and the stallion stumbled. She grabbed Ryven by the collar of his armor, pulling him off the warhorse. His excessive weight made her muscles burn with the pressure of keeping him from his footing even for a few breaths, "I still have yet to see if you are worth this much effort."

Depositing him on the bridge, she shoved her knee into her mare's shoulder and her horse sidestepped again, crushing him between the two. She grinned ferally down into his dark eyes as someone behind her pressed metal against her cheek. The warm start to a trickle of blood, the sulfur and coppery scent tickling her nose as the blade dug in. "I have killed you twice, Prince Ryven."

His lips curled at the corners as his steed moved away, freeing him from the press. "Have you?" He jutted his chin, eyes flicking to his man.

The sword at her cheek receded, and the blood flowed freely from the knick. She covered it with a fingertip, allowing her black glove to soak in her orange blood. With her free hand, she grabbed the tip of the soldier's weapon, cleaning it of her life's vitality. She flicked the blade away, smiling as the soldier just glared at her and returned the threat to near her shoulder, aimed at her neck.

"I have." She answered, returning her attention to the Prince. More of his soldiers surrounded them, ready to protect him.

"Maybe I just like you touching me without my express permission."

More than one of his men chuckled, and the guard pointing his sword at her stated with a smirk, "If you would, kind Prince, leave those things to the bedchambers and not scare us half to death."

Sihfe rode up, "Did I miss something? She lose a boot?"

Ryven placed a hand on her mare's neck. The beast betrayed her, allowing the touch. "Just our Klava being playful. Come on. Sagawa awaits."

She wouldn't let him bait her.

Melted shards of color were within the glass stones that paved the roads within the city. The rough surface of them ensured that neither beasts nor people would slip. Whenever in Sagawa, she attempted to peer past the glass streets to the ground beneath, or through the thick walls of each home or business. Never to see anything, except through the portions that were windows in this city.

Holes to peer out of or windows were molded freely, then made whole again at will because Sagawa's people held glass magic in their blood.

"Fire magic?" Sihfe asked, his head swiveling to look at it all at once.

"No." It was a lot like her own, after she studied upon it. Their hearts were molten cores, like hers, feeding molten glass through their veins. Not all the time. Like hers, they had to activate their magic, and they could only do so by feeding it. Kavkan magic drew its power from heat. She explained, "Glass from molten magic. Sagawan magic is fed by shattered light, not a heat source like most fire magics."

Hence why most Sagawans never left their city, like her people. Pride filled her as they rebuilt admirably throughout the years. Her conquest of them had melted most of the city down to smoky shards.

The city's architects designed it in squares. Each square was a particular district, kept from the next with a wide street, like the one they traversed down. Most of the outer districts were farming and lumber households where the farmers near Sagawa would stay during the selling of their wares. Then the inner blocks were merchants, trades, markets intermingled with some housing districts. The center held those of the government, army officials, and the house Juliant royals used during their visits.

Ryven, as if a native, guided them to the royal house gates. Mylva thought about asking him about it, then decided against it, as she shouldn't show that much interest in him. The long process of dismounts began. Then, a redhead that looked like a curvy version of Sihfe threw open the shining glass gate with a smile.

"Sihfe! Ryven!" She cried, running up to the two and throwing her arms around them.

The brothers hugged her in return, smiling and laughing with her. Klava felt another pang in her chest. Perhaps she would find a new way to feed her magic. Pain. Grief. Maybe with anger, too.

She got down and walked towards the carriage, offering her hand for Pazai. "Do you have a plan for here?" The Queen asked in a harsh whisper.

"No." She bit back a snide remark as Pazai pursed her lips in distaste again. "If you want to get killed, or worse, make a plan of your own."

"Ple-" She faltered, then bowed her head, "I see, Empress. I apologize. I shall be better behaved from here."

"See that you only behave with me, though." She smiled, kissing the back of Pazai's hand as the others watched, "Give them hell."

Pazai's smile was radiant, pleased with Klava's attention, "Thank you, Empress."

Parvis had a grand theater, which the royal family often visited. Pazai took many notes and seemed to be a brilliant actress herself. Mylva never took the time to see one of her acts, but Carlan constantly bragged about his sister in thick letters.

"One doesn't have to guess which is which, do they?" The red head laughed, still standing between her brothers. Then she strode toward Pazai and Klava, "I'm Monace. Sihfe is my twin, and Ryven, a brother that I wished was my twin."

Sihfe rolled his eyes to the bright blue sky. There his gaze caught the white belly of a predatory bird and watched it soar along the thermals above them. Here the winter was a sunny day, for now. Sagawa held mild winters, except for the rare years where they drowned under thick snow drifts.

Klava gripped Monace's arm, as she had Sihfe's upon his greeting. Monace, like her brother, then pulled her into a hug, speaking no words. They handled Pazai similarly, but with more gentleness. "Klava. This is Queen Pazai."

"Fire and...?" Monace's eyes rested on Pazai.

"Metals. Although sometimes I believe Kavkan blacksmiths do better work than us," Pazai said with a wry smile, showing off her better mood, though the force it took made her left eye twitch.

"Shall we eat? You best have a feast prepared, sister." Sihfe interrupted.

"Of course. Anything for my ravenous brothers." Monace waved them inside, striding to the front of the column. "Leave your soldiers to the outer houses here. I have enough of a guard within. It gets too stuffy with too many armor-clad giants." She said this with a glance over her shoulder at Ryven and then Klava.

Klava made sure that Gyrna was at her side before following. Her Bloodsworn walked stiffly. The wagon was not suitable for her for the past few days.

In the entryway of green glass stood a wide basin of constant water flow. Soaps of different herbal scents lined the back rim. Monace motioned to it as they entered, even though Mylva already knew the ritual and had her gloves off. Washing off the road dirt from her hands and face, she sensed someone watching.

Gyrna handed her a towel, and she looked up into Ryven's dark eyes.

"What?"

"Not going to drown me?" He asked, finishing drying his hands and dropping his used drying cloth into a basket at the end of the basin.

"Too obvious." She answered as she stepped into his space to drop her fluffy hand towel into the same basket, "I'm pleased you're trying to be on your toes."

"Though being light on my feet may help, I believe it's best to assume you'll try to harm me constantly."

His breath was warm on her cheek as she leaned toward him, "It is. If I knew you better, I might be proud of you." She brushed the tip of her nose against his, watching as his lips parted. She gave him a winning smirk before she pivoted around him to enter the dining room. Keeping her eyes ahead to ignore Gyrna's mouth agape.

"Kasu." Sihfe said breathlessly at Ryven's side.

She tilted her head, Gyrna quickening her pace to walk beside her instead of behind and to the right. "What is that word?"

"I believe it's a curse. Many of the men use it under their breaths after something causes their heart to pound." The expression Gyrna gave her made Mylva want to cackle.

"She is correct." Monace clarified, stepping from the shadows beside the open dining room doors. "Sex, for instance. If I wanted to have sex with you, instead of asking 'can I have sex with you', I could say 'Kasu?' or something like that." She grinned, tilting her head, "Kasu, tonight?"

Gyrna opened her mouth to say something, but at a look from Mylva, she stepped back to her rightful position just behind her Klava. She muttered under her breath, "It'll bring me great kasu to kill the lot of you."

Mylva raised a brow as she said, "Earn it, Monace." She spoke the words over her Bloodsworn's mutterings.

The redheaded woman frowned, "From what I understand of your culture, it won't be easy to earn, will it?"

"Best every warrior that wants me in the room, and you can have me. Or I choose someone for you to fight, and you have to win." Mylva turned and jutted her chin slightly as she surveyed the two brothers behind her. She returned her gaze to Monace, "Without a worthy warrior, you have to beat me to bed me."

Monace snorted, "As you are truly your own champion." She eyed her up and down with golden eyes, "Perhaps another time." She turned, pushing open the glass door that looked like an insect wing, before entering the dining room.

After settling around the thick, round mahogany colored glass table that took up most of the chamber, they turned the inner workings of the table to fill their plates from the feast within. The compartments twisted up from channels in the table with a turn to the left. Turning to the right moved the serving dishes in front of another seat. The mechanism kept the food warm, or cool, depending on the needs because of the insulative properties of the glass.

Eating her fill with her maroon fork, the color of Sagawa's higher officers, Mylva studied those in the room. Gyrna was to her right, allowed to sit with them. Then Pazai. Monace sat beside the midnight queen, Ryven to her other side. The royals of Juliant refused to eat. As such, there was a vast gap in the table until Sihfe, at her side.

After stuffing his face with what seemed like two platefuls, Sihfe said, "For someone who has taken over much of the world, you are young." His tone was conversational and his lips softened into a slight smile. "Is it correct that most countries on this continent fell under your rule, not an ancestor?"

"Seven are my doing. Those that were indebted to us fell quickly. Juliant was one of three of them who never asked us for anything, so we conquered them." Her work. Her pride. She was still Kavkan and Kavkan her. She was the only one worthy. But not worthy at the same time.

"Your fleet, is it many?"

She shook her head, "Not until we took all of Juliant." Frystwaithe, a formidable city, almost rivaled Edgewhere's resilience. This still surprised her, almost ten years later. She needed them to think she was being truthful. Her fleet was large enough to carry all the people of Kavkan and then some, but they didn't need to know that.

"Hm, perhaps that is something you may learn from us." Sihfe smiled then, rubbing the stubble along his chin. He lounged in his chair, a long feline looking relaxed but ready to pounce.

"Your navy is grand?"

"As grand as they come. As is every portion of our military." He nodded toward Ryven, "Thanks to his doing, partly."

"How is that?" She asked, turning in her seat so she could converse with Sihfe more easily.

"His plan." He waved a hand to continue, "This infiltration and attack is all his plan. He contemplated for an age before ultimately disclosing it to Father. In secret, they worked steadily for ten years before informing us. I saw the building of the armies, but didn't know we were partaking in a scheme like this."

"How many did you use to infiltrate each country?" Her blood stirred again.

Sihfe chuckled, "You mean how many we used to capture yours? Thousands." He leaned toward her, resting on the arm of his chair to contemplate her. "According to our spies, you were to be the toughest. He had every one of us worried we would go to war with you outright. Something we didn't want to do. We wanted to do this as peacefully as possible."

She held up a hand, "Peacefully? You call killing my Bloodsworn peaceful?"

He frowned, his crimson eyes swinging over to Ryven, "He probably did his best not to kill them, if that's any consolation." He stared at Ryven for a few breaths, his head canted to the side, before he returned his gaze to her, red brows drawn low toward his nose, "Bloodsworn? What is this term?"

Mylva shook her head, "It's difficult to explain." His excuse in Ryven's defense tasted like acid on the back of her tongue.

"Try."

At his urging, she smirked, "You're the curious one?"

"Nope, not hardly. But I am curious about you. Your country is quite a mysterious place because your people are… well, they're difficult to get to know, even for that one." He pointed to Ryven, "Which says much as he's practically a mind reader."

"Wouldn't be so mysterious if you prepared." Ryven glared over his chalice from across the table.

"How am I supposed to read through something as thick as my thigh?!" Sihfe waved his brother off before amending, "Not practically, *is* a mind reader."

"How so?"

"Ah, answer me first. What is Bloodsworn?" Sihfe grinned at her.

"We tie ourselves through the sharing of blood." Simple enough explanation for something far more sacred than that.

"Tie how? Like, do you feel each other's deaths? Do you… what?" He shrugged at his own lack of imagination.

"Tie as in a bond. Bloodsworn cannot betray one another to the point of death or maiming. Nor can they swear fealty to another. Their connection to the land, to Kavkan, is as strong as mine." She succeeded in excluding significant details. There used to be three of her. All her Bloodsworn. Her heart ached. Would it ever harden to keep her strong again?

"Does this include the two that were exactly like you? Isn't that creepy? How is that managed? Were they of the same womb as you?"

He was too curious. She gritted her teeth. "Those are secrets of our country," she said, trying to sound diplomatic at best. "Yes, they were Bloodsworn. We shared the same day of birth, but not the same womb."

Ryven sat down beside Sihfe and looked like a kicked animal with a downcast gaze and slumped shoulders. "Her Bloodsworn were formidable. A sacrifice I did not wish to allow them to make for her sake. Bloodsworn are to die before her. If she dies, they die."

The secret pouring from his mouth set her blood on fire again. She stared at him. "How did you find out about such a thing?" Neither Hava nor Nava had told him that before their last moments. Who spoke of it in front of him?

Which of her Bloodsworn had betrayed that dangerous information?

In the past, hundreds of Bloodsworn existed. All the highest officials in her country belonged to those oathed. If the Klavas of the past were to die, Kavkan would be utterly defenseless. Leaderless. The fires in the blood of her people would smolder and turn to ash. Mylva carefully chose only a few to be Bloodsworn to her, ensuring Kavkan's survival without her.

Sihfe shook his head, "I believe that is a tradition that needs to end. No life is more important than the other."

Her background as a warrior from a conquering nation prevented her from fully agreeing with Sihfe. There were lives more important than hers, yes. Hava. Nava. Praedae. Her generals. Gyrna. There were others that were less worthy of life than her. Rapists. Pedophiles. Those who beat beasts and innocents. Her Bloodsworn swore to her of their own volition. Except for Hava and Nava.

They hadn't had a choice.

Glass everywhere was not suitable in the presence of a fire wielder. He felt it in his heart that any moment molten glass would melt him into the bed or where he stood. Sleep eluded him for yet another night. It was worth it. He had to keep telling himself that. Even though there was no sign of her giving in. Even her moments of curiosity he had to take as her plotting his demise. Such was the woman who filled his every waking moment.

He yawned, his jaw cracking, and his sister made a face. "What?"

"Bed her already."

Ryven snorted, "She has to be willing."

"She will." Monace grinned, "Willing to spread her legs and eat you alive with what's between them."

With a roll of his eyes, Ryven downed the strong liquid from his country, feeling the burn of it hit his stomach. With a study of Monace's grinning face, he sighed. He refilled his mug, knowing one would not be enough. "Who did you choose?"

"I didn't have a choice, brother. The King it is. All crying. All whining. King of Juliant."

"What of the general that's next in line? Why not him?"

Monace shook her head, "Seedless."

"That's unfortunate."

"It's why he's next. The royal family likes their seed, but Juliant's royal whiner hasn't had offspring yet. Once he does, the general's status of being the next ruler will be replaced with the child." Monace explained, "Common occurrence. Smart."

"Then kill the brat and take the general's brother." Sihfe said with a shrug and a dismissive tone, grabbing an empty mug and filling it from the almost empty carafe.

"He has one?" Monace raised a brow at Sihfe, who joined them after stretching as he ambled toward them.

"Didn't he?"

"No." Ryven eyed Sihfe, "You suggest this when you know nothing of Juliant like Monace does. Monace, are you certain there isn't another?"

"There is not." Monace's lips dipped down at the corners, "Unless your Klava has something up her sleeve for this country instead?"

"I'm not asking her."

The siblings looked at one another in turn, then all held out both hands, flipping them over and under before placing them behind their back to untie the money pouches.

"Less." Ryven said with a smirk, knowing his siblings were far more stingy than he was. If he was correct in owning the least amount of coin, he'd win.

"Most." Sihfe grinned right back, for some reason betting Ryven would have the most coin.

"Middle." Monace smirked.

The siblings showed their hands pouches open and began counting.

"Five." Ryven went first again.

"Seven." Sihfe raised a brow at his older brother.

"Two!" Monace cried, bouncing on her toes. She turned to Ryven, plucking a hair from her scalp at her temple and grinning. Making him go alone, instead of with Sihfe. Monace won, because she had the least amount, taking the spot Ryven bet on. If the winner had the longest hair as well, the loser had to face the challenge alone, instead of with the other loser.

"Why did you even pull it out? I know you have the longest hair." Ryven muttered, replacing his pouch after giving them one piece each for winning. He shook his head and went back toward the room he shared with the deadliest woman he knew. One of them. He still didn't know who would win. Mylva, or his mother. Still trying to play out the battle between the women in his mind, he pushed open the door and ducked the projectile, barely in time.

The table leg hit the door where his head had been with a loud crack, both woods splintering as the leg stuck in it. He frowned, staring at it for a moment, and decided. Mylva. His mother was a gentler beast than the Klava.

"Nice reflexes."

"I appreciate your praise, but would rather have gained it by my other merits." Ryven retorted, turning to gaze at her. The rest of the table lay at her feet, still intact. Minus the one leg, and the linen tablecloth bunched underneath a few platters of pastries on the floor. "I beg your pardon for the interruption in your meal before we leave, but I have an important question."

"And it is?"

"Is there another eligible heir here after the King?"

Her smile sent both a chill and a thrill through two different portions of his body. "Tired of his nasal complaining already?"

He nodded, not sure how Monace hadn't killed the king yet. The finger tapping on her lip intrigued him. Was that a thing she did when thinking? Or when amused?

"The problem is, Juliant desires steady lineage. They were one country that I nearly destroyed for that reason. Luckily for them, some of them were smart and surrendered." Klava Mylva sat, plucking a berry from a vine still in the bowl that landed upright beside the overturned table. "There is a cousin. Some question her legitimacy, but the people like her well enough." She smirked, "Good luck prying her from Juliant's common fingers."

"Why do you say that?"

"Tuier's like a saint to them. That bridge we crossed, it was all her doing. The castle we're in? It's half her creation. No other. She also has some healing capabilities, oddly enough, too."

"The grown man-babe or a saint worth more than the city?" Ryven mused, remembering reading some about a Tuier in his reports after Mylva said her name. She would be an advantage to have. Better than the king, that was for certain. "Do you have any sway?"

"With Juliant commoners?" the empress snorted, "Always." After spending a few months with the people after taking them under her wing, she'd grown fond of them. Like Kavkans, they worked harder than they should, but playtime was just as challenging.

"Then I shall accompany you to gain her."

"No need." Mylva jerked her chin at Gyrna, who swiftly left. "Give her a moment." She ate another few berries, "Hungry, Prince?"

He debated. Thinking if he sat with her, then that bowl would imbed itself somewhere in his person. If he didn't, another table leg might impale him. Her best option could have both occurring.

Ryven sat at her feet and held the bowl. At least this way it wouldn't shatter on him or in him. The table blocked her from kicking him. He marked it as a win for him, for now.

After the bowl was clean, he set it down and watched the door open. Gyrna stood to the side, head bowed slightly. A woman wearing red robes belted over her chest entered. Her hair was nearly as red as the robes, and she was a wisp of fire through the room. She hit her knees before the Empress, then her forehead rested on the floor next to him.

Her voice was a soft wind instrument, he couldn't remember the name, as she spoke, "Klava, I am humbled to be in your presence once again."

"Rise Tuier. Pack your things. We leave in a few hours at the behest of our hosts."

"I cannot, Klava."

"Why defy me?" Mylva asked as she stood over them both.

"I am with child, my husband awaits me."

Ryven groaned, already hearing the king's whine from here to Rothland in his mind.

"Congratulations. May the seed bear true. You are dismissed." Waiting until Tuier left, she looked down at him, lifted a shoulder, and said, "I tried."

"Please tell me there is another. I cannot bear his voice."

Mylva patted his head, "Only beasts whine, and you complain much."

Ryven watched her leave the room and slumped back against her vacated chair. "I'm dead. I just don't know it yet."

Chapter 7

"Just one night." Mylva's overgrown fingernails dug blood out of the palms of her hands. Blood her people never wanted to see spilled, but she would spill freely for them. She wished for the smells of Kavkan to fill her nose instead of the waxy cotton scent of the tent. "Leave me alone for one night."

"Once we're on the ship." Ryven's words stung, even as his face softened, outlined by the tent flap he held open. "I cannot, in good conscience, forsake you this night."

She snorted, turning from him in case she couldn't blink away the hot tears threatening behind her eyes. She experienced the sensation of a child on the verge of throwing a tantrum. They could use her tears against her. Just like her blood. "Even if I swear upon my life that I will try nothing?"

"Even that will not sway me, Klava." He let the tent flap fall behind him. Ryven reached for her with one hand.

She jerked away, snarling like a glacial bound, ice encrusted black fur covered Braorqer at him. Tantrum it was. She wished she had the long canines and massive jowls of the Braorqer to tear him to pieces with. "I have nowhere to go in this godforsaken part of my empire!"

Desert. It was a vast scourge across Juliant until the air from the ocean lent its moisture to the land beyond the hills that were once high mountains. The heat from the unforgiving sun scorched into her blood, feeding her magic. She felt as if she would burst. Mylva desperately wanted any kind of release. An area to scream, something to tear apart, a tent to herself to process and cry or rage.

And explode she might. She hadn't been alone for a second since the day she put her sisters' bodies into the mountain. Her ears were too full of sounds; the thin fabric of the encampment did little to dampen. Nose was too full of scents. Her eyes burned from the sight of all these people around her, strangers, save one. Enemies, save one.

A string of curses in the ancient language left her lips. Ryven stood there. Watching her pace within the tent they shared. Gyrna had set up her bed in the far right corner, the furthest away she could get from the enemy. She kicked her cloak, that served as her bedding.

"Come with me."

She stared at him as he commanded her. The flames in her veins grew to a roaring forge in her chest and arms. She closed her eyes, breathing in and tamping down the fires so they wouldn't show in the vessels of her neck and face as they were bare to his sight. "What?" She also wished for the deep chested growl the Braorqer warned their enemies with.

"Come out with me," He beckoned, opening the flap.

She narrowed her gaze at him. Either he was brave or an idiot. No sane person would want to get near her like this.

Taking another few deep breaths, she walked past him. He was so close; she imagined what his blood would feel like over her fingers. She cleared the tent and out into the burning, setting sun.

"You. You. And you." He pointed to three men nearby. "Bring staffs." He stepped around her and motioned for her to follow. He led her, with the soldiers and his guards following behind, past the tents and into the open sands.

"Circle." The word was a bark.

The soldiers created a wide circle around Ryven and Mylva once they stopped walking. Then Ryven studied the group and picked one of them. "In." He held out a hand for an extra weapon.

Ryven turned his dark gaze on her, "Rules are simple. No killing. If they yield, you don't hit them another time. Step away. Got it?"

"Yes." She took the smooth staff in her hand as he held it out to her. She watched him go to the edge of the circle. There might be a chance yet.

"First." Ryven pointed to one of his guards, the snide one.

Sir Snide spat into the sand, smirking, and strode into the center, twirling his staff. Once he was there, Ryven called for them to begin. His twirl turned into an attack, stepping into her so that he could use the full weight of his body in the hit.

She dodged with a twist, bringing up the staff to hit the back of his knee with the end. With another spin, she was fully behind him. She let the staff's weight pull itself down on top of his head before he could turn to face her again. Then she picked up the pace, rattling his shoulder plates with three hits.

His knees hit the sand, shaking the fog from his head. His stave came around his body, swinging out at her wildly as he tried to gain his feet. The curse she'd learned in their language leaving his mouth in a huff.

She blocked his swing with her pole, taking a long stride to get within reach and wrapping her fingers around his throat. She grinned as he grasped her wrist, trying to dislodge her.

"Don't yield." She hissed, bringing her staff down onto his toes, and then blocking the movement of his forehead toward her temple. He tried again, and again, his face burning red, the edges of his lips turning blue.

"Yield." He managed through his closed windpipe.

She wasn't a cheat. Klava still had some honor. She gritted her teeth, the fire in her threatening to burn them both alive, taking control of her senses. Mylva wanted to dig her fingers further into the soldier's throat.

"Second!" Ryven growled.

Another soldier ran wildly toward her, swinging his staff down. She stepped away, still holding on to the snide one's neck as she met his swing with her own. "Protect your kind, slug."

He screamed a war cry, kicking out at her as he used his pole to swing his feet up out of the sand, level with her chest.

She picked up the deadweight of his friend, swinging him like a flexible staff, to knock the soldier off course. He landed on his back. She planted the end in his chest, his armor cracking under her power. The air whooshed out of his lungs. With some effort, he swung his staff again, knocking it against the back of her legs.

Mylva dropped the gasping one from her fist as she tumbled to her feet, leaving the snide soldier in the sand beside his comrade.

Ryven. His blood on her hands was a desperate need. She weaved on her feet, feeling the flames shift with her. She could let them loose. Burn them all to the ground.

That was too easy. She still needed to learn how. She still needed to make them all pay dearly. Swift deaths weren't payment enough.

She glanced toward the camp. A crowd gathered there. "Come one, come all, see if you can throw me down."

"Third." Ryven ordered.

The second rolled over, coughing, slowly coming to a stand after leaning on his staff. The third warily entered the circle, eying his fallen friends. He seemed to relax at seeing the chest plate rise and fall in a shallow motion.

The snide one still breathed, much to Klava's dismay. How had the poison not worked by this point? That was another concern. Perhaps in another day's time she would see the results.

Two more soldiers with wooden staffs stepped up to the edge of the circle. Ryven gave them a nod. "Fourth. Fifth."

The other pair crossed the line, circling around Mylva.

A smile parted her lips. Finally, a slight challenge. They might alleviate some anger.

She experienced a high level of disappointment a few predictable moves later. Granted, they would have beaten a lesser opponent. Some flames within had worked their way down. Still, the rage burned in her chest.

Sihfe called from the group at the tents, "Why don't you try it, Ryven?"

The defeated five crawled out of the circle, receiving help from those who didn't dare to approach. Then Ryven took over. He picked up a discarded staff, "Will you allow me the honor, Klava?"

"I think the honor shall be mine when I take you."

He smiled, "If you take me, then you will gain the freedom to go back home."

Something iced the flames for a moment. Those words. The strength behind them. He knew he would best her.

As she had no doubt, she would beat him.

Home.

She heard the whining voice of the Juliant King ask, "What's going on?"

Whispers filled the crowd as she circled Ryven in the ring. He moved in sync with her, down to the length of her stride. An unnerving tactic that made doubt grow.

Mylva and doubt were strangers.

Someone as used to her as Praedae didn't cause her to falter. Why should this male before her?

She stepped in, kicking sand into his face.

He dodged with a flip backward, returning the favor.

Can someone who can't mount their own horse with plate still fight effectively in battle? She smirked, seeing through his ploy. He wanted her to think him immobilized by his armor this whole time.

"I switched armor, as I much prefer your blacksmith's work. I bought it during my second year in Kavkan."

No blacksmith in her nation would forge something with such a silvered appearance. "How did you force them?"

He smirked, "I might tell you, one day."

His next movements were a blur of motion. His staff attacks were precise and powerful, causing the wood to reverberate as she stopped each strike. She met him, hit for hit, and added a few of her own, which he blocked.

It was as if she were sparring with Praedae.

The pain erupted in her chest again. This was the man that killed her sisters. Her Bloodsworn that knew her like she knew them. A lick of flame slid up and down the length of her staff. She peeled back her lips, snarling, allowing it to leave her body in a steady flow.

Release. The pleasure of letting go had her scream a war cry that echoed back to her off the sand dunes. The blood orange of the sun's last rays made her armor look like it was aflame.

Ryven's eyes widened, but then he grinned. "That's it, Klava."

Her teeth hurt as she pressed them together. Her efforts doubled, striking out with everything she had. Staff. Fist. Fist. Staff. Roundhouse kick.

The sun set. Purple darkness spread over the dunes. Long shadows stretched from the camp towards the circle. The torches and campfires lent little light to the fighters.

Her staff blazed.

Her strikes grew more frequent as the fire in her veins blossomed into an inferno. Regardless, she concealed her emotions from her face. They had instilled that kind of control in her since she could walk. Not to let them see. Never let them see her power until it was a last resort.

Ryven grunted as she landed two blows to his ribs, then another one to his thigh. She hissed as he retaliated, beating her shin and then shoulders with his staff.

Rage boiled within. Mylva tried to keep it down.

In that moment, her weapon flew from her hands as a crack thundered in her ears. Ryven had driven his staff through hers. His elbow flew into her nose. She sensed the intense heat of her blood. Bright. Flaming.

He can't see this. Not now. They can't know.

She covered her blood with her gloves. The flames within her automatically retreating in the cold sway of fear. A blow to her head, and her knees sunk into the scorching sands.

Defeated?

Klava stared up at him. Ryven's chest plate rose and fell heavily, his brow and temples wet with sweat. The staff held high in his hands. A killing move ready.

It never landed.

Her vision zeroed in on his face before blackness engulfed her.

Ryven refused to allow anyone to touch her. Not after this. He was a fool.

She was heavy in his embrace as he carried her from their temporary training ring back to their tent. A tent she didn't want to share with him, but he desperately wanted her to accept him in it. Gyrna opened the tent flap, standing in his way as she stared at the limp form of her master in his arms. "She needed the fight."

"You shouldn't touch her!" Gyrna cried as she lashed out.

Ryven pivoted, swinging away from the maid launching herself at him. "Guard!" He growled, his grip slipping on the deadweight in his arms.

He had to back up three strides and then take a fourth step in the sand before the guards grabbed Gyrna to drag her away. "Keep her in with the Parvis Queen." For the life of him, he couldn't recall the woman always in blue, name at the moment.

Entering their tent, he quickly, but as gently as he could, lay the empress on her cloak. After he made sure she was as comfortable in her armor, he moved over to his bedroll and sat. His ribs throbbed with each breath from where she'd landed two blows between the plates.

Ryven thought for a moment, and began shedding his armor, tossing it within reach. Gyrna was gone, and that was a single peril down. The other threat, and the more deadly of the duo, lay unconscious by his hand. If she woke and killed him, so be it. He probably deserved it.

He rolled his head on his shoulders once the metal pieces were off. A pale yellow color caught his eye, and he pulled the pages from under a flap in his bedroll. The small sphere he used for messages tumbled out after them.

Reading the first one, he frowned. The script was something he was still getting used to. A message from a villain or a benefactor, he didn't know, not until he knew if Mylva would work with him. As it stood, it was a missive from a threat. It reminded him of the time he had left to decide.

It wasn't really a decision at all. The option of being between war and conquer was never a choice. He read further and shook his head, tossing the paper down to read the next one. More of the same. The days numbered. Giving them the choice of becoming filial, or of death. The enemy had few words, and they were often always the same.

He was glad he'd instructed his father to send the repetitive messages in one day, instead of whenever Rothland received them. If he hadn't, he was sure his spheres would have been found in no time because of the message one.

With these missives, if he didn't know any better, he could put this threat off as a child's game from boredom.

But he knew better. Too many people had died already. He wasn't about to allow them to be in vain.

He ripped up the slips after reading the last one. Tucking the tiny pieces into the sand beneath his bedroll, he returned his gaze to the woman sleeping in her armor. The pain she gave him was in more than his ribs.

Ryven rolled his eyes at himself. He couldn't help picturing her in that dreadful dress from the other night. How her deep breaths would stretch the fabric taught over her chest. He wanted to know what she tasted like.

He licked his parched lips, his imagination guiding him further down the path he shouldn't take.

Crawling toward her, he stopped at the center support to their tent. He sat against it, resting his back upon the smooth wood. He trailed his gaze over her. Even in armor, she was the most beautiful woman he'd ever laid eyes on. Ryven imagined the pieces falling off. Her smile.

An extra throbbing began with the ones accompanying his breath, and he loosened the laces in his pants.

"I need this. Release is good." He reminded himself in a whisper as he slid his hand into his pants and stretched his legs out toward the woman of his dreams. He let his head fall back to the pole, gazing at Mylva through his lashes.

He curled his fingers over his balls, massaging them as his cock hardened from the base under his palm. Ryven imagined the warmth of her hand on him. How her fingertips would slide up from his sack and over the length of him like featherlight candle flame flickers.

He wondered if her lips would be hot to the touch, too. Warm like her tongue, but not as wet. A kiss from her could probably kill him with fire, but he wanted a taste, anyway. He raked his palm up his cock, wrapping his fingers around the head and swiping down to the base in one quick motion.

She could wake at any moment. What would she do if she saw him like this? Hard for her. Thrusting into his own hand and envisioning doing the same to her.

Ryven gritted his teeth. Desire from the other night quickly drove him to release. He worked faster. Pumping vigorously as he imagined being inside her. His eyes closed. He imagined her in his lap. Taking him in. Riding him. The sounds of her skin slapping his. Her ass in his hands. Mylva's head tossed back, before she looked down at him with those eyes filled with desire and pleasure.

How would her moans fill his ears?

How hot would she be on him with that fire magic running through her veins?

He hissed as seed spilled onto the back of his hand and over his fingers. He panted, the pain of his ribs dragging him back down to reality. A reality where she still slept, and he had a mess to clean up.

She awoke to the scent of salt and wet sand in the air. Birds screamed and chattered overhead from various perches and flights. The sun burned her eyes, making them water as she sat up. The rough scrape of wood against her armor grated in her head. Her brain seemed on the verge of exploding from her skull with each heartbeat.

"Klava?" Gyrna's familiar voice sounded to her right. Her maidservant provided shade with her hands, relieving her headache.

She blinked, focusing on her Bloodsworn, "Frysthwaithe?"

"Yes, my Klava. Just arrived."

The hit had kept her unconscious for two days. Her muscles seemed as though they were loose bands. Her mind was a fog. Pangs of protests and low growls filled her stomach. Her mouth felt normal, thanks to the wet rag and bowl of water in Gyrna's lap. At least she was in a wagon of stuff and not the frilly carriage of Parvis' queen.

The fire within her was out. Snuffed. Klava Mylva, defeated. Dishonored. She was not worthy of her name, much less the blood that ran in her veins.

She looked up, past the large palm leaf Gyrna fixed for her against the barrels she leaned against. The yellow and orange roof tiles in Frystwaithe stood out against the blue sky and white plaster on the buildings. The port city was loved by her mother, before the burdens of birthing and training Mylva fell upon her. Nearly a second home to a parent full of conquest and adventure. How would her life have turned out if her mother had forsaken their ancestors and gods?

A life on a ship, perhaps. Adventuring. Lands to explore. New sights to behold.

"Klava." Ryven's voice grated through her ears like shards of shells rubbing together.

She turned, glancing at the wagon's side to observe his steed prancing beside it. "Here to gloat?" She didn't hear her usual bite and command in her voice. It appeared to be broken.

"No. Here to check on you."

Out of the corner of her eye, she saw Gyrna's fingers flicking a message. Apparently, Ryven hadn't left her side. Gyrna feared he would make a physician run tests. She barely convinced him not to by telling him that once a Klava was defeated, the soul of the Klava rested for days before awakening to seek revenge.

She adored the quick thinking and fortitude of her Bloodsworn. Later, she would need to think of a reward. Could she ever give such a thing again?

"I'm fine." The wagon jolted to the left, and she hated how it made her head hurt that much worse.

"We will stay at an inn before departing at dawn. You should get more rest there."

"I've been asleep for days, why do I need more?"

Ryven chuckled, "You haven't been knocked out much, have you?"

At that moment, the wagon halted, and she peered out. The salt worn inn called Water Tales and Ales towered over them. Smaller crafts' masts bobbed gently with the calm ocean's gentle swells on the other side. A wall of larger vessels, armored and fitted with massive weapons bearing the same sigil Ryven bore on his armor, rested beyond the familiar ships. How had word of these things, his ships, not reached her?

Surely a single spy or Sparrow could have gotten through to her. She frowned, rethinking. It was why she'd only had two Sparrows to release from their duties. Her spies were dead or held captive.

"Hands off, vermin." Gyrna's hiss had Klava returning her attention to what was in front of her.

Ryven had his hands around her Bloodsworn's waist, lifting her out of the wagon. "Calm down. It would be a waste to take you all this way just to throw you into the ocean."

"I want to throw you into a pile of horse dung!" Gyrna spat.

A sudden urge to laugh caught her, and she bit the inside of her cheek.

Then Ryven was reaching for her. She grabbed at her side, nothing but air hit her fingers. Nor was there the small mace at her calf where her other hand slid to. Her armor was still on. Probably thanks to Gyrna. Habits. Always be ready. Even if someone had already defeated her.

"Slowly." He murmured, as she pushed herself up, swatting his hands away. He dropped his hands to his sides, stepping back to watch her slide to the end of the wagon and sit there. "Lean on me."

She glared at him, "I'd rather lean on a pile of dung."

"Then consider me dung." He stepped into her, grabbing her arm and wrapping it around his broad shoulders.

She pulled away, weak as a child, to no avail. Their armor clanged and scraped as he lifted her to her feet, steadying her. The muscles of her legs barely worked. She wanted to crawl.

A musk of old books and rum filled her nose over the salt in the air. She stumbled against him into the inn. He abruptly moved his head towards the soldier at the counter, distributing coins to the thin and leathered innkeeper.

"Your best room?" The soldier asked, finishing his count.

"Down the hall, the door at the end." She waved her hand to the left, intent on counting the coins, "Occupies the majority of the rear and overlooks my garden."

Ryven half carried her, half pulled her to lean on him when she tried walking on her own down the hall. Gyrna fussed and muttered under her breath the whole way, directly behind them. Once in the room, he deposited her gently on the edge of the bed. He turned towards Gyrna, his dark eyes flaring. "Can I see the wound now?"

"No," they both said simultaneously.

"Gyrna can check it."

His jaws tightened, and his gaze burned into hers, "One day, there will be no secrets between us." He straightened, turning to Gyrna, "Make sure it's clean and not infected. Bathe, both of you. There isn't such luxury on the ship on the way home unless absolutely necessary." His eyes returned to Mylva, "I suggest you find sea faring clothing, not that armor. You fall over, you'll drown instantly. No matter how light your blacksmith makes you."

"My horse?"

"Will be stabled here."

"No, she comes with me." She wanted to throw something. Desire for there to be one more thing other than Gyrna with her, she had to have her mare near. If not to have another being burning with fire like her.

His brow twitched, "Any other demands, my future wife?"

"She will not marry you!" Gyrna looked like a bird with talons flexing in the air, readying to strike an unsuspecting prey down below.

"Stop saying that," Mylva said, still not hearing any emotion in her own voice. He'd hit her in the head too hard. Something was definitely wrong.

"I'll be back for our nightly meal. There are some preparations I must attend." He strode toward the still open door, only to turn when he placed his hand on the latch. "Don't get any ideas."

Gyrna waited until the door closed behind him, and his footfalls faded down the corridor, "I have a cousin here. Shall we go visit?"

Chapter 8

"Your leathers will be perfect for the ship." Gyrna kept rattling. Ever since Ryven left, she talked constantly. Every other sentence seemed to ask her permission to escort them to her cousin's house.

Mylva stayed silent, soaking in the lukewarm lavender scented water of the bath. She faced the glass wall separating the room from the fenced in garden. It reminded her of the wild gardens of Kavkan surrounding the statues of her ancestors. Instead of larger-than-life replications of heroes past, the innkeeper's plot boasted of tiny figurines of animals and fantastical creatures from bedtime stories.

As she tried to remember one of those fairy tales, the base of her skull throbbed. The knot there was the size of her fist, but Gyrna assured her it was much smaller than earlier. Her shorn hair wouldn't hide the sore.

Failing was something she wasn't used to.

Did it not make her more of a failure? Not having failures to learn from? Given her age, did that mean she took fewer chances? Everyone failed. She chided herself for acting like a child. Throughout it all, she remained fixated on sulking and wallowing. Torn between being worthy of her name and the desire to reclaim her honor so she would be. Mylva let Gyrna talk as she stood and dried off, letting her Bloodsworn's voice soothe while not comprehending a word of it. She wrapped herself up in the robe provided by the inn. For once, knowing her armor wouldn't do her any good here.

As the sun set over the ocean, the garden took on an orange hue. Mylva watched the door open in the glass's reflection, and Ryven closed it behind him. "Our meal will be here shortly." He stated curtly, going behind the screen to the bath. The clank of his armor falling to the wooden floor filled the room. His servant filling the bathtub washed her self indulgent thoughts away.

"Is Gyrna allowed to go see family here?"

"With a guard or two, yes," Ryven answered readily.

Mylva nodded to Gyrna. She raised her brows as her servant stared at her, mouth open. "Go. Be back before dawn. Remember, I do the planning, not you, nor your cousin."

When Gyrna left, Ryven spoke, "She wants to escape with you to this cousin's home?"

"Yes." With the number of ships that were not hers in the harbor, now was not the time to escape. Neither would when she was on the ship, or in his country. Getting away was no longer a viable option.

"It wouldn't have worked."

"I know." She stared at a particularly ripe set of berries, dark blue like Parvis colors. She didn't know what they were, nor how they tasted. Her eyes fixed unseeing, while the water splashed behind the partition, she let her mind wander again.

One against twenty-one, including the king. Not counting the enemy's servants and army. Few of the royals she knew in her kingdoms could fight. Sacrifices. Perhaps she should kill them off so her empire may be stronger. So nothing like this would happen again. Mylva failed to keep the number of Bloodsworn needed to prevent defeat. It was her fault, not the weaknesses of those under her.

The new era she hoped for, cracking before her. Half because she'd destroyed part of her traditional practices, making them easy prey. And the other half because of her need to protect the future from the pain of being Klava. Chipping away, one piece at a time. The diamond bowl was no more. She would not have it remade. No more women tortured for her and her offspring, like Hava and Nava. And those before them.

Her best course of action would be to choose one of the twenty, go through their idea of courtship and the abomination that was marriage, and return home with them. There, she could regain control. Would her people follow?

She didn't deserve them.

Mylva tried to squash the negative thought. She was a strategist. A Klava. The blood of fire coursed through her veins. No one was worthy if she wasn't.

Her mind kept fighting with her.

Settling in the chair beside her, Ryven sprawled out, appearing completely carefree. What would he have to worry about? He beat her. The enemy won. He could do anything to her.

Ryven carefully slid a small blade beneath each fingernail, meticulously digging out what dirt and grime he found. He was bare, save for the long towel wrapped about his waist that covered down to his knees. Tanned and broad, the soap he used imprinted in her mind, already familiar.

"What are you thinking when you stare at me like that?"

The question startled her enough that she blurted, "Your unscarred skin is like a baby's."

They stared at each other. Ryven blinked slowly, while she couldn't blink. If she'd said that to anyone in her country, it would have been the worst affront she could utter. And she had delivered the insult to the one who had defeated her. She should prepare for the beating, or an equal barb.

"Does that mean you want to touch it? Is that a compliment?" His dark brows drew low over his mischievous black eyes. He chuckled and shook his head, "You Kavkans have odd sayings and… ways. Even after nearly six years, I'm still unsure how to interpret certain phrases I've heard."

"It's usually an insult. Scars are badges of battles fought, and you survived. Of winning and living against an opponent challenging enough to leave a mark. Or of saving a comrade." She explained readily. "You wearing unmarred skin at your rank and age is an oddity. It isn't seen in Kavka."

"I see." He tilted his head, a smile toying with his lips, "I suppose you shall be the only Kavkan to see all of me if this is offensive. Or perhaps you will aid in making me worthy of more scars." He leaned toward her, his eyes flashing, "I know of a few ways you can add your own marks to me."

She lunged, her head screaming in pain at the sudden movement as she pressed her knee to his chest. Her hand gripped the tiny blade, forcing his with the weapon against his throat. Before she could plunge it in, he held her back. The muscles in his neck and shoulders bulged as she leaned her weight in. His breath feathered her cheek and she smelled the gentle scent of pine from him.

"You are determined to touch me. It's making me feel more threatened than flattered, though. Myl, do be gentle from now on, hm?" His voice strained under the pressure of holding her from him.

She bared her teeth at him, jerking his blade away from him. Mylva flicked it through her fingers, driving it toward his rib cage. Stars filled her vision as pain spread from the base of her skull to her forehead. She cried out as his other hand fisted in her hair and yanked her head back. Her body followed.

He did too.

She slammed into the small table, then the wood crumpled underneath their weight. Somehow, her legs were around his waist now. She twisted, rolling them until she was on top. The blade still between her fingers, Klava drove it toward his eye.

He blocked the downward trajectory of her wrist with his.

A fire ignited as his eyes drifted from her face to her flesh. The robe was open. Her skin exposed.

"You have many scars." His gaze softened, returning to hers, "I am horrified at the pain you must have endured."

Time stopped. Her mind stilled for a moment. She felt her body breathing, but it was as if it was no longer hers. Some stranger. A stranger covered in wounds. All bleeding her orange blood. The burning scent of flesh as the fire within poured out. Each arrow, blade, mace, claw, spear, club, and shield that had ever given her discomfort, or a scar, flashed before her eyes.

What a silly thing for him to say.

Horrified at the pain. Was that pity? The heat of his fingers shifted across her hand, relinquishing her hold on the small knife with gentle pressure. She watched in her peripheral the flash of metal as he flicked it away from them.

Mylva clamped her mouth, gritting her teeth to get her mind in the attack. She thought of her next three moves. She didn't need a blade. Her body did not budge. Ice arced through her chest as she couldn't attack, and her lungs stopped working.

Gods. This woman. How marvelous would she be whole and well? His voice, bruising her mind, breaking the ice in her lungs.

"What?" she managed through a gasp.

Ryven blinked, and then his smile was soft. There he lay, surrounded by wood shards from the table. He tugged her down, his free arm wrapping about her. He gently cradled the back of her head with his palm and pressed her temple against his chest. "You best be careful, Myl, falling for you is easy. The heart you hear, I believe it is already yours for the taking, should you choose it."

Smoke and fire, this creature under her was mad. Did he get off on pain? Fighting? Nearly being killed? Mylva took in a deep breath, calming her thoughts to stillness and concentrating on what had just happened.

Since when did he call her Myl?

She didn't know how long they lay there. On the floor. Amid the splinters. She knew only that she quickly stood up when a sharp rapping on the door sounded, shattering her concentration, trying to figure out when he'd first called her Myl instead of Mylva. Her head throbbed more, but the stars weren't as many. She leaned on the back of an empty chair to keep herself steady.

Why was there a towel on the… her gaze zeroed in on Ryven's privates. With that between his legs, maybe he had needed little charm. Just some tight clothes, or wet ones, and he'd have half her empire in line.

He was beside her in an instant. Straightening the robe, closing it over her flesh. "Enter," he said, returning the towel to his hips.

The serving woman carried a large tray into the room, balancing it between her hand and shoulder. She slid it onto the little dining table next to the glass wall. "Enjoy," she said with a bow, "I shall call for someone to clean this up, immediately," she bowed again and left.

The cook had loaded both plates with meat dripping with a spicy sauce that tickled the nose. A small bowl of steamed vegetable to its side offered less flavorful, but a healthy addition to the meal. In the center were two cups and a tall pitcher of ale.

"Do you think you can eat?" Ryven asked her.

"Of course I can eat." She jerked away from him, moving through the mess away from the confusing man. She lowered herself in the chair, grateful the thumping didn't worsen. Mylva filled a cup with ale, drained it, and refilled it before another knock came at the door.

A few boys came in after Ryven bid them, picking up the pieces of the broken table. They refrained from asking questions. And then they moved another one in before leaving them alone. She devoured the meat.

As Ryven ate, he studied the garden.

The silence between them was both maddening and comfortable. She had questions, but didn't want to show him that she was interested. Was she interested? Why? Ryven gave her a nickname. Was that all it took?

Nearly finished with his plate, he turned to her. "Klava."

She paused, her spoon halfway up to her mouth, "What?"

"I may overstep my bounds here, but if you ever need to talk about any of those scars. Tell me the stories, or things of that nature, I will listen."

She narrowed her eyes at him, then snorted, "You overstepped when you came into my country, Prince." Had she given him the impression that she wanted to talk with him about anything? No. "That before." She pointed to the table, "That didn't happen."

His lips formed a thinner line, "You may believe that it didn't, but I know it did. My words and your words will be in my memory. As will the moment I held you. When you're ready to accept them, I'll be right here, with you, waiting."

"You…" She clamped her lips shut. The demand for him to forget everything nearly left her mouth. Foolish. Even her best behaved and eager to please Bloodsworn wouldn't forget a display of weakness, even with an order. She pushed her plate away, "I'm tired."

She hoped he would take the hint and leave her alone.

He stood, walked toward her, and without a word, lifted her from her chair in one graceful movement.

"Stop." Mylva pressed against him, trying to get a foot down out of his arms and onto the floor again.

"No," he countered, holding her tight as he crossed the room.

She frowned as he placed her gently in bed. He pulled the covers from the end of the bed over her. Mylva swatted the covers down to her waist, "What is wrong with you?"

He rounded the end of the bed to get in beside her. "That depends on who you ask." He propped up on an elbow in his pillow, looking down at her, "What do you think is wrong with me?"

"You manhandle me too much." It was what left her lips, but not the first to cross her mind. The others, like him being gentle after cracking her skull open days ago, were dangerous to tread upon. Or how he was so comfortable getting into bed with her.

"I figured you wouldn't object, seeing as how you've been wounded so many times against your will." His brow quirked, "Calling it manhandling is a bit much. I thought a little gentleness might soothe what those injuries did to you mentally. Even if they are part of your traditions." With his free hand, he straightened the covers from where she'd swatted them away. He raised them under her breasts, his fingers smoothing the soft fabric embroidered with tiny flowers before resting just under her diaphragm.

What was he talking about? Strength. Gashes to scars, bumps and bruises, all of those strengthened her. Gentleness weakened. It made the muscles lax, the senses less sharp. Panic set in if the mind wasn't ready for a challenge.

"I see."

Mylva turned her head to see his face more clearly, "What do you see?"

"I see that the Kavkan ways tear you apart on the inside."

She snorted, "Kavkan grows the strongest people you'll ever meet." Which was no longer her, right? Here, sleeping with the enemy?

"Kavkan has made you break under the simplest of kind gestures, Mylva." Ryven said, and then added, "If I were to hold you, what would you expect to come next?"

"Sex." She readily provided.

"You thought I'd make you ride me down there, with the broken table?"

"Yes." She wasn't about to confess that she'd spent that time deciding on whether or not she enjoyed having a nickname. Or why his arms felt like the embrace of her goddess, Kasvuki.

"If I were to touch your face, maybe even kiss your forehead, would you think I wanted sex next?" Ryven didn't make those moves, just spoke of them.

"What else would you want?" What else was there? Coddling? Similar to a mother consoling her child after their fifth year initiation into stabbing?

He sighed, flopping to his back, "You are the perfect weapon, aren't you? The lack of a certain set of emotions makes you plow forward without a second thought. All you have is rage, pride, and loyalty."

"That's what every warrior is." She turned to her side, facing him. "If you love something, someone can use it against you. Look what it's doing to me because you threaten Gyrna."

He snorted, "We both know you'd get rid of her when she becomes too much trouble. It's an act. To keep her close. To give you something of power when you feel you no longer have any."

She stared at him, evaluating his words against her own mind. He wasn't wrong. But he wasn't completely right either. Gyrna was her last Bloodsworn. Her last line of defense before her own throat was cut. She was more valuable than he thought. Her feisty maidservant was all she had left. Her little Kavkan fire of a friend had been with her through it all, more so than Hava and Nava, as Gyrna was always by her side.

"How did it make you feel?"

"What?" All this talk about feelings was about to make her itch all over.

"When I held you?"

She turned onto her back again, her head swimming with the effort. "It didn't."

"It did, or you would've tried to kill me."

She thought harder on that moment she wanted him to forget about. Her body hadn't wanted to move, even though she had the perfect opportunity to end him. Why was that? Was it his warmth? His body was warm. The blow weakened her, and the chilled bath drained even more of her energy.

Excuses. Mylva cursed herself mentally. She remembered, once, her first wound. A mace wielded by Gyrna, a much older child, had sliced open her shoulder. At that moment, her mother had smiled and wrapped her in her arms.

That was similar, like the goddess holding her, and Ryven moments before.

"I suppose you're like my mother." It was the best explanation she could offer, considering she didn't quite know what to think of these things.

He groaned, "That's not something any man wants to hear from his future lover."

Ryven woke to movement in the bed. He assumed Mylva was turning over to her side, but when she yelped, he opened his eyes. Strands of black hair stuck to her damp temples. The sheet rumpled as she gripped close to her heart with white-knuckled fists. Her head jerked, then her shoulder, then her whole body writhed. She pulled back her lips from her grinding teeth, as if trying to snarl, or keep from screaming.

He wound his fingers over her wrist. Hating what he was about to do. When she cried out again, he entered her mind and dropped into her nightmare.

Her scream rent the air as leather cords embedded with metal shards whipped against her back, only for her head to be pushed into the water again.

It was a contraption built specifically for her. A shallow box with deeper indentations for face, chest and feet. Filled with ice water, and leaving her back bare to the whiplashes whistling through the air.

Young. So young. Then the dream shifted. *The screams of her sisters echoing her own. Blood spilling like waterfalls. A diamond bowl swirling in the hands of an older woman with frown lines around her mouth and eyes. The blood poured from the dish as if it were made of flesh.*

Mylva's little hand reached for the woman. Wounds opened on the tiny palm, then closed only to keep spilling orange blood. The woman laughed, the same colored blood coating her teeth.

"Smoke and fog," Ryven whispered, gathering Mylva close to him. Break the dream? Was it healing her? Her subconscious letting her release the wounds? Or was this a nightmare just to have terror again after weeks of peace?

Her pitiful whimper solidified his resolve, and he shook her, "Mylva?" When she didn't answer, he panicked and pinched her arm.

She shot awake, her body bolting upright, nearly knocking him out of the bed. He gripped her harder, sitting up with her. "Mylva."

Her eyes swung to him, wide and distant.

"Listen to me." Ryven's voice was hoarse, tight. "Listen well. You are strong. You will heal. You are more than the torture." He pressed his lips to her hands, the scent of lavender still clung to them, then cupped her cheeks to rest her forehead against his, "You are to be more than those wounds. More than Klava. Klava can die and you, Mylva, will still be Mylva."

He held her long after her breaths steadied.

Her fingers wrapped around his wrists. "Klava shall not die. Ever. We are eternal." She moved away, lying on her side with her back to him.

He watched her eyes, bright and present. A hatred burned within him for the pain she suffered all for the title, for disgusting traditions. No wonder she killed everything in her path that gave any amount of resistance. Ryven held her, wondering when he'd meet the same fate as her other enemies.

Chapter 9

Mylva pinched the bridge of her nose. How can someone be a country's leader while sounding so whiny? The salt spray misted her face and hand as she leaned on the balustrade. Duima, the Juliant King from Sagawa, threw up his breakfast over the edge of the ship beside her.

"Klava, please. You must do something." His nasally voice heightened with the pleading, and he didn't even bother to wipe his pale chin of the spittle.

The siblings hadn't chosen him. Unfortunately, Duima was the only one available. Useless and spoiled resulted from being the only remaining child after a sickness took the rest.

"Pray, tell me what I must do, Duima." Mylva demanded, trying to hold on to her patience with a thin thread.

"King. *King* Duima!" He cried, waving his hands at her.

She growled, grabbing his knee and lifting. His body flipped flopped over the edge before splatting into the sea below. She counted the seconds before his brown-haired head rose back to the surface in the white swells made by the large ship. His waving hands were of use to him as he flailed and screamed.

"Hold! King Overboard!" The crew immediately shouted up and down the ship upon spotting the brat in the wake.

Mylva turned, leaning to watch the sailors scurry about on deck. Surely they would not bring a vessel aft just for the sniveling brat. She tilted her head, looking around the stern. Perhaps the next ship in the fleet coming up behind them would squash him.

One could only hope.

Sihfe whistled long and low as he meandered toward her, "I think we may need you to step from the gunnel and keep away from all edges at all times, especially when someone is near you, oh great warrior empress."

Mylva smirked, looking into Sihfe's amused face. "Let the others pick him up. I'm tired of his voice."

"It's only been a few days," he chided with a smile.

She felt her brows twitch before Sihfe laughed.

"Very well, dearest." He lifted a hand, motioning to the back of the ship, "Let the Regallia get him!"

Two crew members tied flags to a rope and hoisted them up on the mizzen-mast. The large pieces of cloth unfurling in some code for the Regallia to understand. Klava watched from her comfortable spot on the rail.

"Happy now?" Sihfe asked, flourishing a bow, and then grinned up at her with a flash of straight white teeth.

"Exceedingly." She stated with little enthusiasm behind it. If she could get rid of the rest of these annoyances just as easily, she might gladly dance. For once.

Sihfe leaned beside her, "For fear of joining him, I must stay on your good side. Thus, I must ask, what is your favorite food?"

Mylva tilted her head back, letting the wind play with her short hair. She closed her eyes, enjoying the sound of a voice that wasn't from the nose, "Why? Are you a cook?"

"The cook here is fond of me and will go to great lengths to ensure my happiness. And! I extend that fondness, exploit it if you will, just for you." Sihfe said with a triumphant look as he flipped his thick red hair back over his shoulder.

"Hm." Because he was so animated, Mylva couldn't help but watch him. She didn't know what to tell him. A memory flitted through, and she blinked back the burning sensation. "Smoked chicken wrapped in pork strips and fat with a honey-based glaze." Hava's favorite, she could taste it on her tongue as she worked through Hava's memory in her mind's eye.

He frowned, "Not sure she has that. Anything else?"

She chuckled with a shake of her head, "That is my one and only favorite." Lies. Hava's not hers. But it might as well be her own, now. Food was for strength. She never had time to truly enjoy a meal. Only opportunity to wolf it down and pray it wasn't poisoned.

"I'll see what I can do then." He said with another extravagant bow before trotting off.

She watched Sihfe's long strides take him down the length of the ship, and into the hold. Was red hair pretty? Mylva had yet to decide, possibly waiting until she grew accustomed to the shade. Most of the empire held darker tones in hair color, blacks, browns, and a few sun-bleached. Red was a rare sight, as was white blonde.

Sihfe returned to the deck, giving her a grin and rubbing his flat belly.

Perhaps she should choose a favorite meal.

Ryven didn't know which hurt the most. His pride, or his head. They were under way, taking the conquered rulers to his homeland. A plan laid out by himself, years ago, before he'd set foot on the continent ruled by Klava. No matter how much he planned and allotted for mistakes, he still found himself second guessing every step.

Every worry and strife disappeared upon the ship. The most difficult portion of his endeavor was complete. He could rest in his own cabin. Away from the woman who excited him while making him fear for his life with each breath she took. "Is this how Father feels with each of his wives?"

"What was that?"

Ryven jerked, staring at his sibling. The smirk crossing his brother's tanned and freckled features irked him. He'd completely forgotten Sihfe was there. "I daresay you heard me, brother."

"And I daresay I want to know why you said it." Sihfe leaned forward, tapping a slender finger in the center of the desk between them. "Tell me, what do you think Father feels with our mothers?"

"Aggravation."

"That's with us kids." Sihfe argued with a grin, "What were you thinking, oh brother of mine? Do tell, or I'll go ask that fire empress of yours what she thinks was on your mind-"

"Fear and lust."

"Ah." Sihfe leaned back, rubbing the stubble on his chin, the grin still in place. "Both. Definitely. And you're enough like him to have those masochistic tendencies."

"Should I thank you for the compliment or slap you for the insult?" Ryven glared at the redhead, laying the small map carefully inked on the thin, nearly translucent paper atop the larger map on the desk.

Sihfe leaned forward again, placing the addition in its exact place, meticulously matching the country borders with the lines on the smaller of the two. It filled out the larger map with several additional details. "As I am not one to get hard from pain, a thank you shall suffice."

"Hm." Ryven settled for a simple acknowledgement instead, leaning forward to study the map anew as Sihfe tenderly added the adhesive to keep it in place. "The empire is impressive."

"Moreso, that we know more about it now. I don't think I need to tell you this again, but you are a master of the world and deserve to be so with handling all this." Sihfe motioned to the large island comprising twenty countries and the addition of the smaller islands to the east of it. "Rothland can fit in Kavkan, I believe."

Ryven nodded, "That it can." his gaze flicked far to the south, to their homeland. He grinned, "I wonder what those royals will think of our city."

Sihfe snorted, "Your Klava is going to figure out a way to knock it out of the sky, mark my words." He tapped his chin, "The others, well, they might like it. Or we might have a lot of panic at first."

"I had Mother gather extra teas for soothing in case of that."

"Has there ever been a time you didn't think of everything?"

Ryven smirked, "I'll let you know."

A new place, Mylva felt a small thrill spread through her. She trailed her eyes slowly from one end of the land to the other. She squeezed the polished wood of the ship in her hands, leaning upon it as if she could see it better from the fresh vantage point.

Rising from the sea, the silvered city spanned the entire island in view. It shone with a light of its own. The ships docked at long piers, stretching out into the bay. The water was deep and a calm, dark blue that lapped along the white stone piers and the pale sands of the beach. Buildings arranged haphazardly among one another, making streets bend and curve in ways that led this way and that.

A long beam of light stretched to the underbelly of a city floating on clouds of shimmering blues and silvers. The palace shone silver-blue in the sunlight. Powers like that would make her people impenetrable.

Much like her country, there was little difference between classes. As they rode through the winding roads paved with tightly laid bricks, she spotted no beggars. Unlike other cities, these grand streets were devoid of helpless, sick people.

The rulers treated their people well. Or they refused to house those less than ideal. If it was the latter, she could disrupt this city, break it to her will. She would build the disenchanted into allies. She only hoped there was such discord.

Her steed was stirring up enough attention to draw people to her. She smiled to herself, watching as her mare pranced and snorted, revealing the fiery nature that radiated from her short black fur. Attention to attraction. Key elements of finding people she needed.

Ryven was at her side on his wide beast. He sat so stiff in the saddle she wondered if he feared being home, loved being here, or hated it. Another item of interest to tuck away for later to use to her means.

They reached the city center fortress after an hour of winding through the paved roads. Circular walls looked like the ice from her blue glaciers back home. They were smooth, with few indentations, no signs of stones being fitted together like the previous buildings and pathways of the urban area. Magicked? Or carved from what existed before?

Many spires stretched toward the palace above them of different thicknesses. Some were thin, others thick, like old forest trees. All seemed to glow from within, mocking the orange sun by showering the world with their own light.

"Ah, it feels good to be home, eh, brother?" Monace turned in her saddle to grin at Ryven.

"You must be mistaking him for one of our other brothers," Sihfe chuckled darkly from behind them, "Ryven prefers the wilds over civilized places."

"Yes, the explorer poet. How could I forget?" She wrinkled her nose, turning to ride straight again.

"Poet?" Mylva asked, before she could reign her curiosity in.

Ryven gave her a grunt for an answer. His face was unreadable, covered by the shadow of his helm. Once again, he was the silent one.

In the center, directly under the majestic dwelling above, they spread out around the thickest spire. Three stood under the spire's glow, shadows stretching across the floor. A towering beast of a man with long red hair and a bare chest scored in scars caught Monace as she leapt from her horse to him. The other wore a duplicate of Ryven's armor, including the cream crested helm, and stood stiffly. A frowning female adorned in an emerald green dress trimmed in white fur stood between them. The circlet of green emeralds on her brow reminded Mylva of the king of Gagaint's crown.

Her matching jeweled eyes widened as they landed on Klava. "No," her mouth hung in the word's shape. Tears brimmed in her eyes, "If Kavkan and Parvis have fallen… we have no hope, do we?"

"Gagaintian?"

The emerald adorned nodded, "I am Princess Enefa Schidae. I had hoped to meet you, Klava, for the first time, under better circumstances."

"As did I," she said as she dismounted and inclined her head. "I met your father once, many years ago. Is he well?"

Those tear filled green eyes flicked to the redhead, "Well enough."

Monace clapped her hands, "Come, let's not keep the others waiting."

"We are not late," the redhead stated in a voice lighter in tone than expected from someone so tall and broad. "Nadran, Behar, and Mirtes have yet to arrive."

"Mirtes had the least to travel, what could keep him?" Ryven dismounted gracefully, dropping the act he held in Kavkan.

"He was the last to leave." Sihfe patted his horse.

"The youngest, though." Monace added.

Mylva listened in silence, allowing Pazai and Enefa to be on her right and left as the royals conversed through tears together. The rest of the royals the ships brought held their distance, but she could still hear Duima's rotten whine.

Ryven motioned them forward, "Let's go. I'm sure there are plenty of extravagances above for our guests to enjoy."

"And us." Sihfe slapped Ryven's armor twice with a grin. "Maybe even some pen and paper for you to work on your latest travel poem."

Mylva sensed Gyrna's presence at her elbow before the woman whispered, "Let's hope he writes of fire to make his blood taste like it."

"Indeed." Mylva said with a nod and motioned for Pazai to follow Monace's lead into the squat spire of light. Three guards and Ryven waited for her to enter after the rest. She sneered, these guards were new, as the hemlock had finally dispatched the others. Following the Rothlanders, she looked around the single room of the spire. The stones lacked translucency, yet she could observe the surrounding spires from within. She watched as the horses, including her still prancing mare, were being led back outside. Glass, but not. A distant land, new tricks, ignited her desire to explore.

The floor caught her attention. It glittered and swirled like the cloud high above them. Within the roiling gray and silver were blue streaks forming intricate patterns. Sigils. Magic sigils she'd never encountered before.

Mylva crouched, trailing a finger over a sigil. Magic like this was a strangeness she hoped to encounter. Her family and advisors had always implemented foreign magics into their lives in helpful ways.

Was this magic the way Ryven and his army had infiltrated Kavkan so easily?

"Do you know it, Klava?"

She denied Gyrna's quiet question and had to push her shorn hair away from her face as she stood.

"Neither do I."

Gyrna's tasks included learning about other countries. The families in power within them, the religion, customs, and magic usage. The fact Gyrna couldn't help her break the spells or read these sigils could be problematic to their freedom of movement.

An impossible situation loomed. Act now? Or wait to learn their secrets?

If they didn't gain knowledge, then the enemy would repeat their processes until they obtained exactly what they wanted. Returning empty-handed, none the wiser to the abilities of her enemy, wasn't an option.

Fire burned her neck and ears. No enemy had stepped on Kavkan soil since the Heretic War, the fiftieth war of their world, nearly a century ago. Their magic now Kavkan's, and their people hers. She had to do the same here.

Pride. Contentment. Two weaknesses she had allowed herself and her country to have.

Once she returned home, her mother would rise from the lava pit to strike her down for the shame she brought to their bloodline. And she would gladly take it. After she fixed her wrongdoing.

Sihfe began explaining, "Stand nearest the center as best you can. It's best if your feet are shoulder width apart. Don't lock your knees. You'll hover slightly above the floor for a breath or two before it sets you down. Only those of our blood, father's blood, can activate this magic."

All in the spire moved closer together. The runes below glowed like moonlight, creating odd shadows under everyone's chins. Then they began swirling faster, in no pattern, chaotic.

Mylva looked up and noted the self-satisfied smirk on Sihfe's face. And the fresh spring of tears from the Gagaint. She listened and watched the siblings closely. None uttered a word. None moved, not even hyper Monace, who stood ready.

The magic activated.

Soft blue light erupted from under them and lit the path up to the palace. The glittering clouds parted. High above them, a white platform lay bare, waiting for them. Her feet lifted from the ground and her stomach sank as they hurtled up the lit path.

Instinct had her raising her arms, trying to block the crash into the platform. She passed through, feeling only a tingle through her body. The momentum stopped, and then she dropped. Expecting to pass through the platform again, she gritted her teeth with a hiss. Mylva's feet landed on the solid pearl-like stone. She glared as Ryven smirked at her. Then patted Gyrna's hand on her elbow, a sheen of sweat popping up on her Bloodsworn's temples.

Her gaze slid to the Gagaint Princess, who clutched the midnight sleeves of Queen Pazai's travel worn gown. She smirked as Pazai rolled her eyes, but allowed the touch. The Princess was young, barely of age, and Pazai's heart was warmer than her actions.

The palace closed around them. Surrounded by air and amid an enemy she knew very little about. A desperate sort of animal began clawing and picking apart at what little of a plan she had formulated. It wouldn't work. Nothing would work. She was going to be married. Then what?

Sent back to Kavkan with her new husband? Or wife? One of these twenty was doomed. There had to be more to it. Mylva promised herself to reveal it.

To momentarily tame the mauling beast inside her, she focused on what lay ahead.

The substance that made up the walls reminded her of blue-hued pearls. Constructed as if the architect couldn't decide on building type or style. Some curved like half moons before meeting with those formed from haphazardly stacked cubes. Different textures spanned odd expanses between slashes of smooth portions. A squat tower on the right corner of the open entrance, while a beautiful spiraled one hovered over another to the left, with a staircase wrapped around the outside. Not a single gate. How many lived here?

Mylva followed the procession through an archway, following a pearlescent path through a courtyard filled with low flower beds and tall fountains. As the siblings chatted among themselves, they went up a curved set of stairs out of the courtyard that led them to a set of deep ocean blue doors flung wide open to a hall of sky blue. Pillars stretched to the high ceiling, evenly spaced throughout. Between each were closed doors leading to who knew where.

Led by Sihfe, they ventured around the palace halls, and a few doorways. Finally, he led them through another hall into a potential throne room.

People milled about, the chamber filled with the hum of a crowd talking softly. Twenty of them, plus their party.

Ryven joined her and stated sternly, "Do not leave this room"

She watched as he and his siblings disappeared behind a door to the right. Guards blocked six doors on each side of the entrances. She could take them if she wanted.

"Klava?"

She lifted her head, searching for who called her name. Her gaze landed on a teen, gangly with his long limbs, but in silk and brocade finery. The only son of King Ropede of Sevinland, a country to the east of Kavkan. "Binesze."

His bottom lip trembled before he launched himself into her. His long arms wrapping around her, his buttons clacked against her armor. Nava, in her stead, had befriended this young prince as she held discussions with the king about his country. Nava. She gave great hugs.

Mylva did her best, patting the boy's back.

"You will save us then?" He asked, stepping back and swiping his eyes clean with already damp sleeves. The hope in his blue eyes both boosted her tremulous resolve and tattered her own hopes.

"Yes, Benz, I will." She used the nickname Nava made for him. Klava also thanked the gods that Benz was here and not his older siblings. Nava was also famous for her bedroom conquests.

Among the three, Nava made the Memory Meld most interesting. Hava excelled in secrecy, but the Bloodsworn rituals exposed all secrets swiftly. Hava also loved to create odd marks for them to scramble to get. Like the ink on her wrist. Klava had the shape of an Infinity Star flower, Hava's favorite, permanently etched into her wrist. Its petals shimmered blue and red along the lava fields and never died unless pruned.

She hadn't minded the ink. Nor the scars they shared. It was the heartache of seeing Hava and Nava reserve themselves to a fate of loveless loneliness when they were capable of the emotion. They wanted. Desired. Unlike her.

"I love you, Klava." Benz whispered softly in the armor plate at her shoulder.

She giggled, as Nava would have, ruffled his dark blonde hair that was nearly brown, and bit out the words as best she could, "As I love you, little prince."

Sentimentality.

It made her stomach churn. Or was it the constant lack of Hava and Nava at her side? At least she had Gyrna.

More guests poured in the doors behind her. Pazai and Enefa had wandered off to mingle among their favorite allies. The latest additions were known to Mylva by name only. The final group of three to appear, she did not recognize their colors, nor recall any of them being described to her.

A quick head count revealed twenty-four. Four more than the twenty countries she knew. Quickly signing her thoughts to Gyrna, the Bloodsworn nodded and kept her sharp eyes on the strange four.

Mylva quickly returned her gaze to a slip of a girl hiding in the shadows, and her heart broke at the same time it swelled with pride. Revra, the stuttering princess, always kept hidden from the public eye by her family, for they were ashamed of her. Revra was safe, at least. Healthy. Alive, for she often worried the little mouse of a woman would die at the disgusting hands of Revra's strict mother. Princess Revra was the only one of her royals she felt so strongly about. Emotions she wasn't used to having at all, for anyone, other than her Bloodsworn.

Grand doors closed with a shuddering groan and clack behind the last group. The last Rothlanders to arrive vanished beyond the same door Ryven, Sihfe, and Monace had. The king had over twenty offspring of age, it seemed.

There were twenty female royals with her. Four males. Twenty sons and four daughters, then.

Benz unwrapped himself from her, looking about the room with her. "How are there two dozen?"

"I don't know." The island countries under her were barely hospitable. Not enough for a rightful kingdom and filled with chieftains, or rulers of several different sects. Nothing equating a need to marry into.

This one, Rothland, she didn't know about. What else had her country not explored?

As the boy tried to ask another question, a door opened and closed behind him. Foot falls, the swish of expensive cloth as all turned to peer toward the door. A woman dressed in a flowing white gown that covered her from neck to floor strode across the chamber. She ascended the dais in the back of the room, catching Klava's attention, and halted. The circular, tall headdress she wore shimmered like starlight, as did her dress when she lifted her arms.

Silence reigned.

"Welcome rulers of the world, to Rothland. You stand in our capital, the jewel of the sea called Rathala. I am a mere steward, my name is Sian. I am here to introduce you to your hosts, future partners, to our queens, and, of course, our king." She let her arms down. Then lifted the right. "If you would form a long line, beginning here." She pointed to a spot on the floor, which began to glow with a blue star shape.

Unaccustomed to commands, the rulers struggled to arrange themselves in a line. Mylva gritted her teeth, then cleared her throat. Eyes shot to her, and the line quickly formed after she frowned at them. She placed herself in the middle, as it would be easier to pass down orders effectively.

"Thank you, dearest rulers." The woman in white, Sian, said with a smile. "It pleases me to introduce you to our beloved queens. The order of their appearance and introductions is by draw, not by rank. First is Queen Hia."

The same door that Sian entered from swung wide open. A woman, all in black, strode in with ruby and gold crowned head high. Her hair glistened a dark brown with a few white streaks. Her face was smooth, taut, with full lips painted red and matching crimson eyes. The black dress glimmered with gold and red shining threads sparse throughout it. She stopped to the left, below the dais.

"Her daughter, Bealia, matches her in beauty, strength and arts. A fine match." Sian stated as a much younger version of the queen, strode past her mother and stopped directly across from the first of the captive royals.

"Her sons, Faet and Glavin, are masters of many things. Handsome and knowledgeable in matters of utmost pleasure." The two men that entered took after their mother in skin tone, a dark olive, hair color and eyes, but their features were wilder. Feral. They stood head and shoulders taller than their sister and mother, as they stopped to stand beside Bealia.

"Are we to endure this until twenty-four and their mothers are introduced?" The question erupted from the end of the line.

"Yes. May I suggest you sit?" At a clap of Sian's hands, the doors behind the royals opened. Twenty-four servants poured out with large wooden chairs with padded seats, backs, and arms. The chairs were placed directly behind each one. Then the servants were gone.

Many sat. Others watched their Klava.

She stood still, crossing her arms and jutting her chin. The ones looking for her guidance, including Binesze, Enefa, and Pazai, kept to their feet.

The children of Queen Hai and the Queen herself also watched Mylva. One son, Faet, had a gleam in his eyes as he smirked. Klava smirked right back.

"Next," Sian said, "Is Queen Moonapsa." She waited for the queen dressed in a form fitting red dress trimmed in pearlescent beads to enter. Her hair was a golden blonde, eyes the shade of dark honey. Her face and body seemed angular, joints and bones protruding from thin skin. Wrinkles framed her mouth and made bird's feet at the corners of her eyes. "Queen Moonapsa was once a famous assassin before she fell in love with our king. She passed her skills to her children. Manda is world renown for his kills with poison."

Manda was as skinny and honeyed color as his mother, but he still had an underlying strength that made his gait smooth even with short legs.

"Tataro kills with blades and is known for his blade dance at the Ceremony of Warriors." He entered wearing red like his mother and sibling, but he was taller, lean, and slightly darker all over.

"Wolfaren, took after his namesake in the common tongue. He stalks his prey to learn all their secrets before killing them." Another red adorned, honey-colored male entered, much larger than his family though.

Mylva was losing interest. Quickly. None of the Queens nor their offspring were up to par with her measurements. Looks weren't her only criteria. Even the concise descriptions Sian rattled off were too long and boring.

She sat. The others sitting with her. Queen Moonapsa had three more sons trotted out to stand before her. The next four Queens all had sons, four each.

"Queen Jerica caught the eye of our king at a young age as they grew up together. She is an accomplished huntress, tracker, and reader of many books. Her son, Ryven, is the greatest general our kingdom has ever beheld."

Jerica looked much like her son, with black hair, black eyes, and wore a silver dress with black embroidery on it. She had a well-built, sturdy body with comfortable curves. The queen, unlike others, warmly greeted her son instead of surveying the guests.

Ryven was out of his armor. A form fitting long-sleeved black shirt was over black pants. As if it wasn't a special occasion at all. And while they were a bit down the line, his dark eyes rested upon her.

"Nadran, a master of the seas and a great captain, soon to be admiral." Sian continued. Nadran was a shorter, far more compact version of Ryven.

"Mirtes, scholar and singer, captures many hearts with his smile, even at his young age of eighteen."

He wasn't as gangly as normal teens were, but square like his brothers. His height was nearer to Ryven's, but not quite there.

Why Ryven kept looking at her, she didn't know. But she did know the sensation of his hard gaze upon her, having felt it for the duration of their travels. Another son and two daughters joined the throng of suitors for the captive royals.

Monace and Sihfe were the children of Queen Ranamala. The last queen had a single daughter to add to the mix.

When they were all together, Klava observed shared traits among the children, including ticks, weaknesses in movements, and other characteristics. Cheekbones and lips all looked rather similar, and even the skinniest still had square, straight shoulders.

Sian smiled, bowing to the Queens and their thirty children. "Now, may I present to you our beloved? A man of cunning, wit, honor, and tenacity. Rothland's King Licthan Verlite."

Behind the dais, the large wooden double doors opened. Light spilled, casting a shadow on the man in the doorway. His stride was sure, even, and he glided up the stairs and stood in the middle of the raised platform.

He was once dark haired, but the long shoulder-length locks of faint waves were gray and white. His dark gaze swept over those present. He looked like a bear in finery.

Once again, Klava sensed the king was a formidable foe. One she might lose against. Not that she would ever admit it.

"Welcome guests!" His voice thundered through the hall. His lips twisted as the captives didn't stand. Nor did they bow like his children and wives. "The introductions will be the most strain you endure here, if you behave, I promise. I hope you will make yourselves at home once we are done here." He clasped his hands behind his back, the muscles rolling under his embroidered shirt.

"Some of you may wonder why I have gathered you all here, or how I dare to demand your presence in such a… hm, not entirely hostile, but threatening way." He smirked at this, teeth and eyes flashing devilishly. "I am done with war. I never want to see it again."

He waited, looking at the royals. "Some of you are allies, while others have many enemies. Some of you remain undiscovered. Thankfully, a terrible world war hasn't broken out yet. It is on the horizon, unless someone, or all of us here in this room, takes action. Now, or at least, within ninety days."

Mylva stole a glance at Pazai at her side and met her gaze. The queen pressed her lips together, and Mylva nodded. They discovered a well-crafted, years-long plan. However, they couldn't guarantee countless children for this plan. Or the number of her countries. Coincidence?

"Here, you'll find a room, servants, every comfort. You will have ninety days to come to your decision." He paused, soaked up the dramatic effect as many of them began looking at one another. "Wed one of my children, rule with them, bear heirs, and we all become one cohesive world empire. Or you may find yourself conquered, wiped from the world along with your culture, ideals, and people. I have details for you if you want them, or they will tell you." He motioned to his children and wives.

Mylva grinned, her blood boiling within her. She turned and met the heavy gaze of Ryven's with her own. Him, or one of his siblings. Though, it seemed he wanted to lay claim with that stare of his.

"The choice is yours." The king bellowed, "Now, the rules! No harming or killing of anyone while you stay here. If you do, well, we believe in an eye-for-an-eye tenfold. Consult Sian before leaving within ninety days. She will present your case to the queens and me, who will decide whether or not to permit you. You cannot lock yourself in your rooms unless feverish or ailing for more than a day. You must mingle. Furthermore, one meal shall be eaten with others each day." He grinned, opening his arms wide with palms out, "That is all! Follow us to the dining hall!"

Chapter 10

After a delectable dinner, where all sat at a long table filled with delicacies, Mylva and Gyrna received permission to explore the palace as they wished. As they wandered down a hall with one side open to the flame hued sky, Ryven called out to her.

Mylva turned, allowing him to catch up. A slender woman dressed in pinks and whites followed close on his heels. Once he reached her, his idea of personal space was nonexistent, "Have you decided?"

"About what?" Mylva asked, as there were plenty of things for her to decide at the moment. Like whether or not she was going to punch him in the nose so he'd know not to stick it in her face.

His lips twisted up, "Whether you will choose one of us, or go to war." He crossed his arms over his chest as he wandered around her like a buzzard.

"I have ninety days to make such a simple decision, why should I rush?"

"Very well. Here, a servant." Ryven stated as he stepped in front of her again, gesturing to the lady in pink and white.

"I have one." Mylva motioned for the pink wearer to leave as Gyrna smiled, lifting her chin proudly.

"We will give each one of your royals, and you, a native servant. That way, you will not get lost or go without something that Gyrna can't find," he said in a dull, perhaps bored, voice as he leaned against the nearby wall.

A spy. Mylva eyed the woman, "Do you have a name?"

"Basau, at your service, my Queen." She answered, bowing low.

"Empress." Gyrna hissed.

"Do you plan to report back to Ryven or someone else?" Mylva asked, raising a brow when Basau didn't automatically correct herself.

Basau flinched, her shoulders nearing her ears, "I am yours, my Empress."

"She reports to me. Remember the rules. You cannot harm anyone while here. That includes workers or servants." Ryven reminded her with a honeyed smile.

"Kicking her out of my room is not harming anyone."

"Abandonment. Not being suitable to your master is a death sentence here. Do you wish for another one?"

Mylva observed Basau's face go from pristine, to confused, to pale as Ryven spoke. She sighed, catching the lie, but was unable to let the woman suffer with a clear conscience. "No. Allow her to prove useful. Since she reports to you, won't you still kill her if she has nothing of interest to tell you?"

Ryven's smirk made his eyes darker, "Not all secrets can be hidden. For instance, the number of scars that mar your flesh may be extremely interesting to me and my siblings."

Out of the corner of her eye, she saw Gyrna's hands fist at her sides. Her Bloodsworn was ready to launch herself at the Prince. Again. A thought crossed her mind. "Shouldn't I return the blessing?" She motioned to Gyrna.

"I'd rather have a hundred servants underfoot than have one always daring to kill me," He said with a shake of his head before walking away.

Instead of continuing her exploration down the hall, which would make her follow him, Mylva eyed her new servant. "Where is my room?"

Unfortunately, Mylva's plan to avoid following Ryven was foiled as soon as Basau shadowed his footsteps.

Down the passage, at a crossroads of another hallway, they turned right, and walked until they stopped at the door at the end on the left. Opposite the one where Ryven smirked darkly, leaning again, against the doorframe.

"Welcome home, Klava." He purred before closing his door behind him.

"Perfect." Mylva muttered to herself as Basau led them into her new chambers.

Somehow, home found its way to the land of Rothland, at least in her bedchambers. The floor of pearls held adornments of thick rugs in many hues of reds, oranges, and purples, displaying intricate patterns. The furnishings were thick, black wood tables between chairs filled with plush blankets and pillows. A few loungers squatted low near one of the two fireplaces. It begged for lovers to become intimate, with silk pillows and thin sheets in vibrant red hanging from the rafters to provide privacy.

To the right was a set of wide doors, ajar enough to reveal a bed four times the size of hers back home. Enough to sleep fifteen comfortably with as many pillows in various sizes and shapes. More doorways on the left led to a tiled room with a deep bath. The three of them could bathe together in it and not touch each other's fingers or toes.

Opulence.

That was the word for this kingdom. And others under her care like this one. Surely, with all these extravagances, the royal family was soft. She would have to test that theory carefully.

"Bath." She uttered the single noun and Gyrna automatically jumped to action. Basau waited a breath, before helping Gyrna fill the large deep copper tub. Her Bloodsworn adjusted the knobs until she reached the desired temperature. Steam rose from the metal of the bath.

She liked her baths as near to scalding as her rage filled fire.

Gyrna helped Mylva shed her armor, Basau watching closely until she learned the snaps and buckles. She helped Gyrna hang the light metal pieces over a stand near the wardrobe. The layer of leather was next, neatly folded and placed on the bench. Then the soft clothing underneath that helped keep her clean with the magic of a certain family in her country. And finally, the clasped binding around her breasts, thighs, and stomach, for extra security and ease of movement without chafing.

She let her lungs fill fully, for the first time in days.

Her flesh tingled under Basau's stare, "What?"

"You're as muscled as a professional fighter, or warrior, yet you still have curves. Softness."

She hoped her muscles and scars would deter the royals here. Mylva couldn't rely on her foreboding character to make them fear her. This kingdom was far enough away that the legends of her family were unknown to them. They had their own lore here.

Mylva followed the hacked lines and jagged holes of her scars peppering her flesh. These stories of her own saga. She shared these marks once. Not long ago. Now, she was the lone figure to carry them. The only one to know the stories of each mark.

She traced a creased scar of puckered flesh circling her biceps. The worst wound she'd earned had nearly taken her arm off in her second battle. She had to perform the same procedure on her Bloodsworn sisters. A hellish night of screams. They all cried together for the first time because of the act.

She still had the sword that gave her the scar. The severed hand of the woman who owned it wrapped skeletal fingers over the hilt to this day. A woman of fire magic, like her, who wielded flaming weapons.

"Klava."

Gyrna's voice broke her from the memory. She strode toward the bathing chamber as her Bloodsworn motioned it was ready for her. Mylva sank into the steaming water. Supreme pleasure engulfed her as the scorching liquid threatened to tear her cooled flesh from her bones. She'd been too long without true heat. Her blood soaked it in. She closed her eyes, letting the boiling heat fill her body.

Baths and sunlight provided relief, but only lava offered full restoration. The fools didn't know how she replenished her strength. She wouldn't let Basau discover and disclose that to Ryven. If he didn't already know.

Gyrna crouched by her bath, her fingers moving against the sponge as she soaked it. "*There is none here worthy of your trust,*" she signed, keeping her eyes on Basau.

"You don't need your armor," Basau stated the next morning as she motioned to the wardrobe. "According to Prince Ryven's requests, we have prepared clothing for you."

This will be awful, Mylva thought to herself as she wiped breakfast from her mouth with the cotton napkin. She pictured the constraining and sheer clothing stored within the ornate armoire. Yawning away the last of the night, she stretched and headed to the Rothlander. Without her armor, she did not rest well.

Every little sound stirred her ire, knowing her protective second skin wasn't on her. This palace was full of them. Rain scented wind whipped through the open windows, and howled through others. The sounds of glass cracking, although she was pretty sure she dreamed that.

"Let me see, then."

Basau opened the wardrobe with a smile.

Ryven was completely infuriating. She realized he had probably decorated the room as well. Her colors were everywhere. The same with her wardrobe. Blacks, golds, oranges, and reds. She nodded. Then groaned when Basau took that as a permission to choose something.

She produced a red item, too long for a shirt, too short for a dress.

Mylva eyed her armor. "I've changed my mind."

Gyrna entered the chambers swiftly and closed the door. Only, it didn't shut. Fingers curled around the edge, holding it open a few inches and pushing it wider.

"Out! Out you mad thing!" Gyrna struggled, propping her body against the wood even as she slid on her slippers against the slick floor. She picked one slipper off her foot and began whacking the fingers. They didn't give way.

Mylva sighed, picking up an ornate metal vase as thin as a candlestick.

"Empress Klava, please! You cannot harm another!" Basau cried.

The door flung open, and Gyrna tumbled over the rug, sprawling over it. Mylva lifted her gaze from a cursing Bloodsworn to the dark eyes of Ryven. They shone in amusement, maybe triumph, as he watched Gyrna pick herself up off the floor. Then he looked up, the smile fading into an 'o' upon his lips.

"Prince Ryven! Manners!" Basau cried, holding the shirt that was a dress in front of Mylva, blocking his view.

The royals jointly stated her clothing was nightclothes, with Mylva adding, "And what you have there is worse."

Basau made an odd frustrated sound in her throat, before saying, "Until she is engaged, she shall not be pur viewed like stock."

Mylva laughed, "You called her servant, but she's as mouthy as Gyrna."

Ryven sneered, "We treat our servants well here."

"Like family." Basau added, sheepishly, still holding the garment up to protect Mylva's honor.

"Thank you for clarifying that the threat from yesterday is void." Mylva tried to hide the smirk, but it spread anyway. She witnessed the realization sink in before asking, "Are you to claim me, then?"

The prince smiled, "I shall. Are you to accept?"

"I have yet to decide. After all, I've only met two of your siblings officially."

He frowned, then shook his head as if to dismiss another comment. "I came in here to make sure you didn't put on your blasted armor. Some might take that as a threat."

"Others will take that as I've given up on freeing them from your clutches." Mylva nearly spat in his face. She turned to Basau, "My armor."

"Don't." Ryven glared at Basau.

Gyrna humphed and strode over to prepare her master's undergarments. Basau whimpered and clutched her hands together, wringing them as she looked from Ryven to Mylva and back again.

"More instances like this will come, dear Prince." Mylva said with a jerk of her chin "What are your servants to do? Defy you, or follow the orders of the masters you have assigned them? Shall you torture them thus?"

Ryven stepped into her area, taking the shirt? dress? from Basau's hand and holding it against Mylva, under her chin. His warm breath was full of a sweet scent that hinted at mint, but had a nutty or something else mixed in. His eyes roamed down her form, then lifted to meet her gaze, "I believe only Basau should suffer. The others don't seem as stubborn as you are."

"Perhaps you should persuade one of them to choose you, General Prince, to make life easier on yourself." She could feel the warmth of his body through her night clothing, and the thin red thing between them and his own gaping open black shirt. Her flesh wanted to soak in his heat. She tamped down the desire, remembering the rules.

No harming or killing others.

She still had to use him until she discovered the magic to descend from the sky prison.

"I like challenges, not suckling or sulking babes." He replied quickly to her bait, and then added, "Tomorrow, you can wear your armor. I must train my soldiers, as they've been lazy for too long. I would be pleased if you would join me."

"I will wear my armor today, too. Or I will not leave this room." She lifted a shoulder, "If they fight like your other men on the road, they need all the help they can get. I'll join."

"Perfectly fine with me." Ryven grinned, with a spread of his hands. He aimlessly roamed, observing delicate items in Mylva's room. Gyrna frowned, her eyes fixed on him like a bird of prey eyeing a mouse.

She lifted a shoulder, handed the red thing and vase back to Basau, and sat in the low lounger near the fireplace.

"Basau, retrieve one or two of my books from my room. The nightstand," Ryven stated as he rounded the chamber. He picked up her feet, setting them in his lap as he sat down on the same piece of furniture as she.

"Out of all the places here, why did you choose to be on top of me?" Fresh soap and a scent that belonged to him filled her nose.

Ryven chuckled, "Hardly on you, but I can remedy that to make your statement more true."

He seemed loose today. Perhaps he was drunk this early in the morning. She eyed his hand on her shin. It rested there, as if it wasn't a big deal to touch her. As if she was already his. "Have you gotten so comfortable with me in our brief acquaintance?"

Upon the Rothland servant's return, he thanked Basau and took the two books from her hands. He read the titles on the spines before choosing one. "Klava, we are well enough acquainted to sit like this, I should think. Your country is not disparaging of touching or sitting with one another occasionally. Is it just you?" He smirked, "Do I make you feel things you don't like when I'm this close?"

"You must indulge in romance books." No other man would think he had any influence on her feelings unless he fantasized himself as a romantic.

"Some. Don't you enjoy them?"

She made a face before answering, "I haven't had time to listen to or read anything other than reports and papers pertaining to my people that need my attention. It must be nice to have such free time on your hands."

Ryven's hand rested back on her shin once he settled the book in his other. "It's a matter of time management and making boundaries with your advisors, my love."

Her brow twitched as his eyes widened on his book. She spied his ears turn a slight red, along with a blush tinge creeping up his neck from the low collar of his shirt. Mylva replayed the words as his voice entered her thoughts, too. She sat still, listening to what he said inside her mind.

Did I really call her that? I didn't, did I? She missed it, right? His voice panicked mentally as his gaze flicked to the side, toward her, but he didn't turn his head. *Kasu, she noticed.*

He cleared his throat, "I could teach you."

"To love or time management?" She grinned as the red deepened upon his flesh. Why was she hearing him in her head? While abroad, did her powers hint at some new ability? She racked her memories to recall the strange abilities her ancestors had.

None of them were mind reading.

Both. Say both! Kasu. His smile spread as he spoke, "I was speaking of time management, but both are doable."

"Wouldn't that impede your free time?" She was still hearing him.

With you, I'll be happy to never have free time again. Her mind. Gods, her mind, I want to be in it. It makes me want to take her as mine so I can pick her brain for strategies. Will she ever talk to me like that?

Her stomach lurched the more she heard his voice in her head. What was this? Just to make sure she wasn't losing her sanity, she paid close attention to his lips. They never moved. She was going mad.

"I'll make it work." He turned slightly, facing her more, his brows drawn low. His hand spread, a comforting rub on her leg, "You alright? You look pale?"

Does the weather here not suit her? Is she too cold? Her flesh nearly burns mine…

Mylva shook her head, pressing fingertips to her temples. She was unable to tell him. Then again… it might hold him off. He would leave her alone. "I'm sick. Send me home."

"Kasu!" He said vehemently, jerking his hand off her leg.

She eyed him, "What was that for?"

He pinched the bridge of his nose, "Are you truly sick from not being near lava? How did you take the other countries if you got so ill?"

His face held red well, not just his ears and neck. She looked at Gyrna from across the room. The maids were bickering with each other. Her Bloodsworn hadn't been paying a bit of attention to her.

Mylva returned her focus to the enemy holding her feet in his lap, "Yes, I'm ill. What will that mean for me?"

He looked away, staring at the fire for a moment, his jaw muscles working. He collected his thoughts, then looked her in the eye. "You have power via the fires of your domain. If I were to give you more fires, would that help?"

She snorted, "You're not that intelligent. Fires here pale compared to Kavkan, to what I need."

"No." He frowned at her, if he had had feathers they would have ruffled, "I am that intelligent. Gyrna doesn't seem to be worried. She was bossing everyone around when you were knocked out. Why isn't she now, if you are seriously ill from lack of contact with Kavkan?"

A boy. This wasn't a man in her room, but a sullen, sulking boy because she'd just insulted him. She sighed, knowing her lie revealed, "I'm not sick." Or was she? Why was she hearing his voice if she wasn't sick?

"No, I didn't think so." He smirked.

She raised her brows, the smirk on his face needed to be wiped off. Who was being childlike now? "I'm about to show you how mad I can get." Mylva needed to understand his meaning.

"Don't make promises you don't intend to keep, Klava." Ryven placed his hand back on her leg, higher this time, just above her knee.

She gripped his fingers, twisting them away from her, "I'll have my revenge."

His lips twisted, eyes crinkling at the corners, jerking his chin toward their joined hands. "I didn't know you enjoyed being touched at the knee. I'll have to keep that in mind when you allow me to woo you more."

"Thighs." she growled, releasing his hand after placing it on the back of the lounger.

"I like thighs."

She glared at him, "Read your book, Prince."

He chuckled, settling in to read his book while slightly facing her still.

Kasukasukasukasukasukasu. Had it hit her? Had his thoughts entered her mind? Had that been the moment she grew pale, realizing his thoughts were not her own? Or was she truly sick for heat, for power?

His greatest fear had been taking her from her country for too long. But knowing she stayed in battles for years outside of Kavkan gave him hope she would be fine. Then again, he didn't know what practices they held in their battle camps.

For all he knew, she slept in hot coals under a bonfire.

Reading a page, he studied her complexion. Normal. A bit darker around her eyes than when he'd first met her, but normal. Healthy.

Ryven's momentary relief disappeared under the panic of searching what thoughts of his she could have heard. How much had he shared? His plans?

She had some meaty thighs. From their interactions, he imagined what they would feel like bare to the touch. Bad thoughts to have with her next to him. He didn't think he had enough self control to not flirt and cajole his way in between them. The book. He'd wanted them for this particular reason.

"Want me to read to you?" When her eyes shot to his, he realized how odd of a question that could be. It was likely the least suitable book for her.

"Yes, why not?"

He inhaled deeply, then exhaled slowly, flipping back to the first page. She'd either have some deep self-reflective moments in the next few days, or he'd find himself in the afterlife, or worse… nothing would happen.

Ryven had chosen the book to reread because the main character reminded him of her. Dangerous. Malicious. But a tender, tortured soul underneath that needed healed. It was her lover that helped heal her before she killed him.

Not only was she probably going to have some self-reflection, but the book would more than likely give her ideas.

Nonetheless, he'd stepped into this action with his big mouth and momentary panic. It was all on him. He deserved what he received. He'd killed hers, two of them, by his hand. Technically five. It also wouldn't hurt to return the favor. After all, he was fairly certain that the odd deaths of half of his personal guard were all her doing.

Retribution. He was unable to find fault with her. But he wanted to. They were good men. Friends, if one like him was able to possess such. Did she count them even now? Ten of his men for her Bloodsworn sisters and three of her generals.

Where had Praedae, the Warmonger, hid?

He still itched to get into his mind and pick apart what she liked most. And her strategies. However, no one had found Praedae, the monster Kavkan.

As he read to her, his mind flitted back and forth. From paying attention to the present, and pulling apart the past and where his strategy had gone wrong. He had a feeling the big man would cause problems. Eventually. He couldn't predict her actions.

A thrill. A few nuggets of hate. Lust. Wonder and awe. And wariness. No wonder he wasn't sleeping.

The warmth of her flesh beckoned him, and he answered its call. Resting his hand just above her knee, he stammered over the next sentence as her thoughts freely flowed. A mistake.

I cannot complain about his voice. It's decent. The cadence is so soothing that I might fall asleep while he's reading. Is that enough to keep him around? Think, Mylva. To keep him means I would gain access to his mind, his stratagem. I won't have to worry about anyone else gaining him and overthrowing me. She tapped her bottom lip with her index finger through the thoughts.

If I still have an empire. I'm not worthy. No, I will be. Can I gain the Kavkan's trust and my honor back with him? Or will it damage my chances?

With all of her thoughts, her face remained immobile. Her eyes trained on the edge of the book in his hand. It was like he was studying a stone.

His army. His family is at my fingertips to use, as good as an army themselves if my assessments are correct. An offspring from his loins would keep the Kavkan tones in the bloodline.

But that red hair. It was interesting. A wielder of my blood with red hair. That would make legendary stories of their battles.

He stopped reading. Why? Her gaze met his, Mylva's eyes narrowed.

Ryven cleared his throat, carefully keeping his thoughts to himself and what he said as he pressed his fingers into her flesh. He realized there were at least three scars under his palm or near it. "I read a few pages, and then we talk."

"Is this going to be like education?" Mylva raised a brow at him, "The text is rather flowery for a study session, don't you believe?"

"Not at all too flowery." He closed the book and rested it on her calf. "What do you think of the main character thus far?"

"She's impressive." *Weak in thoughts. One of her caliber should not doubt if they are making the correct moves or not. They should be sure of themselves.*

Perhaps her head was a bit too hard for her to have moments of self-reflection through comparison with a fictional character. "She is. Like you are."

Her eyes narrowed, then the novel was in her hands and the spine came down over his knuckles.

He noticed her face was pale again. Had his thoughts entered her? He turned his hand out, reaching for the book. "Do you want me to read more? Or do you want to read to me?"

She snorted, jerking it out of reach by stretching her arm out over her head, "I'd rather read it by myself than read to you."

"Then give it back." This could only go in one of two ways. It was going to hurt. But it might give him delicious dreams that night.

He leaned forward, practically between her legs, his chest to her stomach, his face in reach of her breasts, delicacies he wanted to taste. The next move would determine if he would live to dream, or to taste her and hope for a swift death.

"Hm." Her eyes narrowed on him, and her gaze roamed over the portions where they touched.

He'd moved his hand, using it to balance, palm on the plush cushion by her hip. No flesh touching. His access to her thoughts stopped. Ryven noticed her eyes narrow, and he wondered what she'd realized in that moment, because she returned the book to him without another word.

Chapter 11

Before dawn, Ryven was in her room. A frown on his face, armor on his back, and a sigh parting his lips. That sigh turned into a yawn.

She smirked, "Wanted to find me naked?"

"Asleep. So I could kiss you awake and bring you breakfast in bed." He motioned behind him. Two servants wheeled in a laden tray. A three tier monstrosity of fruity smelling pastries balanced in the center surrounded by plates of steaming fatty meat, a plate of salted biscuits, and one with pads of jam, jellies, and butters on it.

With joy, Hava would melt and dedicate herself to him. If only she lived instead of her. Ryven's life might be easier.

"I would have cut off your lips," Gyrna quipped.

Mylva grinned, "Head butted first, then cut." For emphasis, she picked up the dull utensil, flicking it between her fingers, then twirling it around her hand.

Ryven's brow rose, "With a butter knife?"

"At times, a fork or spoon can do the job." Mylva retorted, baring all her teeth.

He dismissed the conversation with a grimace. "Let's eat and get to the training grounds before my men make up excuses." He sat down at the table, one servant pouring a cup of a dark liquid. The familiar, rich, bitter scent of the coffee made her assume it came from one of her countries. She sat across from him, the servants fixing her drink and plate like they did his. A lot of meat, a little of everything else. How many people did it take to serve two in Rothland? Four, plus the two personal servants, apparently.

"Gyrna, Basau, eat too." Mylva said, motioning to the tray. The strange servants gasped and looked at one another with wide eyes. Then the four that came with the breakfast pressed themselves against the wall to either side of the door. Stoic, except for another glance at each other.

"Not until you eat," Basau stammered at her elbow.

"Defy me again when I give you an order and I shall show you how well this cutlery skins you alive." She watched as Basau hurriedly took an almost empty plate of meat and filled the rest of it with pastries. The Rothland servant retreated to the sitting area before the fireplace. "Gyrna, I know you're not shy."

"I'm not, my Klava, but I was looking forward to seeing your handiwork again." Gyrna's pout turned into a small smile as she filled another plate and joined Basau, probably to torture the other woman more.

She bit back the laugh, but gave Gyrna the sign for 'well done' with a few flicks of her fingers. Eating quickly, she outpaced Ryven, cleaning her plate in five bites. Then she drank down the coffee, delighting in the burning sensation before her blood soaked it in. Leaning back in her chair, she watched him.

"While I appreciate you admiring me, I have to wonder if you're not picking out a place to stick that butter knife or a shard of a broken plate."

"Choking you on a pastry is my favorite idea of the ten so far." Mylva said with another grin.

"You're a morning person." His face said it all. He wasn't.

"Hardly. I'm a meet-my-enemies-at-my-best person."

"She didn't sleep." Basau blurted.

For a moment, Ryven studied the servant from his country, before returning his attention to Mylva, "Why?"

She wondered if he was concerned about the climate's suitability for her again. His little mind powers could prove useful to her. If his voice in her head was his powers and not her losing touch with sanity. Mylva lifted a shoulder, her armor scraping lightly, "New place, new enemies, would you sleep under those circumstances?"

"Like a baby."

"Then you're a fool." She would normally reprimand, but he wasn't her man. He wasn't truly her general.

He chuckled, "I thought Kavkans enjoyed challenges. Do they not? Or is that just you?"

"Yes, but there are no obstacles here. I'm bored. The new enemies are far from ideal for any challenge." Mylva took a long sip of her coffee to finish it.

"I am a challenge." The Prince's lips twisted to one side as his eyes bored into hers.

She kicked the dining table into him. Ryven toppled over his chair amid the clattering dishes and silverware. She pressed the edge into the soft spot, the break in armor at his diaphragm as soon as he stretched back to launch himself. Mylva grinned as his air whooshed out of him, and she slammed her body against the table, using her own chest plate to drive both the weight of the heavy wooden piece and herself into him.

He grunted, gripping the smooth edge. She saw the veins pop in his neck as he strained to get out from under the rib-breaking wood. "Klava," he breathed, "No harm." He barely got out the words.

"Bones breaking is little harm. Sorry you had an accident. These tables are so heavy." She leaned along her edge, petting the table like an animal she adored. The cloth fell away at her urging, leaving the dark black wood bare, and Ryven covered in the white cloth and a few shards of dishes.

She caught the staff member, one of the two to the right of the door by their neck as they dashed toward her. She used their momentum to flip them onto their back at her feet. With a shatter of plates and glass, Mylva released the servant. She twisted, kicking the stomach of

Basau as she tried to run at her from behind. Gyrna had two others drawn away in a tight combat of fists.

The quiet blonde that had stood frozen to the left of the door for a moment surprised her. She should've known better than to dismiss the threat of a silent person. The blonde swept her leg. Mylva grunted, going down on one knee and losing her grip on the table. It rolled toward her, giving Ryven enough room to slip out the other side.

"Water and ice!" Mylva cursed, pulling herself back up.

Ryven leaned all his weight into his side of the table, pinning her underneath and slamming the edge into her temple. Showing his teeth in a snarl, with ragged breath he hissed, "You could've kept it for the training ground."

"What's the fun in that?" Mylva asked, shaking her head to clear the stars glittering around the edges of her vision. She thanked the gods Gyrna had braided her hair against her scalp in three plaits, leaving the rest loose but away from her eyes.

The table slammed into her again and Mylva rolled, jerking her leg free as her greave scraped a huge welt into the dark wood. Somehow, he was over her. The heavy weight of his body pinned her to the floor, slamming her chest plate into the orange rug.

How?

She grunted, trying to twist and press her way out from under his weight. His breath tickled a loose hair into her ear. She shuddered, then her upper body trembled violently of its own accord.

He laughed, "Mylva...what was that?"

His breath moved the hair again, and she shuddered. Her whole body reacted violently. "Stop! Breathing!"

Ryven laughed again, his fingers brushing the strand away gently, "All that for a little hair?"

Klava whimpered, her body vibrating under him as she felt the hair leave. "I do not know what you're talking about."

He brought the strand back, dangling and shaking it in her ear. Her body shook and twisted, desperate to flee from him. So much for getting the best of him. "Aren't your ribs broken?" Where was Gyrna when she needed her? She could hear more scuffling from the back of the room. Were Rothland servants trained in fighting?

"Yes, but they're healing." He said with a smile she saw out of the corner of her eye.

"That quickly?" Were his powers not of the mind, but for healing, then? Was she seeing signs of sickness yesterday, one that twisted thoughts?

He brushed her hair back away from her face, then placed his lips against her jaw, near her ear. She caught in her mind, *One attack for the day down, how many more to go?* As she heard him say, "As long as I can focus, my powers allow me to make my body put forth all effort into something. In this case, healing. And kissing you."

The touch of his lips against her temple sent a strange warmth through her. He was in her thoughts, no doubt. An image flashed in her mind. Them, naked, in this very position. His kiss pressed to her nape as he rammed into her.

They gasped together.

"Gods, woman." He murmured, his mouth rubbing against her cheek, "Do you have any idea what you do to me?"

Unsure if he spoke those words aloud or just played them in his mind for her to receive. This was maddening. What was he doing to her? She'd much rather fight him.

Break bones. Spill blood. Relish victory. Not have her mind invaded.

She threw her head back, slamming her skull into his face. She felt a crack, her ears pricking at the sound of it, and grinned. Her mind was free of his thoughts.

His curse was sharp.

The blood in her body boiled, flowing toward her back and arms. She felt her armor slightly expand with her heat. The warmth made her want to smile again, but she didn't.

He cursed again, rolling off her as his flesh sizzled.

She crouched, watching as he stared at the bare, reddening hands.

Ryven lifted his gaze to hers, twisting his nose back into place. "You can heat it like that? Doesn't it bend it?"

"Sometimes." Mylva stood, glancing over her shoulder to where she'd last seen Gyrna. The two breakfast servants pinned her arms while Basau sat on top of her back. The three on top looked far worse for wear than her Bloodsworn did, but they were victorious. Mylva returned her gaze to Ryven.

Ryven chuckled with a shake of his head, "Worth the risk of ruining your armor just to burn me off you?"

"Yes. And it won't ruin. Yours would, even with it being Kavkan, mine won't."

He dragged himself up to his knees, leaning on a toppled chair, eying her right back, "Magic?"

"Of course. My blacksmith is the best. He knows my powers well." She turned slightly, keeping the three within her peripheral vision while Ryven kept most of her focus.

"And what else can those powers do other than let you walk through lava?"

"Lots of things." She could tell Gyrna was breathing at least, but knocked out.

"Not going to tell me?" Ryven slanted his head to the side, "I have to find out the hard way, hm?"

"Yes. Experience is the best form of education. Like with your men's training." She motioned for him to get up, "They're waiting for their leader, I bet."

"That they are." He grunted as he stood, holding his diaphragm with one arm. "I'll not report this. You should be careful who you attack, though." He pointed to the servants once he found them by looking past Mylva, "Walk it off and don't tell anyone. Clean this up."

"Yes, Prince." Basau and the other two chimed together from their position of sitting on Gyrna.

"No one heard the scuffle?" Mylva asked.

"No. These walls are like your lava. Noises bubble and meld, you can't tell where they're coming from if you perceive anything." Ryven answered, dropping his commanding tone into a conversational one.

That's interesting. She could kill him in his sleep and only she would know. Unless he was lying. The noises last night were muted. She mostly noticed the wind and a handful of loud dogs barking. Perhaps the glass sounds were the palace settling in the wind? That thought would keep her up at night. Mylva motioned for him to lead the way.

Ryven's brows rose slightly as his lips formed a frown. "The look on your face says that we're thinking differently when it comes to things going bump in the night not being perceived here." He stepped out of her room.

Was he brave or an idiot? She never walked in front of an enemy if she could help it. She'd attacked him just moments before, too.

He hadn't checked her for weapons.

She glanced at Gyrna, jutting her chin. Not passed out, like she'd thought, but there was a swollen lump on her Bloodsworn's temple. Basau helped Gyrna stand. She watched Gyrna's gaze drop to her fingers. Through a few motions, she instructed her Bloodsworn on her tasks.

Gyrna promptly signed she understood and left.

Mylva motioned for Basau to get her helm and training gloves before she followed Ryven and Gyrna out of the room.

"Where did you send her?" Ryven asked, guiding her down the hall.

Mylva lifted a shoulder, "She's preparing my chambers for later. Cleaning up the mess."

"The other servants take care of that and she left the room." Ryven stopped, turning on his heel to look down his nose at her with narrowed dark eyes. "Scheming, while it makes life interesting for me, will not be tolerated by many here."

"I'm not a schemer."

He snorted, another rather non-princely thing to do. "Any other lies, Klava? Is that your last one for today?"

She just smiled up at him and didn't step back when he stepped into her personal space.

"Your smiles are like a beast baring its teeth. Your threatening pose challenges me to discover the abilities of your mouth." His pastry and grease scented breath caressed her cheeks, not entirely unpleasant to sniff, but not welcomed either.

"I am rather curious if your mouth can do more than smirk, snarl, and spout nonsense myself."

"We have our lifetimes to get to know each detail. But smoke, I want to know all now." He dipped his head, his lips nearly touching hers before he froze in place.

The butter knife was the perfect slenderness to slip in between plates and press against the tenderness of his manhood. Despite the lack of leverage to cut him, it could still cause bruising and other harm. Making sure he understood the danger, she wiggled it between the flaps men used to relieve themselves while in armor. The heat of his skin washed over the finger she stretched along the back of the butter knife.

"For one revered so, you have little patience, do you?" She slid her tongue out, brushing it along his bottom lip.

Ryven's lips twisted, but the widening of his pupils belied his emotions, "Not going to ask permission to sample me?"

"I certainly don't have approval to almost be touching your penis, but you're not pointing that out."

His brows rose, "Fair. You do not have sanction to cut my cock off. But if you would like to touch it gently, kindly, with an effort to pleasure instead of harm, you have my permission. You may also taste me all you want." He paused, a look crossing his face, "Biting I'll permit, but not the biting off of things upon my person. Is that enough permissions to suit you this far into our relationship?"

"Quite." She removed the butter knife, dropping it beside them. It clattered musically, and his eyes darted to it. She took advantage of his momentary distraction to slide out from under his half block, allowing her to move more freely. "I shall take liberties with you as I see fit, permissions or not." She still needed to decide on how long he would be useful to her. If she needed his bits intact on him, or in a jar.

He sucked in a breath before breathing a sigh of relief, "I would not expect any less." He returned to leading her down the hallways through the palace.

Their boots echoed along the smooth opal flooring. If someone had been in the hall wearing boots that night, she would have definitely heard them. She noticed, since his back was to her now, that he'd cut his hair, at some point, between their arrival and this morning. The back of it no longer dragged along his armor and curled and bent wildly from being creased by his collar. The top was still long enough to fall into his eyes if he ever allowed it to be free of brushing it back.

A few strands refused to lie flat. Scars, probably, as most were in a line. Someone had knocked his helm off in battle. Or, like Praedae sometimes did, he took it off to see better.

Ryven confidently stepped onto the platform, and Mylva attempted to decipher his signal for the magic to descend. Nothing. Again. She frowned. Perhaps mind powers made it work. Her feet hit the swirling opalescent floor below.

"Klava!"

She looked up at a breathless boy trying to hold her snorting mare still. His face was pale, and he shook all over. She strode forward, taking the reins from him, "What's wrong, boy?"

He swallowed and pointed to the back of her steed, just above the saddle bags.

There, glowing softly in the morning sunlight, was a Magmazard.

"How are you scared of it and not the horse?" Mylva asked the boy with a raised brow. She chuckled when he shrugged, "It's alright. Just a stowaway." She picked up the fat lizard that was barely big enough to fill her palm. "Keep it with her, they'll keep each other company." She rubbed her thumb over the glowing spiked ridge in the middle of its flat head. It soaked in the heat of her slight friction, glowing brighter and giving a soft gurgling growl that sounded like a lava bubbles popping. "It will keep your stables pest free, even if there are rats twice its size."

The mare breathed a half snort, turning her head to sniff the lizard in her palm before returning her gaze to Ryven's stallion across the doorway. Her mare soaked up the morning rays, her black fur over the major arteries giving way to a slight dark red glow as she warmed. Mylva patted her neck and placed the Magmazard on the top of her saddlebag where she'd found it. "They both need sunlight, warmth, daily. If they step into fires, don't worry. Just watch the straw and hay to make sure they set nothing else ablaze."

Mylva laughed as the stable boy stared at her with wide eyes.

What things are worse than death? Let's see. Penis-less, that would definitely be worse, particularly because I haven't had her yet. If she removed my balls… would that be alright? Ryven's mind was a flurry of random thoughts. She did that to him, to make him think in circles and spirals rather than strategize along paths of possibilities. The boy pointing out the lizard drew all his attention. "Wakxen."

Mylva turned to face him, her brows arched, "You named her?"

"Yes." Ryven hoped to give the thing to one of his siblings, but had lost it. He didn't think the lizard would find the horse and stay with her. Now he knew, it made perfect sense as both were Kavkan.

"Is it for Prince Wolfaren, Prince Ryven?" The stableboy asked.

"It is." Ryven nodded curtly at him, "I'll let him see it later." He got up on his stallion and waited for Mylva to mount her mare before he guided her through the city. Had Rothland missed him this much? For every single person was out on their stoops and patios. *No, of course not*, he thought, watching his people straining to glimpse the woman behind him on her fiery steed.

"Prince Ryven! Are we going to get fire horses, too?" A soldier, off duty, looked up at him as he jogged beside them.

"I'm not sure. I haven't been able to really talk trade with her yet."

The soldier nodded, reaching up to pat Ryven's thigh, "Blessed victory and all the power of the magics with you, sir."

Ryven bit back a laugh. He'd need all the powers to tame the woman behind him and heal her of her pain. It was a marvel to him how she hid and used her trauma. He wasn't even sure she knew she was emotionally hurting. Or perhaps she had her own way of dealing with it. What healed him wasn't always right for others.

He'd give her more hot baths to soak in, long rides on her mare, and maybe let her keep the little lizard for herself. Would that help her? He clenched his teeth around his questions and focused on the road between his horse's ears.

Now was not the time. Smoke and fire, was ninety days' enough time? He doubted it. One strategy had to succeed, or lives would be lost. Klava Mylva, empress of her known world, was among them. He needed to give her the true world. Let her travel and explore the grandness of it. If they all survived. Mere days to fit this piece into the plan to avoid annihilation and war.

His first plan was the best one. Patience. Also, surviving her attacks would be a boon.

"Fala, here." Ryven called out to a lady on a stoop up ahead as he dug out a bundle from his saddlebag.

"You remembered?" Her hair was grayer, but her nearly toothless smile remained unchanged.

"Of course. I cannot forget the wishes of an old friend," Ryven said, handing her the small bundle. The old woman met him on the path to the training grounds every day before he left. And every day, she had a cloth bag full of dried fruits for him and his soldiers to snack on.

Six years ago, he'd stopped and talked with her for a while. He learned she was from Frystwaithe. Ryven wasn't sure how she'd made it to Rothland, but he knew someone had captured her and moved her place to place before she gained her freedom here. He'd promised her the fruits of her country when she wouldn't go with them. "I'm sorry it is not more, but I feared rot."

She patted his hand, "My Prince, this is more than enough for an old woman. To have a handsome man remember my silly wish will have me waltzing with death without regrets."

"May death not reach you this day." Ryven kissed his two of his fingertips and waved them at her.

The familiarity of meeting Fala set his mind at ease for the first time since gaining his general status in Kavkan. The ache in his temples dimmed, and he rolled his shoulders, then neck to loosen up. The woman's potential surprise attack kept him tense, causing constant pain. Not that he would complain, as he found himself enjoying her company. Attacks and biting remarks included.

He glanced back, following her finger trail over the spines of her helm, and smiled. Ryven remembered he needed to ask her about the sign language, the thought crossing his mind as he kept watching her long fingers. For once, she seemed lost in thought, her armor stiff, but the relaxation in her facial features assured him she was fine. As iced fingers tripped down his back, he realized that might not be a good place for her to be.

Chapter 12

After training the stable boy on how to handle her mare better, she and Ryven left for the exercise field. She had something new to think about. Did they not say only the royal family can manage city-palace travel? These thoughts consumed her mind. Witnessing several people use it at different times had her considering just how big the king's family was, along with surely they weren't all his blood.

She toyed with a spike, resting with a leg thrown over her horse's neck, her helm perched on her calf. Mylva realized she wasn't paying a bit of attention to her surroundings, other than picking up on movement and dismissing it as non-threatening. She looked around.

They were heading west and were halfway through the city by the stronger scent of the salty sea hitting her nose. The streets had become less crowded, not like they were when they first arrived. People were waking. Late risers.

There wasn't a single guard with Ryven.

Fool.

She frowned, feeling the insult burn in her blood. Was she such a minor threat to him? Granted, he'd bested her. Brained her and then pinned her in their last brief scuffle. Still, she could gain the advantage. She had to get the upper hand once.

Klava traced her finger along the spines of her helm, down and back up. Her fingernail plucked the thin metal making it ring like chords on a harp. She perked up once they reached the outskirts. The street broadened, opening up on a plain of white sand. Once the hoof hit it, barely a cloud lifted. The air tasted severely salty.

"Salt wastes." Ryven stated, barely turning his head so his voice floated to her over his shoulder. "Ride correctly, our horses need to stretch their legs and we're late." With a tightening of his knees on his stallion's sides, the beast lunged forward, stretching his long limbs out before his large hooves pounded into the heavy salt.

Her mare tensed. She pulled her leg back to her side, settling in as she put her helm on. "Upsss," she hissed in her mare's ear. In an instant, they went from trotting to cantering, and then galloping.

The salt sprayed up under the horses' hooves as Mylva settled her fingers deep into her mare's thick mane. "Show them what you are, my war beast."

With a neigh that sounded more like a battle cry, her mare lurched into full speed. Surpassing Ryven on his stallion in two strides, Mylva grinned. Her horse trumpeted the challenge again, wanting a race. The veins of her steed burned brightly. She was born in an eruption on a blood moon. The mare's muscles looked like moving plates of cooling lava as she glowed from the inside with her own fire.

Her horse loved to run more than she loved to battle. The opposite of her last one.

Ahead, she saw a squat cream-colored wall, matching the salted sand underneath, built with large square blocks. The sounds of metal clanging against metal reached her ears over the roar of the wind. Training grounds.

If she had her maces, she could ride in and do battle. She and her mare could take out hundreds. They'd done it before. Without the hindrance of keeping those she cared for alive, she could let loose her power and rage. Mylva glanced rearward, Ryven trailing far behind on his blustering stallion.

She sighed, leaning back slightly in her saddle, and her horse snorted her disappointment as she slowed. "I know." She murmured, loosening her fingers from their hold on the black mane to stroke her mare's blistering hot neck. "One day, my battle hungry friend."

Mylva pulled them to a stop just before the wide opening of the training grounds and turned them so she could watch Ryven ride up.

He stopped before them, his eyes wide on her still ignited mare. "When we marry, you'll have to let me have one of those."

As if understanding him, her horse snorted and shook her head vehemently. Mylva laughed, "Can your mind magic keep you from scorching your ass in the saddle?"

"I'll find a way." His words came out breathless, as his lungs still filled shallowly.

"That is, if I choose you." She studied his face for his reaction.

His eyes swept up to her, his lips changing from awe to a smile, "You will. You won't be able to oppose me much longer."

She watched him ride into the training grounds through the open iron gates. Was his confidence rooted in some kind of trickery, or was he truly that convinced she didn't have another choice?

Lust, yes. She couldn't deny she wouldn't mind him under her just to see how well he performed. Marriage, no. The process and cage would never appeal to her, because she knew she was incapable of love for anyone except her Bloodsworn.

She slid off her saddle after following him in and laid her mare's reins over the rail opposite of his stallion. His beast was wet with sweat, panting, but not winded. It at least had stamina. The Kavkan horse pranced back and forth along the rail, begging to be running still.

The sound of metal clanging stopped. Mylva turned, meeting the gaze of hundreds of young soldiers. Then she smiled as she realized they were looking past her to the flaming black steed. That expression was why she loved the war beasts of her people so much. They garnered the unblinking fixation of awe. Then fear once witnessed in action. Such a beast leaves only ash in their wake.

Ryven cleared his throat, "If all of you have time to stare, you have time to fight. Line up!" The last two words snapped through the salted air.

Scuffling, running, and some curses later, there were four long lines of young soldiers before them. Silence filled the pale walls of the training ground as the trainees awaited further instruction. Ryven nodded, pleased.

Klava had to admit to herself that she, too, was impressed.

"Boys and girls and those in between, meet my future wife. Klava."

"Greetings Klava." The voices of hundreds became one in those words.

She rolled her eyes as Ryven smirked.

"Today we're going to train with one of the best fighters I've seen in all my years, and probably in the ones to come. She's deadly. So pay attention to her and you'll learn a lot if she allows you to live." He paced in front of them, his helm under his arm, gloved fingers tapping against his chin as he spoke. His speech flowed like water along the walls, reaching even those in the back.

She must obtain that amplifying trick. So she could modify it within her training grounds, avoiding the need to ascend her towers to address her armies. He could teach her when they married. The thought made her flinch. When they married? His next order pulled Mylva away from the ridiculous idea.

"Form your battle families!" Ryven called out.

Another scuffling mess of soldiers and groups formed. "Each of you not with Klava and I break off into pairs in your families and spar lightly, stretch, and keep warm." He turned to the closest group, "Where's Maey?"

"Still healing, sir." An olive complexion young teen with a ringing voice answered.

Ryven nodded, and motioned to them, "Form a circle."

The one that answered him barked a repeat of the order Ryven just gave to his battle family. A sweet term. Mylva was unsure if the term was appropriate for battalions. Her soldiers were family, but they didn't readily call each other such. Shrugging off her thoughts, she raised a brow at him, "How do you want me to teach?"

"Spar with them. Gently." He added the last word with a bit of bite to his tone. "Show them what it's like to be a Kavkan warrior and how to best you."

She shook her head, studying each of the fourteen in the circle. "Hand-to-hand combat with a Kavkan is no simple task. We are a fire people. We are an ice people. Lava and ice are in our blood. Extremes hold little meaning for us, but they hold everything for softies like you. First of all, you give away too much with your stance."

She plucked the red braid up from a squat armor covered trainee's shoulder, considering the color yet again. "Name?"

"Cale, Klava."

"Cale, you have a pulled muscle in your left thigh. What does that mean for me, your enemy, when I notice that?"

"You will go for my left thigh or take advantage of its weakness by driving me onto it."

"Smart, Cale. How do you not show a weakness?"

Cale frowned, "Stand in a way that you can take no matter what hurts?"

"No. Stand the same as your fellows. Uniformity, like trees in a forest, makes it difficult to see details. My Kavkans are uniform, even the ones using metal arms or legs to replace their original limbs." She demonstrated by standing still in the middle of the circle. "This is ingrained in us, this very stance of loose readiness, since we could walk. Every muscle is prepared, slightly tense, ready for any movement in any direction. People have occasionally told me that they have a feeling of being pulled in a hundred different directions." She lifted a shoulder, "I wouldn't know, this is natural for me."

She moved to stand in front of Ryven, who was part of the circle, "Your very general is in pain. Can you tell me where?"

The young ones looked at one another.

"Speak up. State where you think he's weakest."

"Klava, our superiors will punish us for revealing their weaknesses." A girl's voice answered underneath the too big leather helmet.

She snorted and hunkered down to peer into the girl's face. "Your superior today is me. Where does Ryven hurt?"

The girl shrank back with a swallow, the function audible to those in the circle, "Hips? Klava."

"Close. Next." Mylva dismissed the girl's answer and turned away from her.

"His ribs, Klava." A sandy-haired boy opposite the girl with the too large training helmet answered.

"Good job." Mylva kept her tone dry to not make the students excited.

Ryven glared at her slightly, so she grinned at him. "He says they're healing, but I bet not as quickly as he wants."

"What happened?" One teen whispered.

"I slammed a table into him this morning when he tried to kiss me."

"We were eating. A peaceful breakfast." Ryven interjected with a growl. "If anyone was trying to kiss anyone, it was you licking my lip afterward, Klava."

She grinned, some teens reddened and shifted on their feet. If he desired his soldiers to resemble her Kavkans, they had a considerable distance to cover. The way they blushed and squirmed over a few simple words showed her how easily distracted they were.

"Can Kavkan really annihilate an entire nation with only a few hundred?"

It seemed the one question opened the floor to others. "Yes. Depends upon the country and their army."

"What about ours?"

She tapped her finger on her bottom lip, considering. "If we fought you, you'd be ash. Your superiors might hold us off for a while, but we would eventually best you."

Ryven laughed, shaking his head.

"Numbers mean nothing but fodder against a force as trained as mine. One year or twenty, we will overcome any foe." She stood toe to toe with him for a moment, letting her words sink in. She needed to rely on that, not think of this marriage thing. Right?

"Klava," his voice was low, "Our marriage means an end to wars."

"War is my life. Without wars, I need not live." Mylva studied him as she spoke. Something in Ryven's eyes wasn't right. Like a wisp of fog hiding a bush behind it, he had a secret dealing with this marriage arrangement.

"I'll show you there's much more to live for, if you'll allow it."

"Are we training… or… is this some kind of lesson on how to seduce your enemy?"

Both Klava and Ryven turned to regard the boy. The one who gave the others orders. Apparently, his superiority lended him bravery. He flinched, drawing in on himself, "Sorry."

"Begin. Attack me as one." Mylva stated, waving them forward with outstretched arms as she strode into the middle of the ring.

After lots of sweat, taunts, bruises and a few gurneys to the healers, Mylva sat on a bench to the side and drank down a tankard of water. The little soldiers ranged in different stages of exhaustion and beaten all over the rectangular training grounds. Ryven was talking to five of the instructors in the corner nearest to her table.

A low whistle sounded from across the grounds. Mylva looked over to see a familiar tall redhead striding forward with his long-fingered hands doing a slow clap. The miniature Ryven was close on his heels.

"Klava, that was impressive, even though they are kids. How did Ryven and his men survive in Kavkan? Do tell us the tale." Sihfe said, sprawling onto the bench and leaning back against the table beside her.

"I want to know more about that story as well. The why not the how." The miniature version of Ryven stood over them with his arms crossed. Mirtes didn't wear armor much like Sihfe, and he was leaner in muscle than his older brothers. "Something like infiltrating a country of hard-headed warriors is nothing to Ryven."

"Hard-headed?" She gave them a knowing smirk, "That we are. Care to see how hard my head is?" She made a move to stand. Threatening someone who was in their early twenties, barely out of their teen awkwardness, felt rotten. Then again, she'd just fatigued several actual teenagers earlier in the name of training.

Sihfe patted her forearm with a bit of pressure, "No harm. Especially for the precious baby brother of our world famous general."

"I agree to a spar."

Ryven disagreed, shaking his head and jostling his sibling to the opposite side of the table. "Sit."

"Not a pet," Mirtes huffed.

"Act like a fool and you might as well be one. She can kill you in a single hit, little brother." Ryven sneered, looming over Mirtes even though he was merely two or three inches taller than him.

"You're breathing shallowly." Mirtes eyed Ryven, the threatening pose ignored.

"Ribs are still healing. No time to refocus," Ryven sat beside Sihfe.

"And pray tell us grand, exotic, handsome general, what broke your ribs?" Sihfe's grin was feral and like a kid entering a candy or toy shop all in one.

Ryven merely jerked his chin in Klava's direction.

Sihfe turned his giddy gaze on her, his red eyes flashing in laughter, "What did you do my ferocious queen? Did he not give you an orgasm, and you took your pound of flesh?"

Mylva rolled her eyes, questioning men's one-track minds. "The tables are dangerous in our bedrooms. Quite heavy."

"And they fit perfectly over my diaphragm." Ryven added dryly.

"You deserve punishment!" Mirtes cried, drawing his sword.

Mylva watched the thick blade arc toward her neck. She smirked as both Ryven and Sihfe tried to warn the barely adult boy to stop. Her vambrace catching the blade's edge. She twisted slightly, putting the metal between two fingers and deftly twisting it out of his grip. Flicking her wrist toward herself, his hilt banged on her shoulder plate, as the end of his blade pointed at his jugular.

"Punished by whom? You can't keep your own sword in your hand." She purred, grinning up at him from her seat on the bench.

The students catching the action oohed. Some voiced their desire to know that move. Mirtes stepped back, eyes wide and mouth open. His gaze flicked from his empty hand where his weapon once was, to where it rested on her shoulder.

"Klava." Ryven stated, quiet with a hardness under it, "Do not kill my little brother. There is still much for him to learn about life."

"Yes, Father would not be pleased if his favorite little boy came to harm," Sihfe added, while still lounging next to them.

The men beside her were trying to appear relaxed, but she saw their tension. In a second, Ryven could be between her and Mirtes. Sihfe could swiftly block Mirtes' sword. She played out a few scenarios in her mind.

None of them were in her favor.

"I am not a little boy." Mirtes' voice resembled Ryven's in its arrogance, even if his fists shook by his sides.

"Then stop acting like one." Klava smiled sweetly, sliding the blade along her glove to flip the hilt toward him. "Attacking without the courage to follow through can cause harm or death. Remember that. Always go for the kill with all you have."

Once Mirtes had his sword back in his hand, Sihfe visibly relaxed. Ryven didn't. Mylva noted the differences between the siblings.

"Sihfe, what is your power?"

He smirked as he answered, "Blood, my dearest."

"Is that why your hair is red?" Mylva asked a ridiculous question to give herself time to go through what she knew of that magic. Her country had few blood users; mostly healers, but some were warriors. If those warriors had an open wound on an enemy to work, they were some of the deadliest she'd witnessed in battle.

Sihfe's laugh was a high musical symphony, "No." He sat up, turning toward her and fully blocking Ryven from her sight. "My hair around my cock is red, and it hasn't seen enough bloodshed to make it so. Care to see?"

It didn't take long for Sihfe to return to sexual innuendos. Mylva had to bite back a smile, lest she boost his confidence. "Maybe."

"I look forward to the moment you are ready." Sihfe said with a wink, holding out the palm of his hand. A dark pool of red began, a coppery tang filled the air, then it twirled up and around in quick circles. It formed a small heart with whirls of blood haloing it. It glistened in the sun, and the smell of copper dissipated as it hardened into a glass-like structure. "For you, my very heart, Klava."

Mylva didn't see any visible wounds for him to pull blood. Did he pull from one kid who'd gotten a minor cut from the training? She hadn't seen a trail from the grounds to him. Perhaps Sihfe's bloodline differed from the ones she knew. Able to wield blood without a visible source. A powerful and on the edge of terrifying, if she were to be honest. If he could do that, how long would it take him to drain a healthy person?

"Smoke gods." Mirtes muttered, a look of disgust crossing his features before he turned on his heel and strode to a few students getting back up to start exercises anew. He joined them in training.

Mylva took the heart between her forefinger and thumb. "Thank you, I think. Isn't it odd to be giving your blood to someone?"

Ryven chuckled, "You'll get used to it. He started making things when he was a child. Creepy."

Sihfe frowned. "You never complained about that miniature horse."

"No, I was terrified you'd suck the blood out of my body if I did."

The redhead sighed, deflating slightly. "Says the one who mind controlled me to go kiss our Father's shoe. And! I almost died trying to steal butter cookies from Cook."

"She wouldn't ever use that butcher knife on any of us." Ryven paused before adding, "I don't think."

"Have you already threatened your brother's life, so now he's pouting by training?" Jerica asked, walking up behind the boys with her right eyebrow raised. The fancy dress from day one was no longer present. In its place was a form fitting suit of black, with silver stitching. She had her long onyx hair pulled back from her face and it swung behind her in a whip-like braid.

She strode to her son, cupping his chin in her palm, and made him look up at her. "You're in pain." Her gaze flicked to Sihfe, then to Klava. "Which one?"

"We were fighting like kids. I hadn't realized we'd gotten so old, Mother Jerica." Sihfe batted his long eyelashes at the woman, picking up her free hand and placing a kiss into her palm.

"Where are your wounds, then?" Queen Jerica asked, returning the sweet smile to her son's half brother.

Ryven sighed, "It was Klava, Mother. I advanced upon her too quickly in my rudeness to make her love me and suffered my due consequences. No need for worry, nor punishment, unless you think I deserve more."

With that, Mylva wondered if Ryven didn't enjoy pain. How very Kavkan of him, in a way. And Sihfe's lazy personality act was a lie, then.

Jerica sighed, observing the trio. Then her gaze rested on her eldest, "You are impatient with your emotions. Show her the true you, and she will love you as much as you adore her." She lightly tapped her son's cheek with her fingertips. "If I ever hear of you forcing yourself on anyone ever again, I shall make sure I will have no heirs from you, my son. Is that clear?"

Ryven's face dropped into a pale hue quicker than anything Mylva had seen before, and he nodded, "Yes, Mother. Completely."

Maybe he didn't enjoy pain. Mylva's heart did an odd pattern of flutters before dropping. Memories of her mother flooded through her mind before she could rein them in. Somehow, it was nice to know his mother threatened just like hers had.

Flames erupted with screams from women and a few children, music to Praedae's ears. Not all Kavkans could protect themselves from magic made fire, and he happened to be one of them. Wood spitting and cracking gave way, only the stones holding on to what once was. Heat bled into other houses, the flames crawling along the wooden connections and fighting to break through the hewn rock to get to more timber inside. The pungent scent of flesh burning streamed through the streets after they screamed themselves to ash.

Kavkans in their black flickering armor soaked the fire up into their bodies, keeping the destruction away from chosen houses. Others blocked the roaring flames with ice walls that suffocated the flames in sizzles and spats. As they worked, all kept within earshot of a certain man pacing before a handful of people on their knees.

"Every one of you is useless. She's not coming back. If she does, she is no longer viable!" The wide hand slashed through the sulfuric air like a hammer. "By law, it is my right to take control."

"No, just ruler wants to rule, idiot." Drak spat blood, it sizzled on the stones of the bridge above the slow stream of lava beneath. "You're only good for swinging a sword."

Drak's head whipped back, the blow to his chin cracking his teeth and severing the tip of his tongue. He rolled his body serpent like, staying upright, and hit the other man with a withering glare. "You show your lack of worth by burning innocents."

Thick fingers dug into the graying hair, the poleyn finished what his fist could not as he drove it into the old general's chin. Drak's jaw cracked in musical notes to his ears, and he pulled the gray strands so he could ram into his face again.

A roar tore through his chest and out of his throat as the fire within erupted. "I am Praedae! Our Klava is no more! Swear fealty upon your blood."

The four remaining were advisors. Weak. Not a piece of weaponry among them, much less armor. Not like Drak. Their slim bodies trembled, but their jaws clenched tightly. Praedae growled, grabbing two scalps in his hands, he let the flames help him burn and crush the skulls in his palms. The next duo he kicked like metal cans until they rolled off the edge and fluttered lifeless to the lava flow below.

"Burn them all. All the advisors."

The pair of soldiers nearest him looked at each other, then knocked their fists against their thighs before running away to relay Praedae's orders. A third soldier took Drak's limp body from the bridge and the Warmonger's reach.

Praedae watched the liquid fire of the volcano flow beneath him, the heat within him cooling as quickly as it had roared to life. "Upon my life, if she comes home, she'll be in my chains. Klava's blood shall be my blood." He bit the inside of his cheek, letting the coppery liquid well up in his mouth before spitting it into the stream below. "I swear it."

Chapter 13

"Gyrna, anything?" Mylva asked as she soaked in the boiling water of her bath after their return from the training grounds. They had sent Basau after a meal.

"Not much. Here, the languages are countless, nearly as many as the magics. Each Queen has passed her bloodline magic on to her children. I am not sure which of the families gathered magic from their father, this king, or if he has any magic at all."

"I believe Ryven and his siblings have the king's magic. Considering Queen Jerica's upbringing with him, it would be logical." Villages usually formed from the people wielding the same magics, as they felt outcast by others or preferred to be with those of their own power.

"I shall study upon it more, Klava. The palace, with its winding corridors, can be confusing, but I now know its layout." Something in her Bloodsworn's voice told her that Gyrna wasn't as sure as she claimed in finding her way around.

"Good."

"The magic that controls the doorway between here and the city below, I cannot fathom how it can work except…perhaps with thought." Gyrna offered weakly, fiddling with the towels in her arms.

"Not all of them have mind magic." Mylva blurted before she thought. If it was the magic of the King, perhaps they did. "Unless, they all do. To some extent. Less powerful and trained in it compared to Ryven."

"His many children make the odds more favorable, don't they? Of more of them having his magic?"

Mylva remembered a study that Hava or Nava read once. The researcher hypothesized that all parental magic resided in the child. One side, usually the sire's, was just dormant. "He's awakened all magic within each of his children. Both from him, and from the mother."

"If that is true, my Klava, choose wisely among the sons. If you are still choosing. Perhaps they can give you a daughter with unlimited prospects."

A Klava with mind control such as Ryven's would be the perfect child. Honed into ruling the world. Maybe becoming a god. Combining blood manipulation with fire would be fine, but it appeared less dangerous and powerful than mind and fire. What additional abilities would render her daughter unstoppable?

Air, perhaps. She could burn everything down with a flick of her fingers and a smile.

Something kept bringing her thoughts back to Ryven. He closely resembled the mate her advisors would select. It was essential to retain the black hair, tanned skin appearance of her people. No Klava would ever be mistaken as someone else marching in front of their army.

"Gyrna, find out which family has air magic here." She wouldn't narrow her choices down to just Ryven and Mirtes. What was the other one? Nadran.

"Yes, my Klava," Gyrna stated, just as Basau returned with a rolling tray of food.

"I will have to appear at supper tonight." Mylva thought out loud. "Armor tonight."

Basau shook her head, "Klava, please. If unused, these dresses and other clothing will rot. And you will be ravishing."

Mylva gave Gyrna an amused look before she revealed, "We have considered no Klava as ravishing for fifty years. I shall not break that trend now."

She enjoyed her meal while soaking in the bath, absorbing the warmth of the water. After Gyrna touched it up with another boiling addition, she made her servants leave her. This was the most she'd ever been without her armor. She was losing her touch.

After a brief nap in the bath, Gyrna returned to help her in stretches and a few training practices to keep her in shape. Training with the kids in the morning was fun, but had a minimal impact on her. She turned to Gyrna and raised a brow.

Her maidservant nodded, "There is a family with air magic."

"You speak of Queen Strandai and her kids." Basau added with a smile. "She has four children to choose from. No one is as worthy of your time as Ryven."

As Basau spoke, Mylva remembered the queen and her children. They would do. Their skin was paler than hers, but she was sure her genetics would carry over in that aspect. "What are their tastes?"

Basau smiled widely, "They prefer women with plenty of hips, which you have. Shall I prepare something that shows those endowments off?"

Mylva glanced at Gyrna. Her Bloodsworn's lips formed a thin line as she thought, and then she nodded, reluctantly. She began signing, "*If it gets us back home sooner, make the best choice as only you can.*"

They agreed. If a marriage was her only way out, she'd make the choice quickly. Once she returned home, she'd make her child, and then sacrifice the partner to the Fire.

The dress Basau chose and dressed her in wasn't bad. Stitched evenly in the middle, the bones made her muscles press close to her ribs and hips while pushing her breasts up and center. The rest of the dress flowed from the boned structure down to her ankles in silken swaths that felt like butter against her skin. Her shoulders and arms were bare. Around her neck was a necklace of intricate golden swirls of metal curling toward the center where a ruby glittered in the light.

Her only concern was that if she moved too quickly, it was difficult to pull air in. Even more so than the bindings under her armor. Bending made her chest fall out, and her lungs empty immediately. Mylva chuckled at Basau's mutterings as she stuffed her breasts back into place and moved some laces around that tightened the bones of the corset against her flesh.

The tightening did nothing new. She'd still fall out if she bent over. Mylva sucked in a breath, trying to get as deep as she could, and failed to fill her lungs even halfway. Her eyes trailed to her armor, and she realized how much she missed the metal on her.

"Prince Ryven is making preparations to eat in the dining hall too, Klava." Basau stated with her musical lilt and sly smile.

Basau was Ryven's confidant. Of course, she would try to keep her master at the forefront of Mylva's mind. Not that she could blame Basau. She couldn't deny that Ryven was always on her mind these days. Whether she imagined the hundredth way to kill him, what an orgasm from him would feel like, or why she heard his voice in her head.

After Gyrna tamed her hair in an intricately woven lattice of braids and twists, and then painted her lips and eyes, Mylva made her way to the dining area of the palace. With Basau leading the way while Gyrna was off doing some more investigations, Mylva could try to retrain herself on how to breathe. She didn't have enough time to get comfortable in the dress, because before she realized it, Basau stepped to the side of the dining hall door to allow her to pass inside.

The hall was wide and tall. Tables for two or four were at the room's periphery, adorned with red tablecloths and gleaming cutlery. For larger groups, there was a long table in the middle. The king was there, along with many women, most were his wives that she recognized and others were wives she hadn't seen yet. She wondered, yet again, just how many children the man really had.

Ryven's chair made a loud sound that drew the eyes of many as he stood, including Mylva's. He let his eyes roam over her. His swallow was visible, even from her distance from him.

The dress was doing its job.

"I shall get you a plate if you point out what you want before you sit," Basau said just behind her, with a smile and a slight bow.

"Very well." Mylva moved to the table, Basau at her side. She pointed to mostly meats, and Basau added a few comments about the foods strange to her. The smells alone made her mouth water. "Those and whatever you think is good," Mylva said, giving Basau more free rein over her meal.

She looked at the other tables. Making her way through the ones closest to the buffet. Two of the children from Queen Strandai, the air wielding queen, were sitting at a table with four seats. Hunkered together, she figured they were talking about some kind of strategy. With a hand on an empty chair between them, she asked if she could join them.

Wain was the first to recover from her appearance. He stood, smiling like a merchant seeing their customer's full purse, and pulled the chair out for her, "Yes, of course."

Lenan's eyes remained on Mylva's boobs as she sat. Once she allowed the chair to be pushed under her, with a nice bounce of her flesh, he closed his eyes and mouthed some strange words. His gaze returned to his plate.

"You are beautiful." Wain said as he sat back down, "I'm Wain. I know there were a lot of names thrown around the other day. My brother here is Lenan. You are called Klava, correct?"

"I am. It is nice to speak with you, finally." Their accent made the words of the common tongue light in the air, like they were whispers of the wind through mountain passes.

Lenan cleared his throat, turning to look directly across the room. She followed his gaze, and noted Ryven's glare, making his dark countenance more foreboding than before. Lenan turned back around in his seat, his back rigid. "Likewise," He said, quietly, his wide blue eyes on his brother. A silent plea passed from him to Wain.

Wain grinned, his teeth seemed larger than most others. Basau served Mylva two plates of food and a goblet of red wine as Wain returned his attention to her. "Isn't Klava a title, though?"

"Technically, yes. But that is what we are called by everyone other than our closest Bloodsworn." Mylva explained.

"I see. The country you are from borders the one that uses Bone magic, yes? I see why you are protective of your name." Wain smiled again, "I would be too."

The user achieved the best results with bone magic against the enemy if they had the name. They would drain less of their own energy if they had the name of their opponent in mind or said it out loud while activating their bone magic. Same with blood magic, as far as she knew.

"What is your magic?" Mylva asked with a smile, "Perhaps I shouldn't have even admitted to Klava."

He laughed, "Air. It doesn't work that way. Wide open space makes us the most powerful against our prey."

Battlefields were open. The number of attacks she could use with air and fire tripled in her strategies. More battle plans formed. Imaginary wars fought. "I see. A room like this is fine too, yes?"

"It is as long as others don't mind being ruffled." Lenan stated, his eyes darting behind him again. He picked up his fork, "Please eat."

It sounded as if he wanted this to be over already. Mylva bit back her smile. Lenan feared Ryven, but Wain seemed unfazed by the dark aura across the room. She picked up her fork and ate a few bites. She watched the boys settle into their meals as well, eating as she did. A silent respect for one another passing between them.

"Despite the limited space, we can still utilize our powers effectively." Then he asked, "I'm assuming you have fire magic?"

She nodded.

He grinned, his airy voice launching into a story. "I had a girl once, had fire magic. Man, she wa-" He jerked back as Lenan jerked forward. The brothers glared at one another as Wain reached under the table to rub his leg. "She was something," Wain finished with a roll of his eyes directed at Lenan.

"I would imagine so, knowing my prowess." Mylva agreed, knowing full well the reputation Hava and Nava gave her in bedrooms.

Wain grinned, shooting a look at Lenan, which made his brother sigh. Wain returned his attention to her. "Yeah, but she wasn't Klava. I've heard that all the other countries of your continent pretty much bow to you, anyway. Is that right?"

She lifted a shoulder with a slight smile, "They wouldn't say bow, but that we have understandings with one another. In truth, yes, I am their empress."

"Klava!" Binesze called, rushing to her. The prince of Sevinland practically folded his lanky body into her lap, his head pressed to her breasts.

Wain choked on his drink.

Lenan stared at the boy, mouth working in silent words again. He turned, studying Ryven, and a whimper like a pup would give parted his lips.

Mylva sighed, reaching up to pat the boy's soft dark blond hair, "My little prince, this is unbecoming in this…

crowd." She tried to think of how her Bloodsworn sisters would have worded it.

"I know. But you're always so warm and comforting, like pillows and beds."

Lenan whimpered again, turning to face his brother quickly, his torso as stiff as a board.

"I wouldn't mind sleeping on those kinds of pillows." Wain muttered, his drink sloshing as Lenan kicked him under the table again. "Stop! You're thinking the same thing." Wain jerked, jostling the table as he dried himself off with a napkin. The wine made his maroon shirt darker in splashes.

"Don't be imagining things like that for my Klava." Binesze glared at the brothers, "When I get older, she's going to marry me. And I'm going to keep her where she doesn't have to fight. She can smile and do whatever she wants! Can you give her that?"

Mylva felt a tug in her heart. Another man who wanted to keep her from battle. Was it sweet or threatening? She pressed his ear back to her chest as she leaned back in the chair to give them some more room. "Binesze, come now. Get your comfort while you may, then you must go eat and mingle. And stop pretending you are less than twenty-two in years. That is old enough."

"I don't want anyone here to talk to me."

"You don't have a choice, little prince." She pulled his face up by hooking her finger under his chin. She pressed her forehead against his, a light rain like cologne tickling her nose, "There is someone here closer to your age. And I'm sure there is someone here that you get along with better than you do with me. Right?"

His bright eyes studied her face, "Your eyes are bigger today. Darker, too." Binesze sighed with his whole body, placing his hands on her breasts, which made Lenan whirl in his seat. "How can I tell if a girl my age will have this size?"

She laughed, kissed his forehead, and pushed him off her. Mylva took his hands in hers, "Pick one out. Then study her mother. If her mother has this size, then she might have it too. Otherwise, you'll have to feed her well."

The grin on Binesze's face let her know he realized exactly what he was doing, "Expert advice, my lovely Klava. If I don't find one fitting, I'll still marry you." He kissed the back of each of her hands before trotting off to torture someone else.

"That kid is too young to have such a death wish," Lelan murmured.

Mylva watched as the little prince made himself right at home at the king's table.

"Balls. Large ones." Wain pointed toward his own.

"Indeed." Mylva agreed, her gaze traveling to Ryven. Her captor watched the little prince with his dark eyes, a muscle twitching along his brow and his jaw tight. As if sensing her look, he turned and met hers. Her amusement with his glares and aggravation turning into a small smirk of triumph.

He smiled right back.

The dinner continued with light conversations about the men with her, their powers, and the country of Sevinland and Kavkan. Mylva stood, stretched, and took her leave of the air magic brothers. She took a small plate with cake and wandered to a window. Her thoughts comparing the powers of air, fire, and mind.

"You have a presence about you."

She turned to the voice at her side.

Queen Jerica nodded a greeting. She wore a dress again, of black and silver. Her hair flowed loose to her waist. "Power that comes from fear and respect does that. What is the predominant feeling your people have towards you?"

They both mattered to her, yet Jerica sought a preferred response. She rarely lost respect. She answered, "I suppose respect. At least that is what I hope. Fear can be fickle. A new threat can turn fear to another. Respect is more difficult to lose." Mylva hoped it was, at least.

Jerica made a small sound of acknowledgement in her throat, then took a sip of her white wine. "Klava, I must say this, you are the one Ryven wants. I always make sure my children deserve what they want, and that what they desire is good for them. Ryven desired little. He was content with what was permitted and pursued more if available. The position of general, for instance, he worked hardest for and grew to deserve it. His actions warrant a higher title for his impact on the world." They watched the blue hues of day fade into the oranges of sunset. "His choice this time, you, is another step in gaining what he deserves. Do you desire the same as he?"

Mylva turned, leaning against the smooth column of the window frame, her plate cleaned. "I need the world at my people's feet, Queen Jerica. If that's what he deserves, then he'll have to fight me for it."

Queen Jerica said with a gentle curve of her lips, "My darling daughter, he won't fight you for it. He's giving it to you."

Mylva wasn't sure how she made it to the throne room. Her feet were heavy, her thoughts whirling over the possibilities. She knew what Ryven claimed. What Jerica claimed. It felt different coming from Jerica. It was as if her dreams were solid, concrete and right in her grasp.

Did she bid the queen a respectable farewell, or did she simply wander away?

That was no way to treat her future family.

Wait. What? No. Lasting marriage was not an option. She had duties. Responsibilities. The traditions of her people resting upon her shoulders, and only her shoulders. Marriage meant more. Meant spending time with someone and that meant not working toward gaining all the power. Marriage meant strolling hand in hand on the bridge like enamored teenagers. She didn't have time for that.

"Myl." The word echoed in the empty chamber. That nickname was becoming familiar, almost welcome. But only in that voice.

She was to breed one daughter. Since she destroyed the Mind Meld Diamond, she couldn't afford to have a weak husband. There would be no more Havas and Navas taken from the Bloodsworn families to be tortured. She had to choose genetics that would make her daughter the most powerful being in this world. Seed that would meld with hers to create perfection. Because her world, her people, deserved gods.

Hands closed on her hips.

She whirled into his arms. Ryven's thoughts ratcheted into hers, *Gods, if I could be in her mind, to see her worries. To know her feelings. I love her. I've loved her for five years. Have I really?*

She looked down at them. No skin touched. She gazed back into his eyes, his brows drawn low, creating a crease between the dark orbs. "I can hear you."

He cursed under his breath, "I was…angry. Am angry. I have no control. Not with you."

Mylva lifted her arms, resting her bare forearms on his shoulders. She moved into the hardness of his body. Heard his breath hitch, as his hands slid to the small of her back. "What do you want to do to me?" She dipped her fingers into the short strands of his hair at the back of his neck, pressing her fingertips against his scalp.

Images of them flowed into her. Flashing and quick like lightning. Them kissing. He impatiently ripping clothes off to thrust into her and take her as his. Her riding him, dress still on, skin slapping wildly. Her observing as he pummeled his brothers and the little prince while telling them she was his and his alone. The two of them dancing across this floor, bodies flush with one another, as they talked. Conversations of wars. Questions of her strategy for this battle and that. Watching her train.

"Myl…"

She sighed, slipping her hands further up into the longer strands of hair. "What is it?"

"I think you know." He murmured, a small smile curling his lips. His thoughts giving her more of his emotions and words than he could, "When I get this way, I can't control what I read from you." He drew in a deep breath, his forehead rested upon hers, "Choose me. Release me from the misery of not being yours. I will give you the world. If you want them, I'll steal the stars. The sun, too. To give you true fires to bathe in."

Her core warmed. This wasn't right. He'd killed her Bloodsworn.

He frowned, then turned his head to kiss her wrist. "I'm sorry. If I could've found another way. I would have." *They left me no option, gave me no choice. One of them killed herself. If only I had kept up the facade longer. Maybe they'd still be alive.*

Several pangs of hatred erupted in her for his weak excuse, but they smoothed quickly as she remembered their last memories, as if they were her own. Never a choice. At the last, they had a choice, for once. They made one for themselves. The first in their lives.

They gave her a choice, too. All her decisions, from their death to now, and her future. She had options.

"You are truly behind this? The marrying into all the kingdoms was your idea?"

"Yes. If you don't believe me, you may ask everyone here," Ryven stated calmly.

His mind slowed until she no longer heard his thoughts. He was calm now. Calm in her hands that could kill him.

"What is it like to not have war?"

The smile he gave her was saddened, "Mylva, it is wonderful. In peace, you can love and learn silly things, read. So much happens when there is peace. I want to give that to you. I think I've found a way with this. See it through with me?"

She paused briefly, shifting her bare skin away and resting her hands on his chest. "I'm not sure. You have some terribly cute brothers. There's also the problem that I haven't tested you to see if you're able to please me."

His dark eyes flashed as his hands tightened at her back, "There's nothing I can do to keep them from being cute to you. Unless you want to bait me into destroying their faces." He paused, as if plotting the course of actions it would take to do so, before continuing, "I am more than willing to pleasure you whenever you wish, my Klava."

"Jealousy is not a pleasant face for you. Perhaps one day, when you regain control of yourself, you can bed me." She freed herself from his grasp and strode down the halls and to her room.

Shutting the door behind her, she splayed her hands over the thick, polished wood. Its coolness belied her heat, and she knew the doors could be ash in a breath if she willed it. The palace would melt, all the people falling or flaring to their death.

Shadows of her wars mingled with the thoughts. Blood spatter that was cold against her fiery flesh, the coppery scent before it evaporated in a sizzle of hatred. She loved war. Klavas were bred for war. It was in her blood. Fire and rage.

Creation. Nava's voice wove into the memories of screams and war cries. *Or love*, added Hava's voice, a smile behind it. Several years ago, they'd had this talk. Because war was no more. They had the countries under tight control, again. Before the minor rebellions. Mylva was itching for a fight, a battle, a war to plan for. And they had nothing to fight.

Hava and Nava were trying to find her another avenue to burn her excess fire off on.

Mylva entered, oblivious to the other women, lost in her thoughts. She sat in the window, the tightness of the dress as comforting as armor, almost. Kavkans loved. Kavkans created.

Her eyes trailed to her armor. They fired beauty into useful objects. What other people could make her gear look like fire, even without her blood?

When they were home, not on a battlefield, the giggles and play war cries of children rang loud and strong through the city. Kavkan's loved. It was their love that kept the Klava bloodline and had Kavkan safe from all enemies. Not just admiration.

She brushed her thumb over her fingertips, remembering the rough hairs of Drak's beard when Hava hugged the old bear after a training round. Those dark eyes of her eldest general shone with something. Mylva wrote it off as respect mixed with surprise.

But after seeing how the king looked at his children, she knew otherwise. The old general who trained them all had far more than reverence for them. He loved them.

Ryven called her broken. Was she?

Not all scars were hers. Mylva pressed the heels of her hands into her eyes as they burned. Hava and Nava were tortured because of her. But she realized they thought the same of her. Tortured. Broken. Yet strong and fearsome. Loyalty bled freely from them.

She scrapped the strategies featuring the murder of all in the palace. After all, she'd die in those plans, Gyrna too. Mylva dropped her hands into her lap, tracing each and every scar upon them with her eyes as she began anew. If she was shattered, she'd remake herself. Something stronger. A being to be loved, respected, and feared still, but perhaps, with more emphasis on the love. She'd destroy everything, then remake it all, with herself as the fire, and her chosen blacksmith.

Ryven, with his gifts, was an intriguing path. For the tenth time since her arrival, she played through all the Queens and their offspring, matching them with the powers and abilities Gyrna fed her. Air was still a great additional choice.

Still, the prospect of going with air made her heart drop. While the idea of Ryven warmed her like a steaming bath. And she did enjoy her baths.

The idea of her with one of his brothers irked him like no other thought. There were times where they fought, all siblings did, but Ryven wished he could break their noses and jaws to keep them from being attractive. He wanted Mylva's eyes on him, and him alone.

Ryven paced the throne room after she left. His imagination bringing up all manner of scenarios to keep her interested in him. He kept some. Discarded others.

He liked the idea of dancing with her. If she knew how to dance. He stilled, looking up at the vaulted ceiling of the grand hall. Ryven wasn't sure if she did or not. Nothing about dances was in any of his reports. The only socials he attended in Kavkan did not have one of the Klavas present. If she didn't, all the more reason he should ask her to. He could teach her.

And she could instruct him in the Kavkan sign language.

It was a fair trade, Ryven thought. Then again, not so much. He'd probably be forcing her to do something he wanted. He couldn't do that.

The memory of her studying the sigils in the tower made him smile. That. He could teach her those. A way of communication just like her sign language, that was a fair trade.

One idea down, he moved on to the next.

"Prince Ryven," the call interrupted him.

Ryven turned, watching the blond braids of a messenger bounce behind them as they ran toward him. "Yes?"

"You have a few." The unsexed blonde claimed, before reaching into their bag. They pulled out more than a few, and their eyes grew wide, "Er… pardon me, Prince, but there are a lot."

He chuckled, taking the neatly stacked messages with his name penned on the top on a blank page stuck to the top missive. "No matter, thank you."

Waiting until the messenger bowed and trotted off to find her next recipient, Ryven tore his name off the top and read the first one. He reminded himself to pass the bid for magical messages to begin in Rothland. This was a waste of paper.

Another reminder of the days, numbered in several languages in a line as if they were making sure he understood the slim amount left to them. He crumpled that missive with the page with his name on it. The next was in his code. He moved to the throne, sitting on the arm as he read it.

'Three houses burned in the civilian district. Ten dead, mostly merchants from other parts of the empire. A new

decree in place tomorrow: all women of age to enter the fortress to be given a gift. Gift unknown.'

Ryven frowned, noting the sign off. This was one of his generals he left in Kavkan. Strange. Was the heat getting to him? Why would there be so many dead in Kavkan when there wasn't a war?

He placed it on the bottom of the pile, keeping it to reread in a moment. He hoped others would provide clarification. After reading three more from their obsessive enemy, Ryven found another from the same general.

'Protect what we can.'

He stood, flipping through the messages until he could read all the ones from his soldiers in Kavkan and Parvis. He then sat down on the floor, spreading them out and putting them in order he assumed they came in.

'Praedae. Advisors. Generals. All in the throne room discussing future of Kavkan.'

'Travel banned.'

'Two advisors beheaded. Women gifted harem.'

Since when was there a harem? Had he missed that in his years there? This was a mistake. Drak and the other generals wouldn't stand for the advisor' deaths or a trade embargo. Would they? Ryven reread the first part and shook his head. No. That can't be right.

As he kept piecing the timeline together, dread curled in his gut. He had to tell Mylva once he made sure this was true.

Gathering the slips, Ryven considered telling her as he ventured out of the throne room. He was close to winning her trust, he could feel it, would this damage it more, or make her fall for him at last? He turned down the hall, heading to the quarters of his younger half-brother, not quite mature enough to partake in the marriages, but old enough to have been there at his side in Kavkan.

He knocked and waited. When the boy opened the door, he took in a deep breath before saying, "I know we just got back, but-"

The soldier that accidentally poisoned Hava groaned, leaning against the door jamb, "I'm going back, already?" The light blue eyes searched Ryven's face before the boy added, "What's wrong?"

"I'm getting some odd messages. I need you to clarify what's going on and report back to me," Ryven explained.

"On it. I'll be there…" his little brother paused, mentally calculating things, "Maybe four days. I can't control the ocean, but I can run fast on land." He shut the door in Ryven's face, calling out behind it, "I'll leave tonight!"

Ryven placed a hand on the smooth dark wood of his little brother's door, "Be safe."

Chapter 14

"I could not ask for a better woman for my Ryven." Queen Jerica laughed. The queen summoned Mylva to her chambers for a private breakfast. She pointed to a low seat beside her bed. "He sat right there all night. Ranting and raving about you. He openly shared his desires upon seeing you in that dress. He threatened his brothers and that poor little Sevinland prince. I have never seen him so out of sorts." She grinned at Mylva, lifting her mug of coffee, "Well done!"

Mylva was unsure of the praise or why Ryven, despite his power and maturity, still confided in his mother. It was both disturbing and heartwarming. She'd often wished her own remained alive for such discussions.

Hava and Nava. They were no longer there to know her mind, nor react to her plans as this woman did for her son. Mylva sipped her own coffee, hating how her emotions seemed to control her these days.

"Your sisters, Hava and Nava?" The queen looked over the rim of her steaming teacup as she took a sip, "They shared all that with you?"

Mind Reader. Jerica was the one with the power, but did Licthan have it, too? "More. We were more. They were a part of me." Her throat threatened to close with unwelcome emotion.

"They still are, Mylva."

Rage erupted. Her fingers tightened around the mug, then loosened as she fought for control. How dare someone who hadn't even met them talk of them. Call her name. Their names.

With her free hand held palm out, the Queen spoke softly, "Easy, have no ill intentions. I shall never wound you, not unless you harm my children or those I love like my children." Jerica's eyes were as a bird of prey watching the grass for a meal. Searching. Pondering. "They are a part of you, so let them guide you still. Their choice was to give you the freedom that Ryven offers. For it is freedom for you. It is much more than you had." The queen's lips softened into a smile.

Mylva toyed with the thoughts floating around in her mind. She wondered if some of her musings were from Jerica. Ryven. He was the best option, no doubt. From her experiences in the castle so far, he was all he played himself to be, and possibly more. How much more… she'd have a lifetime to figure out.

"Now, my dearest." Jerica said gently as she set her mug down, "All there is for you to do is keep torturing him until you make the choice. For it is still yours. I hope you choose him. You both have the potential to be exceptional leaders of the world. I judge this by what he's told me of you and your country. I'm pleased that your people have such lives that they need nothing. Well, other than some water, I suppose."

Mylva laughed and explained as simply as she could, "We have glaciers and there is plenty of fresh water from them."

The Queen shook her head as she said, "I cannot imagine such a place. Fire and ice living side by side. I can see it in some of your memories, but it is like a work of fiction."

"When I marry your son, you may see it."

The Queen's eyes lit up. "Your choice?"

"My choice."

Jerica laughed and came around the small table to hug Klava to her. "Now, don't tell him still. Like I said, string him along, my darling. I enjoy watching him squirm! I never imagined him this way!"

"I shall do my best." Mylva tried to wonder why she didn't shove her away. She was still wary that some of her thoughts were not her own, and the Queen was practically a stranger. Yet the embrace was warm. The scent reminded her of Hava and her herbal tea. Perhaps that was why she liked Jerica.

Someone knocked briefly at the door before pushing it open. The King entered, a smile on his face. It faltered a little when he spotted Mylva, but it grew again. "Klava, it is a pleasure to see you getting along with Jerica." He paused as he rested a hand on the crown of Jerica's chair and leaned down, "Darling…you're flushed. Is the news you two speak of really that good?"

"I shall not tell you. Not yet."

"But why?" The King drew back, his face falling into a near pout.

"Because, my dearest husband, you know not how to hold your tongue." Jerica gave a wink to Klava. "Watch, this is where Ryven gets it from."

"Gets what from?" Licthan ran a hand through his long hair, his bottom lip protruding ever slightly more. "Don't make me use my powers to learn what you two speak of." He eyed Mylva before turning to his wife.

"Impatience. It only occurs when the ones they love hide something from them. Ryven gets that from you, my pet." Jerica grinned, sliding her hand along the scruff of her king's face to pat his cheek.

"There are other things he receives from me as well." The king blurted, his chest expanding. "He's intelligent! Well, he gets that from you, doesn't he?" His gaze turned back to his wife, "Ah! He's strong!" He flexed his arms, then looked again at his wife, "That's from both of us. Your father was an ox." Licthan licked his lips, "Ah! His dick!"

"Lict! Please!" Jerica groaned, patting the king's face rather forcefully before dropping her hand back into her lap.

"Oh, right," he chuckled, "His sense of humor. I gave him that."

"His big heart, you gave him that too, my sweet."

Mylva watched the two. Her mind floundered over the fluttering inside her chest before producing the answer at last. Desire. She wanted what they had? How strange for her. Foolish.

Ryven could give her that. She saw it in him. Felt it in herself.

No.

Yes.

She shook her head, "Where's Ryven now?"

"Probably in the library, my dear." The king smiled, finally bending down to kiss his wife chastely. "If he's not training, he likes to read in the morning."

"My dear, may I follow you to your room to change you into something?" Jerica asked, her eyes on Mylva.

She eyed Jerica, the grin on the woman's face was scary, yet challenging. She nodded, and the queen uttered a sound she'd never heard before. Something between a giggle and a squeal. Wait, Hava made that noise sometimes. Made. She'd already become accustomed to using past tense with her sisters.

Mylva allowed Ryven's mother to hold her arm as they walked down one hall and down another until they reached her chambers. Basau worked quickly, following the queen's instructions. The maid had left Mylva's hair unbound and messy. They pulled a short dress over her head, barely reaching the middle of her thigh, and it plunged deep, nearly to her belly button. The deep red reminded her of the color of her lips the other night.

She felt as if a flimsy nightgown was on her, and butterflies fluttered inside her. Since when did she have these sensations? The last time she had wings in her stomach was the first time she'd had sex.

"Perfect." The Queen nodded with a smile. "Seduce him, my dear. You may or may not let him partake, that amount of torture for him is up to you. Your choice."

As she talked, Jerica led her out of her room with an excitedly bouncing Basau and to the library. Her voice dropped the closer they got to the double doors. Jerica opened one of them, stepping out of the way, and waited for Mylva to enter before shutting it behind her gently. Alone.

Not alone. He sat in a window, a low bench fitted into the curve of the glass. His shirt was his usual black, open with the laces as loose as they could be down his chest. His pants looked as soft. Messy hair, bare feet - he looked like he just woke up. Book, thick in his hands, resting on a knee against the panes. His eyes flowed over the pages.

He hadn't noticed her entrance.

She smiled, thankful for her own bare feet as she crossed the carpeted expanse between them. Mylva slid neatly into the space on the cushion at his crotch, her leg resting over his outstretched one. "What're you reading?"

His body was stiff underneath her, his breath had caught. Then he relaxed. Slightly. "An adventure called…" His voice trailed off as she looked up into his face. Her mouth nearly brushed his chin. "Called… did you just wake up?"

"Not an impressive title, is it?" She curled her lips, resting her head on his shoulder as she brought her knee up to rest it against his along the window. The skirt dropped, leaving her leg uncovered.

He swallowed, eyes following the fabric. They rested there on her thigh for a while, before they trailed up the bare flesh of her belly and chest. He swallowed again.

Mylva drew her arms together, folding them under her breasts. They nearly fell out with the motion, but she held them there. She watched his mouth work. Then his gaze was on her lips, as if he had to physically tear them away from her chest.

"It… what did I say?" He squeezed his eyes shut, shaking his head slightly.

This was fun. Why hadn't she done this before? The butterflies faded into a warmth. "You said the title was 'Did You Just Wake Up?' and it's supposed to be an adventure."

"Right. No. That's not the title." He eyed the tome as if it had betrayed him. "It's…ah…It's called Starving…something. Something…" He flipped it over, revealing the name of the book, "Remedies of Starving Travelers."

"Hm." She trailed a finger down the spine, watching his gaze follow the digit as his lips slowly parted. "Tell me about it."

"About…the book. Right. It's ah…" His gaze flowed back to her mouth.

She wondered what his thoughts were. No bare flesh touched on them. Yet. Mylva slid her foot down his leg gently. Her body stretched, her toes found the cool skin of his ankle, and in came a storm.

Kasu. Kasu. Kasu. Mylva's in my lap. She feels so soft. Kasu. Gods protect me. She's about to kill me, isn't she? Is she wearing any clothes underneath this flimsy red thing? Doesn't look like it. Kasu, I could slip my fingers right into her and…

She smirked.

She's going to kill me for sure. That smile. I want to taste her. I want that smile to greet me in the morning. I want to know every mark on her, kiss it away. Please. Gods. Let me be hers one day. What was the book called again?

Mylva let her body relax, her foot dragging back up his leg a little. "Something wrong, Ryven?" She asked as she flipped it open on his knee, her fingers resting over his thumb that he'd used to hold his place.

She said my name. Is this dress part of some ritual where she turns me to charcoal? I don't care. She can burn me alive while I'm inside her. Wait. No. "Nothing's wrong." *Focus. Focus.*

Mylva sighed, trailing her finger down his thumb, and she made herself think of Wain. Naked. A grin on his pale face over her as he pounded into her from behind.

Ryven jerked his hand and the book out from under hers. His irises flashing as he gritted his teeth in a snarl. His body was so taut underneath hers she might slide off the bench and into the floor if he didn't relax. She wriggled against him, turning slightly so her shoulder was more in his chest.

It was cold in the room. Glacial. She thought about pulling some heat from him, but she couldn't harm him. Not while he was like this. She never knew seduction could be fun.

"Seems you're lying to me. Are you angry with me? Am I too close?" She tensed her body, readying herself to get off him.

The arm with the book snaked around her, pinning her to him gently. "No. I'm not angry. Not…" He hissed out a breath, his free hand running through his hair as he closed his eyes. "Wain? Really?"

"What's wrong with Wain? He looks like he'd be fun. Rough, maybe." The flesh of her chest touched his between the thin laces of his shirt.

Take her. Take her. Smoke and fog I'll give her rough if that's what she wants.

He glanced down. His chest expanded as he breathed in deep, his gaze glued to the plunged neckline. He licked his lips. His hand slid down, pulling the red fabric over her breasts, creating a barrier between their flesh. He leaned in, knocking his forehead into hers gently as he closed his eyes, "Mylva," he whispered her name, "Take me."

"Take you where, Ryven?"

Curses erupted in his mind as his breathing stayed deep and even. The image of him flipping her onto her back and diving between her legs intrigued her. Torturing this man was easy.

"Kiss me. Touch me. Mate me. Allow me to do those things to you. Let me take you to pleasure."

"We're not married."

He frowned, his dark eyes flicking open. His irises were wide, like a cat's, as he stared into hers. "Does that truly matter to you? Isn't it a trap to you?"

"Maybe." She grinned.

Another set of curses before stillness. His eyes narrowed on her as he drew back, creating a distance between them. "Your breath smells like my mother's favorite tea."

"Hm." She tilted her head, still smiling.

"What exactly did she tell you?"

"Plenty of things. What are you so worried about, Ryven?" She drew his name out, watching the gooseflesh rise on his neck. Perhaps her breath was hitting him there.

"This for starters." He muttered, leaning his head back to the window frame.

Perfect. She leaned in, placing her mouth on his neck where the goosebumps were. His body froze under her, not a breath. She turned, flipping over to lean over him poised on one knee and her hand on the frame beside his head. She dropped her other foot to the floor, giving herself a steadier stance. "What's wrong with this?" She asked, before planting her lips on him again, this time a little further down on his neck, where his shoulder began.

"Nothing is wrong." He said aloud as his mind stuttered and stammered together into a string of nonsense as it flowed into her mind. Ryven rested his fingers on her cheek, cupping her chin in his hand as he drew her back so he could look into her eyes. "Do my incessant thoughts not bother you?"

"No. I'm used to having other thoughts in my head besides my own." At last, she learned why Hava and Nava had so much fun in these situations.

He chuckled, "How can you be so perfect?"

"Even if I want Wain?"

His gaze grew hooded, before it softened, "Mother gave you permission to torture me, didn't she?"

"I never needed her sanction." Mylva realized she hadn't asked him for his, but she knew he wanted her. Even if she couldn't read his thoughts, he'd told her so several times already. Love? Why did he love her?

His hand slipped on down her neck, threatening, but not. "No, you don't. Mylva, you haven't asked my permission to taste me."

She smirked, "Returning the favor of you kissing my cheek."

"Hm." He mocked the sound she'd made earlier. "You mean the sample of you after you squirmed like a kid when your hair dipped into your ear?"

She sensed a flush of heat racing up her neck, "I didn't give you consent for that."

"No, you didn't. You were too cute to resist." He licked his lips, his gaze dropping for a breath, "You want to sample more of me?"

"Yes." She smirked at the string of thoughts from him before he dropped his hand and looked away for a moment. "I suppose that means I have permission?"

"You have my approval to try me. Touch me, passionately. Do things as a lover does to me, Mylva." His gaze swept back to hers as he spoke softly. "May I have the same permissions?"

"No, you may not." At his frown, she grinned, "Whatever I do to you is only what you may do to me."

"Fair enough," He said with a twist of his lips as he tossed the book to the floor.

"Does anyone else come in here?" Wouldn't that be rich? An audience like the parties in Kavkan she hated. Again, she was thankful they had happened every five years, and not each one.

He snorted, "Only me. And now you."

She kissed his forehead. The tip of his nose. His lips parted as she went down, but kissed his chin instead, under it.

"Hateful, woman."

"Needy, man." She said, kissing his jugular, and the dip between his clavicles. She pressed her tongue there; the heat of his body comforted her. Drawing back up, she kissed the pulse point to the left of his neck before placing her lips below his earlobe.

"I'm not sure I like this game." He said, even as in his mind he was begging for more. Imagining her later in his arms as they had sex.

She bit his earlobe, sucked on it. She relished in him drawing taut under her, like a bowstring. No wonder Nava liked these kinds of things. She frowned, then cleared her mind. No distractions. She nipped the hardness of his jaw and was about to kiss his cheek when he turned on her. Mylva found her lips over his and he tasted sweet, but bitter. Like the coffee he enjoyed. The scent of books and rum filled her nose more as she opened her mouth to him. Her tongue met his before she pulled away.

"Take your shirt off, Ryven." She ordered, resting back on her knee instead of leaning over him.

He eyed her, licking his lips, "I can only do what you do, remember?"

"I guess we're through, then." She teased, only to bite back a laugh at his haste in obeying her.

He leaned up, his shirt tugged off with a ripple of muscles. The black cloth lay over the book on the floor. He sat before her, hands clasped between his legs.

She warmed, content with the sight of him, and settled back. Her fingers danced over the scar on his shoulder that dragged down into his chest. She would learn where it was from later. This day was all about touch, sampling, learning to be with one another. Goosebumps followed the path of her fingers over him as she touched each scar. The roughness of healed skin, observing how some turned from pink to cream.

Skin not as marred as hers.

She chased each touch with a lick. His breathing grew ragged, his muscles tensing under her. His hands kept themselves still, fingers tightly woven with white knuckles.

When she kissed each knuckle, a new bloom of impatience erupted in her mind from him. As she began suckling on his fingertip, she ended up on her back, looking up at Ryven. One hand was behind her head, the other gripped her hip. His eyes trailed down her, irises darkening to the hue of his pupil.

The bulge in his pants rested against her bare thigh.

"My turn." He said, dipping his head down to nuzzle into the softness of her neck.

"Not hardly." She rolled them, crashing onto the floor, and then straddling him.

"Mylva," He half moaned, half groaned as his fingertips dug into the soft flesh at her hips.

"I'll allow that, only because I like it." Since she was hanging out of the top part of her dress anyway, she shrugged it off. Settling over him, a hand on his broad chest holding him down, she focused on his face as she rolled her hips, dragging her center up the length of his hard cock trapped in his pants still.

His intentions excited her as she indulged in his thoughts. She was half tempted to let him. Another day, perhaps. Because she liked the friction, she rocked her hips, and again as she clasped his hands in hers.

His moan was long and low, his eyes half lidded as he watched her move over him.

Dragging his hands away, she moved them above them, pinning them down under her. "Lift your hips." His cock and hips bumped into her pelvis and held there. She rocked her hips into him again. Mylva dipped her head, taking his mouth with hers.

He lifted his head to better have her with his tongue. His own hips meeting her movements. His thoughts focused solely on her. How wet she felt on his manhood through his damp pants. The flash of desire to be inside her. The need to have her breast in his mouth.

Ryven's urge to eat her out before he took her.

She crawled off him, not able to catch her breath or slow her heartbeat. She leaned back against the bench and licked her lips. "Stand. Take your pants off."

Ryven rolled forward into a crouch on the balls of his feet before standing. The move so easily executed left an impression on her. He turned to her, loosening the laces that held his pants so low on his hips. He let the fabric drop; the soft black fabric pooled over his feet.

His penis bobbed. She found him pleasingly sized, her hand's length, maybe a hair more. Nava would have jumped his bones and kept him as a pet for as long as possible. Looking into his eyes, she saw herself, not her sisters. They would have liked Ryven.

"Your turn."

A second of hesitation and then Ryven pulled her to her feet by grabbing her hands. He half walked, half nudged her toward a wall of shelves filled with books. His dark eyes probed hers. His cock bobbing and bumping her stomach between them.

Once the wood pressed against her back, he pulled her arms up over her head, one at a time. His eyes never left hers. He gently hooked her fingers on to the edge of a shelf, high over her head, making her stretch up, her body arcing toward him. "Your hands should only move upwards, towards the next shelf."

She nodded. It was only fair. She'd made the deal to allow him to do things to her.

His head dropped, lips attaching to her flesh under her jaw. His thumb pressed to her chin, lifting and easing her head to the side to give himself some room. He suckled the sensitive skin below her ear, gently at first, then hard enough to leave his mark.

His thoughts came to her seconds before his mouth and hands followed. She knew what awaited, burned for it, craved the action, even if it was just a look. Ryven's hand flowed down her arm in a light brush of fingertips and a warrior's callouses.

Mylva arched into his touch as that hand drifted to cup her breast. She gasped, and his lips caught it. His tongue crashed into hers, tangling for a moment, before he pulled away to kiss her chin.

He flicked her nipple with the rough pad of his thumb and moaned at her second gasp. "My, my, my, the sounds you make, my love." He purred against her bottom lip. "Move your head back."

She obeyed, gazing upwards at the shelf. His mouth kissed down her neck, jumped over to the scar from an axe on her shoulder to kiss there. His other hand dropped to her other breast. She pressed into his hands, begging for more of the gentle circular caresses, the pads of his fingertips over her hard nipples sending little shocks of pleasure, and then the random hard squeezes that sent her gasping.

He took his hand from her, raking the rough pads and palm down her side to her back. His fingertips dipped underneath the waistband of her dress. He dragged the dress down, over the globes of her ass, before he gripped her in his hands.

Her sound thrilled his mind and resonated with hers.

His kisses trailed down, stopping at a few scars, until he took a nipple in his mouth. He suckled, then nipped before rolling his tongue around the hard flesh again. Another half moan, half whimper, tore through him. His thoughts were full of the struggle in not taking her. As hers were struggling not to wrap her legs around his hips and drive him inside her.

"Waited too long." He muttered against her flesh before shoving as much as he could of her breast into his mouth. "Far too long." He breathed over the wet spot, his suckling left. "Five years is too long."

He dragged her body up by her ass in his hands.

She whimpered, struggling to reach for the next shelf until she caught it with one hand. Her other met it, even though she wanted to tangle her fingers into his hair and pull his mouth to her breast again. He licked between her breasts and she swore under her breath. Five years? Did he want to do this a year after being in her country?

He readjusted his grip, and he lifted her up again.

Her thighs pulled over his shoulders. A note of surprise left her as his breath washed over her heat. Her fingers fumbled up the next two shelves. His tongue parted her, and she dropped her hand to his hair as her other finally gripped the edge.

Ryven's tongue dug into her, lapping like she was water in a desert. Then the tip of his tongue found her clit, and she moaned. She heard herself through him, too. She tasted herself through him. To him, she was his world.

His tongue flicked the small bundle of nerves, driving her toward a cliff she didn't know was that close. Her body tightened, dove over the edge with a cry. He lapped up her orgasm, making her body jerk each time he still hit her clit or drove deep inside her, stretching her pleasure out past maddening.

"Let go of the shelf." He murmured, pulling back slightly before nipping her thigh.

She did.

"Open your legs, let me slide you down." Ryven's voice was heavy with need.

Mylva opened her legs, and he brought her downward. She placed her hands on his straining shoulders and helped him handle her. His grip loosened, and she took her weight on until he wrapped his arms around her waist. He kissed her clavicle and turned them. He nudged the chair from the desk and lowered her into it.

Not the best seat for sexual encounters. She frowned, about to crawl out and pull him down on the floor. But he set her foot on the edge of the desk, his mind telling her to wait and see. He placed her other foot on the desk, his hands raking up and down her legs, before he hooked her thighs over his shoulders again. Through the connection, she saw what he planned. Mylva knew how she felt in his hands. What her flavor was on his tongue. The chair creaked back as she gasped when his thumb brushed her clit.

Sometimes his tongue would play with her clit in place of his thumb. Sometimes he would sample her folds. She knew his movements mere moments before they happened. His fingers slid into her, his tongue matching their harried pace on her clitoris. A breathy moan intertwined with each breath she took. Her body writhing under him.

He kept her thighs from crushing him with his free hand as her body went taught as another orgasm slammed into her.

She knew he wanted to know how her orgasm felt while he was deep inside.

Ryven sat on the floor, licking his lips clean before wiping them on the back of his hand. "Your turn."

Mylva glared at him, her muscles twanging. She crawled out of the chair, pushing him to lie down. Dragging her tongue up the length of his shaft made his body lurch underneath her. She wanted it inside her. He definitely wanted to be in her.

She straddled him, raking her wet heat over his cock, when the head of it brushed her clit her body wanted to erupt into another orgasm. Mylva slid her hand between them, parting her folds with the head of his penis, situating it perfectly. She removed her hand, placing his on her hips. His thoughts swirling with hers in a dance of need.

"Hold on." She said with a smirk.

He did.

She slid her body down his shaft and took him in until she felt herself settle at the base. Mylva rode him, slow and deep at first. Then slapping their bodies together as they found their rhythm. His mind in hers. His pleasure hers. Her mind in his. Her pleasure his.

It didn't take long for him to spill his seed as she milked it from him in her third orgasm.

Mylva woke. Her knees were on softness instead of the hard floor of the library. The warmth of his body still under hers made her smile. When had she fallen asleep?

She blinked and rubbed her eyes. Expecting shelves upon shelves of books, she yawned as she realized they were in her room. She sat up, staring as his body stretched under hers as he gave a jaw cracking yawn himself.

"You walked us naked through the hall?"

His hands rested on her hips. His smirk was contagious, "You hid my cock while I had you wrapped in my shirt. Someone might've gotten an eyeful of my ass. Other than Basau and Gyrna." He lifted a shoulder.

She rolled off him, only to have him follow her. They lay side by side. His hand dragged her leg over his hip and he scooted closer. One hand lay on her ass while the other propped his chin, allowing him to look down at her.

"Good morning." He said, the sleep still in his voice.

"Good morning."

"I'm going to love this."

"What?" It was probably the sex, because that's what occupied his thoughts yesterday.

"Waking up next to you. Every morning. Some at night," Ryven said with a squeeze of her buttocks.

"Did I say I'd marry you in my sleep?" Mylva raised a brow, her heart warming to the idea while her mind still debated on killing him once she got bored.

His lips twisted into another grin, "No, my fire, but you dreamed it, and thought of it many times."

"You're gonna have to stay out of my head." She eyed him, finding that a man in her head was far different from having Hava and Nava in there.

"I couldn't help but do a bit of diving into your thoughts. We have a similar one. Where I wake you to take you. I feared it was your dream."

"Was it not?"

"No. And that's good. While we waited a little, now is still a good time." He leaned over, capturing her lips with his.

She moaned, curling into his body heat. Mylva pulled him to her, wrapping her arm around his shoulders. She rolled to her back, pulling him over her.

He moved smoothly with her, resting over her as they kissed, nesting himself neatly between her legs.

Their kisses were slow, as were his thoughts, both growing deeper and heated as they woke each other up. His penis grew ever harder between them and she rocked her hips to help him along with the friction, because it felt good to him. When he dipped his head to suckle on her right after she thought about it, she urged him on with a moan and a hand in his hair. Her hand moved over his back, feeling the ridges of a few scars.

Whiplashes?

She pulled at him to enter her, tilting her hips up to urge him into her damp folds.

His cock slid in and they found a slow, rocking pace together. How good they felt to one another twisting in her mind, twirling into a storm. Then she gripped his shoulders, pushing him faster. He matched her need, thrusting deeper, harder. He propped up on his elbows, watching her and she him. She bounced under him, taking him in so deep his balls slapped against her ass.

He spilled his seed into her, his body rigid over her as she gripped him hard.

Already, Ryven was thinking of taking her again.

"Again." He breathed against her neck. He rolled, pulling her on top of him. With a few thrusts, his soft cock grew rigid again. He drove himself deep inside her, his hands gripping her hips.

She sat up, taking him in deeper and widening her legs so his hips could drive hard and fast up into her. She gripped her breasts in her hands, pinching her own nipples as the image played through her mind from his. He moaned his pleasure at the sight of her, his need driving him up into her harder. She trailed a hand down her stomach, parting her lips to find her clit to rub it with a callous on her index finger.

Ryven's grunts became cries. His eyes were wild on her, dark lust filling them. Just when she felt his orgasm erupt from him, he pushed her away and was behind her.

His wet manhood slapped against her ass as he bent over her. He shoved her down, chest in the mattress. His fingers slid into her hair to grip it in a fist. With his other hand, he rubbed the head of his cock against her slit, then nudged it against her clitoris with jerks of his hips.

She whimpered, him not taking his pleasure did little to stave hers off. She gripped the sheets as her body shook all over with it. As she rode it, he pulled her gently up.

"Watch me take you." He growled, pushing her head down as she held herself up on still shaking elbows. She rested her forehead against the sheets, doing as she was told. He wanted to see what she did. Mylva spread her elbows and legs wide to keep her vision from being hampered.

She saw him enter her. His thrusts were harder as he relished having her watch, knowing what she beheld with their joining. His hips slapped into her ass, making her jiggle all over. When she was about to orgasm again, he pulled from her, his cock bobbing beneath her, leaking a few white droplets along with her juices.

His fingers found her clit, driving vigorous circles against it, and she screamed her release into the bed.

Ryven turned her over, flipping her onto her back. He stood on his knees, looking down at her. Studying her as her chest rose and fell with each labored breath. His hand slowly slid up and down his still hard cock.

Something about him watching her while doing that made her want him again. Desperately. She spread for him.

He leaned over her, propping himself up on his elbows. His hands cupped her face. His lips pressed to hers and he swallowed her moan as he slid back into her.

She wrapped her arms around him; her legs around his hips. The strokes of his body into hers were deep, and like he was stitching them into one. Her breath mingled with his and she met his gaze.

"I love you, Mylva. I've searched the world until I found you." He ran his fingers through her hair as he thrust into her with the gentle rolls of his body over hers. His eyes intent on hers. "Allow me to give you the world as a wedding gift?"

Unsure of the meaning, she felt his desire to marry her through their shared thoughts. To tie their lives together. The world at her feet. He was her best option. From what she saw of his siblings, Ryven was the best out of all of them.

His words rang true. Not a doubt in his mind from what he shared with her. But that was it. How was she to know that he shared all of his thoughts with his powers? Mylva shoved the thoughts to the side, hoping he didn't read them. Her focus returned to the man inside her. The moment.

As his pleasure grew, hers did too. She nodded, "Yes, give me the world and we will belong to one another." Her mind flicked back to her release, refusing to dwell on marriage.

He smiled before dropping his lips to hers. His thrusts became more erratic, breaking the rhythm, but not the euphoria. Ryven's orgasm gave her hers.

Chapter 15

A moment to herself. Finally. In her room, Mylva sat on the small couch by the crackling logs. Her armor warmed with the nearby flames and she soaked it in slowly. It was like drinking a warm beverage before bed. She was able to think.

The flames inside searched and writhed. Unrest and distrust heightening the fire within. There was so much magic around her. She could feel it in the very walls.

At least, she didn't have to wonder if Ryven's powers were seeping into her. According to Gyrna's research, and her own in the library, his powers wouldn't reach through the palace walls. It irritated her at the same time. For they made her less powerful as well.

With his magical abilities, she was sure he used his powers on her. Twisting her feelings and thoughts. Strategically, she couldn't blame him. As a possible mate, she wanted to throw him to the fires, still. But then, when she pictured that, her heart dropped. That was concerning.

Her fingers curled around the flames as she toyed with the fireplace, feeling the tickle against her flesh as she tugged them toward her. The little orange flickers spanned her knuckles and wrapped around them like fiery rings. Emotion wasn't a thing she sought other than rage, for that pulled the fire within her out as needed.

The fluttering. Hava and Nava's thoughts, what they would say, brought tears to her eyes. More emotion. So she closed them, willing the emotion back so she could concentrate. Mylva knew not having them by her side was a portion of her instability. She never imagined life without them. Yet, here she was. Conquered and alone. Being toyed with away from home.

She bit her cheek, forcing herself to rely on the bitter truth.

Fact one: she was in enemy territory and she couldn't best him, much less all of them.

Fact two: even if she raged, she was unable to kill them all with the fires of the goddess within the palace.

Fact three: there was something else underneath all this, and she didn't have a single clue what it might be.

Fact four: the man who made her heart move in odd ways was also responsible for the deaths of her sisters and some of her generals. Praedae, too, perhaps.

"Water and ice," she muttered, taking a few deep breaths in. She watched the flames dance across her palm.

Mental influence was not the same as emotional. Not with one as herself. Mylva was too old for puppy love. She knew she was an all-or-nothing type, always had been.

Was it the fact he'd been the first one to listen after the deaths of her Bloodsworn that made her love him? She let the flame grow, allowing it to cover the entirety of her hand. Mental powers after an emotional blow. It was a perfect storm, was it not?

She grinned, confident she would uncover it with little effort. Years spent melding minds with her sisters allowed her to learn which memories were hers, and which were theirs if she just studied the differences. Mylva began with the latest and worked her way back. Searching for things out of the ordinary.

His thoughts entering her mind in his voice, he did that without even trying. What if he'd placed thoughts that were in her own voice? Anything abnormal, she pulled and tugged, twisted it to check its source.

From what she studied, she didn't think he'd influenced her. There were some memories of him as a general that could've been, but nothing that would tie in with her emotions. Right?

She growled, tossing the flickering flame back into the fireplace. The problem was, she had little to do with her own emotions. And fewer instances of dealing with someone that had magic to influence minds. Mylva started another tactic.

What would she love in a mate?

Black hair, black eyes, tanned skin, smart and muscular.

Was that her thoughts or Nava's? Hava's? Ryven's influence? Her people's?

All of the above, perhaps? Mylva stood, pacing in front of the hearth, tapping her bottom lip. Ridiculous. She'd never ran in circles in her own mind before, not like this.

Was there a plan to gain what she wanted without falling into a trap? She eyed the playful flames and cursed herself. A deeper cage? While the opalescent palace was beautiful, it was indeed a cage. As she stared at the fire, one coal tumbled forward, landing on the hearth and stretching out.

Mylva crouched, poking the lizard from her homeland in its chubby belly. What had Ryven named it? "Wakxen. You are rather good at stowing away, little friend." She chuckled as it rolled over and stretched further, asking for more. She scratched the glowing potbelly with two of her fingernails and continued her thought process.

Her third plan remained available. Marriage to Ryven wouldn't be the worst thing, she assumed. And after a while, she might get used to it. A matrimonial state. With one that wanted to give her the world, so she'd take it. Use him. The sex was the best she'd had, too. Since she was alone, there wouldn't be much harm in sitting back, for now.

Different scenarios played through her mind with the marriage. None were too detrimental. She thought of the worst potential outcome, and it had little chance of actually happening, unlike the others.

"Klava?" Gyrna called from the door when she cracked it open.

"Enter."

"Have you had enough time?" Her Bloodsworn asked, head bowed after she closed the door behind her.

"I have." Mylva stood, amused as the fat lizard crawled back into the fireplace with soft growls and grumbles.

"What may I do to assist you?"

"Help me watch, listen, and learn. That is all."

Gyrna's hands were in tight fists at her sides. "That's what I've been doing. Isn't there anything else? Will we ever be free of this place? Of him?"

"Nothing else, Gyrna. As far as being free…" she frowned, the words caught in her throat because she hardly believed them herself. "I think we are as free as we can be." Because the only things she had to do these days was appear at a meal. There weren't any pressing matters to attend to. No advisors to satisfy. Not a single mountain of reports from all her holdings, and she chose what to do for the rest of her day. The lack of paperwork was both refreshing and worrying. What were her countries doing without her guidance and those of the royals?

"Find out what's happening back home. As much as you can," Mylva ordered Gyrna, "I need my reports."

Ryven hadn't returned for the next meal, so Mylva went to the dining room. She filled her own plate, took up a chair at a table in a corner of the room, and settled in to observe. Wisps of conversation caught her ears, not an important piece of information in the mix.

Then the king entered, looked around, caught sight of her, and grinned. He pointed to the buffet, and a servant scurried to it, filling a plate. Licthan circled the long table, weaving through the smaller ones to sit across from her. "Waiting for Ryven?"

"No, merely eating."

He smiled as he said, "Observing, more like."

Mylva's brow twitched. "That too."

"I'll tell you something you are probably mulling over." He leaned forward, bracing himself on the table with his forearms, clasping his hands together in front of him.

"Go on," she said before finishing her plate and sitting back to listen.

"You cannot kill my son. Not today. Not tomorrow. Not a month from now. Nor years from now."

Mylva tilted her head to the side, taking the time to run her tongue along her teeth. "Can I not? If I ask permission with a smile, may I then?" She hated to tell him she was past that point.

"Your smile is not that sweet, my dear." Licthan said with a chuckle, "In fact, it's downright vicious looking." He waited until the boy sat his plate, drink and utensils down before continuing, "Aren't you going to ask me what will happen if you kill my son?"

Mylva lifted a shoulder, "If I cannot do it, why know the consequence?" She tapped her finger on the table's edge. "Ah, that's right. Tortured for thirty-two years."

He stared at her, fork poised over the pile of white stuff with butter melting on top of it. He chuckled with a shake of his head, "Yes. Very well." Licthan dug the pronged utensil into the creamy vegetable as he said, "And let's not forget, I will have your precious Kavkan." He held the fork up, "I do like mashed potatoes. Don't you? How do you like it here?"

"It's nice." He'd threatened her people with a smile and a potato filled fork. "I've only had them baked." She swallowed back the rage, trying to keep a neutral tone.

"Nice? That's all?" The king asked after swallowing a mouthful of his meal. "I would like to see what would be beautiful to you."

She smiled and asked, "You didn't go to my country with any of your children, then?"

He shook his head, shoveling more food into his mouth.

"Then I suggest you visit after they saddle their rides."

His eyes narrowed, "Is that how you perceive us? Still?"

"Seed from you is worming into every corner of my empire, and more, I assume. What other possibility exists?" Mylva crossed her arms over her chest plate, feeling the pull of a muscle in her cheek as it ticked. "You just stated between bites of your precious potatoes that if I didn't play nice, my Kavkan would be yours. How exactly am I to perceive you?"

"Ryven said Kavkans bled war. I've barely spilled any of your blood through this plan. Very few deaths." The king pushed his half finished plate away and sat back with his wine in hand. "What if we could give your people a life of art, peace, and a way to travel without worry, to explore? Because they were capable. All corners of the world are to be Ryven's soon."

"Then Kavkan will probably be the leader of the rebellion. Little bloodshed is still the blood of my people spilled. What are you to do to soften that blow? Make sure your sons give us six orgasms a day?" She shook her head, feeling feral, "While I see your idea, and commend it. I don't think it's going to work as well as you hope. People are greedy. They always plan to gain more. Like you. You're gaining the world through this. There will be another you. Perhaps not one as virile, but they'll try. Or another like your son, ambitious plans to give himself the world, and more."

"I see." The king tilted his hand slowly in a circle, his eyes on the wine within the cup, "Do you not think my son is smart enough to have fail safes in place? If the peace to come not payment enough?"

Mylva nodded, "Even the most brilliant minds cannot think of every scenario. We are humans. Kavkans. Are you sure there can be peace throughout the world?"

The king grinned, "My darling daughter-to-be, there isn't just one brilliant mind at his disposal, and you will be part of that peaceful world, holding it steady right beside him."

That was what she feared and was part of her three worst-case scenarios. Some form of magic she was unaware of, being used against her from a place in the world she'd never heard of. Ryven brainwashing her and her people. Some other disaster she couldn't visualize.

Her knowledge of the world and types of magic grew with each day she was here. Either submit or face defeat. What would Kavkans do with peace? The countries under her even rebelled from time to time, as weak as they were. How did they think Kavkan would react to this?

She doubted her generals would read for pleasure, but if given the time, maybe they would. The desire to grasp the unknown grew beside the fear of it. Something nagged at her, "Why now?" Ryven wasn't young, and half his siblings weren't either. The king was older. They had plenty of time to begin this, didn't they?

The king frowned, gaze flicking away, then back up to her, "Now is the best time. If not now, when?"

His tone and stiff shoulders made her question his flippancy. "I will find out." Something in her knew there was more to this than what they kept saying. There were too many gaps.

"I have no doubt you will. Until then, I shall keep my secrets." Licthan grinned at her, returning to his more jovial self. He downed his wine and stood. "Enjoy riding, my dear Klava, and ride well."

Mylva saw him exit the dining hall. Her gaze swept over the crowd and an overwhelming desire to turn everything to ash made her blood burn. A shadow appeared at her elbow and she turned, a growl lodged in her throat. The large eyes of the slip of a princess cooled her anger. "Revra."

"K-k-klava, I'm afraid I'll f-fail." Revra's voice was so soft, even right beside her, Mylva had difficulty hearing each stammering word.

She slowed her movements, pushing the chair next to her out gently and motioning to it with her chin, "Fail at what, little mouse?"

Revra's eyes swept the room, growing ever wider before she looked back at the empress. Her fingers fluttered in the path her eyes took in a short, close to her chest wave.

Mylva sighed, "This is not a pass or fail thing. This is a…" What was it? Choose the best option? In Revra's case, which one would allow her to read her books and not beat her for her stammer? Klava lacked the familiarity with them to determine the answer. "It's a make friends situation." That made the woman grow paler. Ice douse her, but she didn't know how to comfort the timid.

Where was a little animal when she needed one?

The clack of the plate against the tabletop shattered Revra's remaining resolve. The princess scurried away like a mouse, and Mylva glared at the newcomer to her table. "For once, you are loud and decidedly annoying with it."

Pazai stared after Revra and shook her head, "I forgot how skittish the child was. Forgive me, I thought we could all have a pleasant chat."

"She's nearly as old as you, Iron Queen." Mylva muttered, watching Pazai's ritual of prim eating. "What is it?"

"These barbarians think they can grab us up, cage us, and then leave us to our own devices without repercussions."

Mylva raised a brow as Pazai's face pale.

Pazai slowly placed her knife and fork tidily on the edge of her plate, "You have repercussions in mind, do you not?"

"Of course I do, Pazai. If you want to die with them." Mylva raised a hand, her glove glowing in flames before she snuffed them out. She found no joy in how the queen trembled. Fear over respect at this moment, and it tasted bitter. "I have found that we may be in need of them."

"Whatever for?"

Mylva drew a breath deep into her lungs and let it out slowly. "There is something underneath all this that has them taking action now, and in this way. They need us. Therefore, we need them."

"Have you seen their armies?" Pazai scoffed, "I'm no strategist, but I comprehend their numbers may exceed yours by ten to one. What do they need us for?"

What indeed? Mylva tapped her fingers against her thigh, taking comfort in the drum of her glove against metal as she had several times before. What lay beyond her knowledge? She uttered words she hated the most, "I don't know."

She witnessed Pazai's fear grow in the tremble of the fingers constantly moving over the cloth, whether it be the blue dress on her person, the napkin, or the very tablecloth. Mylva sat up, reached over the table and captured the pale hand under hers, "I shall do my best to not allow harm to come upon you. But I may need you to attempt to follow their rules and choose one of these…" her lips twisted, "Barbarians."

After a beat, Pazai slipped her hand free and nodded, "I shall endeavor to fulfill your wishes." The queen stared at her plate as if settling her thoughts, before stating, with a glare at her empress, "I will have complaints. And demand compensation in some form for my lengthy disgust and torture."

Mylva bit back a smile and wondered if Pazai would call Ryven's treatment of her torture, "I shall await your entreaties." After a few more steadying breaths on her companion's part, the queen resumed eating in her tiny bites that took too much time. "Any seem less odious?"

Pazai's gaze flicked to hers as she cut off another bite only fit for a rodent, "Shall I marry into the king's harem, you think?"

That was a reach, but probably wasn't completely off the table. An interesting solution for the iron queen, perhaps.

♨ ♨ ♨

"How can someone so intelligent have such a grin on his face?" Monace asked, finger pressing into Ryven's cheek repeatedly. When he slapped it away, she brought it back, "Are you that sure of your charms?"

"No. Not at all." He shook his head with a chuckle, "But there is progress."

"Meaning she hasn't killed you yet," Nadran, the middle brother between Ryven and Mirtes, said from lying on top of the wall beside his siblings, his cap over his face to shield his eyes from the sun. "I commend you, brother, for having nerves of iron and the mind of a bear trap. But I fear even those attributes will still find you in the realm of death. And I am not well versed in the passages to keep your soul from returning for more torture."

"May gods watch." Mirtes mumbled, tossing the hull of a nut at his lounging elder brother, then another piece at Ryven across the table from him.

The siblings took up two of the outdoor tables of a restaurant they all enjoyed. Including a portion of the wall for Nadran, who refused to sit like a normal person. Overhead, long strips of cloth hung between poles to provide swaths of shade. The salt in the air was weak against the scents of spiced meats and sweet baked goods. The plush pillows and rugs provided comfortable seating and lounging around the thick tables on stocky legs.

"Enough of me. What about you?" Ryven eyed each of his siblings. The trouble ones. Half were too clever, while the others were overly picky. When his gaze turned to Wolfaran, his half brother with Moonapsa as his mother, a small feathered head poked out of the man's torn collar. He eyed it, "Please tell me you're actually socializing with the royals and not just your animal friends."

Monace giggled, "We should feather one of the females up, that way he'll talk to them."

"Or starve one nearly to death." Mirtes added.

True to his form, Wolfaran glared at his siblings with a half huff, half growl being their only answer. He fed the fowl in his shirt the husks Mirtes tossed in his direction. The little thing cooing contentedly with large eyes partially closed.

Ryven pinched the bridge of his nose between his thumb and forefinger, the pressure behind his eyes building again for the first time since leaving the empire. "Tataro?"

"I've talked. Socialized." Tataro grinned, his canids sharp, much like his brother Wolfaran's. He juggled a blade between his fingers as he talked, "That little beast you saddled me with at the beginning was not good for my palate, brother."

"He still has wounds." Wolfaran murmured, his eyes flashing as he looked at Ryven, only to soften the moment he returned his attention to the bird.

"It was between you and Wolfaran for obtaining her, and you cast the lowest lot." He reminded himself that he was patient while looking over his siblings again. "I know what you've not done to help, and you?"

Sihfe sighed, his eyes half lidded as he sucked a piece of fruit out of its hardened shell. He chewed, balancing the husk on his lips before blowing it away in a single puff for it to land on the waste pile in the middle of their table. "You took the one I would like to cuddle."

Ryven clenched his teeth for a count to keep words he'd regret spilling from his tongue, "There are others just as tall as she."

The redhead grinned, "Tall yes, but not with those thighs and hips. Sure you don't want to find another for yourself and let me have a ride?"

"You wouldn't survive a day." Mirtes chuckled, finishing his nuts and licking the salt off his fingers.

"Put the red with the animal. Maybe he could blow her mind." Tataro purred, flicking the blade so the end pointed at Sihfe.

"No wonder you haven't charmed anyone. So eloquent." Monace rolled her eyes, "As for me, I'm working on it. I've either got the whiner, the kid prince, or the ghost between my legs within the next two weeks."

"Never know if you'll like a ship until you take her for a spin." A few circular drawings accompanied Nadran's muffled voice in the air from one hand.

"Rovinlan has plenty of ports. Are you not interested in docking there?" Ryven added to the sea story.

"Which one is that?" Nadran asked, still under his hat.

Ryven sighed, "I… she's the small one."

"A shadow of a thing." Glavin, the last troubled one in the group, added from the end of the table, "She's scared. Of everything."

Ryven eyed his brother and raised a brow. Only to sigh yet again when Glavin shook his head. He looked at the other three and felt the first pangs of failure pricking at his chest. This had to go well. The hardest part was over, or so he thought. He put all the fish in a single pond, all they had to do was catch one.

If it didn't work between his siblings and the royals here, perhaps the others would prove worthy of them. He propped his chin on his palm and toyed with his drink. The only problem was, he hadn't a clue when they'd decide to attack. The enemy's threat of numbering their days was a fear tactic, and it worked well for them.

Mylva was the key. The rest were layers of excess security. Should he manage to charm her and endure, then peace would reign. He needed her fire against the darkness coming. Something in his heart and mind knew that.

She had understanding of her people. If his siblings couldn't control the armies of those beneath her, she possessed the ability. His siblings could make things easier for his future bride with the royals. He wanted her to enjoy the world. Not have to stay in a strategy room.

The siblings and the royals he assigned them were ideal matches. There were a handful that would be interchangeable. Glavin was the best choice for Rovinlan because he was gentler than Nadran. Frystwaithe, the largest port, deserved a naval commander like Nadran at its wheel. The lack of interest irritated him, but he couldn't do anything about it. If there wasn't a spark, then the plan would go awry, anyway.

He needed his fire goddess to heal and not burn him in the process.

Chapter 16

A week flew by. Mylva's body became exhausted from constantly teaching the kids at the grounds and Ryven's incessant need to bring her to orgasm. She never complained. Without war tiring her out, sex was the next best thing. Readying to return to the training grounds, she let Ryven buckle the leather that she always wore under her armor, protecting her ribs and chest from being crushed by the edges of the plates.

His hands flowed up, crushing her breasts in his palms as he kissed the back of her neck.

"Don't tell me you're hard again."

"Almost there," he said with a press of his hips against her backside.

She rolled her eyes, reaching behind her to slide her hand down his flat stomach to his crotch. Her fingers pressed against the base of his hardening cock after pushing the fabric of his pants away. "You have the stamina of a teenage boy."

He snorted, biting the nape of her neck before kissing there, "I hope not. Otherwise I'd just spill into your palm."

"That's not necessarily a bad thing."

"Only if you find pleasure in it too, Myl."

He enjoyed saying her name. She liked hearing it in that tone he had when he was about to take her. He untied the strings holding her pants up, even if he'd just helped her put them on. The fabric dropped, and his fingers dove into her folds.

"You're always wet for me." He moaned into her hair, beginning the circular massage of her clitoris.

"Hard to dry up from the last orgasm I had an hour ago." Mylva said with a half laugh, rubbing the width of her palm up and down his shaft. She tilted away from his lips on her shoulder, giving him room. If he couldn't have her breasts, mouth, or cunt in his mouth, he liked her neck.

Once he was rock hard, she leaned forward, urging him to return. When he obliged, guiding the head of his cock to her entrance and sliding in, she placed her hands on the shoulders of his armor, still on the stand.

Sex in protective gear was near impossible. It was too noisy. Too constricting. And she never got to feel the full length inside her with all the metal in the way.

She moaned, Ryven's cock driving her near as mad as his finger rubbing her clit. The hand on her hip flexed, pulling her harder against him with each of his thrusts. Their bodies slapped together, the sound echoing through the room.

The orgasm washing over her made her clutch him. With a few more thrusts, the heat of his release met her pulsing body, pleasure slow to descend. They stood there, his cock softening inside her.

She pressed her face to the coolness of his armor, "By the gods, Ryven, if we don't get to the training grounds in an hour we'll have to stop in the salt flats to rut like animals again."

He chuckled, gently pulling her up to stand flush with him so he could capture her mouth in his. "I truly cannot fathom not being inside you at this moment."

"The brain of the great general strategist is locked in a worthy prison, then." Mylva answered, unsure if him not being able to think of anything else was a good thing, or detrimental.

"That I am." He grinned, kissing her again.

A knock sounded before the door cracked open, "Klava and Sex Toy," Gyrna began, not entering, "The King summons you to the war room."

"Is she ever going to call me by name?" Ryven asked with a sigh.

Mylva turned slowly, allowing him to slide free. "Probably not." She smiled as she said, "I find joy in hearing what she comes up with for the day."

"It will be a problem if she calls me that in front of others."

"Why?" Mylva asked as she pulled her pants back up, "You are my sex toy."

Ryven gave another long sigh, watching her get dressed as he held his shirt in his hands. "True, but not everyone likes bedroom talk in the open."

As she situated the pieces of her abdominal and chest plates for him to buckle in place, Mylva laughed at his grumblings about having to dress. He fumbled with his shirt; the neck catching on his head, causing him to complain even more. She helped him with fastening his armor, as he had hers, and teased, "Poor man-child, you must deal with the restrictions of clothing and the public." Once his bigger pieces were on, she returned to her own, buckling her rerebraces and the rest. Then she asked, her mind circling around to what Gyrna had said, "Why the war room?"

He fixed the last buckle on his vambrace, then rocked from toes to heel a few times. "Mother commented on the lack of effort from the other royals the other day."

"Why do I need to go?" Mylva's thoughts whirled. From getting some strategies, more knowledge of the kingdom and how it worked, and then some. Whatever she could use. Other than Ryven's cock.

His brows rose toward his hairline as he regarded her, "If I go. You go. I won't be alone in trying to motivate others to spread their legs. Especially since half of them are my siblings." His armor clanked as he shuddered.

"My royals spread them readily for me."

243

Ryven cupped her chin in his hands as he said, "Did. Past tense."

She tried to pout, like he would have, but failed. "I don't get to play with my allies anymore?"

He frowned, and his eyes flashed. From his mind to hers, images of a handful of royal beatings flowed. The main show being Benz. The poor boy. "No. Mine."

"Single syllable words coming from the one that's supposed to be the smartest in all the kingdoms. Are you sure you've earned that title?" Had she earned the ability to render him thus?

"While my eloquence may be in question at the moment, I can assure you that I am, indeed, smart enough to hold such a ridiculous title. I can't help that with you, all I have spilling from my mouth are terms of endearment and awe, moans, and, apparently, claims of ownership." He paused, "The last being that you also own me." He shook his head at himself. "I believe I need to read the dictionary again."

"Do you soak words up off the page to use?"

"My powers are fed in that way, yes." He raised his brows at her, "Have I not told you that?"

She motioned toward the bed and then the limited space between them. "Ryven, we've hardly had discussions that do not pertain to mating and what our bodies can do to one another for the past week."

"Yes." He paused, then added, "I would like to say that I shall endeavor to have deeper conversations with you. But I cannot make such a promise only to break it in the next hour."

Mylva rolled her eyes as he kissed her forehead. "Let's go before you get any other ideas. Or the same ones."

He led them down the halls and entered the King's quarters and meeting rooms. The first door on the right he pushed open, letting her enter in front of him, before closing it behind them.

With windows covered in thick tapestries depicting maps, the room was darker than the rest of the castle. She surveyed the first map, drawn ages ago when people preserved knowledge more in spoken words than in writing. She recognized the three maps that followed, but not the last one. The last was new. Broader in scope and housed another three continents and several islands.

"Klava, that is what I'm about to give you." Ryven whispered in her ear as she stared at the map. "Not just the world you know, but the entirety."

"My boy undeniably inherits my charm." The king laughed from his seat at the head of the oval pine table.

Mylva turned, regarding him with a small curl of her lips. Thirteen wives surrounded the king. Queen Jerica stood beside him, her hand over his shoulder and clasped in his, and she too had a smile on her face as her dark gaze flicked between her eldest son and Klava.

Mylva straightened her spine, crushing the sense of being outnumbered in the darkened chamber. There were enough chairs surrounding the table to seat all of them present. At least no one else was arriving after her.

"He needs to remember his place. He's not Worldgod yet," Queen Moonapsa said with a tilt of her head, but there was a curl to her thin lips as she regarded Ryven.

"Yet, Mother Moon." Ryven grinned as he walked to the table and lay a hand gently on her shoulder to lean down and kiss her temple.

Worldgod. She remembered the ageless term. Was that what Ryven wanted? That title? She flicked her gaze to the largest map, wondering if King Licthan truly held the vastness it depicted outside of her own domain. With hers, Ryven truly would be Worldgod after the king passed.

He kissed the other queens the same way, stopping at his mother to allow her to wrap him in a tight embrace. He hugged her back and clasped arms with his father as he did so. "You summoned us?"

"I need your minds, boy, never question my summons." The King pointed to the table. Upon its glossy pale surface were little wooden figures of different colors, holding matching ribbons that flowed from their heads with scrawled letters. One black and one red stood tied together at the edge of the table, near the king's elbow.

"I will always question your summons, as I have since birth." Ryven retorted, studying the peg-like pieces before him. He raised a brow with a slight curl to his lips as he picked up the joined ones. "We're not married yet."

"Just think of it as your dick always in her, son." The King smirked.

"Licthan Verlite." Jerica scolded, smacking the back of the king's head. She took the carvings from Ryven and placed them on the table closer to herself. The other Queens exchanged grins, with some laughing and others suppressing their amusement.

Mylva found it endearing in a way. She kept silent, watching them interact with one another. There weren't any secrets to be uncovered here, other than the drive underneath this entire plan. Other than how to act like a family. If people could call a single man with thirteen wives and innumerable children a family and not a horde.

The King cleared his throat, smiling sheepishly at his favored queen, then he turned his black eyes upon Mylva. "My dear Klava, I would like your insight. Given your familiarity with most of your fellow rulers, and we know our children, aid us in creating… situations, if you would."

Mylva raised a brow, taking the chair the king motioned to across from him. While the table was long, it was narrow, perfect for placing pieces together upon a game board. She noted that the top of it depicted the grounds of the castle. Interesting. Ryven escaped from his mother's grasp and sat down beside her. She eyed the players, picking up the blue of Parvis and twirling it in her fingers.

Ryven was hers. His mind alone was enough to keep him by her side instead of allowing him to do damage elsewhere. But the others… why should she bother? Her royals obeyed her and siblings didn't always get along. She rested her gaze on each queen, then the king, trying to read them and their devotion to this endeavor, to each other. It was like she was looking into the eyes of her Bloodsworn.

Devoted. Ready. And willing to do anything for this plan. Why? What was at stake?

"I know this one the best. Pazai is proud and stubborn about it. She claims to detest butting heads, but she's always rising to the occasion instead of giving in. She's not trained in combat, has little stratagem in war, but is excellent in managing goods, people, and getting her kingdom through moments of chaos."

"What about her tastes?" Queen Hia asked, "Sexually?"

Klava Mylva leaned back in her chair, trying to remember a time where either she, Nava or Hava saw a concubine of Pazai's. Hava had. "Males, mostly. She likes lean, muscled, dark-skinned. The darker the better."

Two queens reached forward, plucking pegs and ribbons and moving them toward the peg for Pazai.

"Did Sihfe not woo her?" Ryven asked Queen Ranamala, Sihfe's mother.

"He has no interest in her. Says she has too many layers to paw through. He'll be exhausted by the time he can dick her."

Jerica pinched the bridge of her nose, "Klava, I must ask this now, my love, do you mind speaking plainly? Or lewdly?" Her heated glares at her husband and fellow queens elicited grins in response.

Mylva waved a hand dismissively as she said, "I do not mind at all. Curse. Speak of dicks. Blood. Speak however you see fit." Biting back a yawn as she studied the names on the ribbons of those nearest to Pazai's. She moved Faet's away, and noted how Ryven's eyes narrowed slightly, watching that orange peg closely.

"Faet is too feral looking." She murmured, giving Queen Hia a shrug. "Tataro?"

"He's mine." Queen Moonapsa leaned forward. "He enjoys playing with blades so the layers can be rid of quickly so he won't tire out." She flicked her gaze at Ranamala with a smug smirk. "He's lean, and while not the darkest of skin tones, he is as I am an even tan throughout. Tat likes a woman who stands her ground. He doesn't want them to just lie about. He enjoys walks. Hands on for the people, is his style. Does she take part in commoner things?"

"Parvis embraced the Kavkan ways, disregarding social classes if they work, or at least try to. The elderly and orphans are taken care of by Pazai and her family. That's hands on, I feel. Enough for Tataro?"

"I think that will make him curious about her, at the least," Moonapsa replied.

The King cleared his throat, "The problem with most of my children is that they are… well, interested in all."

"They take after their father in that." Jerica said with a slight smirk.

"Mother, you've had your fair share of lovers." Ryven chided.

"And that's just among us." Moonapsa grinned. "Who knows what you do in the streets?"

The King smiled too, patting Jerica's hand as the queens teased one another. "One down, twenty-two more to go."

Next was little Binesze. "How old is Monace?"

"Ten years his senior." Ranamala shook her head, "Monace prefers older. She says she's interested in Quintland."

"Guost. He's a fair ruler, and he collects exotic looking things. Monace might fit in that category." Klava hummed thoughtfully, placing the two pegs together, "He likes his drinks stout, and loosens up with a lot of them."

Ranamala nodded, "I'll tell her."

Queen Hia pointed to a peg of maroon, "Bealia for the young prince? She has spoken to him a few times, trying to comfort him, as you have been riding wet."

She would have to remember that term, she quite liked it. "Benz loves acting younger than his age. A mother figure would be ideal, but strictness and teaching capability are also musts. He will soon have to step into his father's shoes." Mylva paused before smiling and studying Hia's torso, "Do you bind your chest?"

"I do, as does my daughter. Why?"

"He likes large breasts. Like these." Ryven said while placing a hand over her chest plate and jiggling it.

"Bealia." Hia nodded and placed her daughter's peg with Prince Binesze's.

Mylva smirked as she picked up the green peg. "Enefa of Gagaint. Her companion must adore green and look fabulous in it, as it is the sole color known to them."

Ryven curled his lip beside her and shook his head. "He doesn't wear green much, but I've seen Enefa looking at Glavin. Is she interested in him?"

"When have you had time to watch another woman, boy?" The king asked with a chuckle. His chair creaked as he leaned back and took a sip from his goblet.

As Ryven lifted a shoulder, Mylva jumped into a quick run-down of Enefa. "She needs a firm hand. A mind rooted in the present and thinking of the future. Gagaint stays stuck in the past. The country has potential, but

249

lacks a leader to drive change." It felt wrong. Wrong to be having fun with this matchmaking. Had they done the same for her before Ryven entered her Kavkan?

Hia waved her hand, "Glavin is not for her. They may play with one another, but I fear Enefa will not do well under their combined powers."

"Mirtes," Ryven stated, "I think the whole green thing will drive the little toad mad, but he might find her challenging enough to fall for her in the long run."

"We don't have long run. We have few days left." Jerica pointed out, "And if Mirtes isn't already interested in her, then she is not for him. Like you, he has to be piqued, challenged, and nearly killed before he realizes he's fallen. Nadran would be a better choice."

Mylva rolled Jerica's words around. Days. They had planned everything meticulously, taking each day into account. Why was that?

"He might be too much of a dreamer for a country needing change, don't you think, Mother?" Ryven leaned forward, grabbing the gray peg that had his brother's ribbon on it.

"For now, but he also has you to guide him until he grows more accustomed to planning toward those dreams." The King smiled at his son, pride shining in his eyes.

The prince sighed and placed Nadran's peg next to Enefa's. "We're going to need to tie them together and throw them in a dungeon to get him to realize she's even there."

"We can do that." The King and two of his queens said simultaneously.

Mylva laughed and shook her head. She sifted through the pegs, picking up one that was the blue of the glaciers in her country, "This might be best for Mirtes." It would also keep that brother close in case his mind became as powerful and as hungry for the world as Ryven's. "Theiu from Hyth."

The king made a face, "He's going to spend his time hissing like a serpent with their language."

Ryven covered his mouth to hide a grin as his shoulders shook with a silent chuckle.

"Well, their royal family is born with split tongues." Klava said with a lift of her shoulder. She glanced around, "What?"

"Just imagining all the possibilities for those." Licthan rubbed his chin, eying his wives, "Especially for my ladies."

"If Mirtes is as jealous as this one," Mylva smacked Ryven's chest plate, "I foresee a problem. They do like to use their tongues in a variety of ways on their partners, and they enjoy having plenty of those. My spies told me that Theiu, in particular, has quite a large harem that she hardly leaves."

"I don't think she will search for many in her harem if Mirtes enjoys her company." Jerica finally took a seat, moving away from the king to sit on the other side of her son. "If he has a partner he likes, he hardly lets his cock go soft, much less leaving the chamber he's captured them in."

It clicked, finally. Mylva turned on Ryven, eying his groin, then raising her gaze to his. "You really mind control your cock to stay hard?"

Ryven's grin was sly, "My dear, I hardly have to use any of my powers with the sounds you make."

"That's my boy!" the king crowed.

Jerica snorted as she giggled into her hand.

Mylva rolled her eyes to the ceiling, disappointed in herself. It took her too long to learn his trick. Ryven was the only man she had ever known who could have frequent and intense sexual encounters. She'd had plenty of men drug themselves to have half the drive as the prince.

She returned her attention to the task at hand, shifting in her seat to lean her elbows on the table so she wouldn't have to watch Ryven's egotistical face out of the corner of her eye. "The others shouldn't prove too difficult."

"Not on your end. We still have three problem children. Four." The king looked at the queens as he named their children, "Wolfaran, Glavin, Faet, and Sihfe."

"It was difficult choosing which countries they could infiltrate, too." Ryven said as he eyed the four pegs Licthan pulled out and lined up in front of him. Storm cloud gray, lemon yellow, fire orange, and cherry red. "Wolfaran, acts before his brain kicks in and it's usually deadly actions. His lovers often whine of his bite marks on them, lasting weeks, and he's fond of taking them from behind and behind only."

"Probably because he hasn't found a face he likes." The king interjected.

"Agreed." Moonapsa said with confidence, she knew her son.

"Is he protective?" Mylva asked, remembering what Wolfaran looked like, and Ryven's comments from before.

"Very," was the consensus of six voices in the room.

Mylva nodded, mostly to herself, as she placed the pegs together. "Princess Revra of Rovinlan."

Moonapsa snorted, "That little mouse? He'll eat her alive."

"Or think he has to keep everyone at bay to protect the slip of a girl." Mylva pointed out, because she'd thought the same thing when she first laid eyes on Revra. Though she seemed sixteen, the woman was in her twenties. Timid to a fault, and she had a slight hesitation in her speech, especially if anyone was looking at her while she spoke. Or around her. In the same building. "Is he patient with timidity?"

She observed the room as they collectively pondered.

"He trains pups." Moonapsa added helpfully.

"That's a start." Mylva didn't think this was going to go well after all. Then she remembered one of Nava's memories with the timid princess. Nava got the girl to talk to her, and relax a bit when she led Revra to a foal. "She likes cute things."

"Wolfaran is not cute." Ryven laughed and shook his head.

"He could be to her. Especially if he's holding a pup." Jerica gave her son a look.

"Revra it is. Someone needs to monitor them to make sure he doesn't scar the girl for life." Ryven gave Moonapsa a look.

"Keep your dick out of your future wife long enough, and maybe she can be a chaperone."

"Maybe I can give them pointers. New positions." Ryven smirked, placing a hand on Mylva's thigh as he spoke.

Mylva thought for a moment and added, "I can be there when they meet, or create the meeting." Ryven was going to have to learn control at some point. "Glavin seems… interesting. He pulled Revra?"

"Glavin? Yes. He took the mouse from her home. It's a good thing that he did, from what I heard." King Licthan leaned forward, "Did you know how abusive her situation was there?"

"Since Revra was born." Mylva murmured, taking Revra's peg and twirling it in her fingers. "It's the stammer. They must have perfection in their offspring."

"Wolfaran will definitely break them of that thinking. He's as feral looking as they come. Not at all perfect in most eyes." Ryven added with a slight smirk.

Hia sighed, "Who is good enough for my Glavin?"

"He's the jumpy one, isn't he?" Mylva tried to picture the man.

"He usually isn't." Hia defended her son, "He fears Ryven, and rightly so after what you did to him."

"I taught him a lesson."

"You broke him."

"Better than him not realizing his own strength and hurting someone." Ryven leaned forward this time, too.

"He was twelve! Of course, he didn't know his own strength! He hadn't grown into it yet!" Hia stuck two fingers in Ryven's face, shaking them.

Ryven's face softened into the most innocent expression it could, taking those fingers and leaning toward her so he could kiss the back of her hand, "How many times are you going to make me apologize to you? Glavin's already forgotten, even if he is still a little scared of me."

"I can have two, can't I? I think their dynamic will be rather entertaining to watch." Mylva watched Ryven as she asked.

His neck above the collar of his armor blushed red, "Me. Mine. You can only have me."

"He's talking like he's broken." Jerica poked her son's cheek. She grinned at Klava, "You're going to have so much fun."

"She already is." Ryven rubbed a hand over his face after swatting his mother's finger away from his cheek. "Glavin. Mate. Who?"

The king spluttered on another sip of his drink. "Yes, let's talk of Glavin so Ryven can learn sentence structure again in the interim." He said with a grin while wiping off his chin on a napkin one of his wives handed him. "I thought the Prince of Wyrn."

"Does Glavin not want kids, or do you not want offspring from him?" Klava leaned back and felt Ryven's arm settle around her shoulders. His fingers toyed with her hair. She wasn't sure whether or not she liked it.

"Hia's children shapeshift. And they all choose to be both sexes at once," Ryven explained quietly, "Though the three keep their appearances leaning toward one or the other according to the company. If the Prince doesn't mind, Glavin can bear the offspring."

"Wish you had told me that before I broke you from being eloquent." She picked up Faet's peg.

Ryven took it from her fingers and set it back down in the line. "One day, you might have permission to play with them."

Mylva wondered at the pegs, the people they represented. Her royals tied to the children of King Licthan. *This could be a world at my feet. This could mean that no one goes hungry. I could do away with the strict ridiculous traditions so people can feel freedom of choice. But what is it that's being hidden?*

What were they doing now other than taking away choices?

"Is this…" she couldn't put it into words.

Ryven took her hand, pressing his fingers into her palm in a gentle squeeze. Gloves separated them, yet she felt reassured. "They still have a choice," he said, "we're just giving them a little push."

"Like you pushed me by knocking me out?"

The Prince flinched before he stated in a low voice, "I did the best I could under the circumstances. My plan did not go as well as I thought. Otherwise, you would have your sisters and more generals waiting for you to come back home."

"Kavkans are a special breed of people to force such plans to go awry." The King murmured. "Forgive us, if you desire. None of us wanted bloodshed. We cannot make up for your loss, but we hope to give you more love and room to heal."

She watched as the queens nodded in agreement and felt Ryven's hand still in hers. Nava and Hava would have fit in with this family immediately. A warmth settled in her chest, and another behind her eyes as her throat tickled. She mimicked their nods, swallowing back the tears. "Glavin and Prince Avy?"

"Do you think they might fit?" Hia asked, staring at the yellow peg representing one of her sons.

"I know little of Avy, but the country is beautiful with a wide range of types of people. The royals there work just as hard as their people and have helped medically when sickness strikes." Mylva stretched her tired muscles; sitting, doing them no good, even if she was torn between fun and wariness.

"We shall see." Hia nodded, hunting down the green peg with Avy's name on it and placing it behind Glavin's. "Now Faet, please."

Mylva studied the pieces on the table. He was daring and feral with the toothy look. Who would go for that of her allies? "Dehdala's Morxas." She picked up the black peg swirled with gray. "She's… untameable."

"Is that the woman that literally tore her room apart?" Hia asked as she looked at her fellow queens.

"The one we are about to have to tie up in one of the common rooms so we can actually know what she looks like?" Jerica asked them.

Ranamala nodded, "That's the one."

Mylva smiled, wondering how the two would react to each other and playing out scenarios in her mind. "Don't tell Faet I saddled him with that beast. If Faet doesn't work and if Wolfaran isn't for Revra, maybe they can switch." She lifted a shoulder.

"Complete opposites?" Ryven asked her.

She nodded, "Her own mother is at her wit's end. Whoever gathered Morxas up and hauled her here probably received a hefty sum as a reward. She is never home, always out in the wilderness. When they gather her to bring her home, it's like bringing in a wild animal."

"Tataro brought her in." Moonapsa stated, "He couldn't give me a clear description of her. Even on the ship, she locked herself up in a room."

"Well, Faet, more power to you, my son." The King chuckled and placed Morxas' peg next to his son's. "Last but not least, Sihfe."

"He seems nice enough. Handsome. Why hasn't anyone chosen him?"

"Because he's lazy." Ryven answered readily.

"Xiexes' queen, or was her sister the heir brought here?" Mylva asked after some thought and scanning the pegs. The scribbles on the ribbons were too small to see on some of them.

"Xiexes…" The King tapped his chin, "Ah, it was the Queen. Queen Rix."

Mylva made a face, "She never sits still. Not even on a hunt."

"Might make it difficult for Sihfe to fall for her. He likes to lie back." Ranamala spoke of her son with a small smile, "Unless you are thinking they could rub off on each other?"

She nodded, "That's what I was envisioning. Even I have a challenging time standing and doing nothing when she's around. She's probably cleaning or doing something ridiculous as we speak."

"We have seen little of her. Perhaps we need her to help mend what Morxas destroyed." One of the Queens spoke up.

"She'd do it. Don't tell her about it. Not sure Morxas would survive Rix." Mylva secretly wanted to get the two in the same room for as long as she knew about them, but she wouldn't admit it out loud.

A Queen, quiet until now, nodded, placing Rix's peg next to Sihfe's. "We have a plan until one of them falls apart with no care between them. The others, I think, will be alright finding love on their own. Rather bland people, but social."

"You're talking about your own children, you know, Mutara?" Jerica laughed.

"I like my boring, no chaos offspring. Far better than any of yours." She flicked her long fingers toward Moonapsa and Ranamala specifically. "Though, they do amuse."

"Are we done?" Ryven asked, hands already braced against the arms of his chair.

"Yes, my son. Go wet your dick. Hurry now, before it falls off." The King chuckled, waving them away.

Chapter 17

After their newly formed morning sex ritual, Mylva bathed for a solid hour. She soaked in the heat, and again when Gyrna touched it up with a bucket of boiling water. Her Bloodsworn boiled the water, so Mylva wouldn't have to waste her magic. Ryven took it upon himself to check how dangerous Morxas truly was and to aid Faet if needed. That left the Klava free to visit Revra, the little princess of timidity.

"She's usually in her rooms. But every other day she appears at the early breakfast, so she won't get in trouble." Gyrna explained, her network of spies grew each day. "Then she scurries back to her room and stays there."

"When does Wolfaran eat?"

"Not until lunch, my Klava."

"Late riser or doing other things until then?" Mylva stood, allowing Gyrna to dry her off and dress her. She chose not to wear her armor this time, but a tunic and pants ensemble that was embroidered to mimic the designs on her gear. Ryven paid attention to the little details. Unnecessary of him, but she admired it.

"I'm not sure. He doesn't have a personal servant attend him."

Mylva made a sound of acknowledgement, very well. She would find a way. She hoped the black wouldn't scare Revra like her protective suit always did. Basau led her to Revra's chambers, and she knocked.

Revra pulled the door ajar a crack, her bright blue eyes wide and bloodshot. The woman, who looked like a child, had been crying. Once she recognized Klava, she opened the door a little further, still not wide enough to step through.

"Klava?" Her little voice squeaked.

"Revra?" she teased the girl lightly, holding her hand out, steady and welcoming.

The little princess stared at her fingers. She rubbed her own hands along her skirt, gripping the thin fabric for a moment before raising a single, trembling hand to rest it in Klava's. "S-so warm." She stammered, redness filling her cheeks even as she looked away, her light brown hair spilling forward off her shoulder to curtain her face from view.

"I always am. Have you been well?"

Revra trembled all over, her free hand fisting in her skirts. The dress was a soft green, like spring leaves and covered her from neck to ankle, but it was of the thin material Rovilans preferred even though they were in the north and half the country held snow most of the year. Revra's was pleated and sewn in such a way that the material became thick, and hid the softness of her body, making her look more like a dress than a person.

Mylva took that as her answer as she saw Revra's full lips working on silent words. "This place isn't too bad with the right company." She rubbed her thumb over Revra's knuckles with a slow swipe. No sudden movements with this skittish little mouse. "Let's take a small walk around. Will you accompany me?"

The curtain of hair swished as the princess nodded.

"Come on then. I'll let you talk my ear off."

Revra snorted, trembling still, but she took a step toward her Klava. Then another. And Mylva gently pulled the door closed behind her before Revra could bolt back inside. She held the royal's small, frail hand and allowed her to take the first step down the hall when she was ready.

After wandering the halls for an hour with Mylva pointing out a funny looking cloud out of the window, or commenting on a painting of the royal family, Revra finally opened up. "I hate it h-here."

Mylva waited patiently, watching the clouds below as they flowed lazily across the blue sky in puffy whiteness. Even up here, she could smell the rain to come. Revra could feel eyes on her just as well as Klava's hand in hers.

"It's w-w-warm. Scary st-trangers!" Revra's hand tightened on Klava's, shaking like a leaf in the wind. "I j-just want to go."

When Revra said nothing more, Mylva squeezed her fingers gently. "I cannot do anything about taking you away. I cannot offer you protection if you step down from this challenge King Licthan has set before us." She said softly, trying to be as gentle as possible. "But I know that there are animals below. Will that make you feel a little better? To have something to hold or pet?"

Revra finally took her fist off her skirt to swipe at her eyes. "Yes."

Mylva led her to the pathway down. She realized they didn't have an abductor in their presence, and the absurdity of her plan became obvious; she looked at the script floating in the glittering cloud of the flooring. "Need to go down?"

She blinked, looking around for the ethereal voice as Revra clamped down on her side like a frightened child. "Yes."

The cloud glowed, and they were at the bottom. Mylva shook her head. She would never get used to this place. Wait. She paused, stepping out of the tower with Revra still clinging to her, but walking on her own. She worked the passage. On her own. She could escape if she wanted, but she didn't. Not anymore. Her plan was superior to any she could populate while on the run.

Mylva followed her nose to the stables and hoped there was a foal or two. When she didn't find any, she frowned.

A stable hand stopped before them, the same boy who liked her mare but feared the little pot bellied lizard. Revra automatically hid behind Klava. "Looking for your horse?"

Hardly. Her mare was unmistakable amid the thick, plain colored beasts. "No, I was hoping to comfort my friend here with something to pet. Something young. Small."

"Cute?" the stable boy offered with a smile. "Come with me." He dropped off a few sheaves of hay into two stalls. Then they were out of the hay and sweat scented building and walking down a winding alley between buildings. After too much time, because Revra was panting like her little body was about to burst, the alley ended at a gate which the stable hand opened. He motioned them through. "It's where we wean and take care of animals without mothers. Have fun!"

Revra ran through the gate before Mylva could thank the boy. She sighed, thankful that Revra was happy. It still didn't help her with finding Wolfaran, so she could make them get along with one another, though. The little princess squealed and began laughing as Mylva made sure the gate was secure behind them.

She leaned against the wall, watching Revra sit in the middle of the packed dirt corral and pull a dust covered little piglet into her lap. She was certainly glad she didn't have to face Revra's parents after bringing their daughter back with a dirty, and probably torn by the time she was through, dress.

Out of habit, Mylva scanned the area. In the doorway to a small, low-roofed building was a shadow. Focusing, her eyes adjusting, she noted it was a man. One hand rested in a band of sunlight, revealing the honey colored skin of Moonapsa's line. It was wide, veins feeding musculature none of Moonapsa's children held other than the one she was looking for, Wolfaran.

She couldn't have planned this better if she had tried.

As if sensing her gaze, Wolfaran disappeared deeper into the structure. Mylva moved slowly toward Revra and crouched beside the woman. Sure enough, she spotted a rip with a little hoof still ripping into it from a deer-like animal with nubby tusks along its snout instead of horns on top of its head. Revra didn't have enough hands to pet all the little ones gathering around her.

"I think I heard smaller ones in there. Thought you might want to check it out too," Mylva said softly, running her fingers over the soft furred head of a rambunctious piglet.

Revra grinned up at her through the curtain of her hair which babies were chewing on here and there. "May I?" Excitement or love of animals cleared up Revra's stammering like magic.

"I don't see why not. Here." She gently helped Revra disentangle herself from the babies and followed the princess at a small distance as she went into the room.

Watching through a window, she saw Wolfaran stare up at the girl from his seat on the floor. Things that looked half pup and half kitten all over his lap as he held three milk bottles to three of their mouths. Revra squirmed, wringing her hands, then one of the little fluffs yawned with a tiny howl and she was basically in Wolfaran's lap and grabbing a bottle to feed it.

Mylva stayed for a few moments longer, making sure Wolfaran didn't run Revra off. Neither spoke. Just keeping each other company while feeding animals, for a while, until Revra began asking questions. Wolfaran's voice was soft, like a puppy growl as he answered readily, those honey eyes of his staring at Revra like she was a gift from the gods.

Her job was done.

"You could've warned me she had claws and a scream like a dying bunny. But louder." Ryven's first words to her came from her bath in her room later that evening. She'd stayed out, surveying the couples forming, and the others that were keeping to themselves. Only returning to her chambers after supper.

"You're a warrior. You're supposed to be ready for anything."

Ryven snorted, touching a rake of clawed open wounds across his right cheek with a fingertip.

"You heal fast, why aren't you using your magic to heal those?" She canted her head as she slid her clothes off and let them drop to the floor. After Basau picked them up, she and Gyrna left the two alone.

"I haven't been able to feed it." His eyes drifted down her body, "Been busy with making you sated."

"Well, I think I've found someone to help you out there." When Ryven sat up in the bath, the water sloshed, and she continued, "Up close, he's something else."

"Who?"

She bit back a smile as he looked just as feral as some of his siblings. "The way he takes care of little baby things lets me know I won't be saddled with all the child care if he gets me pregnant." She slid into the water of the bath, lukewarm, might as well have been ice water to her.

As she imagined Wolfaran manhandling her, she trailed her hands up the taut muscles of Ryven's arms.

He growled, lunging forward to pin her to the other side of the tub. The water splashed out onto the floor with the force of his movement. "What is it I can do to make sure you never picture another man like that again?" His words spilled through gritted teeth as he hovered over her, skin gleaming, muscles bunched as if in the middle of an attack on an enemy.

She smiled up at him, placing her hand on his chest as she pictured both him and Wolfaran pleasuring her. The golden hands cupped and kneaded her breasts from behind, while Ryven's tongue raked from her clit down her slit.

His lips pressed together, forming a thin line as his eyes narrowed on hers. "Wolfaran is as jealous as I. He doesn't share."

"I think I'm good enough to convince, don't you?" She forced herself to picture Wolfaran thrusting slow and hard into her as she wrapped her limbs around him.

Ryven cursed and stepped out of the bath. He grabbed a towel, beginning to dry himself off before wrapping it around his waist. "I'll be right back."

"Where you going?"

"To cut his dick off."

She laughed, throwing her head back and holding on to the sides of the tub so she wouldn't slide down in the water and drown herself laughing. Tears slid down her face as she kept on, not able to stop. The look on his face with his hand on the door handle made it worse.

As she calmed down, he ran a hand down his face. Still giggling between hiccups, she wiped the hot tears from her cheeks. The mirth brought a release in her chest and mind, like something broken was healed a little. She watched him stalk back to her. Mylva reached out and pulled the towel off him. "I'll be disappointed if you make all your brothers celibate. And your strategy will go awry even more."

"Stop messing with me like that, or the plan will be smoke and fog." He said as he bent and lifted her from the bath. After a few long strides, he practically threw her onto the mess of pillows, blankets, and rugs before the fire.

She grunted, the pain of her elbow hitting the floor between pillows dissipated as she soaked in the heat of the low burning fire beside her. Then he was on her. Spreading her legs wide as his mouth found her slit. His fingers opening her.

His tongue and teeth were rough. Little pin pricks of pain melded with shards of pleasure. Her orgasm arrived quick and hard, throwing her body into an arching stretch and she couldn't catch her breath.

Ryven crawled over her. Using both hands, he elevated her hips and positioned a long pillow beneath them. His cock rammed into her. "I'm better than Wolfaran." He stated as he pulled out of her slowly, stopping with the head of his cock barely inside her folds. His eyes darkened as she tried to sit up. He pressed her back down with one hand splayed over her stomach while the other lifted her hips, keeping her down. When his body slapped against hers and he was inside her to the hilt, he leaned over her, growling the next statement, "Way better than Faet."

His thrusts were hard and fast, driving her shoulders into the pillows until they slid out from under her.

Another orgasm was right at her fingertips when he stopped. She clawed at the pillows around her as he dragged himself out of her to place the head of his manhood against her clit. Her hips bucked, searching for the friction she so desperately needed, only to have him still her. "Glavin couldn't do anything like this for you." He raked its length up her clit, then down.

"Smoke be fire, take me!"

"Who am I?"

She stared up at him as he held her still, his cock completely gone from her person. "Ryven."

"Who is the only one that can drive you to completion like I have been the past week?"

"Ryven." She liked this mood he was in. It sent fire and ice through her body in waves as she trembled in her need for him.

"What is the name of the man that's going to give you the world, because you deserve it, and so much more?" His voice softened with the last few words.

"Ryven."

He lifted her onto his thighs, then slid his cock inside her. His arms steal bands around her, holding her vibrating body still over him. Face upturned, he said, "Hold on."

She did, and he gave her stars.

Darkness released the injurious thoughts. Ryven watched her sleep. Her chin length hair shining in moonlight that also made her skin pale compared to its true hue. His woman. The one he chose for himself. The fires of volcanoes embodied.

She hadn't killed anyone lately. That was an improvement. He could feel her power writhing like it had in Kavkan. Therefore, he knew she could do as she pleased. What was holding her back from attacking them all?

He hoped it was him. But all he received from her were thoughts of his siblings in her playful torture of him. A teasing he was sure was progress, but another part of him thought this was a fresh tactic. Testing him to see… something.

As he quietly left the bed, he used his powers to keep her mind in dreams, and pulled his pants on to pad out of the room. He wandered the halls, finding his way into the place he most enjoyed. The library.

He wasn't alone. "Mother?"

"I had a feeling you wouldn't rest this night, son." Her voice was soft, welcoming. She motioned to the small table before her, "Tea?"

It was like he walked into a hug as he listened to her voice. He nodded and sat across from her. "You couldn't sleep either?"

Jerica lifted her shoulders slightly before pouring them both a cup, "Not when my son needs me, no."

They sat in silence for a while, sipping tea, enjoying one another's company. Then Ryven asked, "How do I know she won't kill me when I go back?"

"You don't." Jerica answered, barely a pause between them. "That is why I wanted to speak to you about your wedding. We have the safeguards planted in the ceremony. You must tangle your life with hers soon."

Ryven rubbed his eyes and leaned forward with his elbows on his knees, "Did you feel you were going to kill father all the time?"

She laughed, "Only in certain moments." A sip of her tea, and she set the cup down to gather her son's hands in hers, "Look at me," she waited until he did, "You are in love with her. That alone should be enough to make this work. She's fiery and experienced only battles, you'll need patience. This patience needs protection, though. If not, then your plan falls apart."

"What if I end up creating more damage?" Ryven searched his mother's eyes, "What if instead of showing her what she's missed, I end up shoving her into another cage?" He snorted, "I brought her here, to a gilded cage."

"Ryv, relationships are a partnership. There is give and there is take. Some pain will happen, but with you knowing the breaks, you can heal them properly. You know her wounds from her cages, use the techniques to soothe them. Sometimes you have to re-break a bone to set it correctly, yes? Sometimes, it might feel like that. It's alright. But you must let her choose to heal, and at what pace she wants." She squeezed his hands. "I do admit, I worry for you. You have chosen a terrible beast to tame and mend."

"She's not that terrible." Ryven muttered, watching his mother's hands on his.

"You need not defend her to me, son. I know. And your lives together shall be a splendid beauty incomparable to any we know once you let each other in."

His brows drew together, and he looked up into her eyes, "I have let her in."

She shook her head, "You fear her, still. With that fear and mistrust, there are still parts of you protected from her." Jerica grinned, "Just because you've bedded her, doesn't mean she's had all of you, nor you her."

Ryven rolled his eyes, "Yes, Mother, I understand." He grinned right back at her, "I'm glad I got your brains."

She laughed, "And for Klava's sake, I'm glad you got your father's dick." She patted his hands, then loosened her hold to finish her tea.

"Mother?"

"Hm?"

"Help me get the ceremony ready, please?"

"Of course, my son."

Chapter 18

They worked together for two more weeks, formulating plans for Mylva's underlings and Ryven's siblings, making sure the relationships that were formed were good and not toxic. As best as she could tell by analyzing each person, the pairings would work. Some might even learn to love one another. Before she knew it, there were only twenty remaining. She still hadn't figured out why she and hers had only ninety days to make their choices.

She stared at Ryven from her seat across the window in the library. He liked this spot. Reading fed his magic, and the book in his hands was thick, but he made quick work of it. They had settled into a deeper pattern.

It shocked her to think that she had a routine with him.

Especially one so lax. Wake up, sex. Eat, sex. Bathe, train with the army, sex. Bathe again with probably more sex, eat, check on allies, eat, read, sex, sleep and repeat. She was still trying to get used to the reading. Some books she started she didn't like at all. Mylva found one and was halfway through it, at least. It wasn't making her exceedingly excited to pick it up, but it wasn't terrible either.

"Are you at a stopping point?" Ryven asked.

She nodded, hooking the small ribbon he'd given her for a bookmark into the page.

He leaned back into the window, his eyes half lidded and on her. "I've been meaning to talk to you about the ceremony. I'm running out of time to do it, so I think it best to just get it out there." He drew in a breath, his chest expanding with plenty of room in his loose black shirt. He had a million of those shirts.

"Since these marriages have so much resting on them, each one is performed with a blood swear. It's… complicated." Ryven's jaw worked.

It was unusual for him to be searching for words when she was fully dressed, so she looked down, making sure her breasts weren't hanging out. They were where they were supposed to be. "How complicated? What are the terms?"

"I need your hand." He held his out, his dark eyes searching hers, "I want your opinions right as they come to you as I speak."

That wasn't a good sign. Could she control herself enough to not give all of her thoughts away? Probably not. Her gaze flicked to the book he'd placed between them. She shouldn't have let him read this day. She laid her hand in his. Then again, why did she need to hide anything from him now? "Begin."

"A child must be born between us within the first five years. If there are complications, this part of the pact can be amended as long as both parties agree."

That wasn't so bad. "Agreed." She wanted her daughter by then, anyway. It was time she had an heir.

"Suicide to get out of the marriage will cause anyone you have blood ties with to perish."

That was acceptable. Mylva couldn't stomach the thought of killing herself because of the Bloodsworn. Any one of them could have four to a hundred Bloodsworn of their own. "I don't think I can agree to that. If I go into battle, I fight hard without consideration of my safety."

"That wouldn't be intentional. But I also know you're not the type to commit suicide either, so I wasn't worried about that part. And with all this, we shouldn't have any more wars, Mylva. That's the whole reason for this." He swallowed, looking down at their joined hands.

There was another thing there. Something he was biting back and keeping to himself. Mylva could feel it in her bones.

"Assassination attempts will result in your death, too. Any made by you, or by anyone in your command."

Not thirty days ago, that would have been a problem.

She looked into his eyes, watched as her emotions and thoughts warred with his in those dark depths. Mylva remembered those ideas clearly. Her desire to kill him with every breath until one day, it was only every other breath. Then she didn't want to murder him at all.

"You still want to kill me?" His hand tightened over hers.

No. It surprised her, but it didn't at the same time. Such an odd emotion to override everything she was born with, trained to do, and understood. No. Her heart thudded as she thought about the single word. It was as if the fire within her reached for him, wrapping him in a protective armor of her own creation. Tears spilled down her cheeks. Tears?

"Mylva," he breathed her name as if he needed it to survive.

Was he making her cry? Why was she sad? Perhaps she missed sharing this realization. Or it was the fact that she could feel. Actually experience an emotion other than rage toward a person not linked by blood.

"No, my love. Do you want proof?"

Heat entered her cheeks, the tracks from her eyes drying in a sizzle. "Yes."

A flood. His thoughts roared into her mind, tearing her apart. Her heart burst. Stars and the world at her feet, their laughter together. Hope. Fear she would get sick one day, or get hurt. He didn't want her to even have a paper-cut? She laughed as more emotions spilled down her cheeks.

Madness. Her sanity was breaking.

As soon as he finished sharing his thoughts with her, he pulled them back, leaving her with her own. Her own terror. Her own hope. Her heart beating for him. Her fire burning for him. Only one Klava ever spoke of finding love. She remembered Hava's memory of reading the journals from past Klavas.

It was like this.

Love. She loved her enemy. Ryven.

The one who killed her generals. The one who tore her from her home. The one looking at her right now and with this hand holding hers. A hand that killed her Bloodsworn Sisters.

Sacrilege. Madness.

No. She could hear Nava's voice. Liberty. Nava thought this would be freedom, this marriage. Why did she have to put herself up for death? Why had Ryven taken it when Nava surrendered?

His free hand stretched toward her cheek.

She snapped her head back. "Tell me."

His hand dropped, and Ryven seemed to deflate before her eyes. "We thought it would be best to end their suffering."

"We?" She couldn't deny their hardships. It had kept her up plenty of nights, tore her apart on the inside like a frenzied beast. Worrying about them. Mylva hated hearing their screams and cries as they had to change to be exactly her.

"It was decided between the Mothers, Father, and I." He rubbed his thumb over the back of her hand. "On the outside looking in, it looked like you were torturing them. Given some of the thoughts you've had… I can see it wasn't quite what we assumed. We prepared everything to either kill you and set them free, or release all of you. Then I stayed there. Watched you. Learned about them. It shouldn't have happened like it did. In the end, their end, I wanted to free them. Let them choose, like I wanted you to do."

"It was torture." She pulled her hand from his and covered her face. "Nava thought you brought me freedom, that's why she…"

Nava's final memory flashed through Mylva's mind. The color of the rough black floor and the scrape of her greaves against it as she knelt. Noticing the lifeless green fingertips of Hava out of the corner of her eyes. The hope and idea Ryven had given her. She had a final wish. Nava wanted to see Mylva smile one last time.

Ryven's arms came around her, pulling her into his lap, pressing her against his chest. He rocked her like a child. His lips were on the crown of her head, murmuring gentle words of encouragement to heal.

The sobs burning her ears were annoying. Who was sobbing like that? Why did she feel like she was emptying out poison?

Her tremors wouldn't cease. She couldn't stop the sobs that made her body lurch deep into his embrace. Every scar. Every tear. Every lash of the whip. Every scream of pain. All that she had put them through crashed through her.

Every blow to her own body prompted the immediate thought that she would have to repeat it on Hava. Then Nava.

The sword pushed through the gap of her armor into her lung; the hot gush of blood as her lung collapsed. Mylva realized she would have to make them live it with her own hands. Nava's scream. The warm wash of Hava's blood as it slid down her side and onto her fingers whilst she tried to hold her Bloodsworn still.

Watching them give up everything they could have been to be her.

The traditions prevented her from making her own choices.

Ryven.

Ryven was holding her.

Ryven loved her like no other.

At least, not to her knowledge. She was certain, without any doubt, he cared for her. Deeply. No man in her life would hold her like this as she emptied the poisons of her past. Purged herself of the burden of Hava and Nava's tortured life.

Weak. Broken. Not Kavkan. Not worthy to be Klava.

"Listen to me." Ryven's voice was hoarse again, tight. "Listen well. I love you. You are strong. You may be broken, but you are healing. You will heal. You will be stronger. You are definitely Kavkan and you are worthy of more than you can imagine. Klava be smoke, you are more than that."

He kissed her forehead, and said, "One day, these broken hateful thoughts of yourself will melt away. I hope they will. I will work my best to make them go, to help you heal, to love you like no one else can."

There his lips curled against her temple, "Especially my brothers. They are not at all as loving, caring, and… all those other attributes as I am. All attributes, I am the best. Best choice you can make."

She cracked, smiling through the salty tracks as her crying stilled a moment for her to laugh.

"Sorry. You can keep crying. Let it all out." Ryven murmured, still holding her tightly against him.

Mylva cried a little more, pondered further, and at last regained her composure. Her mind calmed. Her heartbeats were strong, as was his against her ear. Ryven. He was her choice. Her choice. A man she cared for. A man she wanted to be with. Ryven was her decision, want, and need.

She swallowed back the burn of more tears. She didn't think she had any left. Mylva, Klava of Kavkan, made a choice all on her own.

He'd held her in silence for a long time before she asked that. A comfortable silence. One she nearly fell asleep in. Who knew crying like this was so exhausting?

"Anything else?"

"Well, I am putting in a few clauses, still working out the details."

She sat up a little, remaining in the circle of his arms and legs. She never thought there would be a man large enough to hold her comfortably. "Like what?"

"Like… I get to kiss you first thing every morning, and last thing every night on all days. The punishment will be… seven orgasms of nonstop sex?"

Mylva rolled her eyes, and he smiled.

"Alright, five. Five orgasms."

"Be serious." She tried to get her raw throat to hold a scolding tone, but it didn't work.

"I am!"

"Ryven."

He made a sound, half moan, half groan in a scant breath, "I love when you say my name. Ah! You have to say my name at least once a day."

"What's the punishment there?" She shook her head at him, trying to wipe some of the grime off her face and frowning at the mess she'd made on his shirt and chest.

"Oh none. Because I'll make you say it several times, as I have before, with my several talents." Ryven leaned forward, pressing his forehead against hers. His dark eyes staring into her green. "Mylva, promise me something?"

She raised a brow before saying, "Depends on what it is."

His smile didn't reach his eyes which were locked on hers. "Promise me not to keep anything bottled up. If you want or need to cry, do it. If you need to scream, do it. To beat something, inform me so I can at least put some armor on."

Mylva grinned, "I promise." She looked down at his shirt again, "We might need another bath."

"Yes, my Klava. You don't have to tell me twice to get you naked and wet," Ryven said as he lifted her and strode out into the hall.

"I can walk."

"As can I." Ryven smirked down at her.

She sighed and knew that she was going to have her hands full with this man in more ways than one.

Marriage. Most of her hated the idea. A binding ritual. She couldn't kill him.

Did she want to?

She liked him. Again, she thought of marriage, pivoting on her point of view to regard it in another light. Ryven at her side, the world at her feet, and an end to tradition that did nothing but spill the blood of those she loved.

Mylva paused, debating on words before she let her knuckles hit the wood several times.

A slip of a woman opened the door with wide, pale eyes. "Is Pazai in?" Mylva asked, peering past the woman.

"May I ask who calls upon her?"

"Klava!" Pazai's voice cut through the room beyond the door and made the girl jump.

As the servant opened the door for her with a smile, Mylva crossed the threshold. It had to be a mild torture to serve one as picky as Pazai, she thought, poor woman. "Sunrise is grand." Mylva said in a gentle tone as she met the queen's eyes.

"I cannot wait for sunset." Pazai's coded reply was quick before she barked orders, "Out!" The queen, draped in her usual blue, waited with folded hands for her six maids to leave before bowing her head slightly, "I'm at your disposal."

"I am to marry." The consternation on the queen's face would usually make Mylva feel a rather joyous triumph, but she settled for a grin. "As are you."

Pazai huffed, her thick skirts swirling as she paced, then sat down hastily at her vanity. "You are a fool, Klava." She bit out, her face paling with each word.

"I am, perhaps. I recall telling you to choose well, and have you not?" Mylva raised her brows as the paleness reached its peak, ratcheting with each syllable she uttered.

"No, Klava."

Mylva dropped her gaze to the blue one, staring at her through the mirror. The queen only turned her back when she was upset. "Then you shall go with the one I chose for you."

Pazai's swallow was slow, as if she'd been chewing on tree sap. "And who, pray tell, is that?"

"Tartaro."

Blue skirts swished as Pazai was up again, her ghostly cheeks bloomed to red in a few steps. "That aggravating little monkey? I shall not!"

"So you've met? Good." Mylva bit back the laughter and stamped down the blood simmering. Why hadn't she come up with a scheme like this before? It was fun.

"I- you- I'll have a-" Pazai bit her finger, turning to face away from Mylva to collect herself. Her shoulders rolled back, head tilted high, and she turned back to face her Empress. "As you wish, Klava."

The red in her cheeks made her words a lie, but Mylva trusted Pazai wouldn't disappoint. "If he is truly that despicable to you, quickly choose another that is more to your liking. You have little time left, pale queen."

Pazai touched her cheeks, her eyes flashing, "I shall provide you a marriage to the best of my ability. Shall I produce an heir the same night?"

Mylva chuckled while saying, "Come now, Pazai. It isn't that bad, is it?" She watched the queen squeeze her hands together in front of her, then smooth her skirts.

"I suppose not. Tartaro has been making… passes. He seems an intelligent sort, if not… dangerous."

"Make him a few blades with your iron, and he'll fall into your lap at your bidding, I'm sure." Mylva said with a smile as she opened the door. It was clear Pazai would need a moment to fume.

"Klava, are you sure of this? You may gain the world, but what is in it for us?"

Mylva turned back, Kavkan roaring in her veins because she didn't know the one detail she needed to tell the truth. So she lied, "Life. A good one."

The paleness returned as Pazai answered, "Yes, Klava."

Mylva's muscles were tight, and her footfalls were loud in her own ears as she strode down the hall. Pazai was half audacious and the other half ego, a combination that rarely got under her skin, unless both were aimed at her. It was a novel experience, having both hit her while she herself was still questioning a step in the proceedings.

A screech rang in her eardrums before she realized an extra weight upon her shoulders, and claws digging through her shorn hair. Instinct had her plucking the thing off her with one hand, while the other searched for an absent mace. A palm smacked her cheek. The smack of flesh against her chest plate sounded with another shriek, but her armor didn't budge, nor did she. The wild tangles of hair covering a dark face, and her grip on a ragged dress, shared the identity of her attacker.

"Morxas!" she growled in the girl's face, "Calm yourself!"

The girl had too many limbs with four and was far too flexible with all of them. Mylva grasped an arm, tried setting the girl up on her feet, but when she kept pulling her legs up to kick before her toes could touch, Mylva growled yet again. "I mean it, Morxas. I know this isn't your true self. I am a friend, remember?" What had her sisters done to soothe the princess?

Right.

"Little turtle, help me in. I shall forever be your friend."

As the words spilled from her lips in a broken melody, Mylva looked up and down the halls to see if anyone was near. Only the gods, Morxas, and her own embarrassment held witness. She continued, still trying to set the girl on her feet, but having to bring her back up by the back of her dress when those long legs just folded up under her.

On all fours, there wasn't a way to catch Morxas the Wildling.

"Little turtle, some greens for you, see I am your friend." Mylva didn't have a single green thing on her, nor any food, but it was part of the little rhyme Nava had contrived for the wild woman. Morxas stopped slapping and clawing. Her hands folded in front of her, tangling with the ragged shirt hanging off her pear-shaped frame. Mylva let her hang from her fist at her side, "My dearest friend, we shall protect one another."

Another small growl, and the princess grew quiet.

"How are you, Morxas?" Mylva tried to get her to stand one more time, and the legs folded up again. She sighed, switching hands, holding the princess up by the back of her stained shirt to her left, where there was a convenient seat. She plopped the wildling down there and blocked her in.

"Grand. Grand well. You? Oh, you are fire and ice. You are more than grand." Morxas' grin was wide through her hair, her too white teeth large and sharp.

"I suppose I am. Have you been eating? Drinking water?" Mylva brushed back the wild unkept brown strands from the princess' face.

"Yes. Yes. Yes. Morxas eats. Eats all. Drinks all. Wine is good. So's the brown potent stuff."

"Coffee. That's the last thing you need. Speak to me, as a friend, for I am." Mylva watched the green eyes slow in their darting exploration of the area. The shallow breathing deepened. The wide grin softened. "That's better. Isn't being your true self more comfortable here?"

Morxas heaved a sigh, "True self? What is my true self, you call this true? For I am me. All me. All true to me."

Mylva smiled because she wasn't sure what else to express on her face. "True to you, yes. I just mean to make it easier on you. To help you gain friends. Allies. To keep you from… further harm." She remembered the horror her sisters walked in on. First Hava, a decade or so ago, Morxas was barely to her knees and already scalped, scared, and trembling. Then Nava, only three to four years ago, watched as they captured the princess and locked her down on a metal table to draw her blood, test her skin, and make her reach for her powers.

Nava had slaughtered them, the so-called healers and worshipers of Dehdala. And she began singing the song that always calmed Morxas down as she held the girl after the bloodbath. Seeing all that death couldn't have been healthy for her, but Nava was convinced she didn't have a choice.

"You are an ally, still. Yes? Revra, too. Yes?"

Mylva nodded, with a strong desire to growl a warning to not go near the little mouse, but she kept her tongue.

"Am I to think that these dancing glory birds are allies, too?"

Mylva's eyes bulged as she held in her laughter. Ryven appeared in her mind, large shimmering feathers spread out behind him like the birds Morxas described. It wasn't a difficulty to picture the others after that. "Yes, Morxas."

"I can't eat them?"

"No."

The wild princess grumbled to herself before she spoke up. "But if I eat them, they'll eat me and I'll never have to go back." The whites of her eyes grew prominent again.

Mylva knelt, placing her hands on the girl's knees, "Trust me. When you go home, they'll never harm you again. You will have an ally by your side, his or her army at your back. You shall be safe for the rest of your days."

"Until they learn of me. The darkness." Her voice was barely above a whisper, and her body folded in on itself more.

"No. They'll love you for it." Mylva had experience with the horrors of Morxas' bloodline. Every other generation bore a godlike child. While Mylva's goddess blood was of flame, Morxas' was the black of ichor, death.

Silence wrapped them in the moment, before Morxas said in a quiet voice. "They didn't stop. After you killed them. New ones replaced the dead ones."

Mylva frowned, her blood boiling. She figured as much, but she'd hoped that Morxas could control the situation as she was of age, and in her powers. She anticipated wrong. "Forgive me. I didn't protect you."

"You cannot be in over three places at once." Morxas sneered in her face, "You said for me to unleash." The princess replaced the sneer with a pout in the blink of an eye. "I could not. Shall not. Not again."

Mylva wondered if she'd made the right choice in partners for this one. Morxas needed a murderer at her side. "I hope you won't have to. Choose wisely, here, Morxas. A protector for you."

Morxas stared at her slender hands. "I will take the scraps, as I always do."

A voice echoed down the hall from one of the intersections, causing Morxas screeched and frog-hopped over Mylva to run down the opposite way. The empress watched her scurry away and disappear. She hoped it wasn't in to some strange room. But if it was, perhaps it would lead to a prime choice for the girl.

Chapter 19

Ryven read over the oath again for the fifteenth time it felt like. It was probably closer to twenty-fifth. He had to make sure it was foolproof. If anyone could break an oath, it would be his future wife.

Wife.

Mylva agreed to marry him. He grinned. And because his father and mother were staring at his grin, he leaned forward and placed his forehead on the desk in front of him. The pressure keeping his wits about him instead of on the fact that the woman of his dreams accepted him.

"Son."

"I know, I'm getting there. Promise." Ryven couldn't push a groan out, or lace his words with irritation. This was too perfect. His dream was coming true. One of them.

Even though Mylva was made of broken shards tied together with frayed ropes, she was beautiful, talented, and willing to share herself with him.

"Ryven, son, come on. Read it to me." Licthan's voice held notes of amusement.

Ryven did, but instead of reading it, he recited it, word for word. "For all the days and nights, we are as one from this moment forth. If I should die by your hand, so do you and all those that share your blood and oaths. No one person, being, or beast shall come to harm you or I by order or cajoling and if that should occur, the other will die a thousand deaths. Only by accident and natural causes shall we perish without harm coming to the other. If there is question upon our causes of deaths, ten of our closest shall judge, five from I, and five of yours within thirty days' time. By their judgment, the living partner will be freed or join the ancestors. Our love shall bear fruit within five years of this union, unless by nature and the gods we cannot and another stipulation shall be met in the fourth year. Through discourse and support we rule all that falls in our purview."

"I cannot think of anything that does not cover." Jerica murmured after mulling over it again. "If it doesn't cover it, then the contract she's already signed does." She placed her fingertips over the pile of papers in front of her on the desk.

"I believe the same." Licthan added with a nod. He leaned back in his chair, his head lolling to look behind him into the night sky, giving way to dawn in budding purple hues. "She is formidable enough to help us against them. Her army is powerful. We may stand a chance if we do have to go to war."

"Yes, I agree." Ryven finally lifted his gaze to regard his father.

Licthan rolled his head, so he was looking at his son, while still resting it on the chair, "Let's save the world, one vow at a time, hm?"

Ryven grinned, rubbing his eyes and standing, "Let's."

☙ ☙ ☙

The day of the ceremony, Mylva was surrounded by Jerica and the Queens. All. Day. Long.

Across the hall, she could hear Ryven swearing.

Jerica giggled, "My little bear cub is eager to see his bride."

"Bear cub?"

"Yes! Feel free to use that. He *loves* that little nickname."

Mylva had a feeling that using the nickname would have the little bear cub pouncing on her and torturing her until she said his real name.

285

She looked down at herself. The red fabric reminded her of the darkest magma swirling in the pits of her mountains. The top started at her clavicles, a second skin all the way down to her waist where the skirt opened up, flowing loosely around her legs until it hit the floor and pooled behind her. While the sleeves of the dress flared from her shoulders, looking like the curve of a candle flame, before resting tighter around her wrist. Slits opened the sleeve on the back and front of her arms to aid in movement.

Her feet and hands were bare, and would remain that way, as was tradition in her family.

Kavkan mating rituals for the next heir were miniature weddings. The mate was to stay with her and nurture her until she conceived, then she didn't need him anymore unless she wanted more children. During the mate bond, their feet were bare to soak in the heat from the mountain to make the Bloodsworn bond strongest.

She wasn't getting married in her armor. Instead a dress, and no helm.

Red and gold pins with dangling chains adorned the twists in her hair. None were on top of her head, and she idly wondered if Rothlanders wore crowns for ceremonies. Her great grandmother had abolished the use of crowns in favor of helms.

"You are beautiful, my daughter." Jerica said, finally stepping back after she filled her face with the gods knew what in colors.

Mylva stared at her for a moment, then turned her head slightly to look past Jerica at herself in the mirror. Her eyes had red corners, making the blackened green in her irises pop wildly. A light golden powder blushed her cheeks, and her lips were painted a matching red to her dress. For once, she didn't see the slashes on her face. Another twist in her stomach happened before it settled. No scars. What would her life have been like if she hadn't had the scars? She hated them for what the wounds did to her sisters, but she loved them for the memories, and the hardness it allowed her so she could become who she was.

"Thank you." She didn't recognize her own voice. It sounded broken.

The Queens shared a smile, then swooped in for a large, too many people, hug.

Mylva whimpered, "I…while this is…nice? I just…" She couldn't push the words out from feeling suffocated by all the bodies on her.

"Shhh, get used to it," Jerica murmured, then kissed her hair just behind her temple.

A ruckus sounded in the hall. Mylva pictured a chair being thrown at all the clattering and bouncing going on. Then she heard Ryven's voice say that something was uncalled for, before heavy footfalls passed her door. Then her door vibrated, as if someone leaned against it.

"Mothers, are you done torturing my wife?"

"She's not your wife yet, boy!" The king's voice sounded not far behind Ryven's.

The door shook, someone said 'ow' and then Ryven spoke again, "We're heading to the throne room. I'll be waiting, my Klava."

He still didn't use her name around anyone else. The trust that built alone was enough for her to no longer doubt this arrangement. Even if he acted like a toddler throwing a fit outside a room he was locked out of. "What was the fight about, I wonder?"

"I saw Mirtes enter looking like a storm cloud." Moonapsa said as she straightened Mylva's sleeve. "I still think we should've chosen the sleeveless cleavage one."

"We would have seen far too much of Ryven with her in that one, and quite frankly, I saw enough of his little butt and balls when changing his diapers." Ranamala shook her head, speaking of Ryven's impatience and incessant drive.

"He's learning control. Taming down a bit. Slowly." Mylva felt like she needed to defend him.

Jerica adjusted one of the chains dangling from the pins in her hair. "He fell in love with you in the first year he was there, Klava. Did you know that? He has six years of pent up adoration for you, so bear with it just a little longer."

Mylva shook her head, "From the way he talks, he fell in love with me after reading a report about me."

The Queens laughed and Jerica nodded, "Might as well have."

Jerica's smile was wide and her eyes shone as she spoke, "Come. Let's get you married." She leaned in to whisper, "And I hope you especially like the surprise we prepared for you."

Before Mylva could ask what kind of surprise, all the Queens turned at once, as if in a drill, and left the chamber. She frowned, not sure she liked the idea of a surprise. She watched Gyrna enter the room. Dressed in golds and reds herself.

"Is this the best move?" Her Bloodsworn asked, meeting her gaze and holding it.

Mylva nodded, "This is the best move."

Gyrna's lips trembled, and she stepped forward to grasp Mylva's hands, "My Master, my Klava, I think you are in love. I have never seen you this way. I couldn't have wished for a better outcome than to see you smile. Truly smile." She sniffled. "Forgive me for being so forward, but I wish to say something else." Gyrna knelt, still holding on to her hands.

"Go on." How unlike her Bloodsworn to kneel before her and say such things.

"For the rest of my life, I am Bloodsworn to you, my Klava. I shall protect you with my very life. When this ceremony is complete, I shall protect him with my life, as I would you. And when a child is born, that daughter too shall be protected with my life as Bloodsworn."

A repeat of Bloodsworn vows. Simplified, but worth every word. Mylva blinked back the burning in her eyes and rested a hand on top of Gyrna's bowed head, "For my Bloodsworn, I wish you a happy life, that you may still yet find love and more purpose than serving me."

"Never." Gyrna murmured, leaning forward to kiss the back of Mylva's hand she still held, "You are my life. It will always be."

"We will see." She set her face into what she hoped was friendly, and not telling of the light nerves making her breathing rapid, "I guess we shouldn't keep the little bear waiting any longer."

"Little bear?"

"A nickname his mother told me about just now."

Gyrna grinned as she stood. "Use it as a sword, my Klava." She opened the door, and they left the chambers together, headed for the festivities to come.

The palace shone with overzealous cleaning. Banners of bright reds, oranges, and golds mixed with those of black, silver, and white hung from ceilings and long windows to flutter in the calm breeze always circling within the palace walls. A plush red carpet began just outside the doors of the throne room. Gyrna bowed, waiting at the entrance.

Mylva motioned for Gyrna to open the doors, a habit to sign to her Bloodsworn.

The servants pulled them open at Gyrna's soft order. Gyrna bowed low, following the flow of the right door opening so that she was out of the way for those inside the throne room to look at her master. Bright light like sunlight spilled out and washed over her, making the golden and black threads in her dress glisten. A collective gasp, and she stared at hundreds of pairs of eyes turned to her, and just as many smiles.

She'd rather stare out on a battlefield.

Gathering her wits about her, Mylva took the first step of the longest walk ever. She still couldn't decide if she dreaded the crowd that was not her army, or was far too excited. The room was so long and too bright. She couldn't see Ryven on the dais, but she knew he was there. A comforting thought to relax the hold her nerves had upon her.

Claps echoed and bounced off the walls and high ceiling. There were a few whistles. The first face she recognized in the throng of grinning faces from her empire was Pazai's. The iron queen gave her a genuine, almost friendly visage on her usually icy features. Benz pretended to sniffle into a cloth, making Mylva roll her eyes.

Finally, she saw Ryven step up on the dais from the head of the crowd on the right. His black hair gleamed, smoothed back except for a couple of unruly strands that fell over his forehead. His ever present black shirt was more form fitting on this day, with a red vest that matched her dress. Ryven's pants denoted that Ranamala had been wrong about him having a small ass.

She pulled her gaze back up to his as she mastered the first step. Darker than dark irises, like a kitten playing with a toy, completely zoned in on her. His mouth hung ajar, and his hand was out. Mylva took it, and he squeezed her fingers gently as he helped her up the last few steps to stand beside him.

"You're gorgeous."

"As are you, little bear," she said the nickname right as the king, dressed in black and white, stepped up and he coughed to cover his laugh.

"Well," Licthan cleared his throat, covering more amusement as Ryven's brows rose toward his hairline. "My wives, children and their loves, welcome!" The King couldn't help another chuckle as Ryven tossed a glare over his shoulder to his grinning mother just behind him.

"We are here today to witness the first marriage bond between our families," the King continued with a smile. "My son, Lit-" He grinned when Ryven hissed a curse word, "Ryven and his lovely bride Klava are to be joined by Blood Bond for as long as both shall live."

The king stepped forward, ducking his head down to speak into Klava's ear, "May I have your true name? I shall not repeat it loud enough for any other to hear, other than my son."

She glanced at Ryven, surprised he hadn't told his own father her name. Something in her warmed for him, the choice for herself. "It's Mylva."

"Beautiful." King Licthan smiled and turned. He picked up a glass bowl from the table behind him, and a small, thin blade. He turned back to them, presenting the blade to Ryven first.

"With this blade my son spills his blood for the love in his heart. His life be hers, his heart and soul to love and protect her for all the days of his life."

As the king spoke, Ryven kept his gaze on hers as he cut the palm of his hand and spilled five drops, signifying the five years they had to produce an heir, then the three drops for each of the terms.

Ryven handed the handle of the blade to her, a small smirk curling his lips and he mouthed, "Last chance to kill me."

Her brow quirked, "Don't tempt me," she mouthed back.

"With this blade," the King dipped his head so his lips were hidden from the crowd and whispered her name, "Mylva," before speaking to the crowd, "spills her blood for the love in her heart. Her life be his, her heart and soul to love and protect him for all the days of her life."

As Licthan spoke, she cut her own palm, looking at Ryven as she did so, and dropped her droplets of blood in the bowl with his. She listened to the terms once more, knowing she would never break them.

When the king began swirling their blood together, she felt the pull and tug of the Blood Oath sealing itself on her heart. He kept swirling until the magic completed, the blood no longer in the vessel. Licthan placed the dish and blade back on the table, and picked up the red strip of embroidered cloth. He took their hands, pressing their wounds together before wrapping the cloth around their joined hands three times. "For the bond to never break, for the hearts to remain true, for the soul to soar, I bind you with this cloth of red. May you ever know happiness, but if pain shall find its way into your paradise, shall you enter into another state of happiness on the other side with stronger bond, stronger hearts, and souls that soar higher together."

He placed his hands over the binding cloth and smired. "Now, son, this only calls for one. Count. One. A single, solitary kiss. Can you handle that?"

Ryven's dark gaze flicked to his father. "One day, you're going to be old and will need me to care for you. I shall remember this day and all the other moments you thought to embarrass me."

The king chuckled, before announcing to the crowd, "By the Gods and all that is beautiful in this world they created, kiss to bind your love before the eyes of your families."

Ryven cupped her cheek gently with his free hand. "My love," he murmured, "Forever I shall be with you in love."

"And I you." Mylva filled her voice with as much love as she could and fit her lips to his.

Ryven kept it tame. Chaste. For once.

Instead of heading to the banquet hall, Ryven turned back to his father. Mylva followed suit, confused. This wasn't part of the rehearsal. The crowd behind them was cheering and clapping. Weren't they supposed to leave?

"Klava, step to this side for a moment, please." The King motioned for her to go to Ryven's right.

She did so, the binding of their hands feeling a bit more relaxed, until Ryven knelt. She watched Jerica clear the table behind the king. Jerica placed two small trays, covered in silver and black swirled cloth, side by side.

King Licthan held his arms up. The crowd quietened. "This is something that we have worked for years to accomplish. Not only finding someone that is worthy of my son, and he her, but for a world of peace. Where children do not need to worry if their parents are ever coming back from a war. Where parents don't have to send their children away, only to receive their bodies back for death rites. In this very room are some of the most powerful countries in this world. Perhaps the last to follow this plan. We are beginning a new era of family. A new era of peace, soon. We are creating a new world."

His lips trembled as he looked down at his son, a tear streaking down a weathered cheek. "And who better to guide our new world into an everlasting peace than the man who is making it happen? For my son, I gift to you the world. Rule it well. Rule it as family. Love and cherish it as much as you do your new bride."

As he spoke, Jerica uncovered the first tray revealing a helm shaped crown. The base was black, the points a fiery red with gold and silver metallic vines curling all around in delicate detail. The King turned, lifting it with two hands and holding it high for all to see, before he placed it on his son's head.

"Rise Ryven, Guardian of the world, Keeper of Peace, and soon to be Ruler of All."

Ryven stood and turned, not even looking at the room, but at her. He gazed into her eyes even as there were far more cheers and claps for his new titles than there had been for their marriage. He raised their hands together, finally looking over his arm at the room.

Again, it fell silent.

"Father will assist me." He knelt before her again, on one knee. When she tried to tug him back up, he stilled her free hand by lacing it in with his. "To you, my wife, I shall give you the world at your feet, as promised." His features set in a stubborn resolve as he gazed up at her, "Rule with me, keep our family safe and at peace, keep us strong through training and mothering as you see fit. Take the world and make it flourish. By all the gods and all my power, I shall support you and this world."

King Licthan picked up the now uncovered helm from the other side. This one matched the one on Ryven's head, but in the tallest spike was a glistening set of jewels in each color, with a diamond in the middle. She knelt, and the king placed it upon her head.

Together she and Ryven stood and turned, raising their bound hands high to the room amid the laughter, cheers, whistles, claps and chaos that ensued.

They found a quiet moment at the table at the head of the dining hall. Ryven kissed her cheek and asked, "How is my Klava, Empress of the World?"

"I think I'm dreaming." Mylva's mind studied the ceremonies over in her head again and again. Not a single battle was fought, only her blood spilled with Ryven's, and she gained more countries added to her empire.

He chuckled, bringing her hand up to his lips to kiss the back of it. Even though they didn't have the binding cloth on, he held her hand more often than not during the feast. "A pleasant dream, I should think."

"I'm still debating. It might be a nightmare." She grinned at him. "At least I have my little bear cub to keep me warm."

He spat the red wine into his silver cup, setting it down before wiping his chin on a red cloth napkin. "Wine hurts going up one's nose, do you know that?"

"I do now."

Ryven eyed her as he said, "Call me that one more time and I shall not allow you one second of sleep tonight."

"Is that supposed to be a threat? I thought you would already do that." Mylva let her jangling bundle of excitement and nerves out through teasing her new husband.

He grinned, for the millionth time that night, "Two days, just me and you, then."

"Klava!"

Her eyes shot toward the yell, and she stood. Gyrna ran up to her, hand clutched to her chest. "I just received word!" Her other hand rose, holding out a folded piece of yellowed paper.

Mylva stared at the seal of her army on the back. Her fingers shook as she took the paper and unfolded it. Her code stared back at her. A series of letters, runes, and numbers jumbled together, jamming in odd places in her mind. She read it again and still couldn't believe it.

Her butt hit the seat she just vacated, hard.

"What's wrong?" Ryven asked just as his father and mother approached the table from the dance floor, concern on their faces. The room seemed to still as more took notice of their now pale Empress.

"Kavkan has a new ruler."

Ryven snorted. "Ridiculous."

"Praedae." Even as she said his name, she didn't believe the code as she read it yet again.

He stared at her for a moment. "What?"

"My general writes that he's taken the country, wrested it from the hands of the generals and killed the advisors. Praedae is creating rules and laws to fit his needs and wants. He is readying the army to battle. Unless…" she trailed off, reading the last line of the letter one more time.

"Unless what?" Her husband asked.

"I return, as his breeder, to bear him children until there is a son to be his heir." Acid flooded her throat as her stomach churned. Still yet, the fires of rage swelled in her heart.

"Ryven, were you not receiving reports from your army?" The King asked.

His voice was low, murmuring as he told them, "I pulled them back to Parvis, only left a few of my most trusted ones. The last few reports were odd. I thought it was because they knew we were about to end this."

"Odd how?" Jerica sat across from them.

"A few lines of code. One stated the Kavkans were starving. The other is that the harem in the palace was growing." Ryven's lips pressed into a tight line after he answered his mother.

"Kavkans don't starve. And there isn't a harem in the palace." Mylva crumpled the letter in a fist. "I have to return. I'm going to kill that fool."

"Doesn't your Blood Oath keep him from taking the throne?" Ryven asked, his gaze sliding from the fist with the letter to her eyes.

Mylva froze as realization hit the fire within like ice water. "If I am ever seen as less than Klava, Praedae may rule until I produce the next." Her gaze found Gyrna's, and her fear subsided little at the rage she saw in her Bloodsworn's eyes.

"Your advisors probably thought this was planned, as the Kavkans would think it was a normal move." King Licthan sighed, resting a hand on the table between them. "What do you need, my daughter?"

Mylva smirked, the fires returning to her veins as battle neared, "My maces, my mare, and to return to Kavkan."

Ryven made a noise in the back of his throat as he stared at her. "Gods, that look right there is going to give me a thrill for years. But you forgot one thing."

"What?" Mylva raised a brow and watched as he gathered her hand with his.

"Me, my love."

ꝛꝛꝛ

Within a week, he'd know if the blood bond worked or not. Ryven checked his trunk, then his saddle bag one last time. They were traveling light once they disembarked in Frystwaithe. Mylva stated it would provide them with the fastest journey to Kavkan instead of landing at a port in Revinland. Once he set foot in Kavkan, she'd either kill him, or keep him.

He shook his head at himself, knowing his heart soared when he thought of the woman. His bride. Ryven refused to traipse through her thoughts without her knowledge since their arrival at his home. His home, not hers. He reminded himself this wouldn't be the last time they were all together.

"Packed enough books?"

"I won't have time to read, Mother." He turned, taking her in. The drawn expression, clenched hands, and stiff body in black betrayed her worry. "This shall not be the last time you'll see your eldest."

She took in a shaky breath, closing the distance between them to lay a hand against his cheek. "She will not kill you. But I fear this Praedae character."

A small bit of relief crawled into his heart at her words. Maybe Mylva wouldn't kill him. Maybe his mother had peered into her mind and found peace. Or at least love for him in there. "My soldiers are ready. I heard word from one still within Kavkan. It is dire, but they are doing their best to protect the people as they were ordered."

"Then let Klava take care of the rest. She will want to. Do not step in unless she asks, my son."

He smirked, leaning into her hand still on his cheek, "Is that the only way I will survive her? Do all she asks and nothing more?"

"Surprises of little niceties are always welcome. But when it comes to taking back one's home… that is not for you unless she says." Jerica narrowed her eyes at her son, knowing he knew these things. "Take care of her," she added, pressing her forehead to his after she pulled his head down to meet hers. "I shall see you again in this life."

She'd been reading his reports on Kavkan. His sense of pride welled, "I shall see you again, Mother." He kissed her cheek, then wrapped her in his arms and held her for a moment. "Keep me abreast of the mess my siblings make here?"

"Of course."

"Don't let Mirtes find his way out of this. Little brother is the only one that can sweet talk you into anything." Ryven turned and slung his saddlebags over his shoulder, then motioned for the trunk to be taken out.

"He cannot and he will not." Jerica sniffed, her shoulders straightening as her chin jutted out. "He will marry."

Ryven gave a noncommittal sound before walking with his mother out. There wasn't much time for goodbyes. Those he saw of his siblings he held back from giving orders, or demands. His father waited for him by the teleporter. He smiled to hide the dread of leaving his plan before it finished. He knew his parents could handle it.

"Son. Fair journey, and may the gods grant you the home you deserve." Licthan wrapped his son in a tight embrace.

Ryven swore he felt his ribs crack. "Klava will gain her rightful place, and I hope to stay by her side." He tried a grin, but failed as his father pulled away. "Or you will have a rather bloody battle ahead."

"No one says such things with a smile, son." The King shook his head, going down the teleportation tower with him. They stopped, watching Mylva mount her fire mare. "If you are to die, then I hope it's a long time from now and it will be with a smile on your face."

He moved forward, prompted by the clap on his back from Licthan. Ryven gave a nod to his wife, settled his things and himself on the saddle, and they were off. Either to another win, or his demise.

Chapter 20

The trip across the sea and through the countries back to her Kavkan was far shorter, with just the two of them, Gyrna, and five guards. Ryven sent orders ahead for his army stationed in Kavkan and Parvis to be at the ready. While on the way there, Mylva and Ryven made a few strategies. She didn't doubt the first one would work, but also knew that backup plans were always a good idea to have.

The night before crossing the border, she entered their tent and crouched over Ryven.

He rubbed his eyes, already half asleep, "You need rest. Come on." He pulled the blanket off him, revealing his armor that, like hers, hadn't left his person for three days, not since their last bath at port.

She ran her hands up his thigh guards to the buckles underneath the plates over his lower abdomen. Unbuckling them, she slid the metal off his thighs, and then the larger plates of his flat stomach. "I need an orgasm."

"Yes, my Empress." He murmured, motioning for her to take care of her own armor as he freed himself of his pants, dragging them down to his knees.

As soon as she was free, she crouched over him again, dipping her head to his hardening cock as she took him into her mouth.

"Wa- let me." He sat up.

She pushed him back down with a clatter of loose armor. She slid her mouth down the length of him, feeling him growing harder by the second. After a few sucks, and a lick that made a moan tear from his throat, she straddled him. Guiding his cock into her, she slipped down his length.

"Gods, I want you naked," Ryven murmured, his eyes glued to her as she moved on top of him.

She gave him a warm look, rocking her hips slowly. When he met her movements, she stilled him by pinning his hips under hers. "Don't move, you'll make too much noise."

"Is that an order?" His voice was a purr in the night.

"It is." Mylva questioned her sanity as all she could hear was the scraping of metal against metal with every move she made.

"And if I disobey?" Ryven met his question with a few rough thrusts of his hips, driving him deep inside her.

"I'll leave you tied to a tree tonight dressed like this," she hissed through her teeth to keep from moaning.

"Fair enough. No moving for me."

"Arms out from your sides so they don't clank with your chest plate." She raised a brow as he clasped his hands behind his head. He looked all too pleased with himself. So she leaned back slightly, placing her palms on his thighs so her armor wouldn't clank too much. She rotated her hips, ever so slowly, the friction was ideal for her.

She sucked her bottom lip, rocking forcefully, slightly quicker. Her first orgasm hit, and she bit harder to keep from crying out. Klava continued moving over him as her orgasm tightened her and made all her muscles tremble at once.

His curse was a whisper, but loud in her ears.

She smacked his hands when they landed on her thighs with a clank. His arms went back up, returning to their previous place. Since he was being such a good boy, she created more friction for him. Her hips bouncing over him.

The muscles in his neck strained along with those under her hands on his thighs. His teeth clenched. She imagined his toes were about to curl.

She knew hers were. "Give in."

With a few harsh, clattering jerks of his hips up into hers and grunts that weren't so quiet, his body shook taut. She rode his orgasm to find another of her own after a few more rocks of her hips upon him. She patted his chest plate, "Good little bear cub."

Suddenly she was blinking at the ceiling of their tent, then rolled again with far too much metallic noise in the night. The blanket they used for a bed was soft against her cheek. She turned her face slightly, looking back at him.

"Bite down, my love." He said, ridding himself of the rest of his armor with more than a few clanks. "I'm about to show you what this 'little bear cub' can do."

She was sore. For the first time in her adult life, she ached in her legs, her ass cheeks, her shoulders. She swore his hands were still planted on her hips, but only her armor was there. The bastard snored.

His horse was wide enough that he could lie down and stay on its back with no worry.

Mylva debated for the fifth time about planting her boot in his ass and pushing him off the beast. It was her fault. She'd called him little cub too many times. That, and they deserved a distraction from thoughts last night.

She needed the distraction.

Her mind had threaded the dangerous ropes of self loathing. She was not worthy enough to be Kavkan, much less their ruler. Praedae should rule. The thoughts swirled in her mind even though deep within she knew they were lies.

He couldn't rule, not Praedae.

A war against her Kavkans would decimate the country, and the surrounding countries, and the peace

Ryven wanted to give her. There was no escaping war as Praedae sat on the throne. She began her reign at Ryven's side by reclaiming her throne How ridiculous was that?

Her forces were in the hands of another. A victory with the ones she could pull back to her side would not be easy. Ryven kept assuring her his army was just as dangerous as hers, but doubt flooded her mind, knowing the weaknesses of their young soldiers from the training grounds.

Their plan was to ride on the main road into her Kavkan. After all, her people would see her return. From the workers to the merchants to the families of the advisors. If they still lived. New reports stated Praedae had spilled the blood of his own people. Her Kavkans. That was unforgivable.

Upon arriving in the capital, she crossed the Bridge of Konu she swore would drink Ryven's blood and smiled a little to herself. Her mare snorted, feeling her dread and excitement, the veins in her steed's flesh glowed bright, soaking in the missed heat of their land.

"Klava."

She looked down toward the voice, her mare stopping. Wide eyes met hers, dark under thick black brows. A tanned cheek held a cotton cover, the red of blood oozing pin pricking the white cloth in a sharp line. Mylva couldn't remember the man's name, but his hands helped her favored blacksmith.

"Who did this?" She pointed to the wound.

"Praedae has a nasty temper." He stated, blunt fingers reaching up to brush over the covering. His dark eyes narrowed. "Diamaster Farva is dead."

The master blacksmith earned the title Diamaster once she made Mylva's armor, and it held for several turns. Last Mylva saw her, her hair was graying at the temples, and she'd taken on two more apprentices in hopes more would earn her title. A significant loss, for what? "Why?"

The apprentice kept her gaze, Kavkan rage burning in his as he answered, "She didn't make him Klava armor. Refused, even as he broke her feet and killed her son."

Her chest burned, veins soaking in the magic of her land. Praedae had gone mad. Mad with power.

"Klava, I am glad you are back. We thought you might never return. But there are some… I don't understand how he has not been overtaken." The man shifted on his feet, looking up and down the street when a single person or two would appear, then scurry away.

Kavkans were acting like vermin, hiding.

"Is there a safe house?" Mylva asked, unsure whether her Kavkans would remember protocol since none alive had ever been attacked on their land.

"Crater Round. The second house, it's mine. Safe as any place." He motioned for her to follow.

Mylva's mare pranced through the streets. The hooves rang on the black stones, calling out to her Kavkans. Ryven at her side, sitting straight and regal in his saddle, the helm crown on his head matching hers. Kavkan would be hers again.

Few of her people met her on the streets. Kavkans cheered for their Klava. They noted the king beside her, stared with quizzical brows at the matching crowns, and while there might have been confusion, they didn't care. Klava was back.

The damage Praedae created in the month she'd been gone became evident closer to the area they called Crater Round. It was a natural indentation, creating wide spirals of earth down to Kavkan's largest freshwater lake. It boiled some, but it was free of heavy sulfur. The Gods provided for the faithful. The inhabitants crafted each spiral into enough flat land to hold housing, shops, and the like. She stopped staring at the destruction. Houses were melted, smoking stumps of themselves. Charred bones lay in the open, in or around those destroyed houses. Her advisor's families and the innocence of her people were gone.

While she hadn't liked the advisors, she would never kill their children. The next generation was always better, smarter, stronger than the last. Those children of Kavkan deserved better. The remains of her Kavkans were worthy of better.

Feeling her anger, her mare turned to flame, Ryven barely kept control of his stallion beside hers. The surrounding soldiers scattered, their horses trying to get away from the fire. Mylva ran her hands down her mare's neck, speaking softly. "Easy. Not yet," she mostly told herself, instead of her mare, but it worked for both of them.

With her mare calmed to a cinder, Mylva followed the apprentice and then dismounted in front of his house. The entry gave way to a wide room full of pillows and low tables, working as both an entertaining and an eating room. Beaded reeds partitioned off two other rooms and a hall that led back into the mountain.

The commotion they had created called more to the house. In a few moments, the table stood against a wall, pillows piled up as they weren't in use, and there was standing room only. Every eye that caught hers seemed haunted. She bit the inside of her cheek, waiting for another few breaths so the fire within her would keep calm.

Then, with some unseen signal, they all bowed.

Klava Mylva looked out over their heads and saw a familiar, wizened face. His shoulders hunched, hand covering the head of a cane, one leg wrapped in swaths of gauze from thigh to ankle. Another circled his thick neck.

"Drak," Ryven's voice at her side was a mix of glee at seeing the old man and worry. "It's good to see you."

General Drak's eyes darted between the two as he said gruffly, his words sounded odd, "Tell us, and I shall let you know if I share the sentiment."

Mylva could only assume something had happened to her eldest general's tongue.

"Our Kavkan was infiltrated by Ryven and his army. It's his plan is to take over the world, and they have most of it, to generate peace."

"*We* have most of it." Ryven corrected her.

"Yes, we. I am married. The worst of the Kavkan traditions ends with my line. We shall start afresh. The world at our feet. Kavkan strength to rule all the lands across all the seas with the vigor of Ryven's kingdom of Rothland." The words tumbled from her mouth even as she realized yet again what Ryven had given her with each syllable.

Drak's eyes narrowed. "His army, are they as good as he?"

"Some," Mylva began, but was cut off.

"Most, yes." Ryven gave her a look before returning his attention to the elder general. "I came up with the training. I-"

Drak's cane clacked against the stone floor like a snap of thunder. "Boy, how many times do I have to tell you I don't need extravagant explanations?" He glared at Ryven, jaw working, lips a thin line before he sniffed, his nose wrinkling before he returned his attention to Mylva. "My Klava, are you Kavkan?" His eyes were like stones against her heart.

"I am Kavkan." Mylva swallowed, keeping his gaze, and catching the worried whispers making their way across the room.

"Then Kavkan is you and with you." General Drak's shoulders straightened, "What are your orders, my

Klava?" He bowed his head, then stood straight, his lips twisting into a grin, and there through a few broken front teeth was his tongue, tip severed.

"Are there many who stand with Praedae?" Mylva asked over the murmurs of the gathered Kavkans.

"Only to survive his wrath. Once they hear of your return, they will be at your side and breathe their last breath as Kavkan, if need be," Drak answered readily.

Mylva felt the pride again, the pride of her people at her back. "Spread the word of my return. Gather those loyal. Get those under his boots to safety. I will deal with him myself. If he should best me, take him down. He is not Kavkan."

With a nod, Drak shuffled and left the house. Many followed, to tell everyone.

Mylva turned to the apprentice. "Thank you for allowing me use of your home. I shall not burden you further." She placed a hand on his shoulder, "May the goddess house you and fill you."

"Thank you, my Klava." The apprentice bowed his head.

"Now. Let's create a diversion for my people's safety." Mylva said as she grinned at Ryven.

Mylva's mare sprinted up the bridge leading into the fortress, and then through the gates where the obsidian floors began. Up the stairs to the throne room, where her mare kicked the doors open in a screaming rear and flaming front hooves.

They trotted in. The lava rolling and swirling under the glasslike floor. He took up all of the throne, his armor like dark smoke swallowing flames.

"There you are, my Klava. I was worried." Praedae's lips curled as he threw his arms wide. His gaze flicked to the top of her head, then over to Ryven, still at her side. "What's this?" He asked as he stood from the massive stone and jewel seat of power.

"Kavkan is mine." Mylva's anger radiated down through her horse, and a hoof pawed the floor with loud clacks.

"As is the world," Ryven added, before giving Praedae his famous sneer. "Bow, plead for your life and forgiveness, and you might yet deserve to return to the lava of your god. You will find no home in her world."

Praedae's laugh echoed in the high ceilings. "What? The world?"

"All the countries, all their rulers, belong and answer to us," Ryven spoke slowly, leaning forward in his saddle. He pointed to the throne behind the immense man. "That's her seat."

Praedae lifted a shoulder, but didn't move from his wide stance before the chair. "I'm only keeping it warm for her. She can share it when she gives me the mate bond and Kavkan. Afterward, she dies when she produces my son."

Ryven twitched.

"Oh? She didn't tell you? That's why Klavas are daughters. Her bloodline cannot produce males. Every male in her bloodline has been born to a dead mother." Praedae grinned, striding like a trainer giving lessons around the throne to lean on the charred back of it.

"Since you killed the advisors, I have no way of rectifying that superstition." Mylva watched for any remorse to cross his features. Disappointment pricked her heart as there wasn't an emotion in her Warmonger's stonelike face.

"Fact, not superstition," Praedae bit out, fingering a red jewel inlaid along the side as he still leaned on the Klava's seat of power. "Since you have bedded the enemy with intent to mate, you are no longer worthy of this throne. I will keep it. Mate me and rule Kavkan beneath me for years until we have a son. Or kill me and take the throne back."

"You are not Klava. Nor a Klava in your line. You are the least worthy in this room to sit there." Mylva jutted her chin, motioning to her seat.

Praedae unsheathed his ax from its resting place behind the throne. The long handle of a matte black diamond, the hardest source pulled from her lava, held a blade curved wide on one side and a spike on the top and opposite. The best metal, just like her armor, forged the sharp edges. Her gift to him when he became her warrior. "Prove it." A flame erupted in his hand and he tossed the bundle of it directly at Ryven.

Mylva kicked her mare forward, taking the flames in her chest plate. She grinned at Praedae, soaking in the heat. With a turn of her head, she looked over at Ryven and told him, "Get your soldiers out of here. You too."

Ryven barked orders to the guards that had come with them from Rothland, sliding off his horse so the beast would follow his men out. "I'm staying." He placed a hand on Mylva's thigh. "I want to see the love of my life in a true battle. See her genuine power."

"You will distract me." Out of the corner of her eye, she observed Gyrna skirt the walls of the throne room, then slip through the doors in the back. Her Bloodsworn would open the rest of the fortress to Drak. Help the trapped escape and let her army and Ryven's in to conquer those who would rather serve Praedae.

Ryven chuckled, "I promise not to rub while watching you, though it will be difficult."

She slid off her saddle into his arms, fitting her mouth to his. "Sit on the throne, keep it warm for me." Mylva smacked her mare, making her go out the doors after the others. "He takes the best seat in the house for the show." Mylva motioned to Ryven, then pointed at the throne.

Praedae stepped away from the seat with a laugh, bounding down the distance separating him from Mylva while keeping a wide berth between him and Ryven. "He'll bend the knee to me, and I'll cut off his pretty head once and for all."

"My Klava won't fall. And you definitely won't take me." Ryven sat on the throne, sprawling back, then hooked a knee over one jeweled chair arm, making himself right at home. "You've lost to me before, little boy, you will again."

Praedae's veins popped, glowing red with power. "Don't get too comfortable. This won't take long. I might keep you around for a while, let you watch me make a whore of her."

Mylva's dark laugh brought both men's attention back to her. "Your dick isn't good enough for my mare." Her anger erupted. She didn't care. She let the magic flow into every vein, every vessel that carried her blood. Years of pent up rage and pain swelling with flames and releasing into the roar in her ears. Armor sank into her skin as she kicked off her boots. She soaked in the heat of the lava beneath her feet. Relished in the freedom not holding back an ounce of what her magic gave her.

Ryven had given her the choice. She didn't need to burn the world down to make it better. Not anymore. He gave it to her. Shiny, full of culture and magic of all kinds and cultures. She had so much more to learn of the people that were now hers. New continents to explore.

All she needed to do was torture the idiot before her until he begged her to stop. Then she'd feed him to her magic. This male didn't deserve death rites. He hadn't given them to her people, the ones he killed. He hadn't fought for her when Ryven captured her.

Hid. He'd hidden to take what was hers after the coast was clear. "Coward." She hissed at him.

Her body molded itself and her armor into the god her blood came from. She spat lava from her mouth, the liquid landing on his chest plate. It burned a bright weak point into his gear. His was poorly made, compared to hers and unlike his weapon. "Pray you win this because no one here thinks enough of you to give you death rites."

"I am Kavkan." He began circling her, a wildness in his eyes she'd never seen before. His fingers moved rapidly in their sign language, *"Never a coward. You know me the best. I needed to make sure it was you, not the other two. Come back to me."*

"My people smiled and welcomed me back with open arms." She ignored his plea, even with the rough tug of the bond pulling at her heart.

Fear. She'd never sensed that in him before. There was a cold sweat smell to him. She drew it deep into her lungs, relishing in it. He feared her this way.

Few living knew this form existed. Only Nava and Hava had ever seen it and lived. And one man, for a breath, before she killed him for whipping them.

Them. She could feel them. Her Bloodsworn sisters flowing into her from the lava beneath her. Giving her their strength.

Giving their love.

"Beautiful." The soft word flowed through the room like a singing praise of worship.

Ryven. He thought her beautiful as a monster. She loved the fool. Her little bear cub. A man that wanted her well. Healed. Healthy. And not pinned under the nightmares of their traditions.

She flung swaths of lava down her arms to her maces, and then to Praedae.

He dodged them. The bulk of him quicker than he should be able to. He settled into his stance. Weapon up, feet wide and always moving, shoulders loose, and fingers tight. Praedae dropped a hand from the diamond handle to sign, *"Let's attack him! Take Kavkan and his!"*

Praedae swung his ax forward, the crescent blade slicing toward her thigh. He used his full weight, coming off one leg. He flicked a stream of liquid fire toward her with his fingers, not letting her dodge.

Mylva knew the weight of his weapon. As well as the damage it caused, for he fought at her side at every battle she'd been in. While his magic was dangerous, the ax in his hands more so.

He'd never fought her like this.

She took the liquid fire on her chest, letting it melt into her and feed her soul. Mylva moaned, drinking in the delicious heat as she slapped his ax down with her forearm. Her mace blazed a deep red flame as she swung it at his head.

Praedae blocked her, hissing as the flames licked over his gauntlet and vambrace, tickling the side of his bare face.

"Where's your helm to protect that ugly face, hm?" She sneered, leaning into his arm as she used the force of his block to lift herself up off her feet. Swinging forward, she slammed her heels into his chest, falling with him, only to roll behind him and gain her footing there. Another swing of her mace for his temple as she whirled.

The clang of metal rang through the room again as he caught her swing with the spike. He planted his weapon on the floor, swinging himself up on it to kick at her head.

"Predictable." She flipped hers, ramming the handle into his open groin.

Off balance with the blow, he fell to his knees, then onto his face, his armor clattering on the floor.

She grinned, swinging both maces down to pummel him. Two hits landed before he began rolling and jerking out of her way. In his scramble to get away, the dented metal of his armor scraped loudly against the floors.

Mylva caught the spike of his ax when he flailed it up toward her kneecaps. The pain of the edge going through her palm made her grin. Her arm shook as she held his blow off her. Lava flowed in molten rivulets, curling around the metal in her hand and then spreading over the curved blade. "I'm giving this back to our god; you no longer deserve this gift I asked for."

His battle cry rang out, screeching into a scream as some of the lava dropped from his melting ax and landed on the unprotected portion of his calf. Praedae jerked the handle out of the ax head as the metal melted around the black diamond.

The movement slapped the rod against Mylva's temple, and she wheeled away with the force. Staying on her feet, she shook her head, rounding just in time to catch the end of his diamond handle on her shoulder. His free hand came around her neck.

The sizzle of his skin gave the air an aroma of burnt flesh.

Mylva laughed, lifting her chin to let him grip more if he wanted. "You never deserved the title. Unable to absorb my flame, or any. Just a fighter. Brawler. Useless."

Praedae's teeth gnashed together, his arm jerking as he lifted her. He uttered a half war cry, and half scream into the chamber. He couldn't take the burn anymore, twisting his body to slam her onto the floor.

She hooked her hand at the base of his neck as she flew off her feet, taking him down with her. Her back slapped against the floor, the magma roiling underneath the glass-like stone trying to join her. He fell on her. She gripped him close, melting his armor as she spilled her magic to her front, lava flowing freely from her.

"Don't you want to mate me?" She whispered into his ear as he thrashed to get out of her hold. She wrapped her legs around him and dropped her maces to grip him better. "Hear me moan your name?" she asked, breathless, before giving him a sample of her moan. He screamed again, his body bucking as the lava ate through his armor, "Won't you give me a son?" She laughed in his ear, releasing him and pushing him off her with her full strength.

Praedae slid across the floor, howling as he tried to peel his armor off as it melted into his flesh.

Mylva stood, sliding her hand down her chest to pick up some of the lava on her fingers. She let it roll between them and she heard Nava and Hava's laughter in it. She kissed the molten fire, letting it drop back into her heart, where it glowed brightly.

She walked, one slow step after another. Her eyes weren't on Praedae. She watched Ryven, sitting on her throne, his dark gaze locked on her.

She dug her fingers through the inky black hair of the warrior at her feet once he got the liquid metal off him. Mostly. A sulfur scent overpowered as his thin hair evaporated over her knuckles. She pulled him up to his knees and walked around until she faced him. "You know… he likes me. Likes to go down on me. Lick me here. You wanna taste?" She slid her hand between her hips.

Mylva laughed as Praedae jerked back.

Predictably, Praedae's feet kicked her legs out from under her and she allowed herself to fall on top of him. "Didn't think that through, did you?" She asked over his renewed screams.

She crawled off him. Disappointment colored her amusement as she saw the man whom she had thought was hers in a new light. Her Bloodsworn Warrior. She remembered every battle. Every sparring match. When she granted him the title. Klava Mylva recalled every moment of when he watched her back better than she did.

"Maybe I should've made this fair." She murmured, hearing him gurgle in his struggle to breathe. His arm melted through where she had landed on him. His back burned down to the muscles. Wounds cauterized. "I told you to learn to absorb. This would have been way more fun if you had just taken my advice."

Her anger faded with his trembles. The magic spooled back into her heart. Her armor reformed around her. Her skin returned to normal. Charred bits fell off her where her underclothes hadn't survived her transformation.

Mylva sighed, "Now comes the pinching." She made a face down at her gear, wishing there was a way to save her underthings to keep the chaffing at bay. She crouched, resting a hand on Praedae's cheek. "Anything to say?"

His eyes flashed, jaw set, and he stared her down.

"That's what I thought you would do." She slammed her gauntlet down into the floor thrice, the sound echoing and screeching through the throne room. As she waited, Mylva prodded the open wounds, reopening some only to cauterize them closed again.

The man didn't scream. Praedae's remaining strength tightened, his jaw muscles clenching as his teeth ground together. That was a Kavkan trait, not screaming. At least now he was keeping to the ways of their people.

She felt... Kavkan, again. Strong. Capable. Her gaze flicked to the throne and even though another sat on it, she knew it was hers and she had the right to be there. Her doubts were there, probably rear their ugly heads more than once in her future. Without a shadow of flame, she deserved the jeweled symbol of power more than the coward beside her.

Mylva canted her head as Gyrna trotted into the room, answering her metallic summons. "All is well?"

"They are free. Some have stayed to help clean up the mess. Others we took to the barracks for the soldiers to guard." Her Bloodsworn's gaze drifted to the man half-burned on the floor, "I would think they'd like a piece of that flesh."

"I think so, too. Is there a healer among them?"

Gyrna's brows drew low over her eyes, then loosened as realization hit. She grinned, "I'll be right back."

Mylva stood, her bare feet slapping the glass beneath in her heavy stride toward her husband. The weight of the crown still resting on her head. She wondered why it hadn't been destroyed. "Take your badly made weapon and poke at him a bit. I'm done."

Ryven chuckled, pulling her down into his lap. "Done? I don't think you really got the chance to get started."

She hissed as the armor pinched her in places she didn't like. "My everything still hurts, too."

"Ah. I'll massage your everything after I make it quite a bit worse," Ryven said, tilting her face toward him so he could steal a kiss. His gaze then turned to Praedae, sprawled on the floor. He rested his chin in his hand and propped up on the throne arm. "Think your mare would eat him?"

She grimaced at the mental image in his head, wondering where their flesh met for her to have access to him. "No."

"Hm. He'll die on his own with all those burns. Should we give him a show as a parting gift?" Their armor clacked together again. The roughness of his gloves slid under her chest plate and scraped across her nipple, automatically making it pucker and harden.

"No. He's had me enough times."

Ryven's hand stopped, "He has? Is once or twice *enough*? Or was it more?"

Mylva turned her head, finding Ryven's gaze upon Praedae instead of herself. His face was a reading of anger from jealousy. "He was my first. He was also my last, before you. And more, too much."

"Mm." Ryven slid his hand from her and stood. He deposited her on the throne as gently as he could, apologizing as the armor pinched her repeatedly. He kissed the top of her head. "Those signs you do, with him and your Bloodsworn, will you ever teach me those?"

He watched their battle so closely he caught their sign language. Mylva was impressed again. She knew she'd promised him before, but never made good on it, "I will. Now that we will have time."

"We will have all the time." Ryven said, "And we are each other's now. Doesn't matter about who we had in the past." He leaned in, kissing her forehead.

Then he was striding toward the hunched body on their throne room floor. He gracefully swooped up the diamond handle on his way. He twirled it in his hands, then brought it down on Praedae's pelvis with an echoing crack.

The dying man didn't have time to make a sound, and none escaped, other than the whoosh of air from his lungs before it landed on his sternum with another impressive crack.

Ryven walked around him, twirling the staff. "I like this. Can I have it?"

"I'll get you a new one that isn't tainted with him." Mylva held still, feeling the fit of the throne against her. She was home.

"You're the best, Mylva." He purred her name, before turning to watch the shock cross Praedae's pale face. "What? She loves me. Of course she'd tell me her real name." He crouched, leaning on the diamond staff. "You know, you could have led a good life with us. But you had to make a mistake." He tapped Praedae's temple, "Some people shouldn't think above their status."

His fingers fisted in Praedae's smoking hair, "Look at her. You didn't help her. You didn't make sure she healed from the breakings she went through. She could've loved you if you had shown an ounce of support her way."

Ryven sneered, slamming the singed head down on the floor. He stood, crushing Praedae's right hand under the heel of his boot. He knocked the shards of flesh off with the diamond staff.

"Let's get you out of that armor, hm?" her husband said, turning back to her. Then noticed as the healer and Gyrna paused at the entrance. "Or do you want to torture some more?"

Chapter 21

Five days and four nights, Ryven studied Mylva closely. In her bed, he watched her eyes study the other two beds in the circular magma lit room. He waited. Knowing there would be a time, multiple times, where she would need him ready to take on the tears. He'd be there for a few training ground rounds and screams into the void of her mountain, too. No matter what she needed, he was there.

In the middle of the fifth night, Mylva conceded. After walking into their chambers, she studied Hava's bed, and then Nava's. Her body shook and fists trembled by her sides. "I cannot, in good conscience, move them."

"You don't have to." Ryven stated quietly at her side. "Only when you are ready. If that day never comes, that's swell, too."

Mylva turned to him, her dark eyes wide, so the green shone brightly in the dark depths like hidden emeralds. Her eyelids glistened with unshed anguish. "Kavkan's don't waste."

"They're not a waste. They are memories." Ryven tried to think of something else to say, "Besides, one day, if you want, our children can have them. What do you think?"

She stared at him, her lips parted with a retort, then she shut her mouth and nodded, blinking rapidly. The tears finally fell down her cheeks, and she turned into him. Her arms wrapped tightly around his waist, and she pressed her face to where his neck met his shoulder.

Ryven wrapped one arm around her and slid his other hand into her hair. He used his fingertips to rub gentle circles against her scalp as her body convulsed in sobs. As he heard her thoughts, he kissed her temple before saying, "You are not weak. Strength is knowing when to give, and add more to the mix that is you to be what you need to be. You are emptying the tears to make room for other emotions, or for more tears. It is what you crave."

While he had her in his arms, he searched for her healing. He expected trauma still, but he also found something else. Ryven didn't recognize the source, nor why it was there. Perhaps it was how her mind healed. Her body storing away nutrients in a panic at the emotional override? That had to be it.

As her weeping gave way to sniffles and just them standing together, holding one another. Ryven asked, "What may I retrieve for my wife to soothe her throat?"

"Water." Mylva answered with a rasp to her voice. "I need to wash my face."

He stepped back, cupping her face in his palms and swiping the few remaining tears away with the pads of his thumbs. "I don't think I say this enough, but I'll say it again now. You are beautiful, and I love you with all my mind, body, and soul."

She rolled her eyes, "You're a masochist, I don't think you saying tears are pretty counts."

He chuckled, "Come on." Ryven nudged her toward their bed as he retrieved the pitcher from underneath the basin beside her vanity. He poured the hot water into the bowl and placed a cloth in it as he put the pitcher back in place. He squeezed the excess water out before handing it to Mylva.

Ryven crossed the room, opening the door to cross the hall and knock. He raised a brow at Gyrna when she opened up almost immediately. "Water, please."

"Are you going to drown in it?" Gyrna sniped, motioning him to step back before she entered the hall, shutting her rooms behind her.

"Hardly. It will have to be another day we fulfill your desire for my death."

Gyrna rolled her eyes toward the ceiling as she made her way down the way to the servant's alcove, "May the gods fulfill it swiftly."

He waited for her to stop pouring the water, leaning against the wall with his arms crossed over his chest, "I have such great respect for you, too."

Her laugh was a bark, "Good one." She turned, holding a tray with a pitcher full of ice with little water as it would melt quickly enough, and two glasses with the same. "Shall I hand this to you so you may take another of my jobs from me?"

"By all means," Ryven motioned her back toward his chambers with a slight bow and tapping the toes of his right boot on the stone floor behind his other one. As he followed her, he commented, "I didn't know you enjoyed undressing her that much. Shall I allow you in our chambers as I get naked, too?"

Ryven grinned at the look Gyrna tossed over her broad shoulder, then he trotted to make sure he got to the door before her so he could open it. "Madam Gyrna."

"Gods." Gyrna muttered, striding past him with another roll of her eyes.

He listened to Gyrna complaining about him and how mouthy he was to his wife. Watching as the red-rimmed eyes of his beloved grew wrinkles at the corners with a laugh. He hoped the tears would give way to more laughter.

"He's been healed from death's door seven times, my Klava." Drak's voice held an edge to it. Though the odd lisp with the tip of his tongue gone took most of the sting from his gruffness.

Mylva looked up, meeting the old man's gaze, "Are you saying that's too few or too many?"

Her oldest general's face schooled itself into a glare, one she knew well. The expression meaning 'you should know', except she wasn't his student getting regular beatings until she learned how to keep his weapons off her. "He murdered seventeen children, nine women, and eleven men. Non warriors. They were no threat." She put down the letter from Revra. The little mouse was coming into her own, it seemed. Picking up her clay cup, she drank down the warm water, allowing her general time to think.

The dining room of the fortress, formally reserved for parties, had become a meeting hall instead. It was safe for Ryven and his generals, as they wouldn't turn to ash if they didn't keep the wards or magic amulets on them. It was on the main floor, behind the throne room, making it accessible for quick errands and missives. While the thick obsidian table, wide and long enough to hold hundreds of dishes and seat nearly as many people, was a bit much for a desk, it worked effectively.

When she said nothing, Drak added, "We're killers, Klava, not torturers."

"Send him back in roasted pieces and tell your new father-in-law that it's a Kavkan delicacy you sent just for him."

Mylva raised a brow at Gyrna, "Did Licthan hit on you? Offer to make you a new wife? Bite off a toe?"

Gyrna's lips tightened.

"Or he didn't pay you any attention? I assure you, you're gorgeous. Like flames dancing at sunset."

When Mylva's companions all rolled their eyes, she studied her words for a moment. Ryven. She reeked of Ryven and spoke like him. Mylva pinched the bridge of her nose and sighed. "I'll put an end to his misery this evening."

Drak cleared his throat while crossing his arms over his chest plate.

With a sigh, Mylva stood. "Now is a good time, too."

The dungeons were in the middle of the glacier, away from the fortress and the city for protection. After escaping Drak's mutters and glares as he followed her from the newly appointed office to the door, Mylva made slow work of gathering her mare's tack together and getting the horse ready. She gave her mare her head and let the hooves eat up the ground in a smooth gallop through the paths over the glaciers. Steam rose in spurts as her hooves landed, water cascading into the indentions the horse left.

Mylva shielded her eyes from the glare of the sun on the blue ice making up the last half of her country all the way to the frozen northern sea. The run wasn't long enough for her eager mare as the black wall of the dungeon neared. She sat back in the saddle and tugged on the reins gently, slowing them before the gates. They opened without her saying a word and they entered at a trot. Her mare snorted smoke, circling the small enclosure with a toss of her head, black mane flying.

The five men watching the dungeon bowed and spoke in unison, "Klava."

"I'm here to see the prisoner." The only one. They were indeed a country of killing traitors, not torturing them.

"The healer finished up just before we saw you on the horizon, Klava. This way." The youngest of the guards smiled at her, keeping his head lowered and talking too much with his hands.

"Rothlander?"

"Er…yes." The tanned skin was lighter than most of her people, and it held a new red tinge. "What gave it away?"

Mylva waved her hands with a smirk, his cheeks grew rosier. "I didn't know that you lot had already infiltrated so well, again."

"I never left, Klava." He informed her, a hand rising to rest on the back of his neck at the admittance.

She nodded, following him through the narrow hall carved out of the glacier that wound down into the small dungeon. They only had five cells, deep in the recesses of thick ice. In her entire reign, she had only used one of them, as far as she could remember. However, people played many games in the prison. She missed playing pranks on her fellow soldiers. She was sure he'd break out, but he hadn't back then.

Just like he hadn't broken out this time, either.

Mylva stopped in front of the cell, the magic of the partition shimmered red and orange between her and the inhabitant, like a soap bubble caught in sunlight. His hair was gone. The crown of his head bubbled in scars. Newly healed cuts and welts shone pink in the natural light from the ice and magic barrier.

Praedae looked small in there. It had only been a few days. Was he truly this weak? Had she been placing him high on a pedestal? Imagining him stronger, or as something supernatural?

"I shall take my leave. I will be at the ready, if you need me… I doubt you will." The Rothland soldier, now hers, stated with a bow.

Mylva forced the words out between the anger she still felt, and the pity rising at the sight of Praedae before her, "Gather cleaning supplies."

"I'll call for the healer to not go back."

"No need. Let them go home." Klava glanced at the boy, heard him swallow hard, bow, and take his leave.

"Asdui." She said softly, and the barrier popped. She stepped in, standing in the cramped entryway, and watched as her warrior didn't move. "Already dead?"

Slowly, Praedae lifted his head from where it was hanging between his knees. The narrow cot couldn't be big enough for him to lie down on. He sat on it, the covers on the floor, only a thin leaf litter mattress keeping his flesh from the ice. "I was. Several times."

His voice was as weak as a sick newborn.

Mylva felt the pity grow and tamped it down. "I'm sure you've had fun." She sneered into his glare, noting the paleness of his face, the dark circles under his eyes. Dead indeed.

"You haven't. I've looked for you." His body fell back, leaning on the ice wall instead of on his knees. "Finally, here to take more blood?"

"I'm here to end your suffering." She met his gaze, held it, and watched as he evaluated his options, or maybe his life.

"Do you love him?"

She wasn't expecting that. "Yes." Mylva didn't have doubts, not anymore. Her emotions grew stable in the comfort of her home, allowing them to settle where they needed to be. Almost, she still had a lot of work to do on herself.

Praedae snorted. "Smoke and fog, I didn't think you were capable of such a thing." His lips twisted up on the left after he spoke. He stared at her and then looked straight ahead at the wall before him. "I am worthy of the throne. After all I've done. After the lives I've saved. The amount of times I saved you. I deserve it."

"That is not how this works."

"Marriage isn't how it works either, but since you are Klava, you get to do what you want? Now that you don't have two others to think of, to act for?" His eyes shot back to her, darkening, but his magic didn't gather.

"You think you still deserve it after all you did to the advisors? Killing all those children? The innocents and the weak?" She stepped forward, towering over him. He'd gotten smaller, insignificant.

"You speak of killing innocents while I know what blood you have spilled. Young soldiers pitted against you for a king that didn't see your ways or a mob rebelling against your rule… how are they any different from the advisors? Because they were yours? Kavkans?" He stood, making her step back. "You left. An army was in our borders and you left. I stayed."

"Where were you when I was knocked out? When I was under his thumb? Why didn't you attack?" She didn't budge further, the fog from their breath mingled.

"I-I was waiting."

"You hid." Her gauntlet cracked his cheekbone as she backhanded him.

He came back from her slap and raised his hands toward her throat, teeth clenched in a snarl. "What was I supposed to do?"

"Be Praedae!" She brought her knee up, slamming into his groin. His hands shot down to his privates, and as he bent, she threw her elbow down on the back of his neck. He fell to the ice floor and lay there. "You are timid. Weak. I never should have made you Warmonger."

"No," he cackled, turning his head to look up at her, "No, I shouldn't have become that. I should've climbed on you and held on. That's what he did, right? Dicked you into marriage?" He slid, leg sweeping hers.

She caught herself on the wall, turning to slam her foot down on his knee, and then stand on it until the bone crunched. She flopped back, her shoulders hitting the bot as he hugged her legs and pulled them from under her. Mylva growled, sitting up as quickly as she could to slam the edge of her gauntlet into his head.

Praedae rolled and half crawled, keeping her under him as he swiped at her arm.

Fighting in enclosed spaces was not a grand idea with her bulk. It was proving far more difficult than she imagined.

Praedae seemed to return to his larger-than build in a blink. The burn of the ice under her palms fed the fire in her and she slapped her hands over his ears. The sizzle of meat against flames filled the room, along with the scent of fried flesh. His howl bounced around the glacial walls, making her ears ring.

Mylva kicked him off her like wet pants and sat on the edge of his cot. She watched him turn his head, cooling his burning ears on the ice. "My next warrior will know how to absorb, and won't think with his penis. Just because the advisors didn't like letting you have their daughters doesn't mean they deserved death."

"They needed death, like our traditions needed to be absolved." Praedae ground out, then closed his eyes with a heave of his chest. After a few breaths, he spoke again. "We were good together. The four of us," Praedae murmured, still lying on the floor. "We could take over the world without him."

"I can take over the world with him." Her heart ached, and she couldn't bring herself to picture Hava and Nava absent from her sides in battle. "Anything else you want to say?"

He looked up at her, his gaze sweeping down her, then he closed his eyes. "You are a fool. Some traditions are meant to be kept."

"Some, yes. We will see if I am or not." She stood, drawing a mace out and wondering if she had enough room to swing it. Mylva pooled her magic into the handle, pushing it up to the spiked head, and watched him get up on his knees. "I release you as Praedae, from the blood oath you gave me freely, and I took willingly." Her voice cracked, she swallowed and continued, "From this day forth, I will no longer think of you, nor know you, for your crimes are against Kavkan, and I am Kavkan. I, Klava, grant you death's respite, but not the bosom of our goddess in your end." She felt a chain break around her heart and knew the oath dispersed.

As she played her memories of him through her mind, from them as a child training with knives to the practice a month ago, all faded. The moments broke from her consciousness like the oath from her heart. A resolve to kill this near stranger before her grew, and she raised the mace high, to bring it down in a quick pull. The crack and splatter of Praedae's skull split the silence. The hulking body took a while to go prone on the ice with a thud. A coppery scent filled her nose quickly in the tiny room.

Blood pooled, crawling toward her boots, and she watched it, wondering why this man was so special as to deserve a cell, and death by her hand.

Our first time should have been on this throne.

His thoughts were far too distracting. Mylva jerked her fingers from his hold and shot a glare up at him when he chuckled softly. Ryven sat on the arm of her seat, toying with her. She'd love to see Hava and Nava smiling as Ryven teased her.

Her generals shifted on their feet before them. The four of them cast awkward glances anywhere but at their Klava and the man claiming to be her husband. Mylva sighed, pushing herself off the throne; she walked toward them. "One world. One ruler. That's what we have now." She called them together for an explanation of what Kavkan was about to become in the new world. Ryven told her they needed to meet in here for the light.

General Ada spoke first, "That means we have no way to live. We shall perish."

Mylva shook her head, "We are going to be the enforcers. The fire in their nightmares and the fear that causes them to watch for us over their shoulders. Should any try to rebel, we are the crushers of their hopes."

Such was Ryven's plan. He'd made sure Kavkans would still be precious warriors, assassins, and mercenaries. A ready, powerful army should there ever be another threat.

"Has punishment been met?" Another of her generals, Mavis, twirled a small ring that held a razor's edge between her gloved fingers. Her dark eyes were on Ryven.

"My Bloodsworn sisters gave their lives for me so I could be free. I've tortured him enough. Unless I deem him worthy of more in the future… it is at my discretion."

General Tayna's brow created a line between them. "Free?"

"Free to be my own. Not what we each thought the other would do. Each Klava demolishes what traditions she can while building new ones. This is mine. This is a Klava's ultimate ambition. To rule the world, is it not?"

They couldn't deny it, so her generals said nothing. Just nodded in agreement.

"You've fought by my side. You still will. We will have much work to do." Mylva tapped her bottom lip as she added, "I doubt there will be much change in our lifestyles for our generation. But we shall make the world a better place for the next, and the next after, and to eternity. Are you with me?"

"Yes, Klava," the four stated without hesitation.

"Good. First, here is our world." She waved over Gyrna, who unrolled a map like a rug on the floor of the throne room; the lava glowed through, hardening the lines and making the words clearer with its light.

Her generals grinned and began planning how to break the Kavkan army up so the world would remain at peace.

"One moment," Ryven said quietly before adding an extra sheet to one side. Another continent. The borders barely filled in, gaps here and there, and few names. "This is first. Kavkan won't have time to rest, I'm afraid. You shall not fear boredom for a long time, generals."

The need for war burned bright in her soul, and she grinned. "He brings me more of the world to take, I see." She walked around the map, gauging the distance from her farthest shores to the other continent. "We are a barrier." Mylva narrowed her eyes at Ryven.

"A good one, too." Ryven widened his eyes with his sheepish grin, failing to look innocent. "But that is not all I wanted you for. I know a nation that takes others as yours did is a grand ally to have."

Drak snorted, rubbing his beard. "You got lucky, boy."

Ada nodded, "Agreed." Her lips pulled back, her teeth gleamed. "Why don't we take his for us? Then we can deal with the other unknown?"

"His is already ours," Mylva reminded them. "A battle against them while we don't know this larger country is not a risk I'm willing to take."

"Rothland is small?" Drak asked.

"It is." Mylva answered.

"That's not the point." Ryven cleared his throat, eyes flitting between the generals in the room and his wife. "The point, friends, for we are friends and you are my wife." He pointedly glared at Mylva. "The point is that we need each other for the greater foe, here."

"Numbers, boy," Ada barked.

Ryven lifted a shoulder as he said, "Not sure. All I know is that the land mass is twice as big as us, the islands, and Rothland put together."

Tayna sat on the floor in a graceful motion, staring at the feeble attempt at marking the unknown. "If their populace per stride is as ours, we are indeed allied with Rothland. May need more pawns."

"We have thirty-two other countries behind us, with us, plus your twenty-" Ryven began, only to be interrupted.

Drak barked a laugh, "Hardly any of our twenty have military, Ryven, you know that."

"I know, but there are navies, and some armies. More can be trained in the Kavkan way."

"You have a plan?" Mylva raised a brow at him. She would be surprised if he didn't.

"Of course," Ryven grinned, "I always have a plan."

Chapter 22

Almost half a year since he had last been in this room as an enemy to his wife. Ryven gazed up at the black irises painted on the ceiling in chaos that only nature could outdo. The stained glass glowed softly, oranges shifting through the black hues as the sun set. He returned his gaze downward, watching Mylva plop flat onto her back on the smooth clear floor of the dance hall atop the fortress.

"How's your nausea?" He crouched beside her, smiling as her brows drew low over her closed eyes.

Her chest rose and fell in quick shallow breaths, "Worse."

He frowned, "I didn't want to make it worse." Ryven thought a lesson in dancing would help take her mind off whatever stomach bug this was that had gripped her for the past few days. He sat down beside her, sliding his hand up her shirt to rest his palm against her flat belly.

"I know that now," Mylva groaned, stretching out in all directions, before she rested her hands on top of his. "Klavas never get sick."

"That's what Gyrna said, and then she blamed me for it." With a smirk, he wanted to add, but it still unsettled him. The bloodsworn's amusement was never a good thing. He wondered what attack she was planning behind his back even as he took care of his suffering wife.

The first time she lost her meal was when Ryven read her a handful of statistics and messages from his brother and sister, who had finally infiltrated their enemy. He thought nothing of it, as the numbers made him ill, too. Aslotor, the chief antagonist to his peace. Their peace.

Aslotor was a country like Kavkan, except their vassals didn't have any autonomy underneath the steel hand of their emperor. Their numbers were five Aslotorian to one

Kavkan. Two to one with Rothland and the rest of the world added in. But it was the Kavkans that were going to save them.

Their enemy was as deadly as Kavkans.

His mind drew back to the present as something niggled at the corner of his consciousness. The nutrients. He reached for Mylva's mind, searching and wondering at the demand of vitamins going to her…

"You're pregnant." The words were out of Ryven's mouth before he realized what he was saying. He watched Mylva's eyes fly open, the whites showing as she stared up into his gaze.

Laughter bubbled up, and he grabbed her up. Crushing her to his chest, he laughed until the sounds echoed off the walls. "Klavas don't get sick unless they are with child!" He cried, squeezing his wife even harder against him. When her back cracked, he gasped and loosened his hold, "Sorry. Sorry, but no! You're pregnant!" He held her shoulders, looking into her eyes.

Mylva's tears streamed down her cheeks, her lips trembled, "My… our child won't have to go through what I did?"

His joy tempered slightly, until he answered, "No. No, she won't."

Ryven heard Mylva's swallow, and observed her face carefully wash from fear, to reddened delight, back to pale nausea with the blush of happiness. He watched her hands cup her belly, rub it, and a smile spread.

"I'm with child."

A chill suddenly gripped him. Their child would be born soon. Would they be in war? Would they still be alive? Ryven sucked in a breath, battling fear to embrace the moment. He grinned, "You are." He kissed her.

≈ ≈ ≈

"I swear upon the gods, Ryven, if you do not let me sleep!"

He pressed his lips against her temple, tasting the light saltiness of her skin on his tongue, "Good morning, my beautiful wife."

"It's morning?" Mylva yawned, only to break it with a surprised grunt.

Ryven rolled her onto her back. He splayed his hands over her taut belly, staring at where his babes were growing in his wife as if he could already hold them. "Yes, my love." He slid his hands up her scared and puckered skin, to where her nightgown still covered her breasts with a few buttons. He flicked the fabric open, cupping each breast in his palms.

She moaned, "This isn't helping reduce the size of your cock I felt against my ass, you know." Mylva arched slightly, pressing into him.

He chuckled, "I love it when you pretend you don't like sex. And no, since you can't see it over our children, I am more than ready to pleasure you."

"I think you like me better fat."

"Myl, I love you better this moment than the last." Ryven leaned down and placed his mouth on hers. When she parted her lips, he rubbed his tongue against hers. He pulled away, trailing kisses down her neck, listening to her curse him in her thoughts and bemoan sleep. He kissed over her clavicle and chest, then suckled each breast, gently. Her curses became moans, even in her own mind. He returned to kneading them with his fingertips as he rained kisses all over her belly. Then he slid his hands down her sides, her hips, and then pulled her thighs over his shoulders.

He licked up her slit and felt goosebumps rise as she bucked with a moan. "Sounds and tastes like this is why you're in this situation to begin with." He murmured against her thigh before nipping it. Her verbal curse made him want to tease her some more, but he could feel her need ratcheting up quicker than he expected already. Ryven went back to her, parting her folds so he could lap at her clitoris. He suckled on it as she grew damp and then wet under his ministrations.

When she moaned again, he swore under his breath. The ache throbbed. He paused, willing himself to calm down so he wouldn't just take her. Her hips jerked as he breathed on her sensitive nether lips and clit before he licked up her slit. He retraced his steps downward, exploring her as deep as he could before returning to her button and sliding two of his digits inside her.

Ryven took special care to find her pleasure point with his fingertips and began caressing it with each thrust. He mimicked the movement with a swirl of his tongue over her little bundle of nerves. With each thrust of his digits inside her, he listened to her thoughts, adjusting the roughness, what he did with his tongue, as she willed it. Soon, her walls tightened over his fingers as her body grew taught upon their bed.

He sat back on his knees to lick her off his fingers. Ryven grew mesmerized for the thousandth time with the glow of the lava behind the walls, making the light sheen of sweat on her body look like sunlight on droplets of dew. His Mylva was a goddess.

Ryven moved forward, lifting her thighs on top of his. He grabbed her buttocks, squeezing her in his hands as his cock rested in the warmth of her folds. Readjusting, he slid himself inside her, his moan mingling with hers, and he had to close his eyes. The very sight of her stirred his primal instincts.

Another reminder not to be too rough with his wife added to her weight on his thighs. He opened his eyes, trailing his hands over her belly. Ryven leaned slightly, his hands on her sides, forearms on either side of her rounded middle. Rocking his hips into her, he watched her mouth open in a gasp. Her hands cupping her own breasts did little to tame him. Her thoughts didn't help either.

She wanted it rough. He moaned, tightening his hold on her and doing what she wished while supporting her added weight. Ryven was always worried he was going to jostle their kids too much, even though Mylva reassured him he wouldn't. He rammed into her time and again. Each thrust eliciting her cries of pleasure, her thoughts begging for more as she crested. He stopped, holding back as her orgasm hit her. He used the tightness to his advantage as he kept thrusting. Mylva. His grin at the thought of her under him crashed into a grit of his teeth as he spilled inside her.

Spent, he disengaged from her, kissed her again, and lay beside her. He threw an arm over her, snaking his hand back to cup her breast. Their thoughts melded in the panting recovery.

Then she had other emotions. Fear. Then she erased it with the thought of birthing two at a time. Twins. With a desire for both to be healthy.

He searched her mind, reading how her body believed they were healthy. Nothing was amiss there. "They are well. As are you."

Ryven wasn't about to admit to his own fears, hoping he had tucked them well away from the thoughts he had flowing into her. But he knew, as they sauntered unbidden from the back of his consciousness, that she would know them too.

"What if it's a boy?" Mylva said his worst anxiety. Her dark eyes stared up at the basalt and obsidian ceiling laced with the glow of the mountain's blood.

"You won't die." Ryven stated, as if it was a fact. Wishing it was an undeniable truth. Fear made his heart grow ice cold and sink into his stomach. "We've broken traditions. Created our own. This too is of the past. It isn't our-" his voice broke, and he cursed himself, "It isn't for us, that thing about Klavas giving birth to boys."

After a few breaths, Mylva nodded, her resolve like iron in her mind, "It isn't for us."

𝕝𝕝𝕝

Mylva smiled, her fingers flowing through the lava as she squatted. The heated water all around her steamed, hiding her from the view of the pacing man safe behind the glass doors. Her back was to the wall of lava, her hands digging into it. Borrowing the power of the earth's very heart. This was one tradition she couldn't bring herself to give up, even after all the months spent building new traditions for her new Kavkan.

Her god and herself would witness the birth of her children.

She pushed, straining. Pain like she'd never felt before, tearing her apart even as she swallowed and molded the fires inside her to help her deliver her child. Mylva tossed her head back, screaming curses, then praises as her body wrenched her into more agony.

Something loosened. She leaned down, pulling her daughter out of the water, noting the orange veins soaking in the heat. Mylva grinned, smoothing the wet black curls plastered to her baby's forehead. Then another pain ripped through her.

She cursed, clutching her now crying daughter to her chest as her stomach convulsed.

337

Another. She cried out in joy, reaching her free hand into the lava and borrowing more power. Weakness washed through her even as her magic bolstered. Exhausted. Wanted nothing but the warmth of sleep. An additional scream ripped from her throat as contractions tore through her and another child worked its way from her, slipping into the near boiling water.

She gasped for breath as she tried to pull the second child from the water. As she lifted it, she stared. The babe's mouth opened, mewling, then screaming a powerful presence.

Mylva waited a heartbeat. Then two. The warmth of lava flowed through her, live and strong. Life. She still had life. Even though her baby boy roared his presence as his sister screamed hers to be known, too.

Sobs wracked her body as she held both to her chest. She lived. Traditions be damned.

Sacrificing the sacks that fed her children to the god that helped her bring them into this world. And the cords to the lava, for the hope of their life to be long and strong, filled with her love. She stood, dragging herself out of the birthing pool and onto the narrow path that would lead her back to her pacing husband.

"Mylva?" Ryven's worried tenor carried through the birthing chamber from where he stood, protected, just on the outside.

"It is done. We have a daughter."

Ryven murmured, barely heard through the protective doors, "A Klava, as powerful and beautiful as her mother." She could hear the smile in his words and the tears.

"And a son."

After a few beats of her heart, he asked, "A son?" Something spiked in his voice, his palms dark shadows on the barrier between them.

"A son," Mylva tried to add a soothing tone to her voice, but all she forced out was a soft laugh. She had a son.

"Come to me." Ryven's voice cracked as his palm smacked against the barrier.

For once, she did as she was told. Their little family held in a tight embrace. A new world at their fingertips, and in the circle of their arms. Kavkan ready with Kavkan blood rising anew in the babes in her arms.

The End

Dear Reader,

  I hope you enjoyed Capture the Empress. Be sure to leave a review on your favorite site! Soon, there will be more additions to The Capture Series for you to escape to!
  Thank you!

S.W. Lupine

Other books from Carder-Wicker Writing

When her best friend kills the White Boar of Prophecy, he's supposed to become the hero. But when the hero turns coward, his smarter sidekick must take matters into her own hands. Nadachia promises she will take his place – and she never goes back on her word.

With a powerful Stygra Matron intent on using her to gain access to the gods, Nadachia must figure out what's behind the curtain, survive fabled quests, and protect her loved ones – but how far down this rabbit hole can she go before it kills her?

Is a reluctant hero really the hero the world needs?

www.ingramcontent.com/pod-product-compliance
Lightning Source LLC
Chambersburg PA
CBHW061112310726
48974CB00002B/502